STEPHANIE
DENNE

STOLEN BONDS

2
BLACKTHORN
SAGA

Published in Canada by Amethyst Corvid Press, Ontario, Canada.

Stolen Bonds.
First Edition.
ISBN: 978-1-7387272-4-7
Stephanie Denne.

See more books by Stephanie Denne at https://stephaniedenneauthor.com
Editing by Kelly Schaub

Cover Design by Story Wrappers – storywrappers.com

"Jealousy is beautiful only on a young and ardent face.
After the first wrinkles, trust must return."
—Alfred Capus

A Message from the Author

This book contains content that may be unsuitable for certain readers. To learn more about content warnings in the author's work, please visit her website:

https://www.stephaniedenneauthor.com/content-warnings

PLAYLIST

Amber Run – I Found
Ghost – Life Eternal
Digital Daggers – Still Here
Breaking Benjamin – Without You
Chaoseum – Until the End (Acoustic)
Catch Your Breath – Dial Tone
Deftones – Entombed
Bad Omens - The Death Of Peace Of Mind
Lorna Shore – Pain Remains Trilogy

Instrumentals from YouTube (added exact title so they are searchable):

WHEN THE LAST HOPE RUNS OUT – Sad Emotional Music Mix | Powerful Emotive Instrumental Music
Dark Victorian Mansion | Piano and Cello with Storm Ambience
Dark Magic Music – Salem's Secret
Suffocating the Senses – Magic Music
Emotional Music – Bury My Heart
Dark Piano – Sociopath
Minor roles in inspiration (YouTube Instrumentals):

A (really) Dark Academia Playlist. Vol 1
Soundtrack for a Supervillain – Dark and Sinister Music Mix
CURSE | 1 HOUR of Epic Dark Dramatic Villainous Sinister Orchestra Music
"SOLITAIRE" Most Intense Powerful Violin Fierce Orchestral Strings Music
Circles – Ambient Dark Sexy Cinematic Instrumental (NSFW Video)
Invitation – Ambient Dark Sexy Instrumental

Blackthorn Academy Campus

It's easy to lose your way at the mysterious Blackthorn Academy. But with a little luck, and this handy map, I'm sure you'll do just fine… maybe.

1

Fragile Bonds

When she first came to the psychology department of Blackthorn Academy for counseling, Blaire couldn't relax enough to sit back in the chair, but now she had her shoes off and was curled up in the chair like she belonged there. Professor Sinclair's office had become a haven of comfort, filled with plants and mild floral fragrances—just the right amount of aromatherapy.

Professor Sinclair said, "Just keep in mind… new bonds are fragile and easily broken when the wrong hands are at play."

Blaire's brow furrowed. "What do you mean?" She shifted in the plush armchair and brushed her fingers over the mark on her neck, an indelible sign of her connection with Lukas.

"Jealousy played a significant role in the journey to sealing the Korrena bond between you and Lukas. His friend had feelings for you, and you struggled with your own attraction."

Blaire's lips twisted as she averted her eyes, picking at the top of the thigh-high stocking of her uniform while looking out the window into the garden just outside. Guilt still plagued her at how she almost walked away from her powerful connection with Lukas in favor of a fleeting physical attraction to Aiden. The latter was easier to quantify and reject to protect herself, but she'd be lying if she said there wasn't more than that there. She couldn't fully explain her special connection to Aiden, but it was not romantic in nature.

"There's also the issue of Lukas's possessive nature. Of course, that'll go both ways."

"What? I'm not—"

"Perhaps not yet. You haven't faced opposition. Lukas has stayed so close to you there hasn't been the opportunity for another woman to cross his path to threaten you. But it'll happen. It always happens with pairs. Some pairs spend decades battling this particular demon." She tapped her pen on her notebook. The colorful bangles on her wrist that matched her floral maxi dress jingled and caught the light. "It's not necessarily that others seek to break apart bonds; it's simply in a Korrena's nature to feel possessive over their pair. It's a primal reaction that can lead to heights of passion."

Blaire frowned. She rarely felt possessive about anything. Growing up, she freely shared her toys and food with other kids. Her mother taught her that selfishness wasn't the way to live, and her marrying into a wealthy family when Blaire was fifteen had no effect on that core value in spite of the Wilcox's avarice. More important than material things, a person was not an object to possess or share. Maybe that was normal for Vasirian—an overwhelming drive to own their pair—but it resonated as unhealthy to her. Though she liked the feelings of belonging and protection when he acted like that, she wouldn't tolerate it overtaking their relationship. Acting in the same manner herself would be ridiculous.

"You're still in the early stages of your bond; it is fragile. If you allow anything to negatively influence its growth, it can break."

Blaire's understanding was that a Korrena bond was forever. "Break? How?"

Professor Sinclair set down the notebook and shook her head, strands of copper hair falling from the low knot at the nape of her neck. "Not break in the sense that it would no longer exist. Emotionally broken. Like a breakup between a boyfriend and girlfriend. A third party coming between you could jeopardize your growth as a Korrena pair—especially with a bond as new as the one you have. Your being human makes the entire process unpredictable, and it increases the chances of complications if you're not vigilant."

Blaire again thought of Aiden, but they worked that out before bonding. It never occurred to her someone could come between her and Lukas now. She thought with the claiming and everything sealed, the rest would be easy. The Order hadn't caused further problems. Aiden stepped back. Blood sharing was surprisingly not an issue. Maybe she was naïve about the nuances of relationships, but she couldn't see anyone from outside their pairing being strong enough to rock the foundation they worked through over the summer.

Her gaze moved back to the garden outside, where resurrection ferns in the bark of the trees shading the window had perked to life. The rainfall the lower part of the state received a few days ago heralded the change in season away from summer, despite continuing heat. The weather had been unpredictable all week with the tropical storm raging off the coast, but meteorologists expected it to shift and move back out to sea or skirt the North Carolina coastline, missing Georgia entirely. Of course, moving into the thick of hurricane season, that wasn't as reassuring as one would hope. Who knew which storm would decide to head up the Georgia coastline?

The last couple of months, since officially becoming Lukas's Korrena in June, had given her the most peace she'd felt in years. Even storms didn't bother her like they once did. She didn't want to face a reality filled with further hardships, especially regarding her newfound love.

"It isn't something to stress over, I assure you. This is merely a reminder to protect that which you find important to you. Both of you. As always, I'll continue to support you, and should Lukas wish to seek counsel with me, I'd be happy to see him. Both of you, even."

Blaire laughed softly. She could just imagine Lukas sitting in on one of her counseling sessions, sulking at Professor Sinclair's larger-than-life attitude.

The clock on the wall chimed, signaling the end of their session. Blaire lowered her feet and slid them into her polished Italian leather loafers.

"I think we'll have another session before your birthday, right?" The professor flipped through a small appointment book, humming. "It's August twenty-fourth today… Yes, I should see you again at the end of September."

Since April, Blaire's counseling sessions had decreased from once weekly to once per month as she gained self-confidence. She nodded. "Yeah. My birthday isn't until October fourteenth."

"Perfect! Then I'll hold the 'Happy Birthday' song until next time."

Blaire's mouth dropped open, and Professor Sinclair burst into a fit of laughter.

"Oh my, you should see your face." She waved a hand up and down, her bangles filling the room with their tinkling. "I'm kidding, of course. You should know better by now."

While the professor was amazing at her job, and helped Blaire in progressing toward her degree with professional skills, the woman was a wild card personally, always catching Blaire off-guard with a quirky, vibrant nature as in-your-face as her fashion sense. This stood in welcome contrast to the darkness that hovered over Blackthorn Academy like a storm cloud.

She was still getting used to the absence of the nightmare of Caleb's obsession. Whoever oversaw the keeping of the Vasirian secret had altered his memory of that part of their life in such a way she no longer needed to fear his interference, and by extension, the Wilcox family's influence on her life. Yet her new position among the Vasirian as the lone human student came with its own feelings of isolation.

After her therapy session, Blaire went back to the dorm room she shared with Lukas and changed into a pair of jean shorts, a loose-fitting t-shirt, and a pair of flip-flops before going outside to soak up the sun and read the new vampire romance novel she picked up in town last week. For fair-skinned Blaire, soaking up the sun meant sitting in the shade of the palmetto trees along the courtyard; she burned easily. Despite the cool mornings and evenings, and the occasional rain, the daytime heat of summer would wane in October, so Blaire wanted to take advantage while she could.

"I want to borrow that one when you're finished," Riley said, walking up to where Blaire sat on a stone bench near the hedge maze.

Blaire placed a bookmark inside the pages and closed the book as she looked up at her pink-haired friend. "I just got this." She huffed a breath without any frustration in the sound.

"I know. But I've heard great things about this one online, and I've already read the first in the series." Riley shrugged, dropping her bag on the ground. "Besides, Emley Rison is my all-time favorite romance author. She's amazing. Did you know no one has ever seen her face? Like, she doesn't even host book signings or attend events where she's won awards." Riley sat next to Blaire and kicked her legs out in front of her, the buckles jangling on her knee-high boots with buckles up the sides. Still in her uniform, Riley had likely just finished her last class for the day.

"She only came on the scene a couple years ago, and has already released like five books—which I have all of, except that one, thank you very much." Riley pointed at the book in Blaire's hand. "This one has surpassed all expectations. The first book was tense, and you can really feel the obsessive love the main character experiences for the woman he's known his entire life."

Blaire shook her head. She had a couple of the author's previous works and the first one in this second series, but Riley, like a true die-hard fan, put everything into her gushing appraisal. Smiling to herself, Blaire asked, "How's the design course going?"

Riley's enthusiasm dimmed. "It's alright."

Blaire arched an eyebrow. "Just alright?"

"I mean, yeah. It's only the introductory stuff so far since we're only a month into the semester, so it's a lot of technical terms and boring stuff like that. No real artistic stuff happening." Riley looked up at the sky, where a few rain clouds lingered, and took a deep breath. "And I have fewer classes with you guys."

That was the only downside to going into their second year of college. While a few general education classes remained at second level, the friends were all taking courses central to their chosen majors. Riley who chose a field in the arts, didn't overlap classes with the others.

"We still get the free study periods together, and a few general-ed classes," Blaire offered.

"I know." Riley groaned and lay her head back, closing her eyes. "I just thought we'd be together more, now that things are better with you and Lukas." The way Riley pouted about small things like this was cute.

Since they'd sealed their bond, Lukas had kept Blaire to himself a lot more, but with each passing day he settled, like he finally trusted this was real and believed Blaire wasn't going anywhere.

"Things were just rocky… but now that things are more solid between Lukas and me, I'm sure we'll have more time together."

"We better." Grinning, she nudged Blaire's shoulder. "I don't want to have to come after Lukas."

Blaire laughed. She could picture Riley's five-foot-four self trying to fight Lukas, who stood a foot taller than her at six-three. The visual was hilarious and decidedly ridiculous.

"Hey, don't laugh. I'll have you know I can kick ass just fine."

Blaire lifted her hands. "Okay, okay. I believe you."

"When you grow up with Aiden as your big brother, you learn a few tricks." Riley winked.

Riley's other siblings were older, so they didn't technically grow up with her and Aiden. The dynamic was more Riley, Aiden, and friends Lukas and Seth as a family all on their own. Riley, Aiden, and Seth had started the preschool division of the academy together. Their parents were close to one another, and later, when Lukas was five, he joined them, becoming fast friends with Aiden.

"How has Lukas been, though? Even though we're friends, he doesn't really open up or anything."

"A lot better. It took a couple of months, but he's done a one-eighty from what he was like before we sealed our bond. I mean, yeah, there are still remnants of the old him… it's part of his personality, but he's not running hot and cold all the time."

"Thank the gods. He was giving me emotional whiplash, and I wasn't with him all the time."

"Oh, come on, he wasn't that—"

"If you're about to defend him and say he wasn't that bad, you need to take the rose-colored glasses off. All that sex and lovey-dovey stuff has got you overlooking some major red flags from before. Now, don't get me wrong… I understood it. But it was too much sometimes."

Blaire looked down. She wasn't writing off what Lukas did before. He had been a grade-A jerkface. But there had been so much more beneath his mask of anger, resentment, and indifference.

"You're right. I haven't forgotten, but I've forgiven."

After nearly losing her to both the Order and her own misplaced desire to leave, Lukas needed reassurance she wasn't going anywhere—that she wanted to be with him. It surprised her that she needed to reassure him as constantly as she needed reassurance about her own fears. She hadn't known his fears ran as deep as they did. He didn't want to be alone, but he also feared getting too close. His fear that Blaire saw him as a monster had affected their coming together the most.

She forgave him, and they talked it through. Not moving together past it would destroy any relationship, especially one as sensitive as theirs. She would not delude herself; Professor Sinclair was correct in her assessment. With their unique pairing of a human and Vasirian, their bond was going to be more difficult than most.

Blaire looked up and waved at a girl crossing the courtyard toward them in full uniform with a pair of chunky sandals.

"Who's that?" Riley asked, following Blaire's line of sight.

"Rue."

"And she is?"

"Well, Rueanna. I don't know her last name."

"Wainwright," Rue said as she stopped in front of them, smiling with perfectly straight white teeth. "Nice to meet you."

Riley smiled brightly in return. Blaire admired her easy friendliness. "Hi, Rueanna. I'm Riley Easton."

"Oh, you can call me Rue, too. I prefer it." She turned to Blaire as she began braiding her long dark hair to the side of her neck. "So, what's your plans for the weekend?" Her hair was silky smooth and shined in the sun, as if she'd just received a hot oil treatment. With her smooth complexion, honey brown skin, and sharp facial features, Blaire wondered about the girl's nationality. Her English surname didn't give much away.

"Nothing much… maybe read. Maybe visit my friend Charlotte at her mother's clothing shop in town. I haven't seen her moms in a long time."

"Oh! Can I come?" Riley asked.

Blaire shrugged. "I don't see why not."

Riley had taken a liking to Charlotte, but what wasn't to like? Blaire's best friend from high school was sweet as pie. She turned her attention back to Rue, "What about you?"

"Liam's parents are in town, and we're going to Charleston for the weekend, but I'm glad I caught you before we left." Glancing back toward the main doors of the academy, Rue sighed. "I'm sorry I don't have much time to hang out, but he's waiting for me. I just wanted to see if you had the notes from the other day from our Introduction to Abnormal Psychology class. Professor Donohue told me to see if I could borrow someone's notes, since I missed the class."

"Yeah, sure. I don't have them with me. They're back in my dorm."

"That's okay." She waved a hand in front of her face. "I can get them next week in class. I just wanted to make sure I had it taken care of so I didn't stress out all weekend." She looked back as a guy with blond hair slicked back on his head stepped out onto the steps and looked toward her. "Shoot. Gotta go. Thank you sooo much!"

Blaire had to squint through the sun in her eyes to identify Liam. With one last smile to Riley, Rue turned and went to join Liam on the steps before they disappeared inside the main building again.

"She seems nice," Riley said.

"Yeah, I met her and Liam on my first day here last spring. I don't know much about him; he doesn't talk a lot. I think his English isn't the best. He's got a thick accent." Blaire shrugged. "But she's been nice to me, and now we're in the same major. We're in most of our classes together."

"Cool, cool… but is it really okay if I come to Charlotte's mom's shop?"

"I don't see why not."

"Awesome! I think it'd be great to see someone who actually works in fashion design in their element."

Riley had settled on an Art and Design major going into this term, finally putting her passion for fashion into an actual concentration. She wanted to start her own alternative clothing line and open her own shop. Blaire wouldn't have guessed she held that ambition.

"I'll have to call her from the office and see if she's up for it."

"We can text her on my phone." Riley dug out her cell phone.

Blaire wished she had one. Situations like this would be much more convenient. Maybe it was time to finally treat herself to a phone now that she secured a place away from the Wilcox family.

"What's her number?"

Blaire sighed and glanced toward the dorm buildings. "I don't know. I've got it in my planner back in my room. We can contact her later today when I get it."

Blaire looked down at her thighs and groaned at the pinkness.

"Oh, come on." The sun had moved, and now she was getting direct sun on her skin. She glanced at the large clock face on the administration building. The day had dragged, but she wasn't complaining. She'd had enough excitement in the previous year to last a lifetime. But losing track of time came with a cost, if her skin had anything to say about it.

"What's wrong?"

"Just turning into a lobster."

Riley laughed. "What?"

Blaire motioned to her legs. "A moment of silence for those who burn instead of tan." She sighed.

Snorting, Riley stood and motioned to her black opaque tights. "This is why I keep my pale ass covered up."

"I normally don't wear shorts. I just wanted to soak in the warmth, but clearly, I'm incapable of tracking how long I've been out here."

"Well, let's get inside before you crisp like a chicken. We can text Charlotte, you can change, and then we'll go grab pizza."

Blaire wrinkled her nose as she stood.

"What? You don't like pizza?" Riley asked as they walked back to the dorms.

"No."

"Who doesn't like pizza?"

"Me."

"Well, Milanos has pasta and stuff too." Riley held open the door to their dorm building for Blaire to walk through first.

Blaire shrugged. "I've heard of the place, just never could afford it."

Milanos Ristorante had opened a little over a year ago a few doors down from Ricky's Diner, and it was the hot new date spot for couples. They didn't have a dress code, so it wasn't overly formal, but they allegedly had the best Italian food in this area of Georgia. It became a hot spot for the well-to-do members of society around Rosebrook who didn't want to make the trip to Savannah.

"Well, you can afford it now."

As they approached her room, Blaire said, "You know I don't like spending frivolously. The school gives me an allowance, but I still want to use it wisely. They won't allow me to work while I'm a student, so..." She couldn't feel comfortable spending her stipend on dining out when the meals at the school were free. Lukas often bought her meals, movie tickets, and random things when they went into town, but she wasn't fully comfortable with that either. She was so used to making it on her own that having someone step up and take care of her took getting used to, but she was working on it.

She unlocked the door to her room and they stepped inside.

"Blaire, I love you, but you can be a real buzzkill about stuff like this."

"What?" Blaire frowned as she crossed to the nightstand on her side of the room to pull out her planner.

"I'm not trying to be mean, but I'm just saying you need to lighten up. I'm sure the allowance is more than enough to actually treat yourself every now and again."

Riley was right, but Blaire still hadn't fully come to terms with her defensiveness around money. Like the proverbial dropping shoe, she was waiting for the conditions to come down on her, because financial handouts from the wealthy always came with conditions. Her previous relationship with the Wilcox family was more than proof of that. This expectation was yet another thing she tried to work on in her counseling sessions. The terms and conditions were already clear in this case. Conditions she freely accepted without complaint. Bonding with Lukas and completing her degree. It was comical how agreeable the terms were when she expected the worst.

"I guess dinner can't hurt anything."

"That's the spirit! Now, give me the number."

Blaire opened her planner and gave Riley Charlotte's number before sitting on the edge of her bed. Riley fired off a quick message, and then her phone dinged with an immediate response. Riley frowned.

"What's wrong?"

"Her moms are taking her to look at colleges upstate this weekend."

"Ah, yeah… Charlotte was thinking of going to the University of Georgia." Blaire closed her planner. "But it'll be awhile yet. We can always visit Sara's store some other time."

"Sara? That Charlotte's mom?"

"Yeah, one of them."

The bathroom door opened, and Lukas stepped out wearing a pair of low-slung black jeans and nothing else. Riley let out a slow whistle before snorting back laughter. Lukas stood in the doorway with wet hair clinging to his neck and shoulders, water running in rivulets down his toned physique. Blaire swallowed.

Riley made a rude noise. "Yep! I'm out before you two maul each other in front of me. Gross, by the way. Lukas is like my brother. I don't want to picture his naked bits hanging out." She gave an exaggerated shudder then laughed as Lukas growled at her. "Meet me at the gates at five? Milanos fills up fast. Bring Lukas."

Lukas blinked. "What?"

"I'm taking Blaire out for Italian food. She hasn't been to Milanos."

"Really?"

"Nope. Not in my budget." Blaire shrugged as Lukas moved to the closet. "She's making me spend my allowance on it."

"I'm not *making* you. I'm just strongly suggesting it." Riley crossed her arms, her pursed lips making her look childish. "Besides, I'm totally allowing you to bring Lukas… if you want. He doesn't have to come." She pressed her lips together harder to keep from laughing aloud as he glared at her, stepping out of the closet. Riley enjoyed getting a rise out of Lukas as much as she did with Aiden. She was worse with Seth, but that dynamic had a distinct difference.

Lukas shook his head at Riley's ridiculousness. He couldn't stay mad at her. "You gonna ask the others?" He pulled a black t-shirt over his head.

"Yeah, I'll see if Aiden, Mera, and Kai want to come."

Blaire put her planner in the drawer. "What about Seth?"

"I caaan." Riley opened the door and sighed as Lukas laughed, walking toward her.

"I can ask him for you, since I have to go to Aiden's dorm anyway, and we both know he's probably hanging out there. You just ask Mera and Kai."

"You're leaving?" Blaire asked.

"Yeah, I needed to talk with Aiden about something I need to purchase soon, and I need his input on what type."

Riley looked up at Lukas in the doorway. "What are you getting?"

Lukas grunted and glanced at Blaire before looking at Riley with a subtle shake of his head, but Blaire caught it. Her brows crumpled as she studied him, trying to not only get a reading of his body language, but also discover why she felt apprehension.

"Nothing. I'll meet you at the gate at five." He looked back at Blaire. His eyes softened as a lazy smile crossed his lips. "I love you."

"I love you too." The uneasiness she'd picked up on dissipated.

As Lukas and Riley left the room, Blaire pressed her tongue against the inside of her cheek as she considered Lukas's behavior. Lukas often became tense or shut down when he felt cornered. It didn't necessarily mean he was angry, but if he didn't know what to say, he'd either clam up or lash out. Thank goodness he stopped doing the latter as much, at least toward her. What had Riley said to trigger him?

2

Peace

The warm press of lips against skin. The gentle drag of teeth across her shoulder. Blaire smiled as consciousness found her. She slowly opened her eyes to the sun filtering into the room through the open curtains onto the carefully arranged pillows on the other twin bed, which they used more as a couch. Outside, the first autumn-hued leaves blew through the air—early for September. The leaves typically reached their peak, with the brightest colors, in late October into November. While still warm, the temperatures this year were lower than average. Fog had plagued the area in August, and birds were already migrating south. It wasn't unheard of in Southern Georgia, but these things often signaled a hard winter ahead. She would need to unpack her uniform cardigan soon and maybe wear thick opaque tights with her skirt for warmth.

Lips moving down her arm pulled her attention from the window. She slowly turned her head, meeting a pair of seafoam-green eyes. Lukas smiled up at her as he trailed his fingers over her exposed skin, leaving goose bumps in their wake.

"Good morning." His voice still carried the sexy rasp from sleep.

She smiled. "Good morning to you, too."

Blaire shifted to her side and faced Lukas, tucking her head into the crook of his arm, resting her cheek against his warm skin as he held her in the small bed. It was hard to believe that just two months ago she'd almost left the academy and would have lost everything. Staring down those wrought-iron gates in the darkness with the storm looming in the distance, she found the answers to what held her back. Once they let go of their reservations and fears, all the tension held between them for so long, everything came naturally. It was surreal how easy it became. She made the right choice that night in the courtyard when Lukas met her fears with his resolve.

"What's happening in that pretty mind of yours?"

She blushed and shook her head. "Nothing, really. I'm just thinking back to the night before we bonded."

Lukas groaned. "Don't remind me. It was the worst—and best—night of my life."

"I'm not going anywhere. I told you… I love you. I meant that."

Lukas leaned in and took Blaire's lips in a gentle kiss before pulling her against his chest. "Your birthday is coming up next month. What do you want to do? This is the first one I get to spend with you."

Last year, Blaire went with Charlotte and her moms for a weekend to Destin, Florida. She thought herself lucky Caleb had allowed her to go, but she discovered his hidden agenda when she returned home. He made her sleep in his bed for the following week as a "thank you gift" for allowing her to celebrate her eighteenth birthday without him. She was officially an adult then, yet she still had to have approval like a child. The ludicrous situation the Wilcox family trapped her in made her want to both laugh and scream in frustration.

"I normally spend my birthday with Charlotte. It's kinda become a tradition over the years since we were little. We went to the beach last year."

Lukas kissed her shoulder. "That's fine. If she's important to you, then I wouldn't want you to exclude her." He lifted himself to sit on the bed and looked down at her. She dragged her gaze down his naked chest and over his abs to where the blanket barely covered his lap.

"My eyes are up here," he said with a lazy smirk.

Blaire rolled her eyes. "You sure are in a good mood this morning."

"Well, yeah, I get to wake up with you. Why wouldn't I be in a good mood?"

Blaire groaned and covered her face. She had gotten so used to his broody nature that she didn't know how to handle his affectionate side. She loved it, but it felt foreign. He still carried his aggressive personality with him like a shield, but in the months that followed their bonding, the affection he expressed so freely with her in private outweighed the face he showed everyone else.

Lukas pulled her hands away, kissing over the raised scar on the inside of her forearm where the Order's goon had torn a chunk of her skin away. "You know, you're beautiful when you're embarrassed."

"Stop it."

"What? It's true. Not only do your cheeks turn pink, but your neck flushes."

Blaire buried her face in the pillow, groaning her protest.

"So, I was thinking… my family owns a beach house about thirty minutes from here on Tybee Island. I thought maybe we could spend your birthday there. With Charlotte, of course. We can also invite the others, if you want. Make it a weekend thing."

Blaire lifted her head to look up at Lukas. "Isn't the water too cold to swim?"

"It's alright, not too cool yet… it's fine until November."

Blaire hadn't been to the ocean locally in years, and never on her birthday that she could remember, to know anything about the sea temperatures in mid-October. Just because the air felt like summer through the fall months didn't mean the water was warm.

"We can do other things if you don't want to swim. Kayaking, visiting the barrier islands, or just hanging out on the beach and visiting the bars and live shows around."

"You kayak?" She tilted her head to study his face. She couldn't picture Lukas in a small boat gliding through the water communing with nature.

Lukas laughed at the obvious disbelief in her voice. "No, not really, but it's something many people do. I can think of better things to do at the beach." He leaned in and kissed her neck. "Alone." The drag of his teeth over her skin made her shiver. "At night." He leaned back with a self-satisfied smirk. "You know, instead of touristy stuff."

Blaire's eyes opened wide, and she pushed him back, laughing. "You are bad." She forced herself out of bed, turning back to him with a smile. "Bad, but convincing. I'll call Charlotte from the office this week and see if she can get time off from the diner." She crossed to the bathroom as Lukas rolled onto his back with a smile on his face.

She turned on the shower to let it warm up while she undressed then brushed her bedhead. Setting down the brush, she held up her perfume bottle to the light and squinted; only enough for a spray or two. She needed to make a trip out to the Valley Center Plaza soon to stock up on necessities. Maybe she could convince Riley to come with her. Riley loved to shop for clothes and accessories, but Blaire wasn't sure if she would be into shopping for things like perfume and body wash. Not much style and flash to be found there.

She checked the temperature of the shower. Satisfied, she turned to get her razor from her caddy and stumbled over her discarded clothes on the floor. She grabbed the edge of the counter, knocking over the perfume bottle. The glass shattered all over the tiled floor.

"Dammit!" Blaire got down on her hands and knees to clean up the mess as Lukas rushed into the bathroom, getting an eyeful of her backside high in the air.

"Are you okay? What happened?"

"Yeah, I just broke my perfume. It's fine though, there were only like a couple uses left—shit!" She dropped the piece of glass she had been holding and looked at her hand. Blood ran down her finger. "Well, that's just great."

Suddenly, Blaire found herself hauled up from the floor and into Lukas's arms.

"What are you—"

Lukas lifted her hand and dragged his tongue over her finger as he maintained eye contact with her.

"Oh."

He grinned and walked her back toward the wall, careful to avoid the glass on the floor.

Blaire ran her hands up Lukas's chest, wrapping her arms around the back of his neck as her bare back met the cool wall of the bathroom. She laced her fingers into his hair and dragged her nails over his scalp, just the way he liked. He groaned and closed his eyes, burying his face against her neck. The simplest things set off the fire between them since their bonding. Lukas often restrained himself from asking for her blood, which made her feel comfortable and safe with him. He respected her apprehension about it, but she was growing to see it as a normal thing between them.

"I love you. Gods, I love you." Lukas sighed against the mark on her neck.

He trailed teasing kisses down over her collarbone and across her sternum to her breasts, where he nipped at the skin before taking a nipple between his teeth, delicately biting the pebbled bud. She laid her head back against the wall and moaned softly, squeezing her thighs together to soothe the ache already building. Lukas caressed and bit at her breasts, sending bolts of pleasure straight to her core.

Moving up to her neck, he gently sucked on the skin as he ran a hand over her stomach, nudging her thighs apart with his knee. He slipped a hand between her legs, sliding his fingertips over her folds. "You're already so wet for me."

She sucked in a breath as he lightly pinched the throbbing bundle of nerves. He smirked against her neck, and the vibration against her skin prompted an involuntary shiver. He dragged his fingers down and slid a finger fully into the heat of her body.

His finger worked her, and her eyes rolled back into her head. When he crooked his finger forward, Blaire gripped his hair in her hands and moaned low in her throat. She met his thrusts with her hips, riding his hand shamelessly, lost to the pleasure. Lukas dragged the fingers of his other hand over the mark on her neck. A trail of heat followed, and she could feel his hardness against her thigh as he pressed against her.

"More," she panted.

Lukas slid his finger out partly before adding a second finger as his mouth claimed hers. Gasping into his mouth, she arched impatiently into his hand.

She wanted more.

She wanted everything.

Blaire gripped his shoulders and moved one of her hands down to wrap around his erection. He felt hot and heavy in her hand, and when she stroked his length slowly, he groaned, meeting her stroke by pressing his hips forward.

"Is that what you want?" he said against her ear, his breath uneven.

"Please."

Lukas growled and raked his fangs across the shell of her ear, making her shiver. He lifted her, and she wrapped her legs around him instinctively as he guided her to slide down onto his length. Once perfectly sheathed inside her, he shuddered.

"C-condom," she said hesitantly, her head resting against the wall as the feel of him bare inside her assaulted her senses. It might have been a psychological thing, but she could swear it felt different. She had always thought men disliked the sensation of a condom, but she didn't know it would feel different for her. The feel of his hard, smooth length inside her with nothing separating them was incredible. She almost regretted bringing it up.

"I'll stop… I'll pull out," he rasped, shaking against her as he held himself still. She could tell he was struggling with restraint, waiting for her consent to continue without protection.

When they discussed it before, after their first time together when he'd used one, they realized they didn't know if she could even get pregnant by a Vasirian while still human. Professor Velastra had no information to help them. She was just as in the dark as they were when it came to how a human and Vasirian pairing worked. But the general assumption was since they shared the same biological functions, it was possible. They didn't want to risk it. Pregnancy at nineteen wasn't something she wanted. She wanted to get her degree and go from there. Where that would be, she wasn't sure. This world was so new to her that small goals seemed easier.

But she was too far gone. She didn't want to lose the sensation.

"Okay," she said, opening her eyes to stare into sea-glass depths that glowed faintly. "Just this once."

Lukas lowered his head and claimed her lips with his as he slid his hands down her sides, pulling her more firmly up against him as he gripped her backside. He broke the kiss to trail open-mouthed kisses over her neck.

"I'll never get tired of this feeling," he whispered over Blaire's skin, thrusting into her at a steady rhythm, her back sliding over the wall as she clung to his shoulders. He dragged his tongue down over her neck to her breasts, where he sucked on the pale flesh.

"Bite me. Please bite me," she mewled, her nails biting into the skin of his shoulders.

Blaire had become so enamored with the sensations and pleasure that came with Lukas taking her blood, biting into her skin, that she sought it out when caught up in the moment. She never thought in her wildest dreams she would beg a Vasirian to bite her, to drink from her, but here she was.

Lukas growled.

His fangs brushed over her skin as his thrusts grew more demanding, resisting the temptation. She wanted to break his restraint. When he let himself go, he was like an animal. A possessive animal that took what he wanted without hesitation. He never hurt her, always in tune with every sound she made, move she did, or signs of apprehension. He responded to her however she needed him to, so when his control did snap, she relished in the high it brought her.

"Please," she begged, digging her nails into the skin of his shoulders. Her orgasm built, and her thighs trembled against the sweat-slickened hips that snapped against her. The slap of their skin meeting echoed in the bathroom over the patter of the shower that still played as background music to their passion.

Lukas lifted his head from her breasts and looked into her eyes, panting as he stopped moving inside her. A sheen of sweat coated his forehead and chest, and he smelled delicious. She wiggled against him, making him groan. Her lips parted to protest his sudden stop in movements.

"I love you," he said with panting breaths before biting the inside of his wrist. Any protest forming on her lips died in her throat when eyes swimming with lust bore into hers over the wrist his full lips wrapped around. He held his arm up to her, blood running down his skin and staining his lips.

Blaire turned her head and licked the wound, and they both moaned at the sensation. She hadn't tasted his blood often, but when she did, her entire body caught fire. The taste of Lukas's essence was sweet, like her favorite candy and dessert all rolled into one, and it aroused her in ways she couldn't explain.

Lowering his head, Lukas licked again over her breast as he rocked inside her lazily. She moaned and ground her hips against him, urging him to give her more, lapping at his wrist. She wanted him to consume her. When Blaire sucked on his skin, Lukas groaned and sunk his fangs into her breast, blood spilling over her pale skin. She cried out, disconnecting from his wrist as she jerked her hips against him, her head falling back against the wall when he gave her what she'd asked for.

"Don't stop." His voice sounded like he'd swallowed gravel as he thrust harder into her, dragging his tongue over the trail of blood between her breasts.

She held onto one of his shoulders for dear life as she gripped his other hand in hers, returning to suck on the blood at his wrist. She grew drunk on the taste of his blood, the smell of his body so close to hers, and the pleasure he wrung from her body. The double assault of his taking her blood as he railed her against the wall had her climax racing through her as her muscles tensed. When she finally gave in to the pull of ecstasy, falling over the edge, she released his wrist and lay her head back against the wall, her mouth parted on a soundless cry.

Lukas buried his face in her breasts and sucked greedily from the puncture wounds as Blaire rode the last waves of her orgasm. His movements grew unsteady, and his legs shook.

"I'm going to come. I can't hold it. Fuuuuck, I—*Blaire*!"

Lukas dropped her legs and slid out of her swiftly, making her whimper at the sudden loss. He took his shaft in hand, and with a few quick strokes, he painted her stomach with his release. Panting heavily, he rested his forehead against hers with his eyes closed.

"Fuck, Blaire. I love you so much."

"I love you," she murmured through her drunken haze as she wrapped her arms around his neck.

After several moments wrapped in each other's arms against the bathroom wall, Lukas lowered his head again to lick across the top of her breast where he had bitten her, sealing the wound. He lifted his head to stare into her eyes.

The fact that Korrena pairs could seal puncture wounds with only saliva always surprised her. They couldn't do anything like that for any other injury, or to each other, only to their pair. The whole Korrena bond truly felt magical. Unfortunately, when she tried it for Lukas, she wasn't able to, leading them to believe it was a Vasirian Korrena trait only. Another benefit to not being human.

Lukas kissed her forehead tenderly and took her hand, leading her to the shower to clean up. The broken bottle could wait.

3

CLARISSA

"I hate Monday mornings." Riley dropped her head on her arms on the desk with an exaggerated huff.

"It's not like you did anything to be tired over."

Riley jerked upright and spun in her chair to glare at Seth behind her. "How do *you* know what I did or didn't do?"

He looked at her expectantly, the corner of his mouth lifted in a smug smirk. "Because unless you can convince one of them to go anywhere with you,"—he motioned between Aiden and Blaire—"you just stay holed up in your room reading those stupid books."

Riley's face turned red. "I'll have you know I do lots of things. Besides, you're no better. You stay stuck up my brother's ass all the time or in your room doing gods only knows what."

Aiden chuckled at the back and forth and shook his head. Riley turned sideways in her chair to face Blaire, but before she could open her mouth, Professor Jenkins cleared her throat. At the front of the room, next to their English instructor, a tanned girl with straight, golden-brown hair that fell to her waist stood looking around the room with narrowed hazel eyes.

"I've placed your essays from last week on your desks," the instructor said. "I want you to review them thoroughly and provide an outline of how you can improve upon your work based on my notes. I expect these turned in by the end of class, and we will discuss revisions tomorrow. But before we get to all that…" She glanced at the girl standing next to her. "I know it's unusual to get a new student once classes have already begun, but we have a new arrival from the first-year program."

The girl next to her cleared her throat. "Actually, I'm now in my second year. They skipped me." Her voice held a slight Italian accent, and even without her smug grin, her attitude and displeasure rang clear in her tone.

The instructor sighed, nodding. "Apologies, Miss Moretti."

The girl flicked back her hair with her long artificial nails, the little rhinestone accents catching the light, and shrugged. It made little sense to Blaire for their instructor to introduce a new student like they were in high school, but if this girl was someone of importance, perhaps she could rationalize the move. It was still weird. Just something new to add to the growing list of things in Vasirian culture she didn't understand.

"As I was saying…" The professor took a breath, looking back at the class, clearly annoyed with the girl but not addressing her attitude, for some reason. "We have a new student joining us. Some of you may know her already from her father's work on the Order's council, but for those unaware, her name is Clarissa Moretti."

Hushed whispers spread over the classroom, and Blaire looked around at the commotion that broke out at the mention of the girl's name. Blaire knew about the Order, but nothing about who the members were, or their families. While they hadn't tried again to take her blood, a few months hadn't erased the memories she held of the torment they caused. She shuddered.

Riley crossed her arms, dropping back against her chair with a huff, and frowned. "Oh, great. Wonder how the hell she got here."

Blaire raised a brow at her. "What's wrong?"

"Nothing." Riley sighed and shifted in her seat. "I guess I'm just not thrilled with the idea that one of the Order's spawn is here." She ran her hand into the faded pink hair on top of her head and tugged on it. "I just don't get why she's in our class. She's supposed to be a year behind us. I—"

"Can I sit here?" the new girl asked, standing next to the empty desk beside Lukas. She had a large forehead she didn't hide with her hair, keeping it parted down the middle. Her perfect small nose perched over full lips, accented by a severe cupid's bow. Blaire wondered if she'd had work done.

Lukas shrugged, not even looking up from the papers on his desk.

"Great!" Clarissa spun and dropped her designer bag on the floor next to her desk and sat in the empty seat, crossing her legs, her skirt hiking up her thigh. She already wore it high on her waist, so the hem rode shorter than most of the other girl's skirts. With only a pair of short black knee socks beneath, it was obvious she dressed to show off her toned legs. She turned her attention to Riley.

"To answer your question." She rolled her eyes. "My daddy moved me forward because I simply wasn't challenged enough with the workload where I was." She shrugged, looking bored already, and class hadn't even started.

"Your… daddy?" Riley suppressed a laugh.

"Yes. Angelo Moretti. Head of the Order," Clarissa said as if it were common knowledge, her thick brows pulling together, not understanding Riley's amusement. She turned her attention back to Lukas, who now played with Blaire's hair on his desk.

"Do you remember me, Lukas?"

Lukas turned his gaze in her direction and raised a brow. "What?"

"I said, do you remember me?"

Blaire turned in her seat to look back at Lukas and Clarissa. Did he already know her? A pang of possessiveness shot through her, but she pushed it down. He may have known her from high school or earlier. After all, everyone here practically grew up together from babies with Blackthorn's branching school system. They may have been in daycare together for all she knew.

"I have no idea who you are."

Clarissa sat back in her seat, her eyes comically large with the long lash extensions she wore as she balked at Lukas. "B-but… you helped me."

"Yeah, I have no idea."

Riley snorted, and Seth kicked her chair from behind. She glared at him, and Aiden shot her a look from the other side of Blaire's desk.

"Last year, when I was visiting to register for university courses, I dropped my stuff, and no one helped me. But you, you stopped and helped me pick up everything."

Lukas shrugged.

Clarissa frowned, clearly not satisfied with not being immediately recognized. The girl reminded Blaire of the petty girls who clamored for a boy's affections during her senior year of high school at Magnolia Heights. *How old is this girl?*

Lukas tugged on Blaire's hair and she turned back around to face him. "We still on for Haven this weekend?" he asked her, twirling Blaire's hair around his finger, ignoring the pouting girl on his left side.

Before Blaire could respond, Clarissa gasped, and everyone looked at her. She pointed at Lukas.

Aiden raised a brow at her in confusion. "What's wrong?"

"Your… Your neck!" she said, shaking her finger at him as she continued to point. Her mouth gaped open like a fish out of water. Lukas glanced over at her. "Please tell me that's a tattoo."

"No." Lukas shook his head.

"Is that…" Her entire body tensed as she squinted at the offending mark.

Riley laughed. "A Korrena mark? Yep. He's paired." She looked way too happy about sharing that bit of information with the new girl.

"Who?" she shrieked.

Professor Jenkins glanced toward them.

They were supposed to be reviewing the professor's critique of their first essays this term and revising accordingly. Blaire had little to look over—a few red marks here and there, but overall, she was confident in her English essays. She looked over at Riley's desk and saw a paper that held more red marks than the actual writing she'd done. Riley didn't think she needed any of the general education classes, with her focus on art and design, but everyone had been trying to drill it into her head that if she didn't get through general education, she wouldn't graduate.

Riley laughed again, struggling to maintain her composure. Blaire got the distinct impression that Riley got pleasure out of Clarissa's discomfort. She didn't know what to think. She felt tense and annoyed that the girl seemed to be so invested in Lukas. The urge to get out of her seat and sit in his lap to stake her claim alarmed her.

Lukas toying with her hair again calmed her nerves. She suspected he could sense her tension.

Clarissa moved her gaze to Lukas's hands in Blaire's blonde

lengths, then to Blaire. Her eyes narrowed into slits.

Riley slapped her desk and got control of her laughter as the professor glared at her. "Sorry, sorry!" She took a breath and turned to Blaire, a mischievous grin spreading over her face.

Blaire felt a sharp tap on her shoulder. She turned her head as Clarissa leaned across the desk, pulling her hand away. "Yeah?" Blaire paused, taking in the expression on the new girl's face like she was gum on the bottom of her shoe, frowning with her nose scrunched.

"You're that…" Clarissa pursed her lips. "Human, aren't you?"

Blaire blinked. "Yes… I'm human." She wasn't sure where Clarissa planned to take her line of questioning.

"Let me see your neck."

"Excuse me?"

"Your neck. Show it to me."

"What the fuck?" Seth said.

Lukas cleared his throat.

"She doesn't have to show you anything," Riley said, her disdain barely contained. "Who do you think you are to demand anything?"

"My dad—"

"Your '*daddy*' isn't here." Riley glared at her. "This is a classroom, not a council trial. You don't run shit here."

"It's okay," Blaire said, trying to calm the rising tension. She pulled her hair into a ponytail, exposing the matching mark to the one Lukas had on his neck. "I'm proud of my mark."

Lukas grinned, his entire face lighting with pride, and a warm feeling floated over Blaire.

Clarissa clenched her teeth as she glared at Blaire's mark.

"Careful. You might break your perfect teeth," Riley said with a roll of her eyes.

Aiden smirked and shook his head.

Clarissa sat back, crossing her arms, falling silent. She clearly wasn't happy, but Blaire couldn't understand what her problem was. Blaire thought the consensus for bonded pairs was that others were happy for them.

Lukas leaned forward and placed a kiss over Blaire's mark, whispering, "I love you."

She released her hair to fall back over her neck and smiled. "I love you too."

"It's not natural." Clarissa pouted as Lukas fell back into his seat.

Aiden tilted his head at her. "What isn't?"

"That!" She motioned between Blaire and Lukas. "She's not one of us. Humans aren't supposed to be Korrenas. She shouldn't even be here." She sounded like a sullen child who'd had her favorite toy taken away.

"Dude. What the fuck is your problem?" Seth glared at her.

"What? Aren't you all thinking it?"

"No, we're not." Aiden narrowed his eyes at her, his jaw muscle ticking with his agitation.

Riley shot Clarissa a dirty look. "Blaire is amazing, and you need to shut your mouth."

"*Blaire?* What kind of name is that?"

"Oh, for fuck's sake! I'm going to throttle her." Riley rose from her seat, but Seth was fast to react. He reached forward and grabbed her waist, pulling her back down. She gasped.

"Easy, Firecracker," he whispered in her ear, loud enough that Blaire heard him.

Riley fell silent and didn't move, even after Seth sat back in his seat.

Lukas sighed. "Listen, you really need to lay off. I don't know what your problem is, but Blaire hasn't done shit to you. I don't know who you are, but you're making a piss poor first impression."

Clarissa gaped at him, the disbelief that anyone would oppose her opinion written clearly on her face.

Blaire didn't entirely know what to make of her. Clarissa acted like a high school brat who really needed to back off Lukas, but Blaire didn't engage with her because of what it might mean for her with the Order.

She started writing on a blank sheet of paper. Focusing on what little revision she needed to address with her essay seemed like the better option. She didn't want to bring extra attention her way with how peaceful everything had been. With the new semester, she wanted it to stay that way so she could focus on her coursework. Tougher classes were on the way.

After a few minutes of silence, she turned in her seat to face Riley, who still looked like she was stewing but had said nothing since Seth shushed her.

"So, Lukas and I were talking over the weekend about going to his family's beach house on Tybee Island for my birthday before it gets too cold. I was going to ask Charlotte to come too because her birthday is in the same month, and we always spend it together. Do you guys want to come?"

"Hell yes!" Riley squealed in excitement, earning another glare from the professor. Despite being left to their own devices to review their essays, the professor still expected a controlled environment.

Seth shrugged.

"I haven't been to their beach house in a long time. Sounds like fun," Aiden said.

"Better be careful. One shark bite and the poor human will be gone," Clarissa said with an exaggerated eye roll.

Everyone ignored her passive-aggressive comments. A shark could do that to anyone, and shark attacks weren't typically a thing around this area. The girl seemed to be grasping at straws. Blaire couldn't be sure if Clarissa's problem applied with her personally or the human factor, pure speciesism—she never thought she'd use a term like that. Racism was the buzzword before her world opened up to other beings. Was speciesism even a word?

She smiled. "We'll let you know all the details closer to the date. Also, what about Mera and Kai? I still have to talk to Charlotte to make sure she can get the time off from the diner."

"*Another* human?"

The bell rang, and everyone got up to gather their things, ignoring Clarissa's question—Vasirian students couldn't work outside school grounds, so the answer was obvious, anyway.

"I'll talk to Mera and Kai," Riley said.

Clarissa grabbed Lukas's leather jacket as he moved past her to Blaire. He stopped and looked down at her hand on his arm then shook her off.

She smiled sweetly, looking up at him through her lashes. "Since I'm already a month behind everyone, do you think you could help me catch up?"

Riley rolled her eyes. "I thought you were here because you were too smart," she sniped. "Why would you need tutoring?"

Clarissa ignored Riley and ran a finger down the sleeve of Lukas's leather jacket. Blaire tensed, staring at them from beside her desk.

Something stirred in her belly, uncoiling inside her like a snake. Anger she hadn't known she was capable of reared its ugly head as her cheeks flushed red, and she clamped her jaw tight to avoid spilling the vitriol that coated her tongue like acid.

"Don't touch me," Lukas growled, breaking the spell Blaire had slipped under. The unfamiliar darkness retreated into its hole. Lukas relaxed as the tension receded from Blaire.

Clarissa sucked her teeth sharply, dropping her hand. She cut her eyes at Blaire and grinned in a way that made Blaire's skin prickle, leaning up to whisper in Lukas's ear. Blaire jerked at the proximity and stepped forward to put the girl in her place, but before she could say anything, Clarissa snatched up her bag and walked away with an exaggerated hip sway.

"Ugh, she's so fake!" Riley jumped up, glaring at Clarissa's retreating form as Blaire began packing her things, her entire body thrumming with nervous energy. "Everything about her screams 'try-hard' and 'pick me.' Not just her personality."

Blaire sighed. She found nothing inherently wrong with women who made themselves up to extremes or did things to enhance their beauty with artificial accents—some of it could even be pretty when not overdone. Charlotte got her nails done, and Blaire had wanted to try a little pampering herself, but she couldn't imagine getting lip fillers, faux lashes, and an artificial tan—though she imagined the sun-kissed skin Clarissa sported was in direct relation to her Italian heritage. A fake personality, though? Blaire took all sorts of issues with that—especially when it encroached on her relationship with Lukas. Jealousy and possessiveness rioted inside her, and she didn't like it.

"What the hell did she say?" Aiden turned to Lukas.

Lukas shook his head, watching Blaire. "She just said I could be a big help."

Blaire stood abruptly, marched to the front of the class, and roughly slapped down her paper on Professor Jenkins's desk, earning her a raised brow.

"Everything alright, Miss Wilcox?"

Heat traveled up Blaire's neck and over her cheeks. She wasn't sure if it was from embarrassment or anger toward the new girl. "I'm fine," she gritted out between clenched teeth before storming out of the classroom.

"She seriously has no shame if she's willing to flirt with someone paired," Aiden said, rubbing the back of his neck as he and Lukas caught up to Blaire in the hallway.

"What? She wasn't flirting."

Blaire stopped short, twisting to face Lukas, filled with disbelief as she rubbed her brow, squinting with a sudden headache. "Seriously?" She didn't attempt to tamp down the shock and indignation in her tone. "Even I'm not that naïve." She allowed the frustration out in the look she speared Lukas with. "That girl was flirting with you!"

Lukas's brows furrowed and Aiden put a hand on his shoulder, shaking his head before heading down the hall following Riley and Seth.

Lukas ran a hand through his long hair. "Look, she's no one. I don't see what the hell you're talking about, but I'm not flirting with her."

"You let her touch all over you."

Lukas sighed. "I didn't let her do shit."

"You barely stopped her!"

Lukas growled low under his breath.

She knew her accusation that he was complicit would make him angry, but she couldn't stop. Lukas belonged to her, and that girl thought she could just waltz into her space and lay claim? Not happening.

Blaire spun away. She didn't like the way she was acting. She inhaled deeply through her nose and exhaled from her mouth to calm herself before she said or did something more she didn't mean.

Lukas stepped behind Blaire, turned her to face him, and then pressed himself into her personal space, backing her to the wall. He slipped his arm around her lower back, taking her lips in a soft kiss. He was trying to distract her from the irritation, obviously.

"I'm hungry," he murmured against her lips.

Her brows drew together at the non sequitur. "What? Didn't you eat breakfast?"

He met her eyes. The heat she saw there made it abundantly clear he wasn't referring to food. She swallowed hard, and he rested his forehead against hers, closing his eyes.

"Lukas," she groaned and pushed him away. "You can't solve everything with sex."

Lukas lay his head back with a heavy exhale. "What do you want me to say, Blaire? What do you expect from me?"

She bit down on a hundred replies that would only fan the flames.

He threw his arms out wide at his sides. "Do you want me to say you're the only one for me? That I don't even remember what the girl looked like? That having her sickening berry perfume all in my face when she got near me turned my stomach?"

Blaire gaped at him as his voice rose.

"Or how about the fact that all I thought about during class after feeling your jealousy was taking you back to our dorm room and making you scream my name?"

Blaire licked her lips and looked away, her heart hammering in her chest.

Lukas crowded her personal space again. "She's nothing," he said tenderly, leaning in and stealing a kiss from her lips before moving to her jaw and peppering kisses down to her neck.

"Okay," she whispered. Her body was at war with itself, but the longer Lukas kissed her skin, the more that black thing in her belly curled in on itself until only lust remained.

Lukas kissed her neck gently over the Korrena mark, lacing his fingers with hers. “Let’s stop by the room before our next class.” His voice had become raspy, deeper than before. “I can’t wait.”

A throat cleared behind them, and Lukas groaned, lifting his head. “Let’s go,” he said, taking Blaire’s hand and leading her away from a glowering Clarissa.

4

Struggling

Blaire dropped her head onto the thick open textbook resting on the table in front of her and groaned. Only one month into her second year and she already felt at her wit's end with her classes. Last year, a lot of her classes were introductory and prerequisite before she could get into her actual field of study, but there were still a few she had to clear this year to focus completely on her degree.

"Tell me why I thought this was a good idea."

"What's a good idea?" Riley asked.

Blaire lifted her head from the book, pushing her hair from her face, and sighed. "Trying to get a bachelor's in psychology. These classes suck."

Aiden leaned over, looking at the book in front of her. "Actually, you'd have to take statistics with a lot of the majors. It's a prerequisite."

Blaire groaned. "Kill me now." She hung her head back and rubbed her hands over her face.

Lukas leaned over and wrapped an arm around her waist, pulling her to his side. "Don't talk like that," he said against her neck.

"I'm not being serious. It's just… Statistics II is way more difficult than Statistics I ever was. Like, even the explanation of the class gives me a headache."

Seth raised an eyebrow. "What do you mean?"

Blaire pulled out a slip of paper from a binder and held it up. "Well… '*Fundamentals of statistical analysis of experimental and observational data including linear models, the analysis of variance, a priori contrasts, post-hoc tests, power analysis, and effect size calculations.*'—Like, what the hell is that?"

Mera burst out laughing. "I'm sorry, I'm sorry." She covered her mouth to regain composure. "I've already taken both for my bachelor's in Health Science."

Mera was the same age as Blaire but was already in her third year of the university program because of her intelligence. She consistently scored at the top of their classes last year, so over the summer she took the remaining prerequisites to skip her second year entirely. She went straight into a full load of major-specific classes. Kai had advanced as well, which meant both of them would graduate a year ahead of the rest of their group.

Seth's upper lip curled as he shook his head at Mera. "How in the hell can you go into a field like that?"

"What do you mean?"

"Just… the blood and shit. I couldn't do it."

Mera shrugged her petite shoulders, tucking her cherry-cola hair behind her ear. "I'm not sure what focus I'll go into when I'm finished. I have several options available, and not all of them would have me come in contact with human blood. That said, I don't really have a problem with it."

Seth's brows knitted together as he stared at her.

"I suspect I don't have any powerful attraction to human blood because of how often I share lifeblood with Kai… but I can't say for certain why I've never struggled with the scent. Not everyone does, though."

Seth held his hands up to stop her. "Okay, okay. I don't need to hear what you and my brother do."

With everything that happened months ago, Blaire suspected Seth didn't have as much control as the others when it came to blood—at least with human blood. From what she was told, he had to leave the room after the first incident with the Order. At least he was in control of himself enough to know his limits. How he responded to his own kind, she had no clue. Kai smirked at Seth across the table, crossing his ankle over his thigh as he sat back in his chair, eating an apple.

Blaire stared at her book as if the answers to all of life's problems would magically reveal themselves.

Mera rolled her eyes. "You know, I'd be happy to tutor you."

Blaire snapped her gaze up to meet Mera's, her eyes widening like saucers in alarm. Riley told her about Mera's unorthodox methods of study. There was no way she could manage being kept up all night and only set free when it was time to actually take a test—that was definitely not how she learned.

"I… uh…"

She looked around the table and glared at Riley suppressing laughter. Aiden wouldn't even look at her. Even Lukas buried his face against her neck to stifle his amusement with little success, given the puffs of air and the vibration of his chuckle against her skin. They all knew of Mera's study methods either firsthand or through the traumatic horror stories shared by the others.

A deep voice from behind broke through her mental freak-out.

"That certainly wouldn't be necessary." Kai and Seth's cousin Vincent stood nearby with his arms crossed over his chest.

"What the fuck do you want?" Lukas demanded, pulling Blaire closer by her waist. She never could fully understand why Lukas had an issue with Vincent talking to her.

"I couldn't help but overhear our beautiful jewel's dilemma," Vincent stepped up beside Blaire, looking down at her book. "Seeing as I am the TA for the class in question, I am privy to what the expectations are and what she should focus on."

He had a similar cologne to Lukas—an apple and spice mixture, with a subtle addition of something woodsy, but despite having similar scent notes, the blend with his natural scent didn't compare to the intoxicating combination on Lukas.

Vincent turned his attention to her face. He grinned at her, and the way the corner of his mouth lifted while the rest of his face remained passive gave him a hard edge that made the hairs on her arms stand on end. His long black hair fell to the side when he tilted his head to study her. It had grown longer since the last time she saw him months ago, falling to his lower back.

"I offer tutoring services to all the students in the classes I am a TA for, and this early in the year, I have wide open availability. I could see you after class every day until you're comfortable with the material, and then we can switch to a less aggressive schedule for refreshers and test prep."

"Seriously? You'd do that for me?"

"Well, of course. A beautiful jewel such as yourself shouldn't frown and show such distress on her face. I'd be doing a civic duty to ensure you're relaxed and able to breeze through the class."

Lukas growled as Blaire's cheeks warmed. She wasn't used to overt flattery spoken like that. Kai rolled his eyes and set his apple core down on the tray in front of him.

"Can you help me too?" Riley asked, taking Vincent's attention from Blaire.

"Of course, but until I know where Blaire's understanding is, I'll need to meet with her one on one. Afterward, I'd be happy to meet with you the same way. Once I grasp both of your levels, I can design a program to teach you both together, if that's something you'd prefer?" He moved his gaze back to Blaire, waiting for her answer.

"Oh, um. Yeah, that sounds great."

"Excellent. We can start tomorrow. Meet me after school in the study lab on the third floor next to the library, and we can assess where you're at." Vincent turned from the table, not acknowledging anyone else, and walked to the buffet to get his dinner.

"That guy creeps me out. Sorry, guys." Aiden glanced at Seth and Kai.

Seth scoffed. "Don't apologize to me. He might be family, but he freaks me out too."

"What's wrong with him?" Blaire asked.

Kai tilted his head, studying her. "You really don't find his way of speaking off-putting?"

"What do you mean?"

"For example, calling you a beautiful jewel."

"Yeah, what the hell is that all about?" Seth looked at Vincent standing in line at the buffet.

Riley drank from her blood packet and shook her head. "He's been calling her that since they met last year. It's like he sees her as some rare thing because she's human. It's really creepy."

"I think you guys are overthinking it," Blaire said. Sure, Vincent acted differently than the others, and his mannerisms were forward at times, but creepy? Blaire wasn't one for pet names, but she couldn't understand everyone's impassioned reaction to Vincent. They weren't the ones given the weird name.

"I don't like him," Lukas said.

Blaire frowned at him.

Riley laughed. "You don't like anyone, though."

"Look, he's willing to help me, so I'm not complaining."

Lukas toyed with the leather bracelet on Blaire's wrist he had given her. "I don't have to like it, though."

"Yeah, but the less time I spend studying, the more time I can spend with you." Blaire tried to appeal to his obsessive codependence. If she took supplemental lessons with Vincent, then she would spend less time going over material she didn't understand in circles all on her own, effectively opening up more time for them to be together.

"At the expense of some asshole flirting with you," Lukas muttered, but she heard it clearly.

"What? He's not flirting."

"'Beautiful jewel'? Come on, Blaire. I thought you said you weren't naïve."

Blaire's eyes widened. "What is wrong with you?"

"Just yesterday, you were all on my ass about Clarissa flirting with me when I didn't do anything."

"Because she was!"

Lukas pinned her with a look that made her shiver. The anger that thrummed under the surface along their bond made her uneasy. "At least she wasn't giving me creepy ass nicknames." He stood and left her sitting at the table, staring after him in confusion.

"We need to go shopping soon. I need a new pair of boots," Riley said, breaking the silence as she poked at the broccoli in her pasta with her fork.

Blaire appreciated that Riley was trying to diffuse the situation, but she didn't know what to do with the renewed hostility from Lukas. She didn't even want to chase after him. What good would it do? She sighed.

Aiden shook his head. "Don't you have enough boots?"

"Absolutely not. You can never have too many shoes. Especially boots."

He rolled his eyes and pushed his straw into a blood packet.

Blaire stared at the packet in Aiden's hands. It still blew her mind to know they had a monopoly on blood donor packets from clinics and hospitals all over the Southeast. Due to their smooth integration into human society, they had enough Vasirian in the medical field that obtaining a continuous supply to keep the students and staff fed wasn't an issue.

When she asked Kai a few months ago what Vasirian who lived outside Blackthorn Academy did for their daily blood, since harming humans was against their laws, he explained blood packets were easily picked up by anyone. The way he described it made it sound like they went down to the local clinic and brought it home like making a beer run. Their world never ceased to shock and amaze her.

She shook her head. "I'll go, but I'm not sure when because I can't miss these sessions with Vincent." She looked at the book in front of her and chewed on her lower lip, trying to not think about Lukas off somewhere sulking. "I really don't want to fall behind and fail this new class, so I won't be able to spend as much time after school as I did last year."

"Lukas already takes so much of your time since you bonded… I'm lonely," Riley pouted as Lukas returned to the table and dropped into his seat, stabbing a straw into a blood packet, glaring at the table in front of him as he sucked on it.

Kai shifted in his seat and gave Riley a pointed look. "You'll just have to find your Korrena soon so you're occupied."

Riley flipped Kai her middle finger. "If it were that easy, I'd already be paired. I want to find my pair." She sighed. "You think I haven't been open to it?"

Seth shifted in his seat and took a long drink of his blood packet.

"Ugh!" Blaire slammed the book closed and sighed heavily. "I'm not going to get anywhere trying to study in the cafeteria when I don't even know where to begin."

"Don't worry about it now," Lukas said. "You'll be able to start your tutoring tomorrow. Why not enjoy the rest of the night off while you can?"

Blaire looked over at Lukas, who appeared calmer now that he was drinking blood, and sighed again. "You're right." She tucked the textbook back into her bag, then pulled her neglected tray toward her. After twirling the noodles around her fork, she took a huge bite of the Fettuccine Alfredo that had already gone cold. "When I'm finished with this, we can go down into the Valley and visit the shops before they close."

"Hell yes!" Riley clapped, bouncing in her seat.

"I need a new bottle of my perfume and a few other things, and I won't have time to get them later." Blaire sipped her white peach tea and asked Lukas, "Are you coming with us?"

Lukas put his nose to the side of her neck, nuzzling into the Korrena mark before whispering, "Anywhere you want me, I'll be there."

She shivered.

"Get a room," Seth said with an eye roll.

Aiden laughed, and Blaire's face heated.

"Jealousy isn't a good look for you, little brother," Kai said with a smirk.

Seth looked at Kai in confusion. "What? I'm not jealous of them. He's welcome to her." He gave Blaire an apologetic glance. "No offense."

Kai shook his head in exasperation. "I didn't mean that you wanted Blaire, you idiot."

"What the hell do you mean, then?"

"As much as you complain about not wanting a Korrena, I think you do."

Seth jerked in his seat as if Kai slapped him and looked away. "Yeah, no. I don't need someone clinging to me. I don't need to be bound to someone against my will."

Kai and Mera exchanged a look. It still surprised Blaire how they seemed to share entire conversations by just looking at one another. She wondered if the bond between Lukas and her would ever get that strong.

Riley jumped up, startling everyone. "We should get going before things start closing."

Blaire looked at Lukas's phone on the table to check the time before gathering her trash onto her tray and standing. Lukas picked up her tray as Blaire grabbed her bag, then followed her and Riley from the cafeteria.

5

TUTOR

Blaire walked down the empty hallway toward the study lab and her first tutoring session with Vincent. Lukas still didn't want her to be alone with him, but he relented, knowing in the end he couldn't stop her, no matter how much he waved his alpha vibes around. Blaire had gotten used to handling his moods when things didn't go his way. Stopping in front of the classroom, she took a breath and pushed open the door.

"You're early." Vincent looked up from the laptop in front of him on the table.

Blaire shrugged casually as she walked toward him, shifting her backpack strap on her shoulder. "I was in the courtyard reading and wasn't sure of the time. I don't have a phone."

"Mmm. That's a shame. But it's perfectly all right. I'm happy you prioritized your time with me." Vincent motioned with his hand to the seat opposite him at the table.

Blaire lowered herself into the seat. She pulled her textbook out of her backpack and set it on the table with a binder of notebook paper to take notes. "Well, I really want to pass this class, so the extra time can't hurt."

Vincent nodded before brushing his long hair from his face. "So, how has Blackthorn been for you?"

"What?"

"School. How has it treated you?"

Blaire's brows pinched together, and she shrugged, trying to think of what to say. She wasn't sure she wanted to share everything that had happened with the Order before she bonded with Lukas. She still didn't know who she could trust entirely at the academy, and she honestly didn't want to relive everything that had happened to her. Vincent wasn't a staff member, but that didn't mean he wouldn't talk.

"Oh. Well, it's fine. The first year was fairly easy… it's just this class that worries me."

"That's fine. I can assure you that you won't have to worry about this class at all when I'm finished with you." Vincent smirked, his eyes alight with something Blaire couldn't place, which made her stomach sink. Maybe the others had gotten into her head, but she couldn't ignore the creepy way he spoke now.

She opened her binder and grabbed a pen as Vincent explained the outline for his approach to tutoring. It seemed straightforward, and if his methods worked, by the time finals rolled around, she should be able to ace them with no remedial classes or make-up exams.

"So, tell me," he said coolly, as though still on the discussion of her tutoring. "How does it feel to be a Korrena now? The beautiful human binding herself to her vampire lover? Much like the book, no?"

Blaire's cheeks heated and she looked away, fingers stroking her Korrena mark on the side of her neck. Vincent's eyes followed the movement. They were both aware Vasirian weren't vampires; he was referring to the novel she was reading when they met.

"May I see it?"

She snapped her eyes up to meet his, and he tilted his head in question. "I… I guess?"

Vincent stood from his seat and walked around the table. He was tall, and from her place in the seat as he loomed over her, she felt tiny by comparison. He didn't wait for Blaire to move her hair. Instead, he smoothly pulled her hair away from her neck, his fingers grazing over her skin. She shifted, her heart beating with alarm and awareness of the Vasirian next to her.

"Well, would you look at that?" He traced his fingers across the marking on her neck.

She shuddered and pulled away. She didn't want anyone touching her like that but Lukas. Shifting anxiously, she tried to think of something to say to take his focus off her.

"Do you have a Korrena?" she blurted, licking her lips and turning partially in her chair to put distance between them.

Vincent's face clouded with an emotion she didn't understand as he moved to his side of the table, taking his seat again. "No. I wasn't as lucky as some to find mine," he said in a clipped tone.

Blaire tilted her head. "How old are you?"

"Twenty-two. As you can already tell from that, I've given up on the prospect of finding the elusive chosen one and have settled on the possibility of a compatible pair."

"I'm sorry."

Vincent chuckled and shook his head. "My dear beautiful jewel, there is nothing to apologize for. I am content with this choice. More so in the last year than ever before."

"Really? What happened?"

"Ah. Well, that's a bit of a secret, I apologize." He smiled, his sharp, aristocratic features softening marginally. Despite his expression changing, his eyes still held a coldness within. He tapped the papers in front of him with his index finger, his ring catching the light. “Now, back to the topic at hand. This will help assess where you are and where I need to begin with you.”

Vincent passed her a sheet of paper, indicating she should fill it in now. Reading over the material, she recognized problems from Statistics I and tried to remember the formulae to solve each one as she worked down the page.

After several minutes of silence, Vincent asked, “Have you considered becoming one of us?”

His words broke through her concentration, and she looked up at him with wide eyes. Blaire hated any time anyone brought up this question. She had nothing against Vasirian, or even being one at this point, as she had become more accustomed to the idea of drinking blood—though she imagined any other blood that wasn’t Lukas’s would turn her stomach. But she couldn’t wrap her head around giving up her humanity.

Not wanting to share her confusion and uncertainty, she simply said, “No. I don’t plan to.”

“Pity. The Dark Kiss can bring so much that you’ll never have as a human.”

She continued answering the assessment questions, trying to ignore his words, but the term “Dark Kiss” struck her as she recalled the anonymous letter she’d received months ago. As a human turned Vasirian she would live longer and not age the way humans did. She’d heal easier, which would be a bonus considering how her body never healed quickly from anything. She wore bruises for months at a time if they were bad enough. Sighing, she set down her pencil, passing the test to Vincent, who took it from her without a word, studying her face. She hoped he had enough tact to not say anything more about the Dark Kiss when it was obvious she wasn't comfortable with the subject.

He looked up from his laptop after he finished assessing her mock test and smiled at her. "This looks good. You retained most of the information presented in the first module class, so it shouldn't be too much of an issue to fall into this course. The problem most students face with Statistics II is the writer of the book changed. The methods are the same, but the way the author of that book"—he motioned to the textbook on the table—"delivers it is dry, and he often speaks in circles, which leads to brain overload."

Blaire sighed, staring at the thick textbook.

"That said, my approach will use minimal passages from the textbook. I'm more reliant on the notes I took as a student of the course and additional documentation from my time as a teacher's aide." He sat back and crossed his ankle over his thigh, folding his arms over his chest, which stretched his shirt over his biceps. "I think we can absolutely get you to where you need to be, if you would like to continue our sessions. I'm available every day for the time being, and as I said before, once we get you on stable ground, you'll be able to take fewer sessions. I'll follow up with another mock test to see if my lesson plan is a fit for you after a week or so."

This guidance was what she needed. Despite Vincent's nosiness, she could learn a lot more this way than attacking it on her own. She nodded. "I would like to continue, yes."

"Perfect," he said, his voice lowering.

Blaire packed her things into her backpack and stood.

"I will see you at the same time tomorrow. We will continue in the same location."

She nodded, glancing back before opening the door to leave.

Vincent sat staring at her with narrowed eyes. She didn't understand why he seemed extremely focused on her today or why he asked her the questions he had.

In the hall, she stopped short as Clarissa shoulder-checked her as she passed, headed into the same classroom.

"Ugh. Move, *human*."

Blaire glared after her. What the hell was her problem?

6

Pressure

Cracking the window to let in the breeze from outside to air out the room, Lukas looked across the busy courtyard from their room on the second floor. Students were heading in all directions, both in uniform and in street clothes. Classes were over for the day, but Blaire wasn't back yet. She'd had tutoring with Vincent, and while he didn't trust Vincent around her, he didn't think Vincent would do anything in broad daylight in a study lab. But he couldn't shake his unease.

His cell phone pinged on the nightstand.

Lukas chuckled as he read Aiden's latest complaint about Seth then typed a reply.

Aiden:

I'm not sure what the hell is going on with Seth. He's been so fucking moody lately that I'm starting to get annoyed with him around.

Lukas:

He's always moody.

Aiden:

No, it's different. Ever since you and Blaire bonded, he's sulked around and seems to have a huge chip on his shoulder.

Aiden:

What's worse is any time Riley shows up, he shuts down entirely.

Lukas:

You know he likes her.

Aiden:

Yeah, I don't know about that anymore. He's been hooking up with girls around campus who don't have their pairs from what I've heard. Besides, he's been with us since Riley could barely hold her head up as a baby. I don't think he sees her as anything more than an obnoxious little sister.

Lukas:

I dunno. I still think there's something there. I don't think a brother figure would act the way he does sometimes around her. The way he's been acting around Riley recently reminds me of when Blaire first arrived.

Aiden:

Huh?

Lukas:

Nevermind, man. I don't know. He just seems possessive of her.

The door opened. Lukas looked up from his phone as Blaire entered the room, tossing her backpack on the floor at the foot of her bed. She kicked off her shoes and sat on the bed, sliding her thigh-high stockings down her legs as she sighed. He followed the motion with pleasure; she was so beautiful, and he couldn't believe she belonged to him. But that sigh said something was off.

"What's wrong?" Lukas sat up on the edge of his bed, setting his phone on the nightstand, ignoring the chime of another message from

Aiden.

"Nothing. It's just… I don't understand what I did wrong."

His brows pulled together in confusion. "Did Vincent do something?" Lukas suspected Vincent had an ulterior motive of getting closer to Blaire with this studying farce he suggested. Vincent seemed too invested in her, and he could see the attraction in Vincent's eyes as he watched Blaire. It turned his stomach and made him feel violent.

Blaire shook her head. "No. When I left the room, Clarissa was headed inside. She shoved past me and just gave me an attitude. I think she has a problem with humans or something."

He hadn't paid the girl any attention. He hadn't considered others might have prejudices against Blaire for not being Vasirian. It gave him more reason to wish she would accept becoming like him. He hated that she could be treated poorly in his world because of what she was.

"It's probably nothing," he said, hoping to reassure her.

"Maybe. She hasn't seemed too fond of me in class either."

Blaire was right. He had noticed the way Clarissa kept making passive-aggressive comments toward Blaire and tried to interrupt them whenever they got close in class, inserting herself in their lab assignments and trying to partner up with him. The girl clearly was vying for his attention with the way she horned in on trying to do things with him, but there was nothing but disappointment to be found there if she persisted. He only had eyes for Blaire.

Blaire stood and untucked her blouse from her skirt, removed her tie, then undid the buttons as Lukas watched in silence. Her cheeks colored when she noticed his gaze as she slipped the shirt from her delicate shoulders, standing in front of him in nothing but her plaid skirt and a white lace bra.

"Beautiful," he whispered.

She turned away and tossed the shirt on the foot of her bed.

"You know, I'm going to lose so much time with you taking all these tutoring sessions."

Blaire looked at him. "Not really. I'm probably going to have more time because I won't have to spend all my free time with my nose in a book."

Lukas grabbed Blaire by the waist, lying back as he pulled her toward him. Blaire straddled his hips, her knees on the bed. "I still don't like you meeting him alone."

She groaned and rolled her eyes. "Lukas…"

"I know, I know. You need this. I just don't have to like it."

Lukas reached behind her and unhooked her bra before dragging the straps down her arms, freeing her breasts, and leaving goose bumps in his wake. He tossed her bra to the floor.

Lukas ran his tongue over his lower lip as he took her breasts in his hands, squeezing gently. "You're beautiful, Blaire."

Blaire's blush covered her neck and the tops of her breasts as she lay her head back, giving in to his touch over her sensitive skin. He sat up and leaned down to take her hardened nipple into his mouth, twirling his tongue around the sensitive bud, causing Blaire to squirm against his jeans and gasp as the denim created friction against her panties.

Lukas released her breast after biting lightly once. "I need you," he breathed, dragging down the zipper on the back of her skirt.

Blaire climbed off him and let her skirt drop to the floor before lowering her panties, standing naked before him. He would never get used to how she took his breath away. There was no disputing the fact that her body was perfect for him, in spite of how insecure she felt about her body from everything she went through with her stepbrother.

Lukas reached behind his head and pulled off his shirt in one swift movement, then tossed it across the room before wrestling his pants and boxers off swiftly. All finesse went in his desire to reunite with the pale beauty before him.

He reached out again and pulled Blaire aggressively back onto the bed. She gasped and fell over him, moaning when her core made contact with his erection.

Lukas closed his eyes and gripped her hips, whispering into her ear, “Need you.” He opened the nightstand to retrieve a condom and made quick work of putting it on. He didn’t want to have to worry about pulling out this time, even if the feeling of Blaire without a barrier between them had been one of the greatest feelings he’d ever experienced.

Taking him by surprise, she got on her knees and lifted herself, grabbing hold of his cock and lining it up with her entrance. He met her stare with wide eyes; she had never done this before, and he felt ready to blow from her taking control.

Blaire took her lower lip between her teeth as she lowered herself down his shaft. She must want this as badly as he did because he had no problems sliding into her. Once fully seated, she rotated her hips in a torturously slow grind that had his eyes rolling back into his head.

“Fuuuuuck.”

This girl had no idea what she did to him. The power she held over him.

He would give her anything she asked for.

Demanded of him.

Lukas groaned as Blaire lifted her hips and dropped hard, testing his reactions. He could tell she wanted to explore, but he couldn’t endure much more. He wrapped his arms around her body and spun them with ease, pressing her back to the bed.

"Can't," he rasped. "Won't last. Need you so bad."

She had reduced him to a monosyllabic mess.

Blaire cried out as Lukas lifted himself and snapped his hips forward, sinking as deep as he could go with one hard thrust. The sting of her nails biting rewarded his flesh in tingles down to his toes. They had made love this morning before classes, but her spending the afternoon with Kai and Seth's pushy cousin drove him mad with the possessive need to own her—claim her all over again—and made the drive and sensations more intense, as if they hadn't had sex in days.

Blaire scratched at his chest as he took her body at a demanding pace, throwing her head back and moaning so loudly anyone passing in the hall could hear her.

Let them hear.

He wanted everyone to know she was his.

Only his.

Lukas slammed her wrists down onto the bed, dropping his upper body to hers and leaning in, taking the flesh at her shoulder between his teeth, his fangs pricking the skin.

Blaire's back arched, and she wrapped her legs around his waist. "Please," she panted, running her hands up his back and tangling her fingers in his hair.

Lukas loved how she always begged him. Her whispered pleas wormed their way into his brain and did things to his insides he couldn't describe. She owned his world. He wasn't about to deny her what they both craved, so he sank his teeth deep into her soft flesh as he pushed wholly inside her at the same moment he let go. He came with his whole body, filling the condom as she pulsed around him, dragging out everything he had.

Blaire's grip on his hair stung, but he was so lost in the intoxicating taste of her blood blooming on his tongue, and the high of his orgasm, that he didn't care. He wanted to stay lost in this moment forever, but he had to stop, or she would be weak for days.

Lukas reluctantly pulled away from her skin, licking the wound to seal it, and stared down at her blissed-out face. His softening cock thickened again but dinner service was happening shortly. Carefully, he pulled from her body, and she closed her eyes. He disposed of the condom then returned to the bedside. Looking down at her body glistening with sweat, a red flush on her pale skin, made him almost break and go back for more, but she needed to eat. He restrained himself.

"Let's shower before dinner. Do you think you're okay to stand?" She often got dizzy after he fed from her, or with excess blood loss. She'd had a bad cycle months ago and could barely function, which frightened him. He wanted to keep her strength up to avoid a repeat. He didn't think he could handle it.

Blaire looked up at him with a drunk look in her eyes. "Mmm… think so," she mumbled.

He worried he might have taken too much, but she sat up and eased up from the bed. She stepped to him and wrapped her arms around his waist, indicating she would be fine.

"I love you," Blaire whispered against his sweat-slick chest, taking in a deep breath like she so often did. He squirmed inside whenever she smelled his sweaty skin, worrying that he stunk; but he liked that she enjoyed it. Her jasmine scent consumed him; so, if she felt anything like he did in response to her scent, he would let her smell him all day. More than all day. Years. Decades.

Lukas pulled her close to his body and kissed the top of her head. "Forever," he whispered and then sighed heavily into her hair. Regret swamped him at the one way she kept holding back from him.

Blaire lifted her head. "What's wrong?"

He didn't want to ruin the moment, but he couldn't hide his change in mood from her. He slowly eased her back down on the bed to sit and picked up his boxers, sliding them up his hips.

"You know..." He put his hand over his mouth, rubbing roughly as he searched for how to broach the subject. With a sigh, he dropped onto the spare bed across from her, putting his elbows on his knees. "There's a way to resolve all this."

"All of what?" Blaire pulled the covers over her naked body, staring at him with her lips pursed and brows drawn.

"This shit with Vincent. Clarissa."

Blaire stared at him expectantly.

"If you were Vasirian,"—he held his hand up when Blaire's mouth opened—"Clarissa would quit giving you shit about being human. And I wouldn't be as worried about Vincent. You'd be stronger; at least strong enough to protect yourself when I can't be there."

There went the post-sex afterglow. The warm and fuzzy feeling that settled in his belly from her contentment soured. He'd ruined the moment like he feared, and her guard went up.

Just. Like. That.

"Lukas, no."

"Hear me out."

"What else is there to say?"

Lukas sighed in frustration and clenched and unclenched his fists, staring at his hands. "It's more than just those things. I can't stop thinking about what happened to you before the summer. Before we sealed our bond, the Order almost killed you. If you were Vasirian, they would stop coming after your blood."

"They haven't attacked me in months."

"No. But maybe that's because they took enough before and it's only a matter of time before they need more samples. What then?

What if they botch it like before and you're more scarred up than before?" He waved a hand at Blaire's arm that lay across her lap.

With the professional stitch job the health team did, it looked a lot better than it could have, considering the Order's underlings didn't know what the hell they were doing, and instead of taking a skin sample, they took a chunk of flesh.

Blaire's hand brushed the scar on her inner forearm.

"You know it'll be a good thing. You can't even have sex with me without coming away with bruises."

While he loved to see the marks he left on her in the heat of the moment, some of them were the result of whatever strange condition she had that kept her from healing well. She bruised too easily, and that didn't settle well with him. There was a difference in marking each other with rougher sex in a way both parties enjoyed, versus actually hurting the other person because they were weaker than you. In Blaire's case, weaker than most humans. They didn't understand her condition.

"Is that what this is about? We just had sex. Are you disappointed you can't have marathon rough sex with me like you would a Vasirian?"

"What? No!"

"I'm not about to give up being human to make sex easier for you. That's insanity."

"That's not what I mean." He paced around the room. "It's just one of many reasons. My point was everything bruises you. And those bruises last way too long for my liking."

"Oh, I'm sorry my slow healing inconveniences you." She scoffed and wrapped the cover tightly around herself.

"It doesn't. I'm saying that I don't enjoy seeing you hurt. It hurts me."

Blaire shook her head.

Temper pricked, he stabbed deeper. "Fine. What about us?"

She blinked. "What about us?"

"What about the fact that when I'm in my prime, I'll be having to bury you in the fucking ground?"

Blaire sucked in a breath and stared at him with wide eyes. "Don't you dare."

"Don't what? Speak of the reality that hangs over my head every day? Do you not understand how hard it is for me to look at you and know that you can so easily be taken from me? That if you somehow manage to survive all the potential pitfalls that come from just being human, then I'll inevitably lose you to time?"

"I thought we worked this out."

Irritation clawed at his throat, making it raw. "No, I guess we didn't. I can't pretend it doesn't bother me, Blaire. I can't pretend that I'm not scared. And that makes me so angry with you."

"With *me*?" Her head recoiled and her dark blonde brows knotted. "You have no reason to be angry with me."

"You're the one stopping this from happening!"

He was walking on thin ice, but the reality of losing Blaire was too much for him to handle. He told himself he wouldn't push her. But with Vincent watching his Korrena like she was something to eat, he couldn't stop the foreboding sense of disaster that ate away at him. He didn't trust that guy. He had this sickening feeling deep in his gut that Vincent was up to something. Making Blaire one of them was the only way he knew to protect her.

"I said I wasn't leaving, but I thought you wouldn't push me anymore on this. You said..." She sniffed. "You said you wouldn't make me. You said you were fine to live the rest of my life with me. Was it all a lie to get what you wanted?"

"No. I meant what I said."

"Then why are you pushing me now?"

"Because I need you safe."

"I'll be fine, Lukas. And as far as Clarissa goes? I don't give a shit if she thinks I'm trash and keeps running her mouth. Do you honestly think I care what she thinks? What I care about is you and her flirting with you."

Lukas sat on the other bed again and ran a hand over his mouth. "I don't want her. I'm just trying to make things easier for you."

Blaire stood from the bed. Lukas's eyes tracked down her naked body, and he had to shift to accommodate the growing arousal he didn't need her to see, considering the tense atmosphere.

"You know what would make things easier on me?"

Lukas met her gaze, then watched her pull her lower lip between her teeth, curious what was going through her head beyond what she said. Her expression said both she sensed his desire for her, and that the mood she was in wouldn't allow for it to go anywhere.

"What?" He had to clear his throat, his voice raspy. "What would make things easier?" he said, clearer this time.

"You giving me freedom to be who I was born to be."

With those parting words, she stalked into the bathroom and slammed the door. The sound of the lock clicking in place, keeping him from joining her, was like an ice pick to the heart.

7

Found Family

The scent of garlic and herbs filled the air and made Blaire's stomach rumble. It'd been three weeks, but they were finally getting around to going to Milanos. When Lukas had asked Aiden and Seth to go, he found out Mera and Kai had caught some stomach bug. It was strange to think of Vasirian getting such a simple illness with how quickly they healed, but apparently bad blood could make them incredibly ill. Not life-threatening, but something akin to food poisoning in humans.

It turned out that one of the clinics Blackthorn Academy used received a donation from a human with an undisclosed virus that slipped past their testing. The situation was quickly contained and the bad blood destroyed, but not before several students at the academy fell victim. The human in question wouldn't fare as well, from what Blaire heard, but Vasirian healing capabilities burned through it in a week. Thankfully, the donor blood hadn't made its way to other humans. It would have been a PR nightmare. It already cost the clinic a lot of business, and the FDA was breathing down their neck hard for the mistake.

With Mera and Kai long on the mend, and Charlotte back from visiting upstate colleges, they were all at last able to get together for Italian food at Milanos.

Cheese bubbled on top of her oven-baked pasta. While Mera and Kai split a large bowl of bolognese with an appetizer as their dinner, Riley, Seth, Charlotte, Lukas, and Aiden ordered several pizzas, spread over the table like their own pizza buffet. They were just waiting for Lukas to get out of the bathroom to eat.

Blaire had opted for a mouth-watering pasta entrée: shrimp, sea scallops, fresh mushrooms, and red peppers sautéed in garlic cream sauce, all tossed together with cute bowtie pasta and topped with a four-cheese blend the chefs baked to sizzling perfection in their brick oven. She'd already made her way through a whole appetizer plate of mushroom caps filled with Atlantic blue crab and shrimp in a garlic and herb cream cheese mixture, topped with even more melted cheese goodness.

She wouldn't be surprised if they had to roll her out of the restaurant by the end of dinner.

Aiden snorted a laugh from across the table, snagging her attention. She looked up to find both Charlotte and him staring at her from across the table with amused expressions.

"You're looking at that bowl like it's going to run away if you take your eyes off it," Charlotte said with a giggle.

Blaire flushed and sat back. "Sorry. Just hungry."

"You're always hungry," Riley said as she took a sip of Pepsi.

Kai tilted his head, studying Blaire. "I have no idea where she puts it."

Mera put her hand over her mouth to stifle a chuckle.

Blaire rolled her eyes. She wasn't going to argue a point she agreed with. If her metabolism was any different, she'd be much heavier. Though, without the exercise she used to do on the regular, she had put on a few pounds.

"Your hair looks great, by the way," she said to Charlotte. She lifted a breadstick from a basket on the table and took a bite. She'd need to run a thousand laps around the main building on the academy grounds to make up for this splurge.

"Oh, yeah?" Charlotte patted the heavily red curls that now hung below her collarbone, lifted one, and twirled it between her fingers. "I just didn't want them to be coppery red anymore. I wanted a change. Thought adding a bit of dark cherry in there would make them prettier. Make me a little sexier, without the focus on other parts of me." She flushed, and Aiden coughed.

"Well, it looks great. It reminds me of a really dark candy apple from the fair. I'm going to have to come back to work at the diner to keep the assholes off of you."

Charlotte laughed and released her hair. The curl bounced back into place in a perfectly coiled ringlet. "No way! I can handle it. Besides, I don't think I'll be there much longer. I have to get ready to figure out college admissions and all that."

Blaire sighed. Charlotte would soon leave Rosebrook. There wasn't much here for education outside of the public K-12 school system and the private prep school, Magnolia Heights. Blackthorn Academy was a no go for humans. There wasn't even a community college. The closest colleges were in Savannah, but Charlotte doubted she'd stay near the coast. Last they spoke, Charlotte was weighing the University of Georgia in Athens or moving completely out of state to Florida.

Blaire would miss her friend, but there wasn't anything here if

Charlotte wanted to pursue something beyond public sector work and minimum wage jobs without the education to do more.

A smile spread across Blaire's face as Lukas walked through the crowded tables toward them from the bathrooms. She squirmed in her seat. His long legs looked amazing in his signature black jeans with a corded belt and chains hanging from his hips. He paired them with a black, long-sleeved, button-down shirt. He'd rolled the sleeves up his forearms, showing off a few leather straps at his wrists.

His face was hard and focused, ignoring the looks that ranged from lust to uncertainty the patrons gave him. She now understood that the cautious looks most humans gave Lukas and other Vasirian were likely a natural survival instinct to avoid the predators walking in their midst, on guard to the threat they didn't understand.

While they'd never bring harm to the humans around them, they were more than capable of it. She'd witnessed it firsthand. Feared it herself. But with that danger came protection and fierce love. She'd never received that from humans after her mother died. So, despite the fangs and blood, Vasirian were not the monsters she feared in this world. At least, not all of them.

It still didn't mean she was chomping at the bit to be turned into one. While she didn't fear her Vasirian friends, or her Korrena pair, fear slithered down her spine thinking of being drained of her blood—risking her life—to become like them.

Lukas hadn't mentioned his desire for her to change in the last few days, but he was thinking about it. It was in the way he watched her. The way he'd cling tighter to her when she packed up her books to meet Vincent for tutoring, his eyes pleading with unspoken words. He was at least trying to respect her wishes.

Lukas's sea-glass eyes met hers, and his entire countenance changed. A smile split through the hardness, making him appear younger. His sharp features softened, and her heart leapt at the sight.

Dropping into the chair beside her, Lukas leaned over and kissed her lips softly.

"I like that shirt," Charlotte said.

Lukas sat up and shrugged lightly. He normally wore t-shirts and a leather jacket, so the ensemble was outside of his normal look.

Everyone had dressed nicer than usual, which complimented the atmosphere of the Italian restaurant. Even Riley had tamped down her outlandish style, wearing a black maxi dress paired with a hot pink, short-sleeved cardigan with a black octopus design on the front and side.

Blaire held back a laugh at Lukas's reaction. He seemed completely indifferent to the compliment, but now that they were connected, she knew better. It was faint, because the emotion wasn't strong, but she knew he was pleased—content, and maybe a little embarrassed, which showed on his face in the slight pinking of his cheekbones.

"Thought I'd dress a little nicer, since it's Blaire's first time at a place like this." His jaw worked as he looked away from the table to stare at nothing in particular. Blaire placed her hand on his thigh and squeezed. He was embarrassed, and it made her giddy inside to know he cared enough to put extra effort into something so simple.

Blaire swallowed a huge bite of hot pasta, quickly picking up her glass and chasing it with a large gulp of sweet tea. "So." Blaire wiped the cream sauce from her mouth with a napkin before addressing Charlotte. "Lukas and I talked about our birthdays, and he suggested something really awesome. Everyone else seems to be on board with it, but I want to run it by you."

"What did you have in mind?" Charlotte took a bite out of her slice of Italian sausage pizza.

"Lukas's parents have a beach house on Tybee Island." Blaire glanced at Lukas. "Thought we could do a big celebration. We didn't get to do much for his twentieth birthday in July, so it would be a perfect birthday makeup for him. Then there's everyone who had birthdays around the time I went to Blackthorn Academy. With settling in and other stuff… No one really got the chance to do anything."

"What's everyone's birthday?" Charlotte asked.

Aiden said, "Mera turned eighteen in January, and I turned nineteen in February, right before Blaire joined Blackthorn Academy. Riley turns eighteen this coming December, and Seth just turned nineteen on August fourteenth." He glanced at Kai with a grin. "Kai actually turns twenty-one next week."

Blaire tilted her head. "What day?"

"September twentieth."

"Then we'll have to celebrate his birthday too!" Riley declared with way too much enthusiasm, drawing attention to their table. Seth rolled his eyes at her playful behavior, but a smile tugged the corner of his mouth.

"So, it'll really be like a birthday celebration for him too," Blaire said.

"It'll be a gigantic party for everyone!" Charlotte clapped excitedly. "This'll be fun!"

Lukas put his arm around Blaire's shoulders and sat back in the booth, sipping on a glass of ice water. "How did you know it was my birthday in July?"

"Riley told me when it passed and no one said anything." She narrowed her eyes at him. "I'm mad you didn't tell me, by the way."

Lukas shrugged. "Never gave much thought to birthdays."

"Well, they're important, so get used to thinking about them. It's a big deal."

Riley smirked and Aiden ran a hand over his mouth to hide his laugh as Lukas pinned him with a stern look.

Birthdays were meant to be celebrated. It might not have meant much to the Vasirian, considering how long they lived, but to someone like Blaire—a human without her family anymore—it mattered. Time wasn't on her side. She didn't have hundreds of years. It could all be snatched away like the snap of her fingers.

Her eyes roved over everyone at the table. Her found family was on borrowed time. How long would she be able to keep them? If she kept refusing Lukas about becoming a Vasirian, would they still stick with her?

"You never know just how long you have with someone, so you should make the time count," Blaire said, ignoring the way her body tried to freeze at the thought of everything she'd found being taken away from her.

She took a bite of one of the jumbo shrimps, with a scoop of pasta. The table fell silent, and Blaire paused her chewing as she looked at the others staring at her. "Whaa ish ith?" She swallowed. "What is it?"

"I don't… your parents…" Charlotte looked at Riley with her brows pulled together, as if imploring her to say something. Charlotte's face was pale, and her perfectly straight teeth showed when she pressed them together in a grimace.

Blaire blinked a few times and looked down.

Of course, that's why birthdays mattered. She already knew that. She barely got any time with her father and didn't even remember him because she was so young when he died. Her mother always made a huge deal out of birthdays, and Charlotte and Blaire continued the tradition. Maybe it was silly to expect Lukas to share the same enthusiasm, but it mattered to her.

"If birthdays are important to you, then they'll be important to me," Lukas finally spoke, pulling her in tight to his side. "My family just wasn't around, so there wasn't a lot of celebrating."

"We tried over the years to celebrate with him. Me, Seth, Riley… but it wasn't something he seemed to care for," Aiden said.

"Well, I'm excited," Riley said and took a bite of her pepperoni pizza.

"You get excited over anything."

Riley dropped her slice and elbowed Seth in the ribs. "Quiet, you."

He shot her a glare and stole a pepperoni off her abandoned slice.

"Hey!"

Popping the slice into his mouth, he looked at her with a playful grin. "Yes?"

"That's mine!"

"It's in *my* mouth now." He stuck his tongue out; the pepperoni still sat flat on its surface.

Riley surprised the table, and him, when she snatched the pepperoni off Seth's tongue, tossed it in her mouth, and chewed before he could react.

"Did you just…"

"She did," Kai said with a chuckle.

Seth gaped at Riley, who gave him a smug smile.

Lukas pulled his arm away as the server set an appetizer in front of him. He'd eaten only a slice or two of pizza, and then ordered the garlic prawns. He pulled the plate away from Blaire as her eyes fell on the large prawns dripping in garlic sauce. "You had your own shrimp already."

She laughed. "I'm full." She pushed her empty pasta bowl away. "I'm not going to steal it."

"You two are so cute together," Charlotte said with a bright smile. "I just can't get over the fact that you have matching neck tattoos."

She looked at the others. "Did you know I tried to get her to get a tattoo with me after she turned eighteen until she left for Blackthorn Academy, and she refused? Now she's gone all out with a freaking neck tat!"

"You know the crap I would have gotten for that."

"You could have gotten it somewhere hidden. Like, I dunno, your hip?" She looked back at the others. "Do y'all have any tattoos?" Her gaze moved to Seth. "Anyone else?"

Riley shook her head. "Nope. Not yet at least. But I want one."

Seth glowered at her, but Riley was oblivious to it. Blaire wondered what that was all about.

"We have matching ones," Mera said, motioning to Kai. "On our chests."

When Mera didn't give details on the design, or anything more, Charlotte looked at Aiden.

"I have one, yeah."

When he didn't elaborate, Charlotte turned in her seat to face him fully. "Really? I wanna see."

Aiden chuckled and tilted his head to look at her from the side. The corner of his mouth hitched in a half grin. "I'd have to take my shirt off for you to see. Can't exactly do that in a restaurant."

Seth groaned and shook his head.

Charlotte's face turned comically red. With cherry red hair rather than fiery copper, and the blush lighting up her pale skin, her embarrassment stood out like a beacon.

For all the talk about wanting to be sexier, she didn't respond well when faced with genuine charisma. Aiden had loads of it. He wasn't even trying. It was all natural, which made it work for him—one reason Blaire didn't find his mannerisms off-putting. He wasn't trying to be a player or get into someone's pants. He was just naturally charming.

Aiden studied Charlotte without speaking, and Blaire stifled a laugh, speaking up to save her friend. “It didn’t feel like the right time to get a tattoo until I moved away from Caleb, you know?”

Charlotte latched onto the lifeline and nodded quickly, her red curls bobbing around her face. “I get that. It sure is an interesting tattoo though… Never seen anything like that symbol.”

Aiden rubbed the back of his neck and offered Charlotte what looked to be a sympathetic look, but Blaire knew he was uncomfortable, and didn’t know what to say about the Korrena mark. Blaire really needed to talk to Professor Velastra to see if there was some loophole to let Charlotte know the truth about them. She didn’t enjoy keeping her friend in the dark. It kept her safe, but if there was a way for her to be safe and know, it’d make life easier, and she could see her more often.

“Felt right now though,” Lukas commented. “I love Blaire, and we needed something that would signify our love forever. It was perfect. The symbol special to only us.”

Charlotte swooned at Lukas’s words, sighing, and looking at him. “That’s so romantic.” If it were possible, Blaire was certain there would have been hearts in her eyes. “One day I’ll have someone like that. Someone who looks at me the same way Lukas looks at you.”

Blaire smiled at her red-headed friend. “You deserve it.”

8

Mistrust

The sensual beats of the current track pulsed through Blaire as she danced alongside Riley on the dance floor. The writhing bodies around them looked like something out of a hazy dream as they moved in the strobe lights and fog from the machines at the edge of the dance floor.

Blaire hadn't been back to the nightclub Haven since what happened with her stepbrother the night he tried to take her away from her new life at Blackthorn Academy. Lukas had nearly killed him. She wasn't sure she'd be welcome back in the club, but Riley had assured her that the Vasirian who owned the club knew it wasn't her fault and that it wouldn't be a repeated incident. So far, no one had said anything, so she allowed herself to relax and lose herself in the music. She even stopped fidgeting with the short skater dress Riley had insisted she purchase when they went shopping after having Italian food the other day.

The black dress was simple, with its halter neck that exposed her upper back and a slightly plunging neckline. No fancy embellishments like straps, buckles, beads, or lace like Riley's outfit. She felt comfortable in it aside from the length.

Riley wore her usual in-your-face style. A black, tiered skirt with tulle lining the fringe that stopped above her knees revealing torn fishnet stockings and her buckled platform boots. She wore a long-sleeved top designed to be a crop top, but with her short torso, Riley only had a sliver of skin above her waistband exposed.

Rue pushed through the crowd of dancing bodies and handed Blaire a chilled glass topped with a wedge of lime and filled with red liquid.

"What's this?"

"A Cape Cod."

Blaire's nose wrinkled, and she sniffed the drink. She could smell the alcohol. "What's in it?"

"Vodka and cranberry juice. Try it."

Taking a small sip, the strong flavor burst on her tongue, and she smiled at Rue. "It's good!"

"Be careful. It's deceptively strong. Sneaks up on you." She giggled and spun around as Liam came up behind her, taking a sip of her own blue-colored drink. She wore a jumper with sheer sleeves that fit tight to her arms and a plunging neckline in the front and the back that exposed the middle of her torso down to her navel. How she kept it from falling open and exposing her breasts, Blaire had no clue. The outfit was gorgeous, but she'd never have the confidence to wear it herself. Rue paired it with gladiator sandals that tied up her calves and stopped below the knees.

"Oh, you've got to be kidding me."

"What's wrong?" Blaire glanced to Riley, shouting over the music.

Riley was glaring in the direction of the table the rest of their friends sat at, and Blaire turned to see what had her so upset.

Through the bodies grinding on one another, she could just see Lukas sitting at the end of the table talking to someone she couldn't see. He had an impassive expression so she couldn't get a read on what he was thinking, and their empathic connection provided no clue. The unfortunate thing about the connection between them was when she really wanted to tune into his feelings, she periodically found herself locked out. It wasn't a constant pipeline into his feelings, and if they were far enough apart physically, it didn't work at all. Of course, that was a good thing as well, because that afforded her privacy to her own emotions.

But with the tension that had grown between them recently, she really wouldn't mind having access to his feelings so she could try to make better sense of his words and actions. Lukas often acted in ways that didn't align with feelings she felt from their empathic connection. He didn't know how to act sometimes. He was just as naïve to this love thing as she was.

The song changed and bodies cleared the dance floor, allowing Blaire a clear view of Clarissa Moretti, laughing, and laying her hand on top of Lukas's. Blaire had to squeeze the glass in her hand to keep from dropping it as her hand trembled. The room was flooded with red light to fit the current theme, and it made Clarissa's otherwise pretty face look sinister.

Riley gently put a hand on Blaire's arm, startling her. "Let's go."

"What's wrong?" Rue asked as she moved up next to them, Liam holding her hand.

"A bitch who doesn't know her place is what's wrong."

Liam looked at Rue. "I don't understand."

"I don't really either, hon. I don't think it's a language barrier thing this time." She kissed him softly.

Riley looked at Liam. "That Italian brat has been trying to move in on Blaire's Korrena."

Blaire was thankful Riley offered the explanation because she didn't have it in her to explain.

His brows furrowed. "You don't intrude on a bond."

"Tell *her* that," Riley spat.

Just as they moved toward the table, Lukas stood and followed Clarissa away from their friends into the crowd of bodies on the other side of the tables near the bar. Blaire's stomach bottomed out, and she had to swallow hard to dislodge the imaginary object in her throat that suddenly made it hard to breathe.

"Where are they going?" Riley shouted as they approached the table.

Blaire looked toward the bar but couldn't see anything for the sheer volume of people in the space.

"What?" Aiden's brows pinched.

"Lukas and the wannabe homewrecker," Riley said in exasperation.

"Clarissa? She just stopped by to say hello. She's here with friends," Mera said, leaning into Kai, who sipped quietly on his beer.

"So why did Lukas go with her?"

Blaire didn't hear Mera's reply. Her blood rushed in her ears as she stared in the direction Lukas had followed Clarissa. He said he didn't pay the girl any attention, but he willingly followed her in the club? That uncomfortable blackness stretched out in her stomach like a cat waking from a nap.

"Blaire? Hey, Blaire! Where are you going?"

She ignored Riley's shouts as she pushed through the bodies toward the bar to find Lukas and learn what the hell was going on.

The bass she had lost herself to while dancing with Riley and Rue now pounded in her head in a way that made her want to escape the dark club and not look back. With the sweeping red lights, and the creepy fog that curled around the crowd, it was difficult to tell who was who. But she couldn't stop. She needed to find Lukas.

Why was she panicking? Didn't she trust him?

She pushed to the end of the bar near the hallway that led to the bathrooms and glanced around. This corner of the venue held fewer bodies, so she easily spotted a familiar figure sitting at a small two-seater table near the entrance to the hallway. His ringed fingers held a small tumbler in his hand loosely, his eyes focused on the dark hallway. He didn't look much different out of his school uniform. A black vest with a filigree design over a button-down navy shirt with the sleeves rolled up, black slacks, and polished boots.

"Vincent," Blaire called out, approaching him.

His icy blue eyes met hers, and a flash of surprise crossed his face. "To what do I owe this pleasure, jewel?"

Blaire glanced around again at the crowd around them and frowned. "I'm looking for Lukas. Have you seen him?"

"Mm, I have."

She spun to face him again. "Where?"

Vincent's eyes cut toward the hallway he'd been focused on when she first approached. "Not sure you want to know the answer to that, jewel."

Blaire crossed her arms over her chest and followed his line of sight. She wasn't even going to entertain his statement with a response as she moved toward the darkened hallway. She wouldn't have asked the question if she didn't want an answer. She heard his deep chuckle behind her as the sound of the music from the club faded into the quiet of the hall.

"—she's not worth your time."

Blaire paused when she heard a girl's voice.

"I already told you she's my Korrena. That's final. Nothing you can say or do changes that."

Lukas's voice.

Blaire put a hand over her stomach as she crept closer, a sickening feeling setting in.

"I know that. But you don't have to accept the pairing. She's not one of us," Clarissa purred, running her hands up Lukas's chest before wrapping her arms around his neck and pressing herself against him. Her dress was so tight it was a wonder her breasts weren't popping out with how firmly she pushed against Lukas's body.

Blaire sucked in a sharp breath as Clarissa's arms wound around his neck. Lukas's head whipped in her direction.

Before he could say anything, Blaire bolted from the hallway, slamming into Vincent, who stood at the opening to the club. His muscular arms banded around her shoulders as they shook. She didn't even know when she had started to cry, but she couldn't get the sight out of her head of Lukas not pushing Clarissa away.

"Talk to me, jewel."

Pulling from Vincent's hold, she looked up at him, roughly swiping the tears from her cheeks.

While Vincent wasn't much older than the rest of them, he still was in a position like a teacher as their TA. Not someone who fit into the friend mold. She didn't want to dump her drama on him. She didn't know him.

He ran a gentle thumb over her cheek, still holding her arm by the elbow. "What has you so upset?"

Blaire looked away until he gently gripped her chin and turned her face back to him. He leaned down and put his face alongside hers. "He's behind you."

Her body tensed, and she moved to go around Vincent to escape into the club and find her friends, but Vincent halted her movements by curling his arm around her shoulder. She tried to back away, but his hold was strong.

He tucked his head down by her ear again "I'm not going to hurt you. I can tell he's the reason you're upset. Let me help you."

Blaire had no idea how Vincent could help her, and what keeping her here would do to help when all she wanted was to get away before Clarissa caught up. Blaire didn't trust herself not to attack the girl. But most importantly, she wanted to flee from Lukas. He was watching her, and she didn't want to hear whatever excuse he had to give.

"Vincent," Lukas growled.

Blaire felt the vibration of a quiet chuckle in Vincent's chest as he held her close to his body.

"Get away from her."

"Is there a problem?" Vincent's voice held a hint of amusement, but his face was impassive as Blaire looked up at him.

Suddenly, she was pulled from Vincent's hold, and her back slammed against Lukas's chest. "You're damn right there is. She's not yours to hold. She's mine."

Blaire's hackles rose at that declaration. She twisted in Lukas's possessive hold, shoving him back. He stumbled into the hallway as Clarissa came behind him.

She gasped and placed her hand on his arm. "What's going on?" Her tone was the perfect mask of innocence.

"I saw you!" Blaire shouted over the music that had gotten louder as a more upbeat electronic song echoed into the hallway.

Lukas's brows pulled low. "Nothing happened." He jerked his arm out of Clarissa's hold.

"I heard what she said. Is that why you keep pushing me? Because I'm not 'one of you'?" Her nose wrinkled, and she bit the inside of her cheek until she tasted blood.

Lukas had stopped pushing since their bonding until Clarissa came along. Ever since her arrival, he'd been trying to talk her into becoming a Vasirian. He used the excuse of Vincent and protecting her, but it was just another way of owning her. With Clarissa so freely dragging her human status through the mud, Lukas clearly had an issue with it.

Had he always had an issue with her being human?

She ran a hand through the blonde waves Mera had styled into her hair for the night and sighed. "I didn't think you had a problem with my humanity."

"What? I don't." Lukas looked genuinely confused, but she wasn't sure she believed it. Her emotions were too up in the air to rationalize properly. She knew it, but it didn't stop her.

She changed tactics.

"Why were you alone with her?" When he stared at her without answering, she added, "I saw you follow her from the table. I thought she was nothing to you."

Lukas's jaw muscle twitched. "She isn't anything to me. I told you."

"So, you just go off with anyone into darkened hallways and let them rub up on you?"

Lukas glared and opened his mouth to speak, but Clarissa beat him to it.

"Oh, I'm not just anyone, trash. You'd do well to remember that."

Lukas turned to Clarissa. Blaire couldn't see his face, but something in the way he looked at Clarissa had her snapping her lips shut. He turned back to Blaire and growled as Vincent stepped up to her back and placed his hands on her bare shoulders.

"First off, I didn't fucking follow her. I went to the bathroom when she left our table. When I came out, she was waiting for me. And second, I didn't let her fucking rub up on me. If you'd stuck around and not run to his arms, you'd have seen me shove her off."

It had been a long time since he spoke so venomously, but the way he spat his words at her made her skin crawl with indignation, provoking her most primal instinct to lash out at him like she had so long ago.

Blaire twisted, and Vincent's hands dropped. "I didn't run into his arms! He was standing out here when I left."

"So, you just decided, 'oh hey, this asshole is conveniently here, I'm going to hug him.' Do you realize how stupid that sounds?"

"Yeah, asshole. I *do* realize how stupid that sounds. That's why I didn't say it. *You* said it."

Lukas's eyes widened like she had slapped him. She'd never spoken to him that way before. She had to push down the conflicting feeling in her belly that told her she went too far, the hurt on his behalf for her insult.

"I don't know what your problem is with Vincent, but he did nothing wrong. *I* didn't do anything wrong. You're the one in the hallway with her," she snapped, pointing at Clarissa. She had to resist the urge to punch her smug face when she gave a satisfied smile. "Only to come out here and start throwing around the 'You're mine' shit. I'm not your property!"

"You *are* mine."

"Lukas, no. I belong to me." She let out a dry laugh devoid of humor. "Is this a Vasirian thing?" She turned to look at Vincent in question. "Do male Vasirian have this fixation of ownership of their pair or something? Or is this behavior just exclusive to a few select pricks?" She turned her sneer on Lukas. "Are women Vasirian like this? Is this what I'd have to look forward to if I gave up my humanity?"

"Are you telling me you don't see me as yours?" Lukas's tone was angry, but the slight waver in his voice revealed his hurt.

"I told you," Clarissa said, stepping up to Lukas and wrapping her fingers around his leather jacket sleeve.

Blaire bared her teeth.

"She's not one of us. She doesn't understand."

Lukas stared at Blaire, not moving, not removing Clarissa's hold on his arm.

"I don't see you as property. I see a partnership."

"That seems fair. You belong to him, and in turn, he belongs to you." Vincent crossed his arms and leaned against the chair at the table next to them. "Unfortunately, from my vantage point, I simply see a boy trying to control."

Lukas's fists clenched at his side. "Fuck you. I'm not trying to control her." He took a deep breath. "If she were Vasirian, I wouldn't have to worry as much about predators like you."

Blaire's mouth dropped open. "Vincent is a teacher's aide! He's only trying to help me pass my class so I can spend more time with you. I mean, what the hell, Lukas? He's not a threat to you."

"I'm still not going to let you get caught up with the likes of him."

"Excuse me? *Let* me?"

"Yeah. Let you." He glared.

Blaire ground her teeth and stepped forward, pushing her chest against Lukas as she glared up into his sea-glass eyes that burned with just as much venom as she felt coursing through her veins.

"You. Don't. Own. Me," she said in a low, measured tone that seemed to knock the wind out of him, judging by his expression and the way he recoiled at her words, his hand moving to rub his chest roughly.

Lukas groaned in apparent frustration and sighed heavily. "I'm just trying to protect you," he whispered and run his fingers over her cheek. "You might not be able to see it, but he wants you."

Blaire shoved him back, and he stumbled into Clarissa. He clearly hadn't expected her volatile reaction because he could have easily stopped her. If he wanted to hurt her, he could do it. If he wanted to overpower her, he could easily do it. He was so much stronger, and that was without his Vasirian gifts. But no matter how things went down, Lukas wouldn't hurt her physically. It was one of the few things she knew for certain.

"I'm not stupid! Stop talking like I am."

This was getting out of hand. Fast. She needed to stop this. She couldn't.

"See, she just doesn't understand our kind. She doesn't belong."

Lukas didn't acknowledge Clarissa as he stared at Blaire with anger that made her shiver, his eyes glowing at the edge of his pupils. "No one said you're stupid, but even a monkey could see the way he's focused in on you."

"Oh, go to hell. Y'all deserve each other."

Blaire turned and shoved past Vincent, disappearing into the crowd, ignoring the shouts of Lukas behind her.

Naïve or not, Lukas had no right to treat her this way. He needed to rein in his temper and controlling nature fast, because she was beyond over it. There was nothing outside of Blackthorn Academy stopping her from living a quiet and comfortable life now that her step-family wasn't after her. She didn't have to put up with this.

Love shouldn't hurt this much.

"Hey, what's wrong?" Riley called.

Blaire looked up from where she sat on the edge of the large fountain in the center of the plaza outside the nightclub. Rue and Riley were walking toward her.

"What?"

"Have you been crying?" Rue asked, bending forward to get a better look at Blaire's face as she approached.

Blaire wiped her cheeks and shook her head. She just wanted to be alone. While Lukas was completely in the wrong, she hated the way she had handled it. Running her fingers through the clear waters, avoiding her friends' eyes, she sighed heavily. "I just can't seem to get it right."

Riley sat next to her on the fountain's edge and Rue stood in front of her. The plaza was practically a ghost town at this hour of the morning, saving her the embarrassment of being seen so vulnerable. The only movement around them was the bubbling of the tiered fountain, the occasional piece of trash blowing in the breeze, and the rustling of leaves in the landscape trees along the shop fronts.

Blaire had never been out in the Valley Center Plaza at this time of night. Gone were the smells of popcorn from the theater and the delicious foods of the various restaurants, replaced by the scent of blooming crepe myrtle trees in their square concrete structures around the plaza. With the only sounds the water at her back, the leaves, and the muted thump of the bass coming from Haven at the edge of the plaza, peace settled over a location that usually pulsed with life and chaos.

Rue tilted her head, and her long, high ponytail fell over her shoulder. "What can't you get right?"

"All of it. Lukas. The Korrena thing. Vasirian culture. Just when I feel like I have the hang of it—like I understand the expectations—things get tricky."

"What do you mean?" Riley asked.

Blaire kicked off her heels from sore feet and pulled her legs up to sit cross-legged, holding her dress down in her lap to avoid flashing Riley and Rue.

"Lukas wants me to be a Vasirian. Which, yeah, I know you all do… but he's been really pushing it recently."

Riley frowned. "Why?"

"I thought it was because of Clarissa, but he said some things earlier that have me questioning it."

Riley growled and kicked her feet out in front of her. "Like what?"

"He wants to protect me. From Vincent."

Blaire gauged her best friend's reaction to see if Riley believed Vincent was a threat the same way Lukas did, or if romantic jealousy fueled his actions. When Riley said nothing, Blaire sighed. "Lukas thinks Vincent wants me."

"He kinda seems like it, yeah."

"Who's Vincent?"

Blaire looked up at Rue as Riley answered. "Vincent Brandt. Seth and Kai's cousin."

"The teacher's aide?"

Rue took statistics class with Blaire, so of course Vincent was hard to miss.

Blair nodded. "The one and only."

When she first met her small friend group when starting the academy, she thought Kai looked like the stereotypical vampire with a goth rock edge. A cliché. It worked for him because he wasn't a try-hard.

But his cousin Vincent? He blew the cliché out of the water.

Where Kai was tall and slim, with leaner muscle definition, Vincent looked like Kai on steroids. It wouldn't be surprising to find Vincent's likeness on the cover of one of her smuttier vampire romance novels. He was the definition of a dark lord in his mannerisms, appearance, and speech. It was way too much. Blaire didn't like the muscle-bound, dark and dangerous types. While she didn't think he meant her any harm, those characteristics made him intimidating and a little off-putting, where she felt indifference to Kai's appearance and mannerisms.

Rue's lips pursed. "He likes you?" She sat next to Blaire.

"That's what everyone seems to think. I think he's just being friendly. Though his nickname for me is weird."

"Nickname?"

"Yep," Riley said, popping the P. "Jewel, beautiful jewel—creepy stuff like that."

"Wow." Rue frowned. "Doesn't he know you have a Korrena?"

"Oh yeah, he knows. Lukas has almost attacked him on more than one occasion."

"Tonight was no different," Blaire muttered.

Riley sat up and turned her wide blue eyes on Blaire. "Whoa. Hold up. What happened?"

"I caught Lukas in the hall with Clarissa." She swallowed thickly. "She was all over him."

"What?" Riley shouted.

"I ran away before I could see how he responded, admittedly, but I was just so upset. Hurt. Angry. I just needed to get away. I ran into Vincent on my way out, and he hugged me."

Rue whistled, and Riley sat back, slumping her shoulders.

"He tried to comfort me because I was crying, but Lukas didn't see it that way. We got into this huge fight in front of both Clarissa and Vincent. He implied I wasn't smart enough to see Vincent as a threat."

The understatement was a nice way of putting Lukas's response, but Blaire couldn't bring herself to admit everything he said and how it hurt her. She didn't want to create a rift between Lukas and his friends.

"I'll kick his ass." Riley tensed to jump up.

Blaire put a hand on Riley's arm. "It's over. Let it go." *This is exactly why I'm not giving you details.*

Riley deflated and tugged at the rubber bracelets on her wrist.

"Liam and I had a huge fight when we first became a pair," Rue said softly, drawing Blaire's attention. "Liam's cousin didn't know we'd bonded yet. I was meeting the family for the first time, and he showed up late. He thought I was Liam's girlfriend only. He flirted shamelessly, but I took it as a joke. I thought he knew."

"What happened?" Riley leaned forward to peer around Blaire.

"Liam broke Rich's nose and then we argued because I couldn't see what Liam believed he saw in Rich's eyes when he looked at me. Later, Rich admitted to being attracted to me and apologized to both Liam and I because he didn't know we were a pair, but the damage had been done. Liam doesn't trust his cousin, and now we don't see him."

"Are all Vasirian men like that?"

"Possessive assholes?" Rue smiled.

"Yeah."

"Mated Vasirian are. Men and women."

Riley shook her head. "I've seen it. Not sure how I feel about it. But it's kinda par for the course."

"It's wrong," Blaire said emphatically. "People aren't objects."

"It's more than that. It's a need to belong to someone and know they belong to you just the same. Our most primal instincts fuel the Korrena bond. If that isn't something you want, talk to Lukas about it. But you've gotta understand he'll have to go against his nature to be any different."

Blaire frowned. She didn't want Lukas to be someone he wasn't, but he needed to understand when enough was enough.

9

Doubt

Blaire jogged down the empty hallway, slipping with her wet shoes. She was late for her lesson with Vincent, and she hoped he wouldn't be angry.

Another week had passed since her tutoring sessions began, and her progress surprised her. She could afford time to enjoy herself, so after spending time with Lukas in their room, she had been outside in front of the dorm with Riley making plans for the weekend when the bottom fell out of the sky. By the time she crossed the courtyard and found shelter in the main building, she was completely soaked.

Blaire burst through the door to the study lab and stopped, holding her side, and panting heavily. She really needed to work out again; that run should not have worn her out the way it did.

"Well, hello there." Vincent crossed his arms as he looked up from his laptop, taking in Blaire's disheveled appearance. His gaze crawled from her soaked hair down over her white button-down blouse that was now transparent, and smirked.

The air-conditioned room made Blaire shiver involuntarily. She rubbed the water away that streamed down her face from the drenched strands of hair falling over her eyes. "I'm sorry I'm late. I lost track of time, and then Riley stopped me, and—"

"Take a seat. I'll get you a towel." Vincent stood and walked to a closet on the other side of the room before returning and wrapping the warm material around Blaire's shoulders after she sat. She twisted her wet hair into a clip on top of her head and gripped the towel around her shivering body tightly.

He sat across from her and tilted his head, his gaze falling to her neck, and then licked his lips. "What made you so late, beautiful?"

Blaire's face heated, and she looked down quickly. She wouldn't tell him she and Lukas had just made love before she met with Riley.

Despite still being upset about what went down at the club last weekend, Blaire couldn't stay away from Lukas. They hadn't talked about everything yet, but a tense understanding had settled between them. He didn't bring up Vincent again, even when she went to her daily tutoring. And he didn't even speak to Clarissa, no matter how hard she tried to get his attention. Blaire supposed that was progress, but she still felt uncomfortable. Things hadn't been resolved.

"Could that have something to do with it?" Vincent said with a smirk.

"Huh?"

Vincent motioned to her exposed neck.

Blaire touched the side of her neck, feeling the water there, and brought her hand back down. Her fingertips were red. What she thought to be rain running down her neck was actually remnants of blood from when Lukas fed on her earlier. She gasped and pulled the towel up, wiping her skin as she burned with embarrassment.

Vincent laughed enthusiastically. "I can't fault him for his needs, but do try to be more punctual. One shouldn't run after… such exertion."

Awareness lit his eyes. He knew what happened before she came here. There was no way he didn't know. She realized early that feeding was a sexual experience for Vasirian when taking from a partner. She loved it now, but it could be inconvenient if they needed to be somewhere. It was surreal how her perspective on the entire thing had changed in such a short time.

"I can certainly understand why he wouldn't be able to help himself." His gaze moved down from Blaire's neck to her chest, where the towel hung open, revealing her lacy bra through the shirt plastered to her chest.

Blaire pulled the towel closed and Vincent snapped his gaze up to meet hers. His eyes flashed an icy blue glow, and she opened her eyes wide. She hadn't expected that reaction from him. Before she could decipher what the flash meant, her ears buzzed with a low ringing. She rubbed at her temples as a dull pressure began at the base of her neck and moved to her forehead, increasing in intensity with each passing second. She closed her eyes to will the sudden migraine away, and after a few moments of feeling underwater, the feeling dissipated.

Vincent cleared his throat, and Blaire looked up to meet his intense gaze. He looked angry and confused; his lips pressed into a tight line, his heavy black brows pulled down into a scowl. Just as quickly as she noticed the look, he schooled his expression.

"Yes, well, shall we begin?" His voice held an edge that could cut glass.

She fidgeted nervously and nodded. He hadn't questioned her or made her feel uncomfortable all week—outside of that first day—but she sensed he didn't have the purest intentions with the way he looked at her today. His eyes glowing perturbed her. She couldn't shake the foggy feeling in her head. How had such an intense migraine come and gone so quickly?

Maybe it was the accumulation of everyone's constant ragging on Vincent's creep-factor, or Lukas's words of warning, but she was suddenly hyperaware of Vincent's scrutiny.

Vincent reached into his bag and pulled out papers. "I think we should assess where you are after what I've explained so far. I'd like to quiz you weekly this way to see that what I'm explaining is sticking. This way, I know what I need to carry into the following week and focus on, and what information I can set aside, if you are well-versed in—"

The door slammed into the wall. Lukas glowered in their direction.

Blaire stood, wrapping the towel tightly around her body. "What's wrong?"

He took long strides toward them, his eyes narrowed on Vincent. "What did you do to her?" he snapped, smacking his palms down on the desk.

"I have no idea what you're talking about."

Lukas swung his gaze to Blaire, and put his hands on her cheeks, looking into her eyes. "Did he hurt you?"

"W-what? No! What are you talking about?"

"I felt it, Blaire! I felt your distress."

"I—what?"

Vincent sighed heavily and leaned back in his chair, crossing his arms. "I do not have time to deal with the pettiness of your jealousy. We have only just started into our session because she was late after her little rendezvous with you. You couldn't even bother to be discreet, allowing her to bleed freely around other Vasirian."

Lukas looked at Blaire's neck with a knot between his brows. "What?"

"I just had a little blood left… I'm not injured."

Lukas cursed under his breath and grabbed Blaire's arm, pulling her toward the door.

"Lukas! Wait! What are you—my stuff!"

"I'll get it later," he muttered as he dragged her from the classroom, leaving Vincent staring after them.

Once in the hall, Lukas released her and spun around to crowd her against the wall. She looked away from him.

"Tell me what he did to you."

Blaire squirmed against his body as he held her pressed against the wall beside the door. Strong fingers clasped her jaw, turning her head to face him. His probing gaze sent shivers of nervous energy flitting down her spine.

"Lukas. Stop. He didn't do anything."

Lukas stepped back, releasing her, and raked both hands through his hair before pacing the hall in front of her.

"This is why you need to reconsider."

"Huh?"

"I'm freaking out." He stopped pacing to look at her with a plea in his eyes. Gone was the domineering presence that used his anger and physical strength to get his way, only to be replaced with the broken man she knew was deep beneath the surface.

"You're out here with blood on your skin. I'm feeling gods only knows what from you emotionally. I was walking down the hall to meet Aiden and Seth, and it hit me like a sledgehammer to the face. What happened to you in there?"

"Nothing happened."

Lukas stared at her in silence, and while she couldn't feel anything from him, his eyes said everything.

"You don't believe me."

It wasn't a question.

"Fuck." Lukas paced again. "Let me protect you."

She stood taller, her nostrils flaring. "I'm not throwing away my humanity to protect your fragile need to claim me."

He spun on her and slammed his fist into the wall, making her flinch. Maybe the forceful reckoning that Lukas wore like a suit of armor wasn't at rest.

"I'm not asking this to claim you! I'm trying to keep you alive!"

"I'm alive now, aren't I? I've survived nineteen years already. I don't need to risk my life."

"Blaire, please."

"No, Lukas."

"You're so infuriating! Why can't you see how stupid it is to cling to your humanity? You're fragile. Most humans heal better than you do. You're surrounded by my kind, and while it's against our laws to harm you, you know from experience that doesn't stop everyone."

Blaire closed her eyes and sighed, recalling her first day at Blackthorn Academy. She'd been cornered in the courtyard near the hedge maze and nearly bitten by another student. If it hadn't been for Lukas, there was no telling how far it would have gone.

She glared at him. "I'm not stupid. Why do you keep calling me stupid?" Her eyes burned from the unshed tears that prickled her eyes. She was angry with herself that she allowed him to get to her like this. She thought she'd moved past letting his hot and cold attitude affect her so strongly.

"Blaire—"

"You know what? No. I'm not doing this. You're just going to go in the same circles as before. Insult me. Reassure me. Tempt me. Only to repeat it later when I do something else you're not happy with." She took a measured breath. "Newsflash, Lukas. I don't belong to you!"

Lukas stepped back with wide eyes. "What are you saying?"

Blaire sucked in a breath at the sudden jolt of agony that lanced through her.

"I'm not your property," she corrected softly.

She held up a hand as he approached her. Beyond altering her words, she couldn't bring herself to comfort him when she needed to comfort herself.

"I just can't give you what you're asking for."

Blaire looked deep into his eyes, forcing herself to see his pain and demanding that he see hers.

She swallowed the apology that tried to push past her lips.

She wouldn't be sorry.

No matter how much consideration she gave to becoming Vasirian, she just couldn't do it. It was more than the fear of losing her humanity… it was also the realization that she wouldn't even belong to herself anymore.

She wouldn't be sorry for running from that.

Turning away from Lukas, she held her chin high when all she wanted to do was retreat into herself as she left him standing in the empty hallway.

10

Taken

Blaire sat on a bench in the immaculately manicured hedge maze next to a small fountain that marked the deepest part of the maze. The central garden was quiet and peaceful. The upper floors of the dorms and the school buildings were visible over the hedges, but the students milling about the courtyard and their noise were obstructed by the layers of hedge.

She had her book open on a small stone table next to the bench and jotted down notes while she waited for Vincent to arrive to review the mock test he gave her yesterday.

Vincent had suggested they carry today's session outdoors. The evenings were getting colder, and with their tutoring sessions running from the end of classes to as late as sunset, they should take advantage of the warmth while it lasted. Today had been chillier than usual, so she was thankful she'd worn her school cardigan over her blouse.

Their sessions were back to normal teacher and student. Gone were the heated glances and comments laced with innuendo from the day of the rainstorm where Lukas freaked out and cut their session short. Vincent had returned to being professional. His behavior further proved that Lukas was overreacting. Blaire wasn't sure how she'd convince Lukas to let it go, because while he had stopped mentioning Vincent, it wouldn't be long before the subject would come up again. Lukas didn't let things go easily.

"Have you been waiting long?"

Blaire looked up as Vincent approached her across the small cobblestone courtyard that surrounded the fountain. Dappled shadows from the ivy leaves clinging to a gothic statue of a winged creature danced across his face as he neared her.

She shook her head. "Nope. Maybe ten minutes?"

"Perfect. I brought something warm to drink. I didn't expect the temperature to drop."

Vincent set one cup in front of Blaire, then took a seat on the other side of the stone table.

"I have a few questions about the last five points on the mock test, but I went ahead and wrote them out before you got here in case they were related in any way. Hit all points at once, you know?" She passed him her paperwork.

Vincent nodded quietly, glancing over at her drink on the table before taking a sip of his. "So how have things been with Lukas since the club?"

Blaire sighed.

Confiding in Riley and Rue was one thing, but she didn't feel comfortable with Vincent on such a familiar level to share the details of her love life. Then again, he witnessed the meltdown at the club. Maybe he was just concerned.

"About as good as could be expected."

His brow rose.

"He's still convinced becoming a Vasirian is the only way to protect me around here."

"I suppose you think that isn't the solution?"

"You think risking my life by doing something that has shit odds for survival is the solution to keeping me alive?" Blaire scoffed with a sardonic laugh, shaking her head. "I figure the odds are more in my favor sticking with my humanity."

Vincent hummed thoughtfully and motioned to the drink she still hadn't touched. "It's apple cider tea. I hope that is to your liking."

Blaire blinked at the non-sequitur. She guessed he didn't have much investment in the "Keep Blaire Human" versus "Let's Make Blaire Vasirian" debate despite asking her once if she'd considered it. Not that she could blame him. She was sick of the argument herself, and she was the main subject.

"I've never had it, but anything warm is great right now." Blaire smiled as she took the warm cup in her hands. "Thanks." She smelled the fragrant drink and closed her eyes before taking a small sip, the strong flavor bursting across her tongue. "Oh, that's delicious."

Vincent smirked, keeping his attention on the paper as he jotted notes on the side margins.

"This is looking promising, jewel. Exceptional improvement."

She took another drink, getting used to the warmth in her mouth, relaxing as the liquid heated her chilled body. After drinking about half the contents, she set it down on the table and slumped back in her seat, holding her stomach. While delicious, it didn't seem as if the drink agreed with something she ate. The scenery around her spun. She felt nauseated and her head hurt again, but this time it felt different. Rather than a migraine headache, she felt drunk.

Vincent glanced up as he finished looking over her paper. "Something wrong?"

“I don’t feel good.”

“Oh, I hope you’re not coming down with something after being in the rain.”

Blaire shook her head and tried to tell him it was her stomach, but she found speaking difficult. Her lips felt numb, and her tongue lay thick and heavy in her mouth. Was she having an allergic reaction to something in the tea? She needed to tell him.

Vincent spoke to her, and she looked at him, her vision blurring. She couldn’t make out what he said.

His brows pinched together as he stood, leaning forward over the table, concern etched in his features. She couldn’t tell him what was wrong. He continued to speak, but she couldn’t make out anything he said. His lips moved, but no sound reached her ears. The environment around her kept going in and out of focus, and she rubbed her eyes.

Fear overtook her, and she panicked, breathing heavily.

Something was wrong.

Something was very wrong.

Blaire lifted her head, her gaze connecting with a narrowed pair of ice-blue eyes that looked even colder lined in black. As Vincent took his seat across from her again, a slow smile spread across his face. Her heart banged against her ribs like it could escape from her body; it pounded in her ears.

She was in trouble.

The world faded away.

The sound of running water stirred Blaire’s hazy mind.

She tried to grasp onto the sliver of wakefulness there, but it kept slipping through her fingers as she faded in and out of consciousness. Pressure bore down on her head from all sides, as if she were being held underwater. No one was touching her; knowing that did nothing to assist in her fight to breach the surface. The pressure was too much, a heavy blanket pulling her back down into the blackness. Her ears rang and even her breathing sounded distorted in the haze that enveloped her mind.

Focusing proved difficult when her ears had their own subwoofers. A constant pounding reverberated in tandem with the beating of her heart. Was that the sound of her heart, like the ocean through a conch shell, echoing back at her? It didn't sound steady, and that knowledge did nothing to calm the rhythm that now worked double-time as dread crawled over her.

Cold dampness pressed against her forehead. She stirred again as fingertips traced her jawline. Something happened; she couldn't remember what. The situation felt familiar. Waking in a daze, unsure of the events that had happened prior. Nothing good ever came from those times, and she was certain this would be more of the same. She willed herself to wake, for the memories to return to her so she could get it over with. Why was someone touching her? She wanted it to stop.

Darkness found her again.

Waking with a start, Blaire sat up, the cloth that lay on her forehead falling to her lap. She looked down at her wrinkled uniform to the lavish, queen-sized bed she sat on. The burgundy and black linens felt of high quality, buttery soft. She surveyed the room, trying to remember anything, taking in her surroundings for anything that might spark a flicker of memory.

Tapestries depicting gardens, epic battles, and runic symbols decorated the walls in the upscale room. A kitchenette was on the far wall behind a dining table. To the right sat a small black sofa and a coffee table with a beautiful vase of multi-colored flowers in full bloom.

An open doorway past the sofa led into a dark space, and on the wall at the foot of the bed another door had several locks down its side. She assumed it was the door to the outside; to where outside, she didn't know. There weren't any windows to give her a sense of where the room was located, or the time of day. She didn't know where she was.

Nausea roiled in her stomach and a cold sweat swept over her. She needed to find a bathroom. Now. She spotted a bucket next to the bed just in time and hung over the side, emptying the contents of her stomach. The aftertaste was terrible, the tea she had earlier sour on her tongue.

The tea!

She sat up and wiped her mouth with a shaking hand as it all came back to her.

Vincent.

The tea.

His grin as she lost consciousness.

Blaire trembled, the mixture of fear and nausea warring inside her making it hard to focus. Vincent did this, and now she didn't know where she was or what he wanted.

Footsteps caught her attention, pulling her from her panic, and her eyes fell on Vincent as he stepped from the darkened doorway on the other side of the sofa, rolling his sleeves up his forearms.

"Finally awake, are we? I may have put a little too much in that drink, I apologize."

Too much of what? What had he given her that made her so sick? She didn't dare ask for fear she would vomit again.

"Unfortunately, it was a necessary evil to get you here, but I assure you the effects aren't permanent."

Blaire tried to push herself up to get off the bed, but her arms shook in their effort to support her weight. She dropped back onto the bed, closing her eyes as another wave of sickness overtook her.

"Now, now. Don't push yourself, jewel," he chided softly as he sat beside her, putting his hands on both of her shoulders to hold her steady on her back. "Stay."

Blaire swallowed around the lump in her throat. "W-why are you doing this? What's going on?" Her voice rasped like her throat had been raked with sandpaper.

Vincent hummed and sat up. "Think of it like your story."

Blaire squinted at him, her focus going in and out as she tried to understand his words.

"Don't you remember that wonderful story you told me about last semester? What was the title again?" He stared at the ceiling then snapped his fingers, looking back at her. "Ah, yes. *Eternal Claiming*. The beautiful story of the human and vampire lovers. The poor girl sold to the mysterious vampire lord who eventually fell in love. It had such a nice ring to it."

"I… don't understand."

"No, I don't suppose you would, yet." Vincent caressed Blaire's cheek as she tried to pull away from him. "I haven't been able to stop thinking about you since that day, my jewel. I want… No, I *need* to get to know you better."

Blaire narrowed her eyes, her face a mask of disbelief. "This isn't how you go about that."

Vincent shook his head. "Perhaps not for most, but I'm a bit greedy. I much prefer to have you to myself as we get acquainted with one another. But it's okay though. I assure you I will give you the utmost care."

Blaire tried to get up again, but Vincent leaned his large body over her. He rested his forearm across her chest to effectively pin her to the bed. She squirmed beneath him, and fear gripped her to her bones. She didn't understand what he meant but instinctively needed to flee.

Vincent sighed and reached over to lift a glass of water from the bedside table. "I didn't want to do this again."

Blaire's eyes opened wide. "No. Please don't. I won't tell anyone if you let me go."

Vincent chuckled, shifting his weight to keep pinning her down as he held her nose, forcing her mouth open to breathe. As soon as it did, he poured the cold liquid down her throat. She gagged and choked, sputtering as the water soaked her. As much as she tried not to, she couldn't stop from swallowing a large mouthful while trying not to drown.

Blaire struggled, clawing at his arm to get him off her, but he was much too big, and she was much too weak from whatever he had drugged her with. She was slipping again, the same fuzzy feeling overtaking her senses, numbing her mouth.

Hot tears slipped from her eyes and ran into her ears as her eyelids fluttered close.

The last thing she heard before everything went black was his deep whisper.

"Good girl."

11

DISAPPEARED

"Where the fuck is she?"

Lukas approached the table where everyone gathered for lunch, panic in his eyes.

"Whoa. Hey. What's going on?" Aiden stood and grasped Lukas's shoulder.

Lukas shook, gaze darting around the cafeteria. "Blaire's missing!"

"What?" Aiden squinted; his face pinched as he stared at Lukas.

"She didn't come home yesterday after she left to go to her tutoring session. She hasn't been back at all."

Riley looked up, her brows netting together in confusion. "I saw her just before she went to her session. She seemed fine."

"Are you sure she didn't come back to the room, and you just missed her?" Seth asked.

"I'm sure." He sighed in exasperation, rubbing at the side of his neck anxiously over his Korrena mark as he glanced around the crowded cafeteria, hoping to catch a glimpse of Blaire. "I didn't leave the room. I didn't even go to dinner or breakfast this morning." He gripped the back of his neck. "She's gone."

Everyone exchanged looks as Aiden guided Lukas to sit.

Lukas didn't know what to do. He thought the Order had finished their stupid little games. Everything had been calm for months, and now Blaire had disappeared. His stomach roiled with nausea. He couldn't understand why he had felt so sick since yesterday evening, another reason to skip food, but it undoubtedly messed with his head—he felt drunk.

"Can't someone call her?" Kai asked.

"No." A pang of guilt hit his chest. He shouldn't have waited to give her the gift he purchased and hid beneath his bed. "She hadn't gotten a phone yet. I… I planned to give her one for her birthday in a couple of weeks before we went to the beach house."

Lukas swallowed bile down and shut his eyes, trying to fight off the sickness that gripped his insides.

"What's happening with you? You're really pale… even for you." Aiden studied Lukas, his features pinching with deeper concern the longer he stared.

"I feel like I'm going to throw up. I don't know what's happening to me."

Mera frowned. "Is this all because Blaire is gone?"

"No, I don't think so." He ran a hand over his face and cursed. "I don't know. I've felt like this since yesterday, before I even knew she was missing." His knee bounced up and down and he glanced around the room again. Where was she? He shouldn't be sitting here talking. He should be out looking for Blaire.

Kai and Mera exchanged a look.

Lukas growled. "Fucking hell, don't do that. Just tell us whatever it is."

"Well," Mera sighed. "I think whatever is going on with Blaire is likely affecting you. You both have such a strong connection that distance doesn't seem to be a factor like it is with us." She motioned to Kai.

Lukas looked at her, his eyes widening. He didn't want to even think about the possibility of Blaire being hurt or sick somewhere where he couldn't find her. He was supposed to protect her, but instead, he found himself sitting in the cafeteria, sick to his stomach, with no trace of her.

"We could ask Vincent if he's seen her since their tutoring session," Riley said.

Aiden nodded. "Yeah, I can go ask—"

Clarissa dropped her tray on the table and parked herself in the seat Blaire usually occupied. "I'm so sorry to hear what happened, Lukas. I can't imagine what you must be going through." She drizzled dressing over the top of her salad, mixing the vegetable medley before taking a bite.

"What do you mean?" Kai asked.

Clarissa set down her fork, looked at everyone staring at her in confusion, and dabbed her glossy lips with a napkin. "You didn't hear?" When no one offered her an answer, her mouth opened in a silent O, and then she clicked her tongue. "Well, Blaire"—she made a face as if the name repulsed her—"requested a withdrawal from the academy, and Daddy granted it to her."

Riley and Aiden stared at her with open mouths as Kai and Mera looked at one another in apparent confusion. Seth shook his head, his brows lowered as he stared at his tray.

"What the fuck are you talking about?" Lukas grated through clenched teeth as he turned his narrowed gaze on Clarissa. He was sure he'd chip a tooth if he didn't calm down. There was no way Blaire requested to leave. She promised she wouldn't leave him. He trusted her. The Order wouldn't just grant her leave like that.

"Supposedly." Clarissa sipped her Sprite, taking her sweet time, and it was all Lukas could do not to reach out and shake her to get answers. "Blaire couldn't handle being with a Vasirian, the fear of what being a human Korrena meant, and that she didn't want to be a Vasirian, so she left." She lightly shrugged, as if it were no big deal. "Daddy told her he would grant her a pardon in exchange for leaving immediately, so that's probably why she didn't say goodbye."

Clarissa shrugged again before taking another bite of her salad. Once she swallowed, she frowned at Lukas. "Of course, the rest of the Order's council was furious about it because she's human and knows our secret, but Daddy convinced them to spare her life."

"Convinced… them," Lukas said slowly, the words rolling around in his head and falling flat. "That makes no sense." Though it was the head of the Order who'd done the convincing. Lukas wasn't privy to the inner workings of the council, but he assumed the leader would have more pull than the others. It made no sense; they'd been so adamant about Blaire and her blood they wouldn't just let her go and move on as if nothing happened.

"That's bullshit. You're a liar," Riley started around the table toward Clarissa until Seth grabbed her around the waist, pulling her back into his lap and banding his arm around her. She squirmed in his hold.

"Stay. Don't start shit I'll have to finish." Seth tightened his hold on her. "I mean it. Don't. Move."

"I find that hard to believe." Kai cut his eyes to Clarissa. "Blaire is a bonded Korrena. Neither we, nor Lukas, have put any pressure on her to become a Vasirian since they bonded."

Riley glared at Lukas.

"Lukas?" Aiden asked, drawing everyone's attention to Lukas.

Lukas sat silently, staring ahead at nothing. How could this be happening? Just yesterday, he held Blaire in his arms, and she told him how much she loved him. Sure, things had been tense recently because he'd made the stupid mistake of pushing for her to give up her humanity, but to drive her to leave? Nothing Clarissa said made any sense. Sure, Blaire had wanted to leave before for the same reasons, but she didn't now. She said she couldn't leave him behind, but now she was gone. It appeared leaving him was exactly what she chose to do.

His mind was in turmoil as he considered all the places she could have gone. Her stepbrother was on the other side of the country. He doubted her abusive step-family even cared anymore. Did she go to Charlotte? Flee the state? Lukas had finally found the love of his life, claimed his happiness, and now she was being ripped away from him. He tried to rationalize the situation; make a plan of attack to find—and convince—Blaire to return. But if she didn't want to be here, he couldn't force her to be. He wouldn't. He told her long ago he wouldn't force her to do anything she didn't want to. He loved her too much to trap her. But that's exactly what he tried to do recently. Not by forcing her to stay, but by pushing her to become like him. Someone she once saw as nothing but a monster.

When a hand came down on his shoulder, startling him from his thoughts, he released a strangled sound before doubling over. His shoulders shook as he sobbed silently.

"Shit." Aiden knelt beside Lukas, pulling him into an embrace.

"I don't believe it," Riley whispered, a tear running down her cheek, and Seth squeezed her, still holding her in his lap. "Even if you wouldn't back off, I just can't believe it."

Clarissa sighed heavily, and looked at Riley impatiently, pursing her lips. She pointed her fork that held a cherry tomato on the end at Riley. “It’s true. You don’t have to believe it, but she’s gone.” She chewed up the tomato and shrugged. “She didn’t belong here, anyway.”

“Will you shut the hell up?” Aiden growled over his shoulder at Clarissa, still holding onto a shaking Lukas, who cried quietly. “What are you talking about, Riley?”

“What?” Clarissa looked around the table, her face a mask of incredulity. “It’s true, and you all know it. A human has no place here. He’s better off without her.”

“Get out of here,” Kai spat, his voice harsh.

Clarissa looked over at Kai and blinked like she couldn’t believe he had said that to her.

“I said…” He narrowed his eyes at her and lowered his voice. “Get. Out. Of. Here.”

She smacked her lips and rolled her eyes. “You’ll see it’s for the best soon.” She stood, taking her tray in her hands. With one last withering glance around the table, she walked away from the table, muttering about human sympathizers.

Lukas’s stomach churned as the waves of nausea swept over him, adding to the misery that suffocated him, threatening to steal the breath from his lungs.

“I hate her.” Riley finally pulled herself from Seth’s hold and dropped back into her seat beside him.

Mera looked at Riley. “Why do you dislike her so much? I mean, I’m not fond of the girl either, but it seems you already had a problem with her. I saw it on your face the moment she sat down.”

“When we were kids, she always pulled the ‘daddy’ card whenever things didn’t go her way. She got me in trouble a lot. Apparently, nothing has changed.”

Aiden took the seat Clarissa had vacated and released Lukas, who sat back and wiped his face, finally able to breathe without devolving into tears. Being with Blaire made Lukas realize he didn't want to waste a single minute, or have a single regret when it came to their bond—their future. But that future wasn't meant to be. She'd effectively reached into the depths of his chest and ripped away the heart he had given her and discarded it as if were merely trash.

"I can't believe she fucking left me. She *promised*." His voice cracked.

"Yeah, but you wouldn't lay off," Riley snapped. "Do you seriously believe that Italian Barbie? I think she's full of it. She's been gunning for you since she stepped foot in our class."

"Again. What are you talking about?"

Riley looked at Aiden and huffed. "Lukas and Blaire got into it. He's been pushing for her to become a Vasirian." She didn't elaborate, so Lukas didn't know if Blaire had told her everything about their recent fights or not. "Clarissa hates Blaire. She wants Lukas. Don't tell me y'all haven't seen it too."

Glances were exchanged, but no one commented.

"See. You know I'm right. I don't trust her."

"I do find it suspect Blaire would just meet with the Order and request to leave," Kai said, his face void of all emotion.

"Why?" Riley asked. "What about that part is suspect?"

"Think about it." Kai waved a hand lazily. "Blaire is afraid of the Order. They spent the last school year tormenting her, and now they're willing to let her just walk away? I don't think so." He sat back in his seat, crossing an ankle over his thigh. "Furthermore, letting a human walk free with the knowledge of our existence is playing a dangerous game I would think they were smarter than to play."

"But Clarissa said her father convinced them to waive any sort of execution," Seth said.

Kai sighed in exasperation, giving his brother a look. "Do you think that would matter, honestly?"

"I do question the sway the head of the Order has over the council if he could not only pardon Blaire, but also halt any form of consequence for her withdrawal," Mera said, sipping on her blood packet. "Not to mention, while they do oversee the Americas, I doubt King Blackthorn would just allow a human to walk away without at least a memory wipe. But I know nothing about our new king really, so who knows?"

Lukas sighed and held his rebellious stomach. He laughed softly, his mind at war with itself.

Aiden raised a brow. "What?"

"I just remembered telling Blaire last month that the night she almost left, and we bonded, was the worst of my life and the best. I guess I was destined to beat that." He laughed again, but there was no joy to the sound. His features went cold. "This is hands-down the worst day of my life."

"We'll find her. Talk to her. See what's really going on," Aiden reassured him.

Mera frowned. "There has to be more to the story."

Lukas couldn't process what was happening. He didn't know how to handle any of it. He couldn't even chase Blaire this time. If she really had run away, after everything that happened recently, by pulling this stunt, she made sure he couldn't catch her and stop her from leaving.

Did she really want to be rid of him, or was there more to it? Why leave everything behind? He'd respect her wishes and let her go if it absolutely came down to it.

She didn't need to run away from him.

All he wanted was her happiness, even if it wasn't with him. He had meant those words when he told her that long ago.

But he couldn't just roll over and accept it without hearing it directly from her. Without at least putting up a fight for what he knew in his heart was meant to be.

He needed to see her. Speak to her.

He had to find her.

12

Intentions

Blaire had grown to expect pain whenever she woke, but she would never get used to it. The familiar throb radiated from the base of her skull to behind her eyes. How anyone could take drugs on purpose or drink themselves into oblivion to wake like this time after time was beyond her understanding. It was a nightmare.

The whole situation was a nightmare.

Slowly the room came into focus. She was thankful for the dim lighting from the bedside lamp, but it did nothing to tell her what time it was.

"There's dinner on the table. Eat." Vincent's voice carried from the sofa.

She turned her head, squinting, barely able to make out his silhouette in the shadows of the room.

Blaire had grown accustomed to the same routine.

One moment bled into the next and all sense of time became lost.

If not to the drug-induced haze, then to the simple, progressive march of time that never paused for anything. Certainly not because disaster came knocking on her door. No. Time stopped for nothing and no one. One tick of the clock to the next. Time moved forward, stealing away precious seconds until the only thing left after the confusion was oblivion.

People clung to and thrived with schedules, routine, and structure until it was all taken away from them.

But it hadn't been taken away from her, not really. Merely replaced with a new routine. Wake, eat—sort of—struggle, drugs, sleep. Everything that happened in between was a blur. She lost all sense of time while barely conscious enough to ground herself to stability or schedule beyond the basics. Without windows to allow light in, she couldn't even track day and night cycles. Maybe leaving scratch marks on the walls, tearing them into the fancy wallpaper of the elaborate studio room, would have helped her keep track of the times she'd been awake vs. asleep, but she hadn't expected to be locked away in this room for as long as she had. What had she expected? A couple of hours? A day? She didn't own a handbook on how a kidnapping played out. While the exact length of time was lost on her, it had been a while. The smell coming from her body was a testament to that. She desperately needed a shower, deodorant, and a change of clothes.

Blaire's stomach growled in the silence, and she shut her eyes. She was starving, but any time she tried to eat, the drugs in her system rioted with her stomach acid. She would either throw up or dry heave if she hadn't managed to eat before nausea hit her from the smell of the food alone.

Was she going to die like this?

She certainly felt like she was dying.

"Eat," Vincent commanded again, more sternly this time.

Blaire groaned and lifted her upper body from the bed on her forearms, her arms trembling from the weight, her body shaking from the exertion. She felt so weak. Taking a deep breath, she pushed herself fully into a sitting position. Once the room stopped spinning, she swung her legs off the bed and stood on shaky legs.

She squeezed her eyes shut against the assault of vertigo that threatened to drag her to the floor. The pinched expression made her face hurt. She breathed slowly in through her nose and out through her mouth. It took a few beats to recover her equilibrium, but when she felt confident enough, she moved—albeit a bit wobbly—to the table where a bowl of soup waited for her.

She sat at the table and breathed in the delicious scent rising from the bowl in front of her. Her stomach didn't rebel. That was a positive change.

Vincent stood from the sofa and made his way into the kitchenette, switching on the light and illuminating the room fully. He pulled a loaf of bread from the small oven and dropped it into a basket, placing it on the table in front of her.

"This pairs well with the soup."

Blaire studied him. He looked tired; his sharp aristocratic features were weary, shadowed by hair that fell forward when he leaned over the table.

"What is it?" he asked, brushing his long hair from his face as he straightened.

"Nothing."

"Mmm. You know, lying is not a very lovely trait to have."

"You look tired."

Appealing to his sense of humanity—or whatever one would call it in a Vasirian's case—felt like the best possible tactic for staying conscious. Blaire wasn't sure how long she could endure being drugged like this; her body didn't feel right. Beyond it making her ill in the short-term, she feared lasting effects, regardless of his assurances of no permanent consequences. She no longer trusted him.

Vincent lowered himself into the seat at the side of the table to her right. "I suppose I am. Between tutoring sessions, being a TA, and ensuring that you are well taken care of, I find myself a little stretched thin."

Blaire pulled a face, then quickly schooled her expression. "Why not let me return home then? I told you I wouldn't tell anyone. My being here is obviously causing you problems."

Vincent placed one of his ringed hands over hers and shook his head. "Thank you for your concern, my jewel. However, coming home to you each day is what keeps me going. Soon, my schedule will lighten up, and I can spend more time with you."

Blaire didn't like the sound of that. At this point, she didn't know how often he was in the room with her because she kept being knocked out, but to have to interact with him constantly seemed daunting. Pretending to be interested in his words. Resisting the urge to fight and try to escape when there wasn't a way out. Both proved difficult for her in her brief moments of lucidity.

"Now, please eat before it gets cold," he directed again, his voice softer this time, possibly in response to her feigned concern for his well-being. At least her time with Caleb had proved helpful in this situation. As long as she pretended to give a shit, she could be relatively safe—at least she hoped that would be the case.

"What is it?" She peered into the bowl in front of her at a thick, light yellow soup garnished with bacon and spring onions. It smelled good.

"Potato, cauliflower, and leek puréed in vegetable stock. I made it myself."

"Really?"

"Well, yes. Making soup is fairly straightforward. I typically get your meals from the cafeteria or purchase something from the Valley Center Plaza to avoid too many questions, but I can make several things here in the kitchenette."

She was still at Blackthorn. Or close enough to campus if he was getting meals from the cafeteria. He slipped up and offered that information so freely. She had suspected as much, but she didn't know how it would be possible for Vincent to keep her on academy grounds and her kidnapping remain a secret. This room looked like none of the others she had seen on the grounds before.

"I would have much preferred to make a velouté, but unfortunately, I didn't have flour available to make a roux. This, however, is hearty and will give you strength. I've seasoned it with salt, pepper, paprika, and a pinch of cayenne pepper—I hope you don't dislike that?"

"No… That's fine."

Blaire didn't dislike many foods. She loved food. Just nothing at all appealed to her with the drugs in her system. It felt like her stomach was eating itself. She lifted a spoonful, the aroma of garlic and shallots making her stomach growl.

Vincent chuckled and removed his hand finally. Sitting back in the chair, he crossed his ankle over his thigh as he straightened the black vest that he wore over a button-down, black shirt with the sleeves rolled up his corded forearms.

The soup wasn't spicy—despite the addition of the cayenne pepper, which she was thankful for. She didn't know if she could handle anything intense on her empty stomach.

"I do hope it is to your liking. You'll need your strength to replenish your blood." He studied Blaire as she took another bite.

Blaire paused, the spoon halfway to her mouth. "What do you

mean?"

Vincent sighed. "While I am intelligent, I'm not able to pull this off alone."

Blaire didn't understand what he implied. She lowered her spoon.

"In exchange for full access to you in this manner, I had to agree to supply the Order with your blood—properly. I'm capable of doing this without risking your life like those idiots in the spring who didn't know what they were doing."

Blaire paled, horror spiking her pulse.

Vincent frowned at her obvious reaction. "Until now, I have been generous enough to take it while you were in an unconscious state to avoid upsetting you, as I clearly have by just mentioning it."

Blaire spluttered, at a loss for how nonchalant he was about the whole thing. "Oh, well, that's so kind of you."

"Of course." Vincent smiled; her sarcasm was either lost on him or he overlooked her retort. "It has been a service to you, my jewel."

"Smart ass," she muttered under her breath.

Vincent chuckled warmly, a hard contrast to the subject being discussed, and she couldn't understand how he could have such a cavalier attitude about it. He continued, not addressing her biting remarks. "To avoid any lasting damage, I will reduce the frequency of drugging your drinks."

Blaire perked up at that.

"…as long as you agree not to fight me."

Blaire looked down at the forgotten soup. She didn't know what to do. She couldn't fight him off if she tried. Vincent was easily twice her size and built like he lived in the gym. She didn't know where he got the time to keep up his physique with all his tutoring and classes. If she was going to survive this, she'd have to use something more than physical strength to fight back.

"H-how long have I been here?" Maybe if she had a better grasp on time, this overwhelming hopelessness wouldn't eat at her.

"Twelve days. It's October tenth."

Blaire's eyes went wide. Her estimate had been barely a week at the most. It sure explained the smell.

"How can that be? There's no way it's been that long. I—"

"That is precisely why I intend to reduce the drug in your system. Besides, your birthday is in four days. I'd like you coherent to celebrate. I didn't want to resort to such a primitive method, but compulsion doesn't seem to work on you."

Blaire stared at him, blinking rapidly. What did he just say?

Noting her expression, Vincent sighed. "It would seem you're immune to the Vasirian's ability to compel—to force my will. I wanted to bring you here through the power of suggestion, but you resisted during one of our last tutoring session. So, unfortunately, I had to resort to human methods to subdue you."

Blaire rubbed her eyes and chewed on her lip as she tried to recall the days before he'd brought her to this room. After several moments, her eyes locked on his. She remembered. Vincent's eyes had lit up just like that bully Aryan's had on the first day at the academy when he attacked her. She didn't remember being frozen in place, but she remembered the headache that followed. Vincent scowled shortly after it subsided, and then he'd given her the tea. The pressure she'd felt on her head like a migraine must have been him trying to compel her. She wasn't sure why she was immune to compulsion when it was possible to paralyze her. Did Vincent know she could be affected by that? If not, she would not volunteer the information.

Vincent shifted, putting his foot down and crossing the other over his opposite leg. "But yes, I intend to reduce the drug in your system, if not entirely cease administering it. How else can we get to know one another properly if you are passed out for most of the time? Besides, you're starting to lose weight by not eating, and it's not very attractive."

He stood, not giving Blaire the opportunity to say anything in rebuttal. He pointed at the foot of her bed to a neatly folded black garment. "You need to bathe. Through the door over there, you will find the bathroom—"

"Wait. If I've been unconscious for two weeks, how have I gone to the bathroom?"

Vincent sighed. "You've been semi-conscious enough to be taken to the bathroom to do your business, and with your lack of appetite, there haven't been many occasions where you've asked to go. When you've been conscious enough to where you could go to the bathroom, eat, and the like, you've not exactly been lucid—which is obvious by your lapsing memory. It's disconcerting, to say the least. More reason to cease drugging you."

She had no recollection of ever asking to go to the bathroom or much of anything else. The memory of her time spent in this room was fuzzy.

"Now, in the bathroom, you will find everything you need for a proper bath. Please change out of that unflattering t-shirt and put that on." He motioned again to the clothing on the bed. "At this point, you have developed an unpleasant smell. I apologize that I have not adequately tended to you, but that will change."

Blaire hadn't even had a sponge bath in two weeks? The oversized white t-shirt he'd stuck her in did nothing to mask the smell of her unclean body. While she no longer wore the uniform he brought her here in, that was the least of her concerns. She was too afraid to ask where her bra and panties were.

She quietly got up from her chair and moved over to the bed, picked up the silken garment, and made her way through the doorway

Vincent directed her to. The large bathroom housed a black claw-foot bathtub with polished gold feet surrounded by black candles in the middle of the room with various bath products alongside it on the marble floor. A black marble counter with a single sink stood against the opposite wall with a black toilet positioned at its side.

Again, she was faced with a room lacking windows.

The bathroom wasn't as extravagant as the room she came from, but the materials looked posh, nonetheless. The bedroom and bathroom décor screamed opulence, and she wondered what purpose the rooms served. They certainly didn't fit a university setting.

Of course, many things about this academy didn't quite fit the all-American university aesthetic, but she hadn't seen any living accommodations on campus quite like this. The bathroom alone was larger than her dorm room. What use did Blackthorn Academy have for something like this? Where the hell was she? Was this Vincent's home?

The color scheme aligned with Blackthorn Academy's uniform and linen colors throughout the school and dorms. Burgundy and black linens. Black towels. Fabric in shades of black and burgundy draped over the walls and hanging from the ceiling around the bath to give the room an intimate feeling. Everything screamed Blackthorn Academy.

Blaire set the silk nightie on the counter and removed the smelly t-shirt, dropping it to the floor. She stood staring at herself in the mirror, taking in the state of her body. She swallowed hard and took a deep breath as she raked her gaze over the purple, blue, and green blotches on her pale skin.

Despite the frequency of being littered with bruises from her stepbrother, it had been a long time, so seeing them again unnerved her. She hadn't fought Vincent while being drugged out of her mind, so she could only speculate where the bruises came from. Unable to do much, maybe she got hurt by his handling of her.

Her gaze moved to the bruising on her arm. It was obvious where those came from if Vincent was working for the Order. While nothing like the bruises she wore when the Order had taken blood and skin from her, the minor bruises still made her feel ugly. She traced her fingertips over the scar where she had received stitches to repair their damage.

She moved to the steaming bathtub Vincent had apparently prepared for her, and slowly eased herself into the water's depths. She sat back against the back of the tub, resting her neck against the soft cushion positioned against the hard surface, and shut her eyes.

She couldn't catch a break. She wondered if this was the life she was destined to have. She had finally escaped the Wilcox family's hold—she'd heard nothing from them since Blackthorn took care of their memories—only to be forced to fight for her life against the Order. Now she was caught up in whatever Vincent wanted.

He could have gotten to know her like a normal person during their tutoring sessions. She didn't have a problem with him in the way Lukas seemed to have with him—other than mild discomfort at how he talked to her on such a personal level at times; he had seemed harmless. Until now.

Lukas.

Blaire swallowed hard and opened her eyes, staring at the fabric that hung above her. She wondered what he was doing at that moment. Her chest hurt with the longing she felt to return to him. The one good thing about being in a drug-addled state was not being forced to face the fact that she couldn't go to him. Her lip quivered as hot tears spilled down her cheeks.

She didn't even know how to reach out to him through their

bond if that was even possible. No one had ever said it was, except speculation of a telepathic link between certain pairs. Unfortunately for her, that didn't apply to them. Though she strained with every nerve, she was too far away to feel any emotion Lukas felt. All she could feel was her own sorrow.

Taking a deep breath, she finished bathing, taking advantage of the expensive body products left for her use to wash away not only the filth, but scrub as if she could wash away the discomfort.

She dried off and slipped the silken material over her head. It was a simple, knee-length black nightgown with lace accents along the top of the bust. At least Vincent took modesty into consideration, despite his obvious leering at her. She quietly padded across the marble floor on bare feet and emerged from the bathroom to find Vincent sitting on the sofa waiting for her.

"Beautiful." He stood quickly and moved to her side, his eyes roaming her body. He placed his hand on her lower back and guided her to the bed to sit with her back toward the pillows and her feet on the bed. Blaire did as directed, unsure what his intentions were now that she had bathed and eaten. He said he didn't intend to drug her as much, so how would this play out?

He reached down beside the bed and lifted a metal cuff attached to a chain bolted to the footpost of the bed. She had a vague recollection of being chained to the bed this way before, but her memories from the last two weeks were hazy. He wrapped the cuff around her left ankle, securing and locking it before attaching the key to a chain with several keys he wore around his neck, slipping it beneath his shirt. Blaire squirmed and pulled at the chain, but it was useless. Vincent slid his hand from the cuff up her bare calf, stopping when he reached the hem of the nightgown at the back of her knee. He held her leg and stared up at her face. Blaire couldn't understand the look in his eyes, but it unnerved her. His touch felt invasive and dirty. She wanted Lukas.

Vincent released her after a moment of silence and reached beneath the bed, pulling out a wooden box. When he opened it, Blaire gasped, shifting away from him. The box held several vials, multiple syringes, and other medical items. She knew his intention. She tried to slide up the bed to get away from him farther, but she couldn't go far with the chain around her ankle.

"Easy now, my beautiful jewel." He placed his hand on her leg again. "It is better this way—I can protect you this way. They won't kill you if I do it like this. If I take only a little at a time in this manner, you can recover easier from the effects."

Blaire's gaze darted around the room in desperation for anything she could use as a weapon. She had to find a way out of this while she was still of sound mind. Her gaze fell on the locks lining the length of the doorframe; more than one took a key from the inside to open. She assumed the keys to those locks were the others Vincent had attached to the chain he put beneath his shirt. Even if she managed to break free from the cuff around her ankle, how could she get through the door?

"Do not make me drug you again," he said sharply, drawing her attention back to him. When he took in her expression, he softened his voice. "Please. I don't wish to make this more difficult than it needs to be."

Vincent caressed her leg before setting the box on the floor, then turning toward her and bringing his knee on the bed as he leaned toward her. She hated his touch, but she feared being drugged again. It wasn't as if she'd never felt the touch of someone with a few screws loose or been locked in a room she couldn't escape, but being kidnapped and chained to a bed? That was a first. A first she wished she'd never experienced.

Blaire winced as the needle pierced her arm, but she didn't move. She feared moving would make it worse. If it didn't bruise her badly, he would drug her for fighting back. The situation felt hopeless.

Placing the filled vials into the box, Vincent turned and lifted her arm, dragging his tongue slowly over the crook of her elbow, his eyes rolling back into his head as he groaned like a man in ecstasy. Blaire shuddered.

"It is even more delicious than I imagined," he whispered, licking his lips.

Blaire stared at him in horror, and he shook his head at her.

"I will not bite you. I simply didn't want to waste good blood." Vincent winked at her, standing to his full height from the bed and gathering the box in his arms. "Sleep now. You must get your strength back."

"Where are you going?"

"I have been sleeping on the single bed in the adjoining storage room. I will not be far. You'll be safe here."

Blaire almost laughed at his words. It wasn't being alone in the room that she feared—it was him she needed to be safe from.

Vincent clicked off the bedside lamp before moving toward the doorway on the other side of the sofa, turning off the overhead light and plunging the room into darkness. Blaire lay back on the pillow as her tears burned her tired eyes. She didn't know how to get out of this situation.

She needed Lukas.

13

Searching

Tightening his grip on the box in his hand, Lukas sighed. Today was Blaire's nineteenth birthday, and so far, his search had turned up nothing. Professor Velastra was handling business with the high school branch this month, so he couldn't seek her out, and Blaire's professors all corroborated the story of Blaire withdrawing from the academy. Any students he asked were just as in the dark as he was.

Even Rueanna Wainwright—someone he hadn't spoken to often despite growing up with her—who found herself pulled into Blaire's orbit like the rest of them had, didn't have a clue what happened to Blaire when he asked last week.

He tucked the box into its hiding place beneath his bed, though hiding it was pointless now.

Opening his message app on his phone, he stared at Charlotte's name. He'd stolen the contact information from Blaire's planner in her nightstand a few days ago, but he hadn't messaged her yet because he didn't know how to broach the topic. He was getting desperate.

Two weeks.

Two weeks had passed since the bomb dropped that Blaire didn't want to be there, and it still didn't settle right with him.

Blaire left everything behind.

Lukas's eyes found the framed photo of Blaire with her mother on their nightstand. She wouldn't have left that behind. He knew it deep inside.

Lukas:
Hey
Charlotte:
Who's this?
Lukas:
Lukas
Charlotte:
What's up? Oh! Tell Blaire Happy Birthday! I thought she'd call me about the Tybee Island plans, but I haven't heard from her in a couple weeks. I guess her classes this year really are kicking her ass.

How did he handle this? He wasn't any closer to knowing how to explain things to her without revealing their secrets.

Lukas:
Yeah, she's had to get tutoring this year.
Charlotte:
Is something wrong?

Shit. Was he being that obvious? Of course he was. He'd never contacted Charlotte in the entire time Blaire had been at the academy and had only spoken a few words to her whenever they met up outside Blackthorn. Without Riley, Blaire, or Aiden as a buffer, he was floundering.

Lukas:

Uh yeah. I guess.

Charlotte:

Is Blaire OK???

Lukas cursed under his breath. He was so bad at this.

Lukas:

We had a fight.

Charlotte:

What happened??

He started typing out a response, explaining how everything was a big misunderstanding and he had gotten jealous of Blaire's tutor, but shook his head. Deleting the entire paragraph, he roughly tapped at the screen.

Lukas:

I don't exactly know.

Charlotte:

...

Charlotte:

What does that mean?

Lukas:

It's personal.

Charlotte:

Okaayyy... then why'd you text me?

Lukas:

I don't really know.

He grimaced when his phone started ringing in his hands, his camera opening up on the screen. He cursed and hit the button on the screen. Charlotte's wide green eyes greeted him.

"What the hell happened?"

"You haven't spoken to her?"

Charlotte huffed. "I just told you I haven't talked to her in a couple weeks since Milanos."

Lukas scratched his head and held his hair tightly at the back of his neck as he propped his elbows on his knees, feet planted on the bed in front of him. "We started arguing before then."

"You guys have been fighting for weeks? Why didn't she tell me?"

"Not fighting… Well, sort of. Shit. It was stupid stuff to start with. Well, no, I guess not stupid to her, but it wasn't a big deal."

"You're not making any sense." Charlotte moved and sat down. The camera shifted, revealing her diner uniform.

"Are you working?"

"Lunch break. Don't change the subject."

Lukas resisted the urge to growl at the snappy demand. Just barely. She frowned at whatever expression she saw though, so at least she knew he didn't appreciate the tone.

She sighed and her tone softened. "What happened? What didn't seem like such a big deal to you?"

Lukas fell back on his bed, head sinking into his pillow as he held the phone above his face. "There's this new girl. Apparently, she knew me from like one brief interaction. Blaire was convinced she was flirting with me."

"Was she?"

"Well, I didn't think so at first. But now? I know better." He looked to the side. "Especially after she cornered me in Haven," he muttered.

"She did what now?"

He groaned.

"Come on. Spill." She took a drink from a water bottle as she waited expectantly.

"I went to the bathroom, and she followed me."

"Into the men's bathroom?" she shouted, her freckled cheeks flushing.

"No. She was waiting for me in the hall when I came out."

"Okaayyy."

"She was trying to talk to me about Blaire."

"What about her?"

"Uh..."

Lukas really didn't think this through. He couldn't explain to Charlotte that Clarissa had been trying to convince him that Blaire being human was a bad thing, and that she didn't belong in their world. Not when he couldn't tell Charlotte about their world even existing in the first place. He exhaled with a grunt of frustration.

"I think she was trying to convince me to leave Blaire."

"That bitch!"

Charlotte's cheeks were the color of a tomato, and if Lukas wasn't so upset, he'd laugh. She and Riley would get along, he mused.

"Yeah... But I'm not leaving her. It's just..."

"Just what?"

"The big problem was when she touched me and put her arms around my neck. Blaire walked up just in time to see it."

"Oh my God, no." Charlotte's words faded on a whisper.

"Yeah," he said with another heavy sigh, swallowing hard. "She didn't want to hear my explanation. And then she ran into Vincent, and he was holding her, and—"

"Vincent? Holding her? What the hell are you talking about?"

Lukas covered his face with his hand, cursing under his breath.

Trying to walk on eggshells with a human to avoid bringing down the wrath of the Order, or worse, the Blackthorn Clan themselves, was difficult. He had to approach everything he said differently, and it kept him from being able to give all the details that might make a difference. He now understood even more why Blaire was frustrated with not being able to share everything with Charlotte and why she didn't meet with her as often as she seemed to want to.

"Vincent is her tutor. He's got this thing for her. She doesn't believe me when I tell her he does though."

"And you're saying he held her?"

"It's what I saw when I chased after her."

"Okay… context. What else was going on?"

"Huh?"

"Did you see her go to him and allow him to hold her?"

"Well, no. I came out and he already had his arms around her, whispering shit in her ear."

Charlotte huffed loudly and rubbed her eyes. "God, men are so obnoxious sometimes. No wonder my mothers prefer each other."

"What?"

"You're in a nightclub, Lukas. Loud, right?"

"Well, yeah."

"So, maybe he was just being close so she could hear him."

Lukas could tell that Charlotte was trying to rationalize the behavior, but the arms wrapped around Blaire's back said Vincent had ulterior motives. He sat up on his bed and brushed his hair from his face. "Yeah, maybe. But you really haven't talked to her?"

"Nope. Listen, you need to sit down and talk with her. I know Blaire. She's not a cheater. Sure, she hadn't had a boyfriend in the time I knew her, but she didn't like people who stepped out on their partner. She wouldn't do that. Isn't your relationship like really new?"

"I guess."

While they hadn't cemented their bond until late June, and it'd only been closing in on four months since that, it had been building between them since Blaire joined the academy in April. While five months wasn't exactly long to humans, with a pairing, it felt like years. The intense emotions and whirlwind of events that happened during that time made it feel as if he'd known Blaire as long as the others.

"Well, you apparently need to learn a bit more about our girl if you're questioning her faithfulness."

"I'm not—"

"Yeah, dude. You are. You might have issue with the other guy, but if you trusted her, you wouldn't have the doubts you have."

Lukas stared at the redhead on the screen in stunned silence. He thought he trusted Blaire. He didn't trust anyone, but he was certain he trusted Blaire. But Charlotte was right. If he really thought about the way he approached Blaire about everything with Vincent, it was obvious he was acting like an insecure asshole.

"Shit."

"Yeah… Relationships are hard. How many girlfriends have you had?"

Lukas's eyes flew up to meet hers through the screen and she giggled at his expression.

"Not many, huh?"

"None."

"What?"

"I've never bothered with a girlfriend. Too annoying."

Charlotte's mouth formed an O. "Wow. That's… surprising."

"Huh? Why?"

"Have you looked at yourself? You're hot."

Lukas choked. "What?"

"You're not *my* type, but I can appreciate that you're attractive. I like my men without all the"—she flapped her hand about her head, motioning to her hair—"hair. Long hair isn't my thing. But I will say Blaire loves it."

"She does?"

"Yep. She told me. She loves your hair."

Lukas felt his cheeks warm and he looked at his lap to hide it from Charlotte.

"Listen, if you've never been with someone before, you might not know how it all works, but trust? It's important."

"I know that."

"Well, it's easy to lose sight of things when you're angry. Talk with her. Explain what you're thinking. She'll listen. I know she will." She looked over the phone and huffed a breath as a man's voice spoke loudly in the background, but the words were muffled by the sounds of clattering dishes. "Breaks over. Gotta go before Ricky gives himself a heart attack." She rolled her eyes. "Let me know how things go. And tell Blaire to call me. I want to properly tell her Happy Birthday."

Lukas grunted his acknowledgment as the screen went black.

He couldn't tell Charlotte that Blaire was gone. Clearly Charlotte hadn't seen her, or this conversation would have gone very differently.

So now he was back to square one. None of their friends knew where Blaire went. Rue was at a loss, so that would exclude her Korrena as well. Professor Velastra left before Blaire disappeared. Charlotte was a dead end.

He threw his phone across his bed. He was going to have to confront the one asshole he didn't want to. Vincent Brandt.

"What are you going to say?"

Lukas looked at Aiden as they approached the study lab. He didn't want to confront Vincent alone because he didn't trust himself not to put his fist through the smug bastard's face; and as satisfying as that would be, it wouldn't help him find Blaire.

"Just going to ask him about the last time he saw Blaire. If she mentioned leaving."

"Why would he know though?"

"Well, after speaking with everyone I can, I'm positive he's the last person to have seen her before she left Blackthorn."

Aiden rubbed his neck. "Think she told him she was going?"

"Don't know."

"I still don't think she withdrew."

Aiden stopped and looked at his sister, who'd come up behind them. "What are you doing here?"

"I want answers too." Riley crossed her arms over her chest, her bracelets clanking against buckles on the belted leather harness she wore over her uniform's white button-down shirt.

Lukas turned toward her. "Why don't you think she withdrew?"

"Because Clarissa has always been an opportunistic twat and a liar. If she says Blaire withdrew, then I call bullshit on that alone." She waved a hand. "Not to mention that for some insane reason, Blaire's in love with you. Why would she just walk away from that?"

Lukas slumped against the wall and crossed his arms. "Because we've been fighting."

Aiden sighed. "Fights happen. Even if we don't fully understand the way humans think, I'm sure they don't just decide to uproot their lives and leave school over a fight with their significant other."

"Maybe. Unless they think you've cheated."

Aiden's brows pinched. "What?"

"It's nothing."

"Oh hell no," Riley stepped in front of Lukas as he started to walk down the hall again. "You're gonna have to elaborate on that one."

"Fuck. Listen. Clarissa has been pushing me, and Blaire witnessed it at the club."

"Oooh, that."

Lukas blinked. "You know about that?"

"Yeah. Blaire was outside in the plaza, and Rue and I went to check on her. She was upset. Told us what happened."

So, Blaire had revealed more to Riley than just his push for her to become a Vasirian, after all. At least Riley had the decency not to spill all the information to everyone. After what happened when she told Aiden and Lukas about what Blaire's stepbrother had done to her, Riley had been wary about saying or doing anything that would break Blaire's fragile trust.

"Well, nothing happened. She caught Clarissa coming on to me, but I pushed her away. She missed that part."

Riley tugged at the leather strap of her harness. "So, what's the plan?"

"Talk to Vincent. I think he was the last to see her. I talked to Charlotte a couple days ago, and she hadn't talked to Blaire since we went to Milanos."

"Yeah, I know. I visited her at the diner yesterday. She said she spoke to you already, and still hasn't talked to Blaire."

"You didn't tell her Blaire left the academy, did you?" Lukas moved around Riley and started back down the hall with Riley and Aiden following.

"No. Didn't know how to explain that one if she hadn't talked to Blaire."

The study lab was empty and quiet when they entered. The lights were turned off except a lamp on the desk in the back corner of the room where Vincent sat in front of a laptop typing, occasionally glancing at a stack of papers next to him. When the door closed, he glanced up and his brows lowered, his lips pressing flat, before he schooled his expression. It looked like Vincent didn't want Lukas here as much as he didn't want to be here himself.

"Something I can assist you with?"

Lukas rolled his eyes. He hated how Vincent talked like he was so much older than them, like he was in an authoritative position. Just because Vincent was a teacher's aide didn't make him an actual teacher. He was only a couple years older.

"Yeah. I want to know where my Korrena is."

"Come again?"

While Vincent managed to keep his face impassive, the fists that rested on the desk on each side of his laptop tightened. The bastard knew something.

"You heard me clearly the first time, asshole."

"Mmm… that's not very nice." Vincent sat back in his seat and folded his arms across his chest. "You would think you'd have toned down your bark with such a lovely jewel in your life now."

Lukas's neck and face heated, and he glared at Vincent. Aiden stepped to his side and clamped a hand on his shoulder.

Vincent tilted his head, long black hair falling to the side as he chuckled. "Trouble in paradise?"

"Where is she?" Lukas bit out, clenching his fists tightly at his side. He had been right. If Aiden hadn't come with him, he'd have wiped that smug expression from Vincent's face. With his fist. Repeatedly.

"Who?" Vincent tilted his head in the other direction. "Ooh." The corner of his mouth turned up in a smirk. "You mean Blaire?"

Riley huffed loudly, drawing Vincent's gaze. "Listen. Yes. We're looking for Blaire. We think she was last with you a couple weeks ago for tutoring, but no one has seen her since. Have you heard anything?"

"Did she tell you anything?" Aiden added.

Vincent frowned and waved his hand at nothing in particular. "I don't know anything. She stopped coming to my tutoring sessions around two weeks ago. I haven't seen her since."

Lukas studied him through narrowed eyes. Did Vincent really not know Blaire had left?

"Clarissa said she withdrew," Riley said.

"Clarissa?" He genuinely looked as if he didn't know who Riley was talking about, but Lukas knew better. He'd witnessed the explosion between him and Blaire at the club. He was certain they'd used Clarissa's name and she was standing right there. Hadn't they? He couldn't remember.

"Angelo Moretti's daughter," Riley elaborated.

"Ah. The head of the Order's daughter. I've met her, yes." Vincent's eyes briefly cut to Lukas. "But I haven't heard anything about a withdrawal. I'm sorry I don't have more information."

Riley put her small hands on her hips. "Blaire really didn't say anything? Not even to tell you she wasn't going to be in your tutoring anymore?"

Vincent shook his head. "I'm afraid not. We had a full lesson plan. She'd given me no indication she was leaving." He paused and tapped fingers against his bicep. "Well, but in our last session…"

Lukas growled when he trailed off.

"What?" Riley huffed impatiently.

Vincent sighed. "She lamented how her Korrena keeps insisting she become a Vasirian like us."

Lukas flinched and Aiden tightened his grip. Blaire had confided in Vincent about their argument. Had she told him everything? Just how close had she become with Vincent?

The door opening had them all turning.

A group of students filed into the room with books in their arms, turning on the bright overhead lights and moving to desks near the front of the classroom.

"I'm going to have to ask you three to leave for now. I have a group study session to run, and my schedule is packed, so I am unable to postpone it to assist you further. I apologize for my lack of information." He stood and stepped around the desk, but paused as he stepped past Riley. "Though I will say this… If you have been pushing our jewel to change who she is, then judging by what I witnessed at the club, I am not surprised to hear she withdrew from the academy. I don't think I could commit myself to a child playing at being an adult, either."

Aiden had to wrap his arm around Lukas's chest and pull him back as he lunged at Vincent, drawing the attention of the other students.

"Let it go," Aiden said in a low voice, pulling Lukas toward the door.

14

ROOMMATE

A few days after the confrontation with Vincent, Lukas opened the door to his dorm room to find Clarissa unpacking a suitcase on Blaire's bed as several members of staff loaded things into boxes on dollies.

"What the hell is going on?" he demanded, watching them roll Blaire's belongings from the room.

Clarissa dropped the shirt in her hand to the bed—*Blaire's* bed—and turned to face him. "Well, since the human isn't coming back and all that,"—she waved a hand with indifference—"and didn't even bother taking her things, they are moving everything to a storage locker until someone can come to claim them. Can you believe she wasn't even decent enough to clean her things out or have someone get them? Did she expect you to do it? No class."

"What?"

The girl said everything so rapid-fire fast that he couldn't keep up. In one breath, she managed not only to explain what was happening, but also insult Blaire. His jaw hurt from how hard he clenched it in his irritation at having to deal with her.

"I assume her family, or someone, will come and pick up everything," Clarissa shrugged and turned back to the designer luggage that was open on top of the bed. "I doubt she'll set foot back on academy grounds, all things considered."

Lukas growled. "What the hell are you doing here, then? Why are you unpacking?"

He honestly didn't have the patience to deal with Clarissa's flighty responses and superficial attitude. The girl had been grating on his nerves over the last month in class and had gotten worse since Blaire's departure; his composure was about to snap. Clarissa continually vied for his attention in some way or another, and holding his boundaries against her wore him out. All he wanted was to come back to the room and sink into sleep, where Blaire waited for him in his dreams.

With every lead he had thought of resulting in a dead end, he was on the verge of giving up and letting her go, because no matter how he looked at it, all signs pointed to one thing: Blaire wanted to leave so badly that she left everything behind. It hadn't made sense before, but nothing else was making sense either.

Lukas felt pathetic. But if dreams were the only way he could have the love of his life until he found her, then so be it. He'd lose himself to the dream world where the cruel reality imposed on him didn't exist. Swallowing back his emotions, he forced himself to listen to Clarissa's explanation.

"What?" he asked; he missed what she said while lost in his thoughts.

"I said," she huffed, "I'm your new roommate."

"Why?"

She rolled her eyes. With a loud exhale, she turned entirely toward him, placed her hands on her hips, and tilted her head to the side. "Well, since they moved me up in the university program, they didn't have a permanent room for me yet, since I came straight from the high school branch academy."

Did they not have a room ready for her first year? Why did she need to change whatever room she'd been in up to now just because she moved to second-year courses instead? Blaire's bed was barely cold. He couldn't bring himself to sleep in it without her, so he'd taken the extra pillows off his bed, returning to using it again. It'd only been around three weeks. Before Lukas could ask any of his questions aloud, she continued.

"So, until they have something different, they put me in the only empty spot available—with you."

Her explanation was bullshit. All the other strangeness about the situation aside, other rooms were available. "Riley has an opening."

Clarissa shook her head, tucking her hair behind her ear. The rhinestone on her faux fingernail glinted in the room's overhead light. "Riley and I don't get along." A sheepish smile crossing her face as she said softly, "I prefer to be in a room with you since I know you."

"We don't know each other. I don't even remember you."

Clarissa's smile dropped and she looked as if she had sucked a lemon. "Well, now that we're roommates, that's easily solved! We'll just get to know one another." She smiled merrily and turned to continue unpacking her suitcase, humming a tune he didn't recognize.

He genuinely didn't care about anything anymore, so it was useless to argue the point or try to drive her away. He didn't have the energy. He collapsed back on his bed and stared at the ceiling.

Professor Velastra had summoned him for an advisory meeting when she returned from her trip two days ago. A meeting he hadn't bothered to attend yet. He knew she wanted to lecture him about his grades dive-bombing this term, but he didn't care. Soon, his parents would be contacted. What would they do about it? Tell him to behave or he'd get a spanking? He scoffed and rolled onto his side, facing the wall with his back to the girl who moved about the room like she owned the place.

Lukas was a grown man—twenty years old. While still in the academy, students remained under parental scrutiny, but it wasn't as if his parents cared. He hadn't seen them since last Christmas, a few months before Blaire showed up. Sure, he'd spoken to them a couple of times on the phone since Blaire had come into his life, and his parents seemed to genuinely care about the situation, but they had never made a point of expressing their expectations of him. He doubted they would be too disturbed by his grades slipping a little. It wasn't as if he were inheriting the family business or anything.

He pulled his cell phone from his jean pocket and scrolled through his contacts, stopping at the familiar entry for his mother. They didn't know yet he'd lost his Korrena. How was he going to explain that? His mother seemed so happy he'd finally found his pair. But if Blaire wanted to leave in the end, it would have been better if his parents had never known about her. It would have been better if they continued to believe he still hadn't found the one. He could have lived his life like the unlucky few who never find their pair.

The problem was he knew what it felt like to have his other half. The taste. The smell. The touch. Everything resonated on a level that couldn't compare to anything he'd ever experienced before, and the loss devastated him.

"—nice to share a room with someone older. We could go to the movies, or maybe that club you mentioned a couple of months ago!" Clarissa's yammering eventually broke through his downward spiral, cracking the shell of dejected thoughts he'd started building around himself. Did she ever stop talking?

Lukas let out a heavy breath and shoved his phone back into his pocket. He rolled onto his back again as Clarissa moved to the nightstand and opened the drawer, placing a diary inside. The gaudy design made him roll his eyes. It looked like a little girl's diary with its sparkly pink surface and heart-shaped lock. He closed his eyes and tried to tune her out again. He didn't want Clarissa's presence to start erasing that Blaire was ever there.

Clarissa rushed to the bathroom, several bottles in her arms.

Lukas stiffened.

Blaire.

He sat upright and looked around frantically. He could swear he smelled her. The scent was unmistakable.

"What's wrong?" Clarissa eyed him carefully from the bathroom doorway, taking in his expression as panic seized his throat. She walked toward the bed, grabbed a tablet, and placed it on the nightstand.

Lukas sniffed the air again and scrunched his brows together. Clarissa moved away, her long hair swinging behind her with her quick movements. The scent of jasmine hit him in the face again. Without thinking, he grabbed hold of her wrist. She gasped as he tugged her toward him to where he sat on the edge of the bed but came willingly.

"W-what is it?"

Lukas lifted her arm and smelled her wrist, and then leaned forward to smell her body. It was the same perfume Blaire wore. More artificial, with another underlying smell unique to the girl herself, but the aromatic jasmine hit him like a gunshot to the chest.

"Do you like it? I just got it."

Snapping out of his daze, he looked up at Clarissa's smile. He shook her wrist from his hand as if it were on fire, not wanting to even touch her. She knew he would respond to the scent. He had done it reflexively, not because he wanted to be near her. What a sick joke the world played on him. Just as Blaire disappeared, his new roommate tried a perfume that smelled like her. No, not exactly like her, but enough to torture him.

He almost laughed—almost.

Instead, his eyes filled with tears. He pushed Clarissa away and turned before she could see them. He grabbed his leather jacket from the desk, and with a longing for the love he lost gnawing at his insides, he left the room without a word.

"You look like hell," Seth said as he and Aiden approached where Lukas lay on a concrete bench at the edge of the forest lining the back of the academy.

Lukas turned his head as Aiden shoved Seth in the side.

"Seriously?" Aiden shook his head. "You have no tact, man."

Throwing an arm over his face, Lukas tuned out their back and forth, listening instead to the birds in the trees. He didn't know why he messaged Aiden. Part of him didn't want to be alone. But at the same time, forcing himself to interact with others was a monumental task.

The grass crunched beneath Aiden's boots as he stepped up to Lukas and tapped his legs. Lukas swung his feet off the bench and sat up, scrubbing his face with his hands. He felt so tired.

Aiden sat next to him and studied his posture. "So, what's up?"

"I dunno… I just needed to get out of there."

"Where?" Seth raised an eyebrow.

"That damn room. They're taking all of Blaire's things away to storage."

Aiden cursed under his breath and rubbed his hands together. "I'm sorry, man. I can't imagine what that must be like."

If well-meaning words could bring Blaire back, then he might find solace in them. But instead, they filled him with bitterness. It wasn't as if his friend spoke only to placate him; Aiden genuinely meant well. The words did nothing for the ache inside. Resting his head against the tree behind the bench, he sighed heavily.

"I couldn't even process it... especially with that obnoxious mouth with legs there."

Clarissa wouldn't shut up long enough for him to even register what was happening. Had he been able to take time and focus, he probably would have kept something of Blaire's belongings. Something to remember her by. Maybe the picture of her with her mother in a field of sunflowers. The thick binder of photos she kept as memories of her youth. Something. Anything. If it had been anyone else, he would have thought the idea silly, but she'd changed something inside him.

Aiden's brow lowered in confusion. "Mouth with... legs?"

"Yeah, that girl Clarissa." Lukas raked a hand through his hair and huffed a quick breath.

Seth leaned against the tree nearest the bench and crossed his arms. "What the hell was she doing in your room?"

"That was my question, too."

"And?" Aiden motioned with his hand to prompt Lukas to finish when he stopped talking.

Lukas slapped his hands on his thighs. Sitting forward, he slid his hands over his legs to rest his elbows on his knees as he hung his head. "And apparently, I have a new roommate."

Lukas felt sick, and Aiden's confused face would have been entertaining if he felt like laughing. Seth cocked his head to the side and wrinkled his nose at the words that hung in the air like the smell of rotten garbage.

"You can't be serious?" Seth asked.

"Do I look like I'm in the mood to joke?"

"Shit." Aiden wrung his hands. "Can't you get it changed?"

"Don't know."

"Are you going to try?"

"Probably."

Seth crossed his arms. "Probably? Dude. Let's go see what the housing department says."

"Went there before coming out here." Lukas grunted. "Closed for the day."

It wasn't even sunset, and he already was done with the day. He felt bad that he couldn't give his friends better words or a sunnier disposition, but he just felt so tired. He pulled his cell phone from his jeans and stared at the screen before opening his text app to the last conversation he had. He didn't talk much with Blaire's friend Charlotte. He really only engaged with her when Blaire was present. When he reached out to her on Blaire's birthday, she helped him realize one important thing, and it might have been one of the catalysts that pushed Blaire into leaving—he hadn't trusted her as much as he thought. His insecurity and fear of being abandoned again pushed him to cling too hard and suspect everything. He was self-sabotaging. Robbing himself of his own happiness.

"What's up?" Aiden asked.

"Huh?"

Aiden motioned to the phone Lukas had been staring at, as if it held all the answers.

"Oh." He tucked the phone away in his pocket. "Just checking if Charlotte said anything else."

"Anything else? You talked with her?"

"Asked if Blaire said anything. Said we had a fight."

Aiden rubbed his jaw. "Does she know where Blaire is?"

"Nope. I didn't tell her Blaire left."

"Why not?" Seth asked with furrowed brows.

Lukas could understand the confusion, but he didn't want to stir up anything if Blaire was hiding from him—a thought he hadn't considered while talking to Charlotte before. If Charlotte wouldn't tell him where Blaire was, then Blaire either didn't want to be found, or Charlotte didn't know where she was either.

Lukas shook his head. "Didn't know if she knew everything, and if Blaire wasn't with her, I didn't want to make her worry." Normally Lukas wouldn't care, but in protecting Blaire, he'd become protective of things that mattered to her, too. The redhead from the diner mattered to Blaire. "If she does know where Blaire is… well, then that means Blaire's avoiding me after all, and I'm not going to be the asshole ex-boyfriend who demands to see her."

Aiden clapped a hand on Lukas's shoulder.

Seth made a sour face and shook his head. "If it were me, I'd—"

"You don't know what you'd do." Aiden cut a look at him. "Neither of us knows what we'd do in a situation like this. Neither of us has a Korrena. We can't say how we'd behave if they left us."

Lukas's stomach turned at Aiden's words, and he pulled away from his hand. None of his friends would understand how those simple words that acknowledged Blaire leaving him felt like a serrated knife digging into his heart.

"I need to go get this shit fixed." Lukas stood. "When housing opens tomorrow, I'm going to see if I can do anything about getting my room changed or something."

"You can always crash with us until they change it. Though, since Seth moved into my room this year, there's only the floor."

If they could go three to a room, even if it was on the floor, he'd take it.

"Yeah, I'll ask."

15

Secrets

The sound of birdsong filtered into Blaire's ears, stirring her mind. Warmth had her nestling into the soft moss beneath her, and a gentle breeze caressed the exposed skin of her arms. When her fingers caressed the ground and found nothing but air, she jolted upright.

She had been sleeping precariously close to a cliff edge near a verdant forest unlike anything she'd ever seen.

Blaire rubbed her bleary eyes as she tried to make sense of what was happening around her. How did she get here? Where was here? The valley below the cliff comprised strangely unique sections of forest scattered over grassy plains in variable clusters to either side of a river. One section of trees looked thick and abundant, while another had bare branches with snow on the ground, despite the grass surrounding the trees beyond the threshold of the copse. Another section of trees was tall and thin, and the trees swayed in unison to a wind no other trees felt. On the opposite side of the river, a section looked charred and burnt, as if a forest fire had laid waste to the entire thing. As the thought occurred to her, the trees regrew their foliage only to be consumed by flames in the next breath in what appeared to be a never-ending cycle.

Before she could get wrapped up any further by the variety of changing woodland below, Blaire's gaze followed the river into a dark and foreboding forest unlike the rest. The trees lurked in shrouded darkness, and the fog that flowed from the depths of the barren trees threatened to consume anything that wandered too close.

As she stared at the forest, she felt the strangest pull inside her chest to go to it. The surrounding warmth faded, and the birdsong disappeared. Nothing remained but the mysterious pull of the darkened forest on the horizon.

Rustling behind her snapped her out of the trance she'd slipped into, and she sucked in a sharp breath as she stood on the edge of the cliff, looking down at a massive drop into the valley below, small rocks crumbling away from the edge beneath her bare feet. She scrambled back away from the deadly fall and looked back at what saved her from certain death, her heart pounding frantically in her chest.

At the edge of the lush forest stood a large deer, whose massive rack of antlers had so many points she was surprised it could hold its head up. Thick moss dripped from several parts of the impressive rack, and the deer's dark eyes were ringed in the brightest gold. Caught in the strangely attentive gaze, Blaire gasped as a rippling sensation passed over her skin and electricity raced down her spine before fizzling out, leaving her feeling hollow and bereft.

The deer's head snapped around to look into the forest behind it just before a woman's singing caught her ear. The song had words but no words at the same time; an echoing lament Blaire couldn't understand, but she felt the pull toward the voice just the same. It soothed the strange emptiness she now felt after whatever had passed between her and the deer faded away. She took hesitant steps toward the forest, mindful not to scare the deer that returned its keen gaze to her again. She didn't dare breathe a word for fear of disturbing the fragile peace that enveloped the bluff she shared with the woodland creature.

As she passed into the forest, no longer able to see the deer, the song grew louder, but still the words didn't become any clearer in her ears. Climbing over fallen logs and pushing through thick vines blocking her way, Blaire quickened her pace as her anxiety grew around what she would find at the end of her quest.

She stepped into a clearing, where a woman wearing a long white gown sat on a stump, staring in the opposite direction. The woman's blonde hair cascaded in waves down to her tailbone. She was the source of the beautiful song.

As soon as Blaire's bare foot touched the grass of the clearing, the woman turned toward her. Hazel eyes ensnared hers, and she sucked in a breath. She had to be seeing things. "Mom?" she choked, before swallowing thickly as emotion rose inside her.

The sorrowful lament the woman sang faded away, and she smiled. "Is that who you see when you look at me?"

The question threw her. The woman sitting on the stump was clearly her mother, but she was dead. If everything she'd experienced so far hadn't told her this was a dream, this certainly did.

The woman gave a melodic laugh. "It is a dream, but it is not."

Did she say that aloud?

"No. But here, in this space, you don't have to."

Blaire took a deep breath through her nose and exhaled slowly from her mouth to ground herself. This was surreal, even with everything she'd gone through this year so far. Had Vincent drugged her again? Was this another drug-addled trip?

"Come, child." The woman who looked like her mother beckoned with one hand. "Sit with me. Let me ease your confusion."

Blaire took hesitant steps forward until she stood before the beautiful woman who looked so much like her mother but not, tears brimming in her eyes. She lowered herself to the ground and pulled her knees to her chest, wrapping her arms around her shins.

"You are asleep beyond this space. Your physical body remains on the other side of the veil. But this is more than a dream, child." The woman looked around at the scenery, and Blaire glanced up as the woman's gaze stayed on something overhead.

High in the sky, kissing the clouds, a colossal beast with massive wings cut through the air as gracefully as a small bird. Was that an honest to goodness dragon? With a roar, it swooped down until the sun caught on individual golden scales. She gasped as it disappeared into the clouds. That definitely was a dragon.

A soft tinkling of laughter made her look back at the woman.

"This space… I wish I could explain to you what this space is, but I'm afraid I cannot. Something limits my ability to share this with you, what it means to you and the future of your kind. But know that it is more than a dream, young one."

A gentle breeze blew across Blaire's skin and stirred her hair. Tucking it behind her ears, she asked, "So, why am I here if you can't tell me anything?"

The woman looked at Blaire for a long moment, her soulful eyes searching Blaire's face for something. "I wanted you to see this place. In time, it will make sense. But first, it needed to be given a home in your mind somewhere. Your fight matters to this place."

"My fight?"

"There is more to your blood than a lover's bond eternal. A long ago buried secret. An unknown history stained crimson. A balance broken to hold control and power. The stars have aligned; your awakening is nigh. The Dark Kiss is the key, but the consequences are shrouded. A child born of a love tested and won holds the key to salvation for a king bound," the woman said, her voice echoing around the clearing as she recited the words of the message Blaire had received at the end of last term.

"You sent that?"

The woman looked at Blaire again, her eyes flickering from a glowing blue to the familiar hazel of her mother's again, and a ghost of the sensations she felt earlier caressed her exposed skin like a lover's touch. She shivered involuntarily.

"I did. I can only share with you what I see, and of that only what the Celestial Conclave allows."

"Celestial Conclave?"

"In time, child. They are not important to your mind yet." The woman clasped her hands on her lap. "When Adrian Blackthorn—the current king of the Vasirian—ascended to the throne after his father's two hundred reign ended, the secret within your blood answered the call of the stars, prompting the Celestial Conclave to ensure Lukas Virtanen crossed your path."

"What secret? What's so special about my blood?"

"Do you not feel it?"

"Feel what?"

The woman hummed and closed her eyes for a long moment. With a shake of her head, she met Blaire's eyes again. "It isn't time. Soon."

Again, time dominated everything, leaving Blaire helpless to the perpetual stream of events out of her control that spurred her forward toward the unknown.

Blaire chewed her lower lip before finally asking the question niggling the back of her mind, "Why do you look like my mother?" This wasn't really her mom. Not only did her mother die in a car accident, but also this woman behaved nothing like her mother did.

"In this place, your mind has given me the mask that is most comforting to you."

"But why?"

"Perhaps if I were in my corporeal form as I am in the waking world, you would not take to heart what I have said and what I still wish to say."

"What is that?"

"Don't give in to despair."

Blaire gave the woman a flat look, reminded of motivational posters with a kitten hanging from a rope saying something silly like "hang in there."

"The time of great suffering will come—soon—where what you've endured thus far will pale in comparison. The void will consume you, heart and soul, but you mustn't allow it to blacken your mind. You must stay alert and have faith. The balance depends on you."

"I don't understand."

"Unfortunately, I cannot elaborate and disturb the path of fate. While it pains me to know you must go through what I have seen, the outcome depends on the choices you make and the trust in your heart."

Blaire pinched the bridge of her nose, trying to make sense of the cryptic words, but she suddenly winced as pain radiated from her forearm.

"My time with you is up for now. But we will meet again. Until then, hold this place secret in your heart. Tell none of what you've seen and heard here."

Before Blaire could question her words, she awoke in the bed Vincent had made her prison to find him tucking away vials of her blood in his little box of at home phlebotomy supplies.

16

Missing

Lukas opened the door to Professor Velastra's office abruptly, and she looked up with a start, clearly caught off-guard by the interruption.

"Explain yourself, Mr. Virtanen."

Lukas cringed when she addressed him by his surname. The only time she used his name like that was when angry with him as a child or when the situation was serious. He shook his head. He didn't have time to think about things like that.

"I'm sorry," he mumbled. While he was genuinely sorry for startling her, his tone didn't match.

The professor cleared her throat and closed the folder in front of her. She sat back and crossed her legs as she studied his face. The shadow of heavy bags beneath his eyes stood out in sharp contrast to skin pallid from lack of nutrition. He couldn't help it. He had no appetite.

Sighing, the professor relaxed her tight expression. "Sit." She motioned to the black leather chairs in front of her large desk, softening her tone. "Why haven't you come to see me as I requested?"

Lukas dropped himself into the seat, throwing a leg over the arm and running his hand through his long hair, exhausted. Despite sleeping, he didn't rest. His dreams were filled with Blaire, but they were turning into nightmares. Waking in the night and smelling jasmine perfume in the air messed with his head. During the day he felt nauseous again.

He took a deep inhale through his nose and his shoulders slumped forward as he looked away, avoiding her analytical gaze. The woman had a way of reading people that always made him uneasy. "I haven't had time… I've had other things on my mind."

The professor frowned and gave a terse nod. She didn't push, for which he was thankful.

Before she had the opportunity to get into a lecture about his grades or anything else, he looked up at her and wet his lips. "Where's Blaire?" he said so quietly he wasn't sure she would hear him, sounding as broken as he felt.

The professor's face morphed into one of pain and sympathy, her lips parting as she considered her next words. "I… don't know. But if I did, I wouldn't be at liberty to provide such information because of the privacy clauses in place in the student contract."

"Don't give me that bullshit." Lukas glared at her, his voice rising marginally. "Blaire is my Korrena, and I have every right to know where she went." She wasn't his Korrena anymore, really. While he still bore the mark on his neck, which showed they still were bound to one another, it didn't matter if she wasn't there physically. It was just a tattoo, a permanent reminder of what he lost. The confusion surrounding everything made it hard for him to focus.

The professor sighed and closed her eyes. She schooled her features, the mask of a firm advisor returning to her expression, the brief glimpse of discomfort disappearing. She locked russet eyes with his. "I understand, but unfortunately, I don't know. I was just as blindsided by this as you when I returned from my stint at the high school branch. I was sent to substitute for the liaison there when she fell ill, and upon my return I heard that Blaire withdrew. I spoke with the head of the Order, and he informed me they offered Blaire a pardon if she left immediately. I tried to learn more, but they…" Her lips twisted and she grimaced. She didn't look pleased by whatever happened, but Lukas didn't push.

Lukas hung his head back and shut his eyes, ready to give up. The pain that gripped his gut and hollowed out his chest had been wearing him down for weeks. He didn't know how much more he could take. He didn't want to believe Blaire could abandon him without so much as a goodbye, but the more he thought about it, the more clear the reality became. No matter how much his heart fought him and tried to convince him it wasn't true, his mind faced it rationally.

If the Order told Professor Velastra the same thing Clarissa said, he had to face facts.

"When I spoke to Angelo, he informed me Blaire is lucky to even be alive."

"What?" Lukas looked at the professor, slack-jawed in confusion. Panic bubbled below the surface and a dull ache pressed below his sternum. Had something happened to Blaire?

As if reading his mind, the professor shook her head. "I mean, if several of the members of the Order had their way, Blaire would have been terminated for wanting to leave Blackthorn Academy after knowing our secrets. As Angelo is the head—and the longest-standing member of the council—he was able to sway their decision in a different direction. To be honest, I'm not sure why they wouldn't just compel her to forget her time here when they dismissed her. The solution would be infinitely simpler than…" The implication of her unspoken words hung in the air.

Lukas shut his eyes, taking solace in the news even for a moment. He looked back at the professor. "Why would she want to leave?" He was looking for any reason beyond the one he was too afraid to face. The one reason that told him he was to blame. That he drove her away by pushing her to become Vasirian. By not trusting her.

"I don't know."

He swallowed and shook his head. "Before we bonded, Blaire tried to leave because she didn't want to grow old and leave me."

The professor's eyebrows rose.

"She also didn't want to become a Vasirian, but I thought we were past that. I hadn't pushed her to become one of us even once until recently, and I screwed everything up… but I hadn't thought it was so much that she'd leave me. The Order hadn't tried to take her blood in two months before her disappearance." He rubbed his hands together and muttered, "I thought things were finally going to be okay."

"I don't know, Lukas. Something seems very peculiar about the situation, if I may speak candidly. Blaire didn't even reach out to me before meeting with the council, which I find very odd. But if this all happened in the span of time I was away, perhaps she couldn't speak to me if the condition of survival was to leave immediately."

"She left everything." Lukas shifted restlessly in his seat. "They hauled it all to storage today, and now I'm stuck with a new roommate as if Blaire never existed!" He slammed his hands down on the armrests of the chair.

"What?" Professor Velastra tilted her head to the side as small lines formed between her slender black brows. "Who?"

"Clarissa."

The professor leaned back, her head recoiling in apparent surprise. "Clarissa Moretti?"

"Yeah, I think that's her last name." He shrugged. "Something Italian." He honestly didn't care.

"Angelo's daughter," she said with a frown. "I didn't know any of this, and I should. This is truly surprising."

Lukas held his head in his hands. "But what does it even mean?"

"Again, I don't know. However, I'll see if I can find out anything regarding Blaire's well-being now that I've been brought up to speed on the situation, especially considering who her family is. I truly wish I had known about this when it happened and not just a couple of days ago. Even if she is no longer a student of Blackthorn, I have grown fond of the human girl. I would hate to see her fall back into the clutches of the Wilcox family, even if the threat of being bound to her stepbrother is a non-issue."

He didn't want to consider that possibility. Lukas nearly killed Blaire's stepbrother, with Blaire actually by his side. He couldn't imagine what he would do if he had to face any member of her family, if they were behind it, without her. Blaire's grandparents hated her for being beneath them on a socioeconomic scale. They hated her for being the daughter of the woman who married their son.

The professor clapped her hands, startling Lukas from his thoughts. He hated when she did that in an effort to steer the conversation where she wanted. "There is nothing more we can do right now, so let us move on to the real reason I needed you to come to see me weeks ago."

Lukas groaned. "I already know what you're going to say. My grades are shit."

"Yes. While you are still passing, your grades have taken a massive hit, and it's unlike you." She pulled a folder from a drawer to her left and opened it, examining the papers within. "I know for a fact you are capable of better than this. Your future depends on it." She motioned to the open folder in front of her.

Lukas looked at her incredulously. How could she even think he could focus on schoolwork and perform as he had before he knew what it was like to have a Korrena and was now denied her presence?

She held a hand up. "Though, now hearing everything that has taken place, it makes sense. When I originally called you for the meeting, I hadn't spoken to Angelo. I had no idea this was happening. But while I understand, I still have to make you aware this is not ideal, per administrative orders. Any student who falls below a certain percentile must be counseled."

Lukas sighed. He didn't care about the future set for him. He didn't know how long he would live, but he knew he would spend forever longing for the beautiful blonde human who had filled his world with sunshine.

The professor sighed. "I'm not asking you to ace the classes, Lukas, but you are steadily falling with each assignment. I can only assume that if this trend continues, you will reach a point where you will be so far behind that you will fail. Then the Order gets involved. I do not want them meddling further into your life." She offered a clenched half-smile. He hated the look of pity in her eyes. "If you can at least maintain a passing grade, that will be enough. Can you do that for me?"

Lukas shook his head, rolling his stiff shoulders. "Yeah, sure. I'll do what I can. I'll try."

"It's all I ask."

Silence descended between them.

He shook his head. "Can you do something about my room

situation? I've already talked to housing this week, and they said transferring me is impossible."

"Impossible?"

"Yeah. I don't know why, but they said a transfer this far into the year wasn't possible. I wanted to stay with Aiden and Seth, at least until I could get something permanent."

"I don't see where that should be an issue."

"Well, apparently it is. Having more than two room occupants is against some sort of regulation. I even asked to stay with Riley. But no. They flat out refuse to move me." He threw up a hand with a heavy exhale before shaking his head again. "Stupidly, I popped off that I'd just unofficially stay with the guys." His brows narrowed. "They told me it wasn't allowed. That staying more than a week was against some policy they had."

"I've never heard of this policy."

"Apparently, it's new." He rolled his eyes.

Professor Velastra's eyes narrowed as she studied Lukas's face. "That is peculiar indeed. I will see what I can do, but until then, I ask you to stay in the same dorm room you always have. The current peace with the Order is not something I want to disturb. I don't want to give them any reason to get further involved in your affairs. It was the only reason I addressed your grades today, given the situation."

Lukas sighed. "Yeah, sure… I get it." He honestly wasn't positive the professor could do anything, but something had to give. Clarissa was driving him crazy already. He stood from the chair and met the professor's eyes. The sympathy he saw there gutted him. He didn't want pity. He wanted to forget. Wanted to disappear. He strode to the door.

"I'll do what I can to find out how she is. It's the least I can do," the professor said softly as Lukas exited the room.

17

Blood Ritual

Blaire poked at the meatball on her plate with a fork. While she had started eating more now that she didn't feel ill constantly from the drugs in her system, her appetite was practically non-existent. Vincent side-eyed her from his seat, taking a sip of his wine as they ate in silence. After trying to force a few additional bites, Blaire gave up and set down her fork, looking at Vincent. No matter how much she tried, she couldn't hide her sadness.

"How is he doing?" she murmured, chewing the inside of her cheek, not sure if it was safe to ask about Lukas, considering the intensity of Vincent's obsession.

The only sign that her question displeased him was the muscle in his jaw ticking as he met her eyes. "Lukas?"

Blaire nodded quietly, not tempting fate by saying anything more.

Vincent gave her a pitying look and shook his head. "Unfortunately, I hate to be the one to share this with you, but Lukas is glad you're gone, my jewel."

Blaire's mouth parted, and her eyes widened. "What? I don't believe that." How could he say something so cruel? Lukas loved her. While she couldn't sense him anymore, he was out there. Even knowing the callous words weren't true, hearing them stung like a slap to the face.

Vincent set his wineglass on the table and took his time dabbing his mouth with a napkin as she stared at him incredulously. He had more to say and was dragging it out. His eyes gave nothing away as he reached across the table and placed his hand over hers. "No one wants to hear that someone they love doesn't want them anymore, but it is true. I'm sorry."

"How could you say that?" Her voice cracked as her eyes filled with tears. She couldn't stop her physical reaction, even if anger burned at her core. "Lukas wants me. You don't know anything about our relationship."

There was no way that Lukas didn't want her anymore. They were bonded. They had made plans together. She even considered accepting the Dark Kiss after everything that happened recently—though the idea of that process terrified her. She strongly considered joining him so that age and death wouldn't take her away from him. But she didn't get the opportunity to tell Lukas any of that before Vincent stole her away. The sadness that crept in fueled the buried anger as she glared at Vincent.

"Is that so? You said yourself he's been insistent about you becoming a Vasirian. I was there when you fought at the club. It was only natural the differences between you would come to this. Lukas realized that trying to have a life with a human was simply too much for him when you were doomed to die long before he would."

"He wouldn't say that. Lukas loves me," she snapped. How dare he imply Lukas was that cruel? Sure, he could be an asshole, but he was her asshole. He loved her and wouldn't do that to her. When she proposed that same argument before they bonded, he rebutted it without a second thought. He wouldn't suddenly feel otherwise—would he?

"Does he?" Vincent questioned with an arch of his heavy brow. "You've been here for how long now? We are closing in on a month, and he hasn't once mentioned you. Never asked if I've seen you, when I'm sure he knows I am one of the last to see you. Don't you think if the words you say are true, he would have come for you by now?"

Blaire recoiled with wide eyes. All the anger dissipated, leaving a sense of dread intermingled with pain burrowed in so deeply that her stomach clenched, and her breathing quickened. Vincent's next words dug deep into the black tar that corroded her heart and shattered her.

"You wouldn't accept being a Vasirian, so he felt dissatisfied." He shrugged. "You rejected him."

Blaire started to say something, but her words caught on the strangled sound she made before she doubled forward with her arms wrapped around her middle, sobbing. It was all her fault.

Vincent's chair hit the floor behind him as he leapt up and moved to her side. He pulled her shaking body from the chair, wrapping his large arms around her, caging her against him in a tight embrace. His entire demeanor changed. The cruelty and biting aura disappeared, replaced by empathy. She sagged against him, unable to fight as sobs racked her body, making it impossible to stand under her own power, much less push him away from her.

After an eternity, Blaire's cries settled and turned into faint whimpers against his chest. She couldn't let this man manipulate her feelings like this. Coming to her senses, she tried to push away from him, shaking her head rapidly. "I-I… I don't believe it. I can't believe it."

Vincent tightened his hold on her, pulling her close, and spoke against the top of her head. "I can prove it."

His tone made a cautioning shiver race down her spine. Foolishly, she didn't heed the warning. She was too distraught to trust her physical reaction.

Blaire lifted her head, meeting his gaze with glazed eyes that made it difficult to make out his features. "How?" she whispered as Vincent ran a thumb over her cheek, wiping away the dampness. Another tear fell free when she blinked away the blurriness.

"There is a ritual that can break the Korrena bond." He paused for emphasis. "But only if one of the two truly wills it to be broken. If Lukas doesn't want the bond, then it would break because *you* want it, correct?"

"I do, but..."

"Then it won't hurt to see, because if he wants your bond, then nothing will happen, right?"

Blaire's stomach swam with nausea, her dinner threatening to make a reappearance. Her mind was in turmoil, and she didn't know if she should believe Vincent. Nothing he had said over the time she'd known him could be trusted, but his words made sense after everything that had happened between her and Lukas lately. She held her throbbing head. She didn't know what to think anymore.

What purpose did telling her Lukas didn't want her serve? Vincent had her here, trapped, so he didn't have to try to convince her Lukas was bad, or manipulate her to get her to stay. She couldn't walk out the door if he said something she didn't like. He didn't have to convince her to stay. This wasn't something she had a choice in. She couldn't pack her bags and leave because she didn't want to be in the situation. Accepting this ritual would confirm if he was just trying to manipulate her or was telling the truth.

Lukas had been right all along about Vincent.

"Shall we try it?" he asked softly when Blaire hadn't answered, bringing her attention back to him as he released her from his hold.

Blaire pulled back from his embrace, sitting up in the chair and staring at the abandoned food on the table, rubbing her arms uneasily. If he was wrong about Lukas, then everything would be fine. The problem existed with her not wanting to face the potential reality that Lukas may, in fact, want her gone after everything that had happened. It couldn't be easy for him to be with a human. All the time that passed with her held prisoner in this room, with not even the slightest sign that anyone was looking for her, made her stomach sink—maybe Vincent was right.

She nodded quietly. If she tried to say the words, she would break down again.

Vincent took her hand and pulled her from the chair to lead her to the bed. Kneeling before her, he slid his hands up her legs, lifting her nightgown. She gasped and stepped back, but he gripped her legs to hold her still.

"This isn't sexual, my jewel. I need to access your skin for the ritual." His icy blue eyes focused on her face, and he offered a soft smile in what she could only assume was him trying to provide comforting reassurance, but it was hard to feel any sort of security with someone who held her captive. "Trust me."

Blaire hesitated and glanced around the room. She wet her lips and shifted uncomfortably, hyper-focused on the way Vincent's hands—that hadn't moved from her legs—made her skin crawl. Clenching her teeth together tightly to distract herself, she finally relaxed her stance. With a tilt of his head, he murmured praise—once again calling her a good girl—before gently sliding the gown up her body as he stood, slipping it over her head and tossing it to the foot of the bed. His gaze lingered on her bare breasts as she stood shaking before him, trying vainly to protect her modesty with her hands.

"W-why do you need me naked if it's not sexual?" While shaky, she finally found her voice to speak the doubts rolling around in her mind. Thoughts cemented by the way his revolting touch lingered, and his eyes burned into her bare flesh.

"Lie on the bed," he said, his voice deep and raspy in a way that made her more nervous than she already had been. He cleared his throat. "I need to have your skin bare for the runes."

Blaire hesitated and stepped away from him, her arm still around her breasts to shield herself. "I… I don't think I want to do this after all." She reached for the nightgown he had set on the foot of the bed and flinched when his hand wrapped solidly around her wrist. She looked at him, and her eyes widened as her heart rate spiked.

Vincent's narrowed eyes were glowing dimly. "Lie down," he commanded firmly.

Blaire tried to pull her arm away from him, and he stood to his full height, looking down on her and tightening his grip until she winced in pain. She shook in fear. His eyes were cold and glowing fiercely, and that familiar sensation crept over her until her body locked. The disconnect of her brain's signals to her body terrified her. Not having control. Not knowing what was going to happen. Knowing she couldn't stop it. How Vincent knew she could be manipulated like this when she couldn't be compelled, she didn't know.

Vincent lifted her, then lay her on the bed on her back, her arms cooperatively limp at her sides. "Now, we're not going to have another problem, are we? I told you I abhor the idea of using manmade drugs to get your compliance, but that doesn't mean I won't use them."

The hold on her body released, and she sucked in a large gulp of air. It wasn't that she couldn't breathe when she lost bodily autonomy, but the sensation that swept through her when her body came off lockdown felt like surfacing from a deep abyss, and she could finally get air that she'd been denied. Once she had her wits about her, she whipped her hands up to cover her private bits.

Vincent sat on the edge of the bed holding a black box he pulled from beneath the bed. "Be a good girl and cooperate with me, won't you?" He opened the lid, and then with a small ornate knife cut open his palm.

She sucked in a breath, her eyes widening. "What are you doing?"

"The blood of the one performing the ritual is required for the runes to work." He turned on the bed to face her body, using his uninjured hand to move her arms away to rest at her sides, exposing her fully.

She flushed and looked toward the kitchenette, trying to focus on anything else. While everything in her screamed to fight back, the idea of losing her senses and time itself in a drug-addled haze... compliance seemed like the lesser of the two evils.

Vincent dipped a finger into the blood pooled in the palm of his hand and dragged that finger over her thighs, marking her in sticky, wet patterns on her skin. She couldn't look at them. The feeling of him touching her was bad enough; she didn't want to see what her body looked like painted with his blood. He moved to her stomach and over her breasts, dipping his finger periodically into the gathered blood in his hand as he wrote the symbols over her skin, which cooled and made her shiver.

"Turn your head toward the wall," he demanded in a hard tone.

Blaire did as instructed, and he moved the hair away from her neck, exposing her Korrena mark to him. She could have sworn he snarled savagely. She swallowed hard.

She felt him cross out the mark on her neck with an "X" and shut her eyes. Something about the action hit her like a rock plummeting into the depths of her soul. The sensation overwhelmed her, and she barely heard him saying something would hurt a bit as he took her hand. For the second time, she questioned going through with the ritual. Did she honestly have a choice at this point? She needed to appeal to his sense of reason. Who knew what the ritual would do to her?

"I think maybe this was a bad ide—Ahh!" Blaire cried out as Vincent sliced open her palm.

She looked at him with wide, tear-filled eyes. Her blood ran down her arm from her hand as he held her arm up, but his focus wasn't on her face. She cringed when he took her bloody palm and placed it against his, joining their blood as he recited an incantation in a language she didn't understand.

Blaire stared at the ceiling as her neck began to burn. She shut her eyes so tightly that they hurt as she tried to ward off the pain, telling herself it would be over soon. More pain started from her toes and worked its way up her body. The areas where he painted her with his blood tingled and heated.

Images flashed behind her eyelids—images of Lukas.

Their first meeting. Lukas protecting her against other students, against the Order, against her stepbrother. His laughter. Lukas holding her in his arms and swearing that he would love her forever—that she was his. Making love to him. Shoving him in the club. Clarissa wrapping her arms around him. The fights that ripped her apart inside. The images grew hazier, and her mouth opened in a silent cry as tears ran from her eyes, across her temples, and into her ears. Lukas was slipping away from her, and she couldn't stop it.

"No," she croaked, but the word sounded broken to her ears as she struggled to swallow.

Her neck was on fire. But the physical pain was nothing compared to the all-consuming agony burrowing through her body.

As the last image of Lukas's face faded into black, she released a bone-chilling scream, and her back arched from the bed. The reality of what this meant grabbed onto her like a poison sent only to ruin. She squeezed her eyes shut as she howled in torment until her voice gave out. The life was sucked out of her, the loss reaching deep in her spirit.

She couldn't breathe.

Blaire thrashed against the bed to fight off the invisible threat stealing away her bond. Powerful hands held her tight to the bed as she wailed with a hoarse voice, kicking her legs harder. Her world was breaking into pieces, and she wanted it to end.

"Please!" She gulped at the air. "No more!"

When her anguished cries reached a fever pitch, the fire extinguished from her skin, leaving hollowness in its place. Her body went limp in Vincent's hold, and he eased her down onto linens she could no longer feel against her skin. He released his grip on her body as she stared blankly at the ceiling. Seeing, but not seeing. She felt utterly empty. Slowly, her gaze met Vincent's, and he gave her a pitying look, his gaze falling on her neck.

She knew what it meant.

The Korrena mark was gone.

"I'm sorry," he whispered, his face a blank mask.

Vincent had told her the truth. Lukas didn't want her anymore. Curling into the fetal position, wrapping her arms protectively around her body, she closed her eyes.

Was this what the mysterious woman from her dream meant? For the first time in all the years she fought so hard for her life, she truly wanted to die.

18

Severed Bonds

Lukas woke with a start.

Something was terribly wrong, and he felt it to his core.

Gasping for breath, he gripped the covers at his sides as sweat rolled down his back between his shoulder blades. His skin was on fire, the sensation traveling up his body and stopping on his neck. Everything looked distorted as he frantically looked around the moonlit room, trying to focus on any one thing but failing. He couldn't get enough air into his lungs. He thought he was suffocating, but nothing blocked his airways.

Lukas needed to get up, needed to move. The covers tangled around his legs in his panic to scramble out of bed. Freeing himself, he rushed into the bathroom to see if he was having an allergic reaction, or to find what else could possibly be happening to him, stopping short when he reached the mirror.

His eyes widened in horror as the Korrena mark on his neck faded away before his eyes.

No. It can't be.

Lukas leaned forward, pushing his hair back and scratching at the side of his neck that already burned where the black mark had once been. He had to still be asleep. That's what this was—a nightmare again, nothing more.

He slammed his fist on the counter as he stared at his neck in the mirror, rubbing aggressively at his skin as if it would magically make the mark reappear, digging his nails into the flesh until blood ran freely down his neck.

Why couldn't he wake up?

He wasn't asleep.

Lukas released an agonized wail as the implications hit him full force. His voice broke. Shards of glass pushed into his knuckles and sliced across his hands as he drove his fists into the mirror, unable to look at himself any longer. He dropped to his knees on the floor as shards rained down around him.

She was gone.

The most precious thing in the world to him was gone.

Dead.

A gasp grabbed his attention. Clarissa stood in the doorway staring at him with wide eyes. Her hands went over her mouth as she took in Lukas slumped on the floor surrounded by broken mirror shards, his hands covered in his own blood.

"What happened?"

"She's gone!" His voice cracked again as he tried to force himself to speak, panic gripping him.

Clarissa's brows pinched together in confusion, and she took a hesitant step forward.

"The mark… it's gone." The words had barely left his lips when he fell forward, holding his head as sobs wracked his body. He couldn't get enough air into his lungs.

Clarissa rushed to his side and dropped to her knees, careful to avoid the glass. She hugged Lukas close as he tried to take in air in short, convulsive gasps. Too far gone to really grasp what was happening, he didn't fight her.

Lukas didn't know how long they sat there before he calmed down. But when he glanced up, he could have sworn a smile dropped from Clarissa's face. At least he thought she smiled. It made no sense, though. He had to be seeing things in his state of panic.

Clarissa placed a hand on his cheek. "I'm so sorry, Lukas. Humans are fragile… so easily erased from this world. I'm so sorry." She hugged him close again. "I'll take care of you," she whispered, caressing his face gently.

He suddenly felt empty. The tension he held in his stomach all month released, and in its place, a hollow pit remained. It felt like a piece of him had been removed, and he was no longer dying. He had died.

Lukas pulled from Clarissa's hold, the impropriety of their position hitting him suddenly. He didn't need—nor did he want—her comfort.

"I need to see the professor," he muttered, scrambling up from the floor and leaving Clarissa sitting on the bathroom floor in the mess he left behind.

He threw on a pair of jeans over his boxers and tugged a long-sleeved black pullover over his head. He slid on socks and leather boots, not caring that he got blood all over everything. Stepping out of the closet, he walked to the nightstand and grabbed his phone, hitting the button on his contact list for his best friend's number as he exited the dorm room, not bothering to spare Clarissa another look as she stood in the bathroom doorway watching him in silence.

The entire courtyard was dark, the moon going into hiding behind the clouds as thunder rumbled and echoed around the deserted yard. Lukas's hands shook as he approached Aiden, who waited for him in front of the staff building housing Professor Velastra's office.

Lukas needed to be focused to get to the bottom of what happened to his mark. He didn't want to entertain the idea of it possibly meaning Blaire was gone from this world.

He'd never heard of someone losing their mark before, but he'd never spoken with someone who lost their Korrena to death. At least, not about their mark. Did Professor Velastra still have her mark? Her Korrena was dead. Moments like these made him wish he had paid more attention in the class they took as pre-teens about the Korrena bond. He had been a cynical idiot who only cared about fighting and hanging out with Aiden then, and now it came back to bite him in the ass.

Thunder rumbled louder as lightning split the sky. He wondered if Blaire could hear it. Was she afraid? She had become better at coping with storms, but he had always been with her during those times. Blaire had managed before him with storms, but knowing she felt comfort by his side had given him a feeling of purpose. Like he was meant to protect her.

Lukas shook his head as he closed the distance to his best friend, trying to rid himself of his thoughts. While the thoughts shoved away the idea that Blaire was dead, they weren't helping him figure out anything to the contrary.

"Whoa, man. What happened?" Aiden took in the blood and gashes on Lukas's hands that hadn't fully healed yet.

Lukas no longer felt the pain from his skin being torn open. His entire body had gone numb.

"Let's go inside. I can't say this more than once." He cleared his throat as he passed Aiden to enter the small building. His voice kept cracking any time he tried to speak. Breathing already felt like a chore.

They knocked on the professor's door and waited. Lukas had asked Aiden to call the after-hours line and have her meet them there. Aiden asked if he wanted the others to join them, but Lukas didn't think he could stomach being surrounded by a bunch of people—friends or not.

The professor opened the door and stepped back to let them enter. Her eyebrows rose as she took in the state of Lukas's hands, a look of concern crossing her face.

"Before you ask, it's my blood."

Relaxing, the professor shut the door and walked around her desk, settling into the high-back leather chair, and crossing her legs. "What happened?"

Lukas took in a lungful of air and tilted his head, pulling his long hair away from his neck. He shut his eyes as he exposed the nightmare he currently lived.

"What the hell?" Still standing beside him, Aiden studied the bare skin.

"I don't know," Lukas whispered, letting go of his hair. "I woke up earlier and felt like I was dying." He looked up at Aiden with stinging eyes. "It burned so badly, and I couldn't breathe. I thought it might have been an allergic reaction, but I've never had anything like that happen before."

"Can we even have allergies?" Aiden asked, looking at the professor. It wasn't something Lukas could recall learning about, so he felt as clueless as Aiden looked.

"Well, yes. It is possible, but we have a strong immune system, so it is rare to experience adverse effects to stimuli other than disease."

Aiden dropped into a chair as Lukas stood in place, unable to sit. If he stopped, he wouldn't get back up.

"When I went to the bathroom, I actually watched the mark fade away. It just... disappeared." He rubbed at the side of his neck. "I really thought I was dying until I saw that."

Professor Velastra raised a slender eyebrow. "Dying? I don't understand. You seem fine now. Your mannerisms, that is. It's rather confusing."

"I'm not fine. Far from it. It's hard to explain. Not long after the mark faded, and I broke down in the bathroom, it was as if something switched inside me." He rubbed at his chest to chase away the hollowness that settled there. "Everything I've felt since she left—the pain, the tension, the sickness—disappeared. Replaced by this disgusting, numb feeling. Something is gone, and I don't know what it is." Lukas ran a hand through his hair and met the professor's eyes. "Please tell me she isn't dead."

If the professor confirmed Blaire's death, that was it for him. He would follow her, because it wouldn't have been her choice to leave. Death wasn't a choice. He wouldn't consider the idea that she took her own life. He refused to accept that fate for her. He didn't want to live in a world where she didn't exist. It sounded irrational and melodramatic, but it made sense to his grief-addled brain. A world without the light Blaire brought him wasn't worth living.

Aiden stared at Lukas with wide eyes, then snapped his gaze to the professor, anxiety written all over his face.

"No. While I haven't been able to find any information on Blaire's current whereabouts, her death would not have brought about the Korrena mark's disappearance."

"How do you know?" Aiden scrunched his brows in confusion.

"I've seen pairs join, and then one side passes away over the years, and never did the mark disappear. I still have my mark, for example."

Lukas had forgotten to ask about her mark; her pair died when he was a child.

"Honestly, this is the first time I've ever encountered such a thing. I didn't know it was possible."

Lukas took a steadying breath and looked up at the ceiling. He could at least take consolation in the fact that Blaire wasn't dead. Unfortunately, it brought no real comfort to his empty heart.

"It's almost as if Blaire has disappeared off the face of the planet," the professor said, shaking her head. "This doesn't happen. In seventy-five years, I have never encountered this." She crossed to a bookshelf on the left side of her office and ran her finger along the spines of several books until she stopped on one. She pulled it from the shelf, walked back to her desk, and then opened it, falling silent as she scanned the pages.

"I can talk to Charlotte," Aiden said.

Lukas raised an eyebrow at him.

"I'll have to go to the diner to catch her, but she's Blaire's one friend outside of the academy."

Lukas knew who Charlotte was, and he wasn't sure she had any information. At least she gave none when he spoke to her. He hadn't thought Aiden had any connection to her outside of Blaire.

"She's bound to know something," Aiden insisted.

"That's actually an excellent idea." The professor looked up from her book. "In the meantime, I'll look into how and why the bond would be broken, because I've honestly never heard of such a thing."

Lukas's stomach dropped. "Broken?" That the bond might break, instead of just something being wrong with Blaire, stole his breath.

"Yes. I would suspect that the disconnect you felt after the mark disappeared signifies a separation from the bond. The connection you built as a bonded pair severed at that moment, and it is likely why you feel like part of yourself is missing. We don't even teach that it's possible, because unless there's something buried in the archives from the days of old, there's simply no information in our modern culture that lends truth to a bond's severance." She shut the book. "But what you describe logically sounds like that's what occurred. Perhaps this is in relation to her being human."

Aiden cursed, looking back at Lukas, whose blood had drained from his face.

He hadn't considered the possibility the bond could break. Did this mean that Blaire really wanted to leave him, and she'd rejected the bond? Was it possible to want to separate enough you could will it away? He couldn't accept that. Even if she was upset with him from the fight. She said she wanted freedom, but had she really meant she couldn't be with him anymore? Had her words sealed their fate?

He rubbed his hands over his face. Blaire had clearly told him she couldn't give him what he was asking for. If he'd known it would have sent her running, he would never have opened his mouth.

"I will research and let you know the moment I know anything. Until then, don't do anything rash." She sent Lukas a knowing look.

"What do you mean?" Aiden asked.

"While Lukas seems fine on the surface and feels empty within, it won't last. When the reality of what has happened hits him, I don't want him to do anything drastic to himself or anyone else."

Lukas tensed.

Aiden stood and put a hand on his shoulder. "I'm with you, man. We'll figure this out, I promise you."

Never in his life had he thought of harming himself. Lukas always thought people who took their own lives were weak. It was another reason he didn't believe Blaire killed herself. She was strong, stronger than she gave herself credit for. She had survived so much and still gave him sass when challenged with his admittedly overbearing personality.

Lukas sighed. He couldn't imagine doing anything to end his existence. Even as he stood on the edge of the abyss and even feeling the temptation to follow Blaire if she had died. He had heard tales of Korrena partners ending it all when their other half disappeared from this world. Was he destined to follow the same fate? His desire to move forward had his entire foundation shaken. He didn't know what he was capable of anymore.

19

CHARLOTTE

Aiden pulled his coat around himself, zipping it up as he leaned against the clock post in the middle of the plaza in view of the doors of Ricky's Diner. A cold front had moved in a few days ago on Halloween, and while the weather folks expected a shift back to milder temperatures later in the week, the air was unusually crisp today.

He'd been coming to the diner all week, but he kept missing Charlotte. He didn't want to go inside after everything that had happened before with Blaire and her boss—especially if no one knew Blaire had left the academy. He didn't want to bring unnecessary attention that might put her in danger.

He didn't know where Charlotte lived; the only time they all met up was in town. Charlotte hadn't been to the academy to visit for obvious reasons, and they'd never seen her home. He could have asked Lukas for her number, but he wanted to see her in person. Gauge her reactions up close to see if he could tell if she really didn't know anything about Blaire.

The bells above the entryway banged against the glass. He looked up from his phone as Charlotte stepped out. Her red curls wafted across her face in the chilly wind taking her breath cloud away. She threw her charcoal gray trench coat over her white sweater and skinny jeans that hugged the curves of her petite body. Every time he saw Charlotte, he couldn't help the strange sense that he knew her from somewhere other than the diner.

He pushed off the pole and stepped toward her, lifting a hand. "Hey."

Charlotte whipped around and looked at him, caught off-guard as she finished buttoning and tying off the trench coat that fell to mid-thigh. "Oh. Um. Hi." She glanced around to make sure he was actually speaking to her.

Aiden laughed and shook his head. "I'm here to see you."

Charlotte's cheeks warmed, the flush of her skin rivaling the fire of her hair. "Oh. Okay then." She pointed back at the door. "I'm just getting off shift, though. I can't be your server today."

Aiden laughed again. With everything that occurred with Blaire's stepbrother, they hadn't visited the diner much. While he hadn't seen her lately—not since Milanos—her animated ways still amused him. He thought her flustered reactions were cute. When she frowned at him, her brows drawn together in confusion, he cleared his throat and held up a hand. "Sorry, I don't mean to laugh. I'm not here to eat."

Charlotte tilted her head, a stray curl falling across her forehead.

"Can we talk?" he asked.

Aiden looked back at the diner. Ricky watched them through the window, standing at the counter with his arms folded across his round belly. Aiden sighed. Charlotte glanced back through the window, following his line of sight.

"Jackass," she muttered, and then stepped toward Aiden. "I know where we can talk, if you don't mind walking."

"That's fine."

Charlotte rubbed her hands together and started walking, Aiden falling into step beside her as they made their way into the busy crowd.

It was only the first week of November, but the town had already decorated the entire plaza for Christmas. Most places across the country waited until the day after Thanksgiving to start decorating, but Rosebrook made such a big deal out of the holiday season they started early. Pine garland wrapped around lamp posts with large red bows and multi-colored lights gave the entire plaza a colorful glow. Storefronts were all decorated differently, so a few shop owners were outside their storefronts with boxes filled to the brim with decorations. One shop hung simple lights and faux snowflakes in the window while another displayed a full ensemble of porcelain village buildings with trains and little villagers in makeshift snow. Even merchants who didn't celebrate Christmas added lights to their windows to provide a consistent sense of community.

It was all a build-up to the biggest holiday event in the area. On Christmas Eve every year, a foot parade wound from the public high school on the other end of town to the Valley Center Plaza, ending in a large Christmas party. He usually missed it. A couple of years ago, Riley had asked to go because she hadn't seen it since they were children, and he couldn't deny his little sister's annoying pout. His feet hurt after an hour, he disliked seeing horse poop, the public high school's marching band hurt his ears, and one could only eat so many hard candies tossed by Sunday school kids. It confirmed parades weren't his thing.

They walked down a side street and stopped in front of a store that had a small Christmas tree out front decorated with flashy ornaments, multi-colored lights, and presents underneath he assumed were fake. Not that Rosebrook had a high crime rate—in fact, they barely had any criminal activity to note. It seemed like the logical choice in case the weather turned sour. Paper-wrapped boxes wouldn't withstand a downpour.

Charlotte turned to him with a bright smile. "Here we are."

Aiden cleared his throat and looked at the storefront again. He took in the bright purple backsplash of the sign and the feminine font of the store's name—Uniquely You—in white.

"Come inside. It's freezing." She rubbed her hands together as she had done several times on their walk over to keep her small hands warm. Why didn't she have gloves? It wasn't really that cold, but he could see where someone as small as she was would have difficulty with the drop in temperature. Riley was roughly the same size and didn't seem to mind, but maybe humans were different.

Charlotte pushed the door open and jingle bells attached to a stuffed Santa head door knocker rattled against the surface of the door. Aiden followed her inside and looked around the store. Clothing racks stood everywhere filled with clothes of various colors. Each rack held a different color in varying shades, creating a rainbow across the room. The shelves on the sidewalls held folded garments in the same layout, a gradient of color moving across the wall.

"Mom is a bit OCD about this sort of thing." Charlotte laughed, taking in Aiden's open-mouthed stare. "Creative types tend to have quirks."

"I prefer to call myself eccentric, no matter what my doctor says."

Aiden followed the voice to a tall, willowy, Native American woman of about five-eleven gliding toward them. She looked to be in her late thirties, with straight black hair that fell to her waist. Her deep brown eyes assessed him, and he glanced away. Her soulful gaze made him uncomfortable. He was sure she read him with a glance.

Charlotte touched his arm, and he flinched, causing her to pull back. "Oh! I'm sorry. I wasn't thinking." She flushed bright red again.

"No. Sorry. I didn't expect it." Aiden rubbed the back of his neck and looked back at the woman who stood watching them in silence. She could see through him, and he didn't like it. Normally, he didn't think twice about people's reactions to him, but this woman was different.

After a long moment, she nodded at him and held out her slender hand. "Sara," she said with a smile. "Sara Walsh."

He shook her hand. "Aiden Easton. Nice to meet you."

"Aiden… a powerful name. Little fire."

"Huh?"

"Moooom." Charlotte glared at her mother then turned to Aiden. "Ignore her. She's really big into names, horoscopes, and all sorts of deeper meaning type things."

Sara laughed and shook her head. "Don't pretend it doesn't interest you too, my love. I find it interesting that Aiden here has a name rooted in Irish mythology."

"It is?" Charlotte's entire face changed, lighting up with excitement as she looked at Aiden, the green in her eyes sparkling like emeralds. He had no idea what was happening, but she seemed suddenly thrilled by that information.

"Charlotte is Irish. Adopted," Sara said, noting Aiden's confusion.

"Yeah, my mom"—Charlotte gestured to Sara—"is Seminole, and my other mom is Canadian."

"After Elizabeth and I married in Vancouver and moved back to Florida, where I'm originally from, we adopted baby Charlotte from Ireland. We moved to Georgia when it was time for her to start school."

"Oh." Aiden rubbed his neck. He didn't know what to say to all that. Charlotte and Sara were so open and friendly, and he didn't expect it. He wasn't used to those who freely shared things about themselves, or their history, without at least a little prompting or familiarity. They didn't know him.

He should have suspected it, considering how Charlotte behaved around Blaire, but Blaire had been so withdrawn when they first met. Not to mention his mind wasn't in the right place to put pieces of anything together.

He had to find Blaire, for Lukas's sake. His best friend was barely keeping himself afloat, whether or not Lukas would admit it.

Sara placed a hand on Charlotte's shoulder as she studied Aiden's face. "Why don't you both go into the back room and chat?"

"What?" Charlotte looked up at her mother, who gave Charlotte a look Aiden didn't understand.

"I think something is on the boy's mind."

"Oh!" Charlotte turned to Aiden. "Right. Okay. Let's go this way." She motioned toward the counter where a doorway stood on the other side that he assumed led to the back.

"It was nice meeting you." Aiden nodded to Sara and followed Charlotte behind the counter.

"A pleasure, little fire. I'm sure we'll meet again."

Charlotte's mouth twisted like she tasted something sour, and she cut her mom a look.

"Alright, alright. I'm going." Sara's melodic laughter faded as she went deeper into the racks at the front of the store.

Sara had a way of speaking that unnerved him. He followed Charlotte into the back room. She took off her trench coat and hung it on a coat rack in the corner before motioning for his coat. He unzipped his jacket, shrugged it off, and passed it to her. They sat on a small bench against the wall next to each other.

After a long, awkward silence, he looked into her eyes. "Have you heard from Blaire?"

Charlotte tucked a few wayward curls behind her ear, exposing a crescent moon earring curling her earlobe. "No, I haven't talked to her since late September, actually, which normally would be pretty weird, but ever since Blaire started Blackthorn Academy, it's become harder to talk to her."

He looked down at the small hands she was clenching in her lap. It clearly bothered her that she lost touch with her friend. Blaire wanted Charlotte around more too, but the risk of their secret being exposed was too great to have her visit the academy grounds.

"Lukas was going to give her a phone for her birthday to help with that, but seeing as she left, that fell flat." Aiden frowned.

"Left? What do you mean? Lukas asked me on her birthday if I had heard from her, but I thought he wanted to poke around and find out if she told me about their fight." She thumbed through her phone and held it up showing a text conversation between her and Lukas from the fourteenth of October. "Has she not been around at all, not even for classes?"

Aiden frowned at the look of worry that crossed Charlotte's delicate features. He speared his hand through his black hair, making the long strands on top messier than before. "The last week of September, a couple weeks before her birthday, she just up and… left. The school administration said she requested a withdrawal, and they granted it. No one knows what she was thinking when she did it, and we're worried about her."

Charlotte looked at him, her forehead wrinkling in concern. "I thought she was dating Lukas."

"They are—well, were. Blaire didn't tell him anything. She just disappeared overnight, leaving everything behind."

"She left everything?" Charlotte's brows pulled together in a frown. "Pictures and all?"

Aiden nodded, rubbing his hands over his thighs on his jeans.

Charlotte gave a quick shake of her head. "Blaire wouldn't just leave everything like that. She has this one picture with her mom she would never leave behind."

"The sunflower one?"

"Yes! They took it just before her mom died. She would never leave that."

"She did," Aiden said quietly, studying the confused look on Charlotte's face. "I'm trying to figure out what happened."

"Wait. She's been gone for over a month and you're just now searching for her?" Her cheeks flushed and her eyes sharpened. "What the hell is wrong with you? What if something happened to her!"

Aiden held his hands up in a placating gesture. "No, I'm not just searching for her now. We've asked everyone we know. Lukas has been all over the school asking anyone who might have information. It's one of two stories: either they don't know what went down, or they insist Blaire voluntarily withdrew."

"Christ." Charlotte bit the side of her lower lip in contemplation. "Do you think Caleb, or his grandparents might have something to do with it?"

"I don't know. I don't think so." Charlotte didn't know about the Vasirian's ability to compel others to change their memories, so they had to play it carefully around her. "As far as I knew, Caleb lost interest and moved."

Charlotte frowned. "Blaire told me that in September, the last we talked. He moved to Seattle. I hope that means his grandparents will leave her alone."

"Have you seen them?"

Charlotte shook her head, then looked around the room as if someone might hear her, before settling her gaze back on Aiden. "The Wilcox family is not to be messed with. It's always better you don't see them, I think."

He shrugged. "Listen, I need to get back to the academy and check on Lukas." He pulled out his phone and held out his hand. "Give me your phone."

"What?"

"Your phone."

"Um. Okay." Charlotte crossed to her coat. She pulled out a phone with a celestial design on a black background, before unlocking it, and passing it to him.

Aiden tapped on her screen, and his phone pinged in his other hand. "There. Now you have my number. Save it. Contact me if you hear anything at all."

Charlotte took her phone from him, programming his number in from where he had used her phone to contact himself. "Wait a second," she said as he moved to the coat rack.

Aiden shrugged on his coat and turned to look at her. "Yeah?"

"Let me take a picture of you."

Aiden raised an eyebrow, confused by her request.

Charlotte giggled and shook her head. "I save all my contacts with an actual picture. I don't like just having letters or whatever for contacts."

"Okaaay."

Charlotte blushed and looked away, waving a hand. "It's fine. That's really stupid of me to ask. You don't even know me."

Aiden chuckled and shook his head slowly. "No. I don't mind. I'm just a little scatterbrained with this thing going on with Blaire.

Go ahead."

Charlotte nodded quietly and held her phone up, snapping the photo when he smiled at her. "Thank you. I know it's probably weird, but thanks."

Aiden shook his head. "Not weird at all." Though he did think her adoptive mother's eccentric organization had rubbed off on her if she kept her contacts arranged to all have photos. He wondered how she handled saving doctors or businesses. Did she take photos of the stores themselves? He smiled and pulled his phone back out of his pocket, holding it up in front of her.

"What?"

"It's only fair."

"Oh my God, no."

Aiden burst out laughing as her face turned red, making the smattering of freckles across her nose and cheeks stand out more. He snapped a candid shot of her flustered face. "This is perfect."

"No! Delete it now!" Charlotte squealed, reaching for the phone that he held up high. Aiden didn't need to hold it high at all. He easily stood a head taller than her. She was the same height as his little sister, which made playing with her come naturally. When she threw herself into his body, one hand gripping his shoulder as she jumped to grab the phone, he had to put his arm around her lower back to steady her, laughing as she nearly knocked him over.

Charlotte suddenly froze, and he stopped laughing, glancing down at the top of her head in confusion. She wasn't looking up at him or moving anymore.

"Charlotte?"

Vibrant green eyes met his, and he swallowed hard as he took in her flushed cheeks and heavy breaths from the exertion. He was suddenly aware of how soft she felt against him. He let go of her back as if burned and stepped away.

"Sorry. I... yeah, sorry." He rubbed the back of his neck as Charlotte adjusted her sweater.

"You can keep the photo," she whispered, turning away from him.

Giving a curt nod, Aiden turned and walked to the doorway. He wasn't sure what that was all about, but it definitely didn't feel like playing with his sister. He didn't have time to think about it when he only needed to focus on the task at hand.

"Let me know if you hear anything," he said, his voice catching in his throat. He quickly passed through the door before Charlotte could say anything else, or he could embarrass himself. He was thankful her mother wasn't in the storefront as he left.

20

Nightmare

The bed creaked and shifted; a weight pressed down beside Blaire as she stirred awake. When more aware of what was happening, she jerked and tried to scramble away from the shadowed silhouette that moved toward her on the bed, but the shackle on her ankle held her in place.

"Shh. It's me."

"Lukas?" Blaire gasped and lunged forward, wrapping her arms around his neck, breathing in the apple spice scent that she missed so much as she buried her face in his long hair. Lukas wrapped his arms around her back and held her close, kissing the side of her head.

"How did you find me?" She looked up at Lukas with tears in her eyes, barely able to make out any of his features in the shadows of the room.

"It doesn't matter. I've got you," he whispered, leaning in to kiss her tenderly as tears tracked a path down her cheeks.

He tasted different.

"I thought I'd never see you again." Blaire choked on her sob as Lukas held her shaking body against his. She couldn't believe he came for her. He rejected their bond—it was broken. Did he regret it? She looked up into his shadowed eyes, but couldn't read anything on his face, the room too dark to rely on anything other than touch.

Lukas leaned forward and kissed her jaw gingerly, his full lips dragging over her skin until he reached her neck, where he took the flesh between his teeth in a gentle bite. She gasped and arched into him. It had been so long since he touched her, but her body immediately responded to him—bond or no bond.

"I need you… but we need to get out of here before Vinc—"

Lukas's growl cut her words off, and he shook his head. "I'm not waiting. I need to reclaim you now."

She gave in to his eagerness, allowing Lukas to push her back onto the bed and lift her nightgown to her waist, goose bumps rising on her skin where he touched. He ran his hands up her thighs, grazed delicately over her core with his fingertips, causing her to suck in a quick breath, before moving to rest a palm on her stomach. His touch was maddening. Saying nothing, he worshiped her body with his hands. He dipped his fingers between her legs, caressing her slick folds.

But the scent of his body soured in the air with every minute that passed, and her nose wrinkled at the unfamiliarity of it, her focus moving away from the pleasure his touch brought her.

Blaire squirmed, her back arching, and she all but forgot about the odd scent as he slid a finger inside her, but he promptly removed it after her attention focused on him again. It was as if he only did it to keep her focus on the moment, not to prepare her. She whined at the loss. Something about his touch felt off—strange. There seemed to be a disconnect in the way he touched her, how quiet and composed he held himself; it was unnerving. This wasn't like Lukas at all.

If they had been apart for so long, wouldn't he be more urgent?

He was always insatiable in his hunger for her when they spent every single day together. This didn't make sense.

Lukas got on his knees over her body and quickly unbuttoned and unzipped his jeans, pulling himself from his boxers. Stroking lazily over his length, he stared down at her. She squirmed at the discomfort in her stomach that the look in his eyes gave her. He grabbed her hips roughly, and she winced at the bite of pain as he pulled her partly into his lap. Before she could tell him to be gentler, or even mention protection, he leaned forward and buried his cock deep inside her body in one swift thrust.

Blaire cried out, throwing her head back against the pillow. The mixture of pleasure and pain from how long it had been, and lack of foreplay, made her dizzy. Tears pricked her eyes. She gripped the covers as Lukas took her violently. Her screams and moans as her body shifted from pain to pure pleasure echoed in the room.

"Please. It's too much. I-I can't!"

She reached out and scratched at Lukas's chest. He growled, stopping his movements. Reaching behind himself, he pulled a switchblade from his back pocket and opened it. She understood the meaning behind the action and prepared for the bite, for the taste of his blood—for being his again. She closed her eyes, readying herself as she panted, trying to catch her breath. Despite the strangeness of the situation, her body anticipated the pleasure. Wanted him.

"I love you," she whispered, needing to tell him everything she felt but unable to find strong enough words to express how much her soul longed for him, despite the undercurrent of wariness beneath the surface.

The bed shifted, and something sharp pricked her neck, but it wasn't the familiar feeling of fangs. Blaire's eyes flew open as she stared at Lukas, who now held the knife to her throat. She couldn't speak without pressing harder against the blade. She didn't understand what was happening, but the sneer on Lukas's shadowed face was terrifying. The hatred that radiated off of him was nothing she had ever seen.

"I *don't* love you."

Blaire gasped and reached for his arm that held the blade. He slid the blade across her skin.

He was trying to kill her.

Not only did he not love her anymore, he wanted her dead. The warning bells going off in her mind made complete sense. The smell. The taste. The touch. It was all so different to what she knew. Had the shift happened as a result of the bond being broken? She screamed as he increased the pressure, then gurgled and choked on her own blood as she thrashed against him, her body weakening.

The room filled with light and she jackknifed up in the bed, looking around wildly before reality sank in. She released a gut-wrenching wail.

"No! You will not cry for him!" a deep voice boomed across the room before powerful arms took hold of her, pulling her against a hard body.

She shook and cried until her voice went hoarse.

"It's just a nightmare, my jewel. Only a nightmare. You are safe. Nothing can get you here."

Vincent's voice cut into her panic. She forced herself to release the breath that had locked in her chest, threatening to send her back into despair. She looked up at Vincent and inhaled sharply when she took in his half-naked state. He wore a pair of loose black lounge pants, leaving his bare torso on display. The chain around his neck that held the keys to her freedom glinted in the light, taunting her. The fog started to lift from her mind, and she tried to pull away from Vincent to not be in such an intimate position. He hesitated before eventually letting her move to a more comfortable distance.

"How did you know?" she croaked, her voice raspy from her screams.

"Know what, my jewel?"

"That I dreamed of Lukas."

Vincent's expression hardened, and he sat back against the wall, crossing his bare feet at the ankles. "It's not difficult to guess what would wake you in such a hysterical state. You've suffered a loss. It's understandable. What I don't know are the specific details of your nightmare. Care to enlighten me? It will help you move past it."

Blaire frowned and twisted the long strands of hair around her fingers, not meeting his eyes. "It's stupid. It's over now, so we don't need to talk about it."

Vincent placed his hand on Blaire's shackled ankle, and she looked up at eyes full of pity. His gaze also held an edge of authority, and she felt like a child being scolded for lying. She huffed and looked away again.

"He tried to kill me," she said blandly.

"I'm sorry to hear that, my jewel. Is that everything that happened?"

Blaire's skin heated, her cheeks turning pink. She shook her head, and Vincent watched her, waiting expectantly for her to continue. Over the time she spent with him, she learned that when he wanted her to provide him with information, he didn't use words—he didn't need to. Vincent only needed to watch and wait her out until her discomfort became too great and she spilled her guts. She didn't like how he could manipulate her with a look, but it worried her what the consequence would be if she rejected him altogether. She rationalized that if she continued to talk, giving him little wins that way, he wouldn't press for more. As long as he kept her talking, maybe he wouldn't touch her beyond the blood removal for the Order.

"We were… intimate?" Blaire's brows pinched at how her statement sounded more like a question, but talking about sex with Vincent made her squirm.

He nodded, humming his understanding, and removed his hand from her ankle. "I suppose it would be rather terrifying to go from bonding to attempted murder."

Blaire hung her head.

"It wasn't real, my jewel. Don't dwell on such horrors."

Vincent shifted on the bed and slid over to sit beside her, placing his hand on the side of her face. She stared into his pale blue eyes. Without the black eyeliner around them they were bigger but still held the icy edge she'd always seen in them. At first, she thought the makeup was what made his eyes intense and scary, but she now saw that they were naturally menacing.

He tenderly ran a thumb over her jawline and leaned toward her. She gasped. A kiss with Vincent could not happen. Even if Lukas didn't want her, she couldn't allow someone else to touch her that way. It would be wrong. This man was her kidnapper, not her lover—not even her friend. Her stomach twisted, and she pivoted her head as he came within inches of her lips. His breath feathered her cheek as she shut her eyes tight.

"Please don't do that," she pleaded softly, swallowing the lump in her throat.

Vincent growled low, and she shuddered, a tendril of fear passing through her. That wasn't what he wanted to hear, but she couldn't allow it to happen. The grip on her jaw tightened, and he pulled her face hard until she met his eyes.

"I have been very patient. I have taken care of you." He grinned, a sadistic glint in his eyes. A flash of fang made her heart thump erratically as her breathing quickened. She tried pulling away from him, but his grip got tighter. She winced at the pain. "I think by now you know you can trust me. I promise to be gentle. While I assured you I would not"—his gaze trailed down her body—"force myself upon you, I am but a man. I simply must know what you taste like."

Blaire sucked in a breath. He took that opportunity to lean in and capture her lips, plunging his tongue into her parted mouth. Throwing her hands up, she pounded his chest with her fists in an effort to separate them. He shackled her wrists with his hands and pressed her back to the bed, kissing her roughly.

This couldn't happen.

She bit his tongue. He jerked back with a hiss, his eyes blazing as he lifted his weight from her. The look in his glowing blue eyes made her body tense as he held onto her wrists in a bruising grip. She didn't know what the repercussions would be for fighting back, but she hadn't thought about consequences in that moment. She needed to stop him.

He stared at her in silence, his long black hair tickling her skin as he hovered above her, her wrists still bound in his hand in a firm grip as the tension in the room rose. When it seemed he finally got control of himself, he released her wrists and sat back on the bed beside her. "Do not do that again," he said with a sharpness to his tone that brooked no argument. "You won't like what happens if you do."

She shuddered and swallowed audibly. He closed his eyes briefly, before looking at her face again. The satisfied grin crossing his lips surprised her.

"But I must say, you are quite delicious, my beautiful jewel."

Blaire turned her face away from him, disgusted. Tears fell from the corners of her eyes and slid over her temples. She shuddered when he leaned down to lick them from her face. She squeezed her eyes tight to will the tears away. Anything to make him stop touching her.

"Please stop."

Vincent smirked and nodded, pulling away from her. "Very well. But you do not know how I have wanted that. Thank you for allowing me such a pleasure."

Blaire snapped her gaze back to his, her eyes narrowing. "Allow? *Allow?* I didn't allow anything! You took!" Her anger rose to replace the fear from being pinned by such a large Vasirian.

"Semantics."

She looked at him in disbelief, not understanding how he didn't acknowledge that what he did to her was unwelcome. He understood; Vincent wasn't a stupid man. "Please get off me," she said, her voice cold. All she wanted was to go back to sleep and pretend the entire night hadn't happened.

"Of course. After."

"After what?"

Vincent's grin turned wicked, and that tendril of fear from earlier blanketed her again as he leaned in toward her. She leaned away to avoid another kiss, but his self-satisfied smirk said that had been the wrong move. His fangs ran down the column of her throat. She froze.

"No. Don't do that. Anything but that." Her voice broke with her plea.

"Don't worry, my jewel. I will not kill you, and we cannot bond this way," he whispered against her skin, kissing her pulse point lightly.

It wasn't possible to bond with another person. She remembered reading that long ago. Only one Korrena existed for each person, but the idea of another Vasirian drinking from her the way Lukas had, shattered her heart.

"While we can be compatible pairs, I can't make you my Korrena," he confirmed, nuzzling against her pounding pulse. "I just want to see if you are as sweet as that tiny taste from before suggested."

Blaire squeezed her eyes shut and cried out in pain when his fangs punctured her neck. She breathed deeply through her nose, trying to ward off the tears burning her eyes as he drank from her. The sensation brought no pleasure the way it had with Lukas.

Disgusting.

Dirty.

Blaire felt violated in a way that made her wish he had taken her body instead, like he said he wouldn't, because this was so much worse. In her time at Blackthorn, she had come to understand the significance of sharing lifeblood with your pair. It was a sacred thing, the most intimate connection one could share with another, and Vincent was destroying that.

When satisfied, Vincent sat up and released her wrists, but Blaire didn't move. She lay and stared at the wall as he watched her. He thankfully didn't say another word, getting up from the bed and making his way through the side door, turning off the light as he went, leaving her in darkness to drown in her despair.

21

Despair

Blaire frowned at her bare wrist, tears running down her face as she cried in silence. It surprised her she had any tears left to cry; crying was all she ever did anymore when Vincent left her alone. Her wrist felt naked without Lukas's leather bracelet. She had been wearing it the day Vincent took her, but she didn't know what happened to it. Another loss—another confirmation Lukas was gone from her life.

She wondered what Riley was doing at that moment; if her friend missed her. Blaire would do anything to be able to hear the little pink-haired pixie yammer on about clothes and milkshakes. At this point, she would be fine to go back to the diner so Riley could have the best in Rosebrook, even knowing she'd encounter her old boss. The things that her stepbrother had done to her were trivial compared to the nightmare she now lived. All the therapy with Professor Sinclair went up in flames.

Nothing felt right anymore. Despite what came with being

someone's prisoner, the regular blood offering, and now being a regular meal for a twisted Vasirian, what really felt wrong deep inside was the emptiness that accompanied the blood ritual. Blaire experienced such pain and distress when thinking of Lukas, only for it to fall into a hollow pit in her stomach. In those moments, it was as if she no longer felt anything. It drove her mad, and she couldn't get a handle on reality when the veil of despair lifted, leaving her numb and broken. Add to that being stripped of her autonomy, and she struggled to maintain any will to fight.

Wiping her eyes, Blaire looked at the new nightgown at the end of the bed next to the shackle Vincent removed from her ankle before he left, instructing her to bathe before he returned with dinner after classes. She didn't know when he left, or how soon he'd be back. Her sense of time was seriously skewed by being in a room with no windows, no clock, and no regular schedule or milestones to signify the passage of time—like class finals, holidays, and birthdays. How many weeks had passed since he took her? The weakness she felt between her loss of appetite, and Vincent drawing her blood for the Order, made her disconnect with time worse—and now he was also feeding on her every day.

With a sigh, she stood on shaky legs and picked up the dark purple gown, dragging herself to the bathroom. She set the gown on the counter before running a bath, adding coconut-scented bath salts to the hot water. In any other situation, she would appreciate a hot bath with scented goodies in the water, but it was a means to an end. Anything to ease the ache in her weak muscles.

Blaire walked back to the counter and slipped the gown she wore over her head, dropping it to the floor, and took a shaky breath as she stared at her reflection in the mirror above the sink. She had grown used to seeing her skin bearing shades of purple, blue, yellow, and green. The bruises no longer brought dismay on sight. She resigned to this being her new reality. What she couldn't accept—and every time she saw it, anything she ate threatened to expel from her body—were the bite marks that covered her arms, shoulders, and neck.

At least Vincent hadn't touched her body again since the ritual. She supposed she could be thankful for small favors. He had kept his promise to not force himself on her in that way. Biting her was still forcing her, no matter how much he tried to paint the picture that he was being respectful of her by not defiling her body. Drinking her very life essence felt more debasing than sex ever would. She couldn't understand why this was happening to her, or why Vincent insisted on doing this. His words made no sense. He gained nothing from keeping her captive that she was aware of. She would never return his affections. This would not end like that stupid book that she regretted ever talking to him about. It was as if it planted a seed in his head, and he expected her to fall in love with him based on forced proximity.

Blaire ran a shaky hand over her neck where the Korrena mark should have been. The overwhelming emotion that came with the reminder of that loss gripped her, and her knees nearly buckled as she held the counter to steady herself, breaking down in tears once again. The pain was so awful that she longed for the emptiness that would eventually come.

She loved Lukas so much, but she couldn't understand why he would abandon her like this. Why wouldn't he look for her? Why wasn't anyone looking for her? Did they not care about her because she refused to become like them, like Vincent had said Lukas felt? She didn't think it was fair. She had no family. Her friends and pair had abandoned her. What was even the point?

Turning away from her reflection once she gained her composure again, she stepped into the steaming water, easing herself down until the water came up to her shoulders. A sigh slipped from her lips as she lay her head back against the cushion on the tub, closing her eyes, hoping to slip away into the darkness that had become a welcome friend.

The passage of time felt more meaningless than it ever had before. Minutes, hours, days, weeks… none of it mattered compared to the nightmare the darkness was a prelude to. The nightmare operated on its own schedule. Haunting, stealing all awareness and reason until the only important thing remaining was darkness. Darkness that allowed the body and mind to disappear, if only for a little while. For a small snippet of time. She clung desperately to those moments of reprieve.

Startled by the sound of the door opening, Blaire opened her eyes. She must have fallen asleep in the bath. The water had gone cold. She shivered as Vincent stepped into the bathroom and sat on the edge of the bathtub. Blaire drew her knees up and crossed her arms over her chest to preserve her modesty.

He shook his head at her, bemused. "I've seen it all, my jewel. There is no reason to hide from me."

She frowned at him, and his brows narrowed as he reached out to touch one of her knees above water level. She fought against her instincts, letting him touch her. If she fought against him, he would take what he wanted anyway, and maybe more. She had the bite marks all over to prove it.

"You're freezing." He ran his hand over the goose bumps on her skin to dip his hand into the water. "How long have you been in here?"

Blaire looked away. "I guess I fell asleep."

Vincent rolled his sleeves up his forearms and reached into the water's depths to unplug the drain.

"I haven't even had a chance to wash."

"I'm refilling it. You can't stay in water like this, you'll catch your death."

Blaire normally would have laughed at a statement like that, considering the situation he trapped her in. Malnourished, losing weight, a regular blood donor in more ways than one. It surprised her she hadn't already died. How long could a human survive under these conditions? She didn't know. Part of her welcomed it. Her eyes watered again, and she fought against the urge to cry. She said nothing, not wanting to provoke him in any way.

Once the water drained, Vincent began filling the tub again with hot water and dried his hands with a hand towel. His eyes met hers and he frowned. "Why are you crying, my jewel?"

Blaire hated the pet name. He started calling her a jewel from the moment they met last semester, and while it seemed charming the first time, it had become creepy. She turned her head away and swiped her eyes. She wasn't about to open up to her captor.

"You know I'm here for you, right? There is no reason to shut me out. I won't abandon you the way Lukas did."

The tears Blaire fought so hard against ran down her cheeks.

Vincent caressed the wet skin of her face. "I promise I will take care of you. Just give it time and trust me." He took a breath. "I love you."

Blaire snapped her head around, glaring at him. "You can't love me," she said icily. "You don't know me."

Vincent gave her an endearing smile, but it did nothing for her. "When you know, you know. And I've always known. The rest is just details."

Getting to know someone before declaring you love them seems like pretty important details to completely gloss over. She couldn't believe how serious he sounded.

Vincent stood. "I brought dinner from Happy Panda. I know you well enough to know you like their food. Crab rangoon, yes?" He winked at her, and her forehead wrinkled in confusion. "I've done my research, Blaire. I know more about you than you realize."

"What?"

"It was easy to get Professor Velastra's files on you. She did extensive research on you and your circumstances before joining Blackthorn Academy. It was quite informative. Added on to my own study of you in your time here, I think I can say I know what I should."

Blaire blinked and had to bite down hard into her lower lip to keep from yelling at him. How dare he invade her privacy like that? Did he know about Caleb? The Wilcox family? Did he know about her friend Charlotte? Would Charlotte be in danger? Her head swam with anxiety.

Vincent walked out of the bathroom and Blaire sunk into the refreshed water's depths, submerging herself in a temporary escape. She couldn't keep going on this way.

Lifting herself up from the back of the tub, she quickly washed her body, got out, and then put on the sleeveless aubergine nightgown that fell to her ankles. Although she hated the man, she wasn't about to turn down the crab rangoon, even if unsure she could stomach it.

Lukas's skin tingled, and something tickled his chest. He scratched at his abs and reached for the covers to pull over himself again when he started to come to. Taking a deep breath, he inhaled the scent of jasmine and groaned. Soft hands ran over his bare chest, down to his abs, and back over his arms. He shifted on the bed. Warm breath fanned over his skin and he shivered when long hair slid across his body.

Blaire had come back, or he was dreaming.

He didn't want to open his eyes and lose it if it was a dream.

Lukas reached up and held the back of her head, tangling his hand in the soft strands of hair that skimmed his body, driving him mad. His breathing came in heavy pants. When he pulled her hair gently and a moan echoed in the room, he froze, finally waking up fully.

This wasn't Blaire.

His eyes flew open, and he stared down at Clarissa wearing nothing but a skin-tight peach t-shirt and a pair of lacy boyshort panties of the same color.

"What the fuck are you doing?" Lukas growled and released her hair, glaring at her.

Clarissa ran a hand over the front of his tight boxers, lightly gripping his hard cock. He tensed and his nostrils flared. She smirked in satisfaction and squeezed him again. "I'm taking care of you." She slid her tongue over her lips as she looked up at him from under her fake lashes, her mouth hovering inches above his covered hardness.

She didn't arouse him. The only reason he had a hard-on at all was because he'd thought Blaire was touching him. The perfume she wore drove him insane. Even with the other scents mixed in, it still reminded him too much of his lost love. The long hair and the small hands on his body had done nothing to discourage the fantasy that Blaire had returned to him.

Clarissa's fingers wrapped around the waistband of his boxers, those annoying nails dipping inside. When she started to pull down, he jerked, making her pause.

"Back the fuck up," he snarled, sliding to sit up on the bed with his back to the headboard out of her reach.

"Oh, come on." Clarissa crawled up the bed and straddled Lukas's lap, pressing her body against his. Her hardened nipples rubbing his chest through her thin t-shirt made him clench his jaw in frustration. Why wouldn't this girl understand he didn't want her? He'd made it clear.

She leaned in and whispered against his ear, "I can take real good care of you." She ran her tongue over the shell of his ear. "We would make a perfect compatible pair. I smell like Blaire, right?"

Lukas clenched his fists at his sides, fighting the urge to throw Clarissa from the bed. He didn't want to hurt her, no matter how angry he was at the asinine suggestion.

"You will never compare to Blaire," he said through gritted teeth.

Curling her upper lip in a sneer, she stared at his face before composing herself. "Just close your eyes. Imagine it until you get used to me." Her voice was breathy in a way he assumed she was exaggerating for appeal. She just sounded like a porn star faking it. He almost laughed at the thought.

Clarissa ground her hips against his waning erection, a soft moan leaving her lips. He no longer felt aroused, and her movements made his irritation grow.

When she couldn't get a rise out of his body, Clarissa sat back and glared at him. "Lukas. It's been over a month. You deserve to be happy, not pining over some pathetic human."

Rage flashed, and he grabbed Clarissa's hips in a bruising grip to stop her movements.

She moaned.

The girl had absolutely no restraint, and it disgusted him. For months she had been pushing him, trying to be close to him. Aiden tried to tell him Clarissa wanted him. Blaire had tried to tell him she flirted. Lukas had been blind to it all until she moved in. Now he couldn't get away from it.

Clarissa always found one excuse or another for them to work together in class. She had weaseled her way into all of his classes. He didn't even know if they shared the same major. In the last couple weeks, she had amped up her efforts, and it became clear to him it wasn't curiosity or some sort of savior worship from when he helped her out. People could get caught up in someone who did something nice for them, but as more time passed, he realized she was infatuated with him in ways he didn't understand.

Clarissa had also tried to worm her way into his friend group, much to everyone's distaste. On more than one occasion, Riley had to be stopped from attacking the annoying girl. Seth did a relatively good job of keeping her restrained; no one else seemed to have the power to stop her.

One of these days, Riley was going to find herself in front of the Order having to explain why she messed up Angelo Moretti's little girl's face. It wasn't a position he would want to find himself in, but Clarissa kept pushing Riley's buttons and made it worse with insensitive remarks about Blaire. Riley was fiercely protective over Blaire, and Clarissa always referred to Blaire as some derogatory term or as "that human"—never her name. It didn't surprise him that Riley felt nothing but contempt for the girl. Passive aggressiveness wielded as a weapon, Clarissa pretended not to understand why anyone got angry with her.

He'd had enough.

Lukas leaned in slowly and her breath hitched, drawing his attention to her lips. She thought he was going to kiss her. Before he got near her face, he moved his head to stop beside her ear. "Get. The. Fuck. Off. Me." Lukas spoke low, enunciating each word to make his wishes absolutely clear to the clueless girl, his voice dripping with venom.

Clarissa leaned back and smirked at him, a look of condemnation and arrogance. The girl really thought she was better than everyone.

She licked her too-full lips again and climbed off the bed, walking to the bathroom door. Before she went inside, she put her hand on the doorjamb and looked back at him. "Just… think about it. I can give you everything you need."

Before he could reply, or throw anything at her like he wanted to, she disappeared into the ensuite, shutting the door.

Lukas grabbed his cell phone from the nightstand and opened his photo gallery. Nothing. He had no photos of Blaire. The only photos he had were things others had sent him and he saved. He never bothered with things like taking photos. It wasn't something he enjoyed—having his picture taken. But at that moment, he wished he had taken photos of her every day. Photos of the looks that were for him only when they were alone, not candid shots or smiles with friends. Wished that he had something tangible to hold on to so Blaire didn't fade from his memory.

He chuckled and shook his head at the ridiculousness of the thought. Nothing would ever make Blaire leave his mind. His brain was branded with her smiling face. The cute way her nose slightly crinkled when she was annoyed and glared at him in an attempt to be stern. Her sleeping face.

Lukas slid down on the bed until he was flat on his back. Closing his eyes with a shaky breath, a tear escaped his closed eyelids. "Where are you, Blaire?" he whispered, his voice cracking on the words.

He prayed for the numbness to return. The empty feeling that sometimes overtook him after he broke down. The numbness had become a bitter reprieve from the mess of his mind and the despair gripping his heart. Everything in him wanted to hunt Blaire down and demand answers, but he'd learned to respect her boundaries. If she no longer wanted to be with him, he had to respect her wishes. Even if it killed him inside.

22

CONTROL

Stepping out of the bathroom after taking a hot bath to soothe the ache that seemed to be a constant in her limbs nowadays, Blaire stopped short when she didn't see Vincent in the kitchenette.

"Vincent?" she called, her eyes shifting to the door. He never left her alone in the room unchained after a bath.

She crossed to the doorway that led into Vincent's room and flipped on the light switch. The room was basic, and obviously a storage space. Nothing like the opulence of the studio style room she slept in, or even the marble bathroom. Plain walls, no windows, the same hardwood flooring from the main room, but lacking in any area rugs or decoration. Large paintings rested against the wall in a stack, and stacked chairs occupied the far corner next to boxes and several pieces of old pottery. The only part of the room that looked lived in was a single bed in the back corner that was neatly made with simple burgundy and white linens.

This couldn't be Vincent's home. Why would he have a room with all this junk stored? And why would he be sleeping in the smaller bed and not the larger one that occupied the living space? He could have kept her hidden away in this room. She was sure it wasn't for her comfort that he gave her the other bed.

Blaire turned from the room after switching the light off, disturbing nothing. She didn't want to do anything that would poke the beast in Vincent. It was obvious he left in a hurry, otherwise he wouldn't have forgotten to chain her to the bed. Or perhaps he thought her bath would take longer? Either way, she would not pass up the opportunity to use the time to her advantage.

She rushed to the door and tried the handle. Nothing. What had she expected? Vincent wasn't foolish enough to leave the door unlocked. With a sigh, she jerked hard on the handle in frustration and one lock rattled, the bolt in the wall wiggling where it wasn't screwed tightly. She licked her lips nervously and pulled on the door once more, before pushing and pulling sharply to pop the lock. If she could disable one, maybe it would make things easier to pry open. It wasn't the most ingenious idea, but it was all she had.

She looked around the room frantically for anything that could help her pry off the hinges. Her body vibrated with nervous energy as she ran into the kitchenette and rifled through cabinets and drawers. The cabinets held dishes and glasses, but the drawers held no silverware or tools. Where did he keep everything? She groaned in frustration. Did he think she would stab him with forks and butter knives? Okay, that was a fair thought. She'd have done it if he hadn't kept her chained up.

Slamming a drawer in defeat, she paused when she heard a rattle as it caught on something, not fully closing. She pulled the drawer out with a hard yank, removing it from its track, and peered into the darkened cubby that housed it. *Bingo.* Blaire reached into the space and pulled out a butter knife.

She aligned the drawer back on its track and slid it back into its cubby, stumbling over the chair at the dining table as she spun around to run back to the door.

With shaking hands, she began jamming the knife into the loose hinge to get it to give. With a lot of back and forth, that required her to continuously stop and wipe the nervous sweat from her hands on her gown to keep from dropping the knife, she finally popped the hinge on one lock. She couldn't contain the giddy squeal that rose inside her. She was going to get out of there.

In her excitement to free the next hinge that wasn't loose, and required a lot more effort, she overextended the knife. With a snap, it broke in two. The part she had jammed into the hinge clattered to the floor. The soft clatter may as well have been a gunshot with how loud it echoed in her ears, marking the end of her escape with a finality that made her chest ache.

No. No, no, no. This can't be the end.

She had a chance. She couldn't fail now.

After several minutes of rocking the door and getting nowhere, she threw her shoulder into the hard surface. Ignoring the pain that lanced through her bruised arm, she slammed herself into the wood repeatedly as she called out for help.

"Please! Anyone! I'm trapped in here!" It was like wailing into the void when only silence answered. Blaire threw herself against the door again with her whole body before she heard the locks disengaging.

She stepped back with a gasp as Vincent threw the door open with a look of rage twisting his features.

"Let me out of here!" Blaire charged at him in a desperate bid to slip past him into the freedom on the other side.

Strong arms wrapped around her waist, halting her escape, and her body was hoisted up effortlessly as the door slammed shut. "What are you doing?" Vincent bellowed, his eyes glowing so brightly they were almost white instead of blue. "Do you have any idea what would happen if someone heard you?" When he set her down on her feet again, Blaire scrambled away from him to the middle of the room.

"Answer me!"

A sob caught in her throat, and she shook her head rapidly. "I… No, I don't know. Please let me go."

Vincent turned his back on her as if she posed no threat to him as he locked the door again. It was true. She had a sorry excuse for a weapon, and because of her lack of physical activity and nutrition—which was her own damn fault, because Vincent kept bringing her all her favorite things to eat—she was weaker than ever. Even then, his body was built as if he were born to bench press cars.

"If someone had heard your screeching before I had, they would have taken you away from me," he said, the rage from before startlingly absent as he casually bent down to pick up the broken hinge and sharp end of the knife that had fallen to the floor. He turned to her and raised a brow as he held them up.

Why couldn't he understand that was exactly what she wanted? Recognizing she was clearly at a disadvantage in this situation, she bit the inside of her cheek to keep from saying something smart or laughing like a lunatic. She was losing it, and this asshat couldn't see she didn't want to be there.

Vincent tossed the broken pieces into the small garbage can near the entryway and folded his arms calmly over his chest. "Take it off."

"What?" Blaire's brows furrowed in confusion.

Waving his hand up and down, Vincent said, "Your gown. Take it off, my jewel."

She took a step back and shook her head. "What? No. You said you wouldn't—" She looked down at the broken knife in her hand. Could she use it?

"Take. It. Off," he growled before stepping to her and snatching the broken handle from her hand. "You seem to misunderstand. If you still think it's appropriate for you to leave this room until we can go together, then you clearly don't deserve such privileges."

Blaire rubbed her aching arm and pulled a face. "Privileges?" How was wearing clothes a privilege?

"That silk is some of the finest money can buy. I would have my jewel in nothing less. However, until you have learned to appreciate how well you have it. How much I love you… Well, you can do without such fineries."

She didn't know what to say to that. He was insane. She didn't want his silks, his love, anything from him.

When she didn't comply, he arched his brow at her. "Come now. We will not have to regress to using manmade products to get you to comply again, will we?" He waved a hand once more in a silent demand.

Blaire lifted her chin, glaring at him, as she reached up to slip a strap from her shoulder. She would not allow him to see her humiliation. As she slipped the other strap from her opposite shoulder, her fingers trembled, betraying the fear that still lingered as she relinquished control to this man. She clenched her abs and hip muscles to stand rigidly upright and raised her chin. She would not allow him to make her feel shame.

When the gown slid over her body to the floor, she met his heated gaze with one of her own. But the heat in her eyes was pure hatred.

Vincent glanced at her bed, and she held her head high as she walked calmly to the bed, keeping her arms at her sides and doing her best to show him this wasn't affecting her.

As soon as he came through the door, she should have tried to stab him with the broken knife. She was so distraught her mind had blanked. She gritted her teeth in irritation with herself.

He chuckled as she got into the bed and pulled the covers over her body to hide her nakedness. He knelt and picked up the ankle cuff, then took her foot in his hand. Once he secured the cuff, and she could no longer leave the cage without bars that had become her home, he turned and picked up her discarded nightgown.

Without looking at her, or saying anything more, he went into the other room, turning off the lights and leaving her in the dark, hopeless and frustrated.

Blaire walked through the trees and into the familiar clearing where a pair of crows nestled together next to the mysterious woman, who perched on the same stump as before. She sat in the same position, her gown spread over the grass in such a way that it appeared as if she hadn't moved since Blaire had last seen her.

She glanced down at herself. At least her dream granted her the courtesy of clothing.

"You're giving in to despair," she said simply, with no accusation in her voice.

The fact weighed heavily on Blaire's stomach. She wouldn't insult the woman who gave her a sense of comfort, an anchor in her waking nightmare, by denying the truth of her words.

"I'm sorry."

"Do not apologize to me, child. It isn't your fault, and one cannot blame you for what you feel. A broken bond is unnatural."

Blaire shook her head, wanting to not think about what the loss of her bond meant. "Why are we here again?" she asked, trying to divert conversation from the sensitive subject.

"In this world?"

"No. In this same place. What is that beyond the cliff?"

The woman sighed and looked up into Blaire's eyes, a strange sadness swirling there. The pair of crows at her side huddled closer, as if comforting one another. "My memories… Rosendo Blackthorn locked them away long ago."

"Who is that?"

"King Adrian's great grandfather. He died a century and a half ago, and his son Luciano took the throne at age fifty in his place. I wasn't even born when Rosendo first became king of the Vasirian. It has been four hundred and fifty years since he took the throne, and no one can remember anything from his three-hundred-year reign or the time before he came to power. Not because their memories sit locked, like mine. The information has simply fallen to time's decay, and records have either disappeared or have been destroyed."

Blaire nodded. She had asked Lukas about Vasirian history, but he said the schools didn't teach anything prior to Rosendo's reign. Destroyed records made sense, much like the Dark Ages of European history, but only if they'd had a single civilization in only one locale on Earth.

"King Luciano enacted laws to protect humans when he came into power based on my guidance. I don't know how I knew, but I felt so strongly that something terrible had happened under Rosendo's reign that his son would have to do something to ensure nothing more could happen. To protect your kind."

Blaire shifted uncomfortably. She struggled to imagine life hundreds of years ago. She was sitting in front of someone old enough to have personally witnessed the history of the Vasirian as far back as when the Pilgrims landed in New England. She still hadn't gotten used to the idea that her new friends would live for so long. It was no wonder they wanted her to give in and join them.

"With my memories locked, I can only access bits and pieces, but they guide the prophecies I give to those who need them in an effort to restore the balance."

Blaire's brows furrowed. "Wait." She shook her head. "Guidance? Prophecies? You… You're the Oracle?"

The crows fluttered their wings as if laughing along with the woman in front of her. "You are correct, child. I am the only Vasirian alive that lived during Rosendo's reign, and with the lock on my memories, I cannot see through the thick miasma that blocks my mind to access what I need to help our people. Only what the Celestial Conclave grants me the power to unlock reaches me."

The somber tone of the Oracle was heartbreaking. For someone so powerful, her helplessness in this moment stirred a response inside Blaire. The skittering electricity she felt in this dream world made her fingers twitch.

Riley had said the Oracle was the oldest living Vasirian. Obviously, Vasirian history went back a lot farther than Rosendo's reign, just as human history stretched back hundreds of thousands of years. Truly, had it all been lost? All traces of their entire evolution and civilization erased?

"What can I do to help you?" Blaire asked. There had to be a reason the Oracle kept reaching out to her. Was she the key to unlocking this powerful entity's memories?

"The future is uncertain. I can reveal what I can as it comes, but I cannot provide you with everything, even then."

"Why not?"

"It doesn't work that way. To reveal everything is to potentially alter the course of fate in such a way that would bring divine punishment from the Celestial Conclave. If one knows the exact course of events as solidly as saying, 'You will need to go to the bathroom in one hour,' then they may deviate from the path to ensure it comes to pass without knowing the alternate future connected to the original, necessary path."

Blaire sighed. It all sounded extremely complicated.

"We have free will, and there are a variety of paths we can take that spread out like spiderwebs through our lifeline, but they all lead to what the Celestial Conclave has cast in the stars for us. But if we make certain choices that take us away from what the Celestial Conclave wills, then things become unbalanced. The Celestial Conclave can set events in motion to try and force what they deem to be the appropriate path, but it ultimately falls on us to make the right choice. This is why revealing too much can be dangerous."

"It sounds like religion. An all-seeing god that shapes the future but gives us free will. I'm not sure I ever believed in that."

If there was a god, why did he take her parents and put her in such a dangerous situation with a monster for a stepbrother, and how could that god allow her to suffer what she had at Vincent's hands?

If there was such a thing as a god, he or she must certainly hate her. But why make all the other good people in the world suffer? If she had the power of an all-knowing god, she'd do something about world hunger, pedophiles, abusers, and people's suffering in general. What kind of god would not do that?

Blaire sighed. "So you're telling me that no matter what I do, I'll end up in the same place, no matter what, if this Celestial Conclave pushes hard enough?"

The idea that once again something wanted to snatch control away from her was infuriating. Energy coursed through her veins in response.

Caleb and his grandparents.

Blackthorn Academy and its rules and regulations.

The Order.

Lukas.

They all wanted to control her in some way or another.

The crows cawed excitedly, flapping their wings before taking off into the sky. The Oracle looked at Blaire curiously as she clenched and unclenched her fists.

"You feel something."

Blaire's gaze snapped up, and the Oracle gasped.

"What?" Blaire asked.

The Oracle held out her hand, but when Blaire only raised her brow, the Oracle sighed. "Come now. Give me your hand."

Blaire slid her hand into the soft palm. The Oracle's eyes widened and glowed a vibrant blue that glazed over the hazel until even her pupils disappeared. Blaire tried to pull her hand away, her hand burning, but the Oracle's grip was surprisingly strong. After the burning sensation spread over Blaire's entire body, the Oracle released her with a gasp, as if surfacing from deep water. Blaire fell back onto the soft grass, panting.

"There is no doubt: you are the key to restoring the disturbed balance. The Celestial Conclave has confirmed that unequivocally. Whatever wrongs Rosendo set in motion hundreds of years ago… only you can make right, child."

23

Seeking Answers

Lukas stood in front of Professor Sinclair's office in the psychology department. He had no idea what he was doing there. Well, that wasn't exactly true. Blaire had regular visits with the woman, and they talked about him, among other things. Maybe she could give him answers to help him get closure, or at least understand what really drove Blaire's decision to leave him. To want to be away from him so resolutely that the bond they shared broke.

"Are you going to knock?"

Lukas oriented on the sweet voice that spoke hesitantly behind him. A woman in a floral blouse and black slacks stood there with a stack of papers in her arms. If not for her attire, Lukas would have thought she was a student, and not a student at the university level, either. With a baby face, round doe eyes, and standing shorter than Riley, she looked barely old enough to be out of grade school. But he knew never to guess ages in their world.

Shaking away his distracted thoughts, he swallowed thickly. "I don't know," he answered honestly.

A soft smile crossed her face, making a dimple pop on the right side of her cheek, further adding to her youthful appearance. "It's okay. If you're not ready, you can always come again." She responded as if she were used to his hesitance. Maybe she was, considering this was a place many came to get counseling. Not everyone approached it with an open mind.

Lukas shook his head. If he left now, he wouldn't set foot back in the department. It was hard enough to be there knowing Blaire came to this wing for a majority of her psychology courses, but also to get counseling? To share possible concerns about him that she hadn't expressed to him when he thought they'd gotten to a stage where they were open with one another? It would be too difficult to come back. He needed to deal with this now.

"No, I…" He glanced back at the closed door. "Is she in?"

"Dr. Sinclair just finished lunch—"

"Candace," a woman said from behind Lukas as the door to the office opened. "What have I told you about calling me Doctor?"

The small woman flushed then nodded. "I apologize. It takes getting used to."

Laughing, the taller woman with copper hair braided over her shoulder waved her hand quickly in front of her face, as if swatting a gnat. "Oh, don't look so serious. You've only been working as my receptionist for a couple of weeks. I don't expect you to change your habits after working with those stuffy old bags at Emory."

"So… I don't think this student has an appointment, but…" Sad eyes met Lukas's. "I think he needs to see someone."

Lukas must look poorer than he thought if she assumed he needed help. He could have easily been there for classwork or something else. He rubbed his tired eyes.

"That so? Well, you're in luck. I just finished my lunch, and I don't have any obligations for another hour. Come in." Professor Sinclair stepped aside and waved her hand toward the open office, which looked like an indoor jungle for all the house plants.

Lukas tucked his hands in the front pockets of his jeans and made his way into the room that smelled heavily of nature. He stood awkwardly in the center as the professor passed around him after closing the door. She motioned toward a large armchair and a black leather chaise lounger. He wasn't sure he could sit, so he remained standing as the professor took a seat in front of a coffee table with a large floral arrangement on top.

"My name is Professor Sinclair, as you heard in the hall, or Professor Isla, if you'd prefer. Of course you can leave off 'professor' if you'd like and just call me Isla. I hope my assistant wasn't too chatty. She's from Emory University. My last assistant had to transfer to Arizona for his wife's job. Shame to lose him. He was all business. Stayed on top of things like a champ."

Lukas was sure she was trying to make him more comfortable, but he couldn't relax. He gave her a short nod, looking toward the large window off behind a desk on the back wall. Orange leaves brushed against the glass from the sugar maple tree outside. The window was still damp from a rare shower that had fallen on the area. They had entered the dry season, but it seemed as if the sky knew things weren't how they were supposed to be, and the clouds were crying on his behalf. He didn't have tears left to shed.

Sighing, Lukas turned from the window, after finding nothing to distract himself, to find Professor Sinclair studying him curiously.

"So, tell me… what brings you here?"

Lukas balled his fists in his pockets and looked up at the ceiling. "Have you spoken to Blaire?"

"Pardon? Do you mean Blaire Wilcox?"

"Yes."

"I'm afraid not. Not since her regrettable withdrawal from the academy."

Lukas dropped onto the plush cushion of the armchair, putting his elbows on his knees and his head in his hands.

"Lukas?"

When he lifted his gaze to meet the professor's, she frowned. "So, you're Lukas Virtanen, her pair," she said with a nod, as if confirming the fact to herself.

"Was, but yeah."

His chest tightened. He hated referring to what they had in the past tense, but it was a fact he had to face. If he continued to deny the crushing reality, he could never move forward. It felt like he was lying to himself when he thought of moving forward. He knew that wasn't an option. Even fifty years from now, he'd still fixate on that beautiful human who came into his life like a whirlwind and made him feel things he couldn't turn off anymore.

"Was? What do you mean?"

"Blaire left me. Our mark is gone."

"I don't think I follow."

"After she left, the…" He swallowed the lump in his throat. "After a month of searching for her, the Korrena mark disappeared. She rejected the bond."

The professor sat back and folded her arms across her stomach, the bangles on her wrist clanging against the large belt she wore over a royal blue jumpsuit. "I didn't know that was possible."

"Story of the year." Lukas sighed. "No one knows what the hell it means, really. But they say Blaire couldn't handle being with a Vasirian and all that came with it… I think that's an obvious rejection of the bond, don't you?"

Frowning, the professor shook her head. "Not necessarily. Just because Blaire may have felt apprehension about this world, and what we are, doesn't mean she wanted to reject you and the bond you shared."

The words rang hollow in his ears. If they were true, Blaire would still be by his side. Instead, he had to find out from the obnoxious spawn of the head of the Order—the people who'd nearly killed Blaire—that she didn't want him anymore. While he hadn't wanted to believe her words, having Professor Velastra confirm them by speaking directly to the Order...

He rubbed his eyes.

"I can't disclose anything we've talked about, but I can at least assure you that Blaire loved you very much, Lukas."

Lukas lowered his hands and shook his head. "That's why I came here. I wanted to ask if she'd said anything about leaving. Had she been planning this? Did she give any warning at all that she wasn't happy with me?"

The look in his eyes must have been pitiful because Professor Sinclair sucked in her lips, and it looked like she was chewing the inside of her cheek. She looked conflicted, and for once, he felt grateful that he looked like hell; maybe it would get him answers.

"Blaire never mentioned leaving, other than the time that I'm aware you know of. The night you both joined your bond completely."

Lukas's gut flipped at the memory. He'd almost lost Blaire that night, and to have it end with her in his arms, and the Korrena mark so proudly—and what he thought as permanently—displayed on her neck, had filled him with so much joy he couldn't put it into words.

"I can also confirm that she wasn't planning anything of the sort. No warnings, or any expressions of discomfort regarding you or your pairing after you claimed her."

"What about before that?"

Professor Sinclair shook her head. "As I said, I cannot share what I discuss with my patient. I can tell you what wasn't said, but not what Blaire tells me in confidence."

Lukas tensed at her words. The implication that Blaire talked about discomfort regarding him and their pairing prior to that night got to him. If Blaire had said nothing, the professor would have confirmed it like she did for the rest of everything else. It was as good of confirmation as any. But it wasn't news to him. That night, they discussed the discomfort and fears she had. It was likely the same stuff she spoke with the professor about.

"Blaire went through a lot to get to where she was at the time of your claiming. Not just while a student at Blackthorn, but long before that."

"I'm aware."

"Yes, she told me she shared her history with you. But what I'm trying to get at is a mind that has suffered trauma as she has, from losing her family to… well, the rest of everything that led her to accept Professor Velastra's proposal to join Blackthorn… Those kinds of things can weigh on the mind long after the threat is gone. Long after the situation resolves itself. If Blaire made the choice to leave, I believe it had nothing to do with you and everything to do with her own efforts to protect herself from a threat."

"But I'm not a threat to her," Lukas bit out, unable to keep the irritation out of his voice.

"No. We know you're not. But for a mind that has experienced trauma, threats don't have to be real. Imagined threats can be just as terrifying. But again, this is all speculation. I was under the impression at our last session that Blaire was making incredible progress. I saw no signs of flight behavior." She shifted in her seat. "When Blaire first arrived at Blackthorn and came to me, that behavior was her modus operandi—"

"What now?"

"Her way of being. How she operated. When Blaire first came, she overread the room. The slightest look from you made her suspect the worst. She was hyperaware of so much that she stayed a ball of tension. I can't go into detail, as I've told you, but she was constantly in a fight-or-flight mentality and never had the opportunity to relax. While she might have seemed calm on the surface at times, deep in her psyche she was being stalked by a Bengal tiger, and it kept her hypervigilant about everything."

Lukas sighed heavily and put his elbow on the arm of the chair, holding his forehead. "So, she wasn't being honest about her feelings?"

"Oh, no. You misunderstand. Blaire is an incredibly honest person. But that trauma… she had the ability to push it away and compartmentalize it. When something would happen around her that she didn't understand—or couldn't control—it would surface, and she would act accordingly. I don't believe she was even aware at first of this type of behavior. But if she hadn't been able to push it aside to live in the moment, Blaire wouldn't be as strong of a woman as she is today. She would have broken long ago before you or I ever met her. That became a source of strength, but it also kept her from dealing with it healthily until this year with me."

Lukas understood, but didn't know what any of this meant for why Blaire chose to walk away from him. Had his insistence and mistrust in her, along with the threat of Clarissa, finally proved too much for even Blaire to handle?

Had she really not overcome things and fooled even herself into thinking she'd grown? Did it all finally become too much and crash down on her when he tried to push her toward a decision to give up her humanity? Had Blaire always been broken, and he just didn't see it? It didn't seem the case. He would have felt it through the bond when they were together. But if she had always been broken and hid it, maybe not. It's not like he understood the bond any more than he did before he claimed her in the bonding ritual.

He felt sick to his stomach as the guilt clawed at his insides. This was his fault.

Professor Sinclair checked her watch. "I'm really sorry to cut this short, Lukas. I have a meeting in the staff building and another appointment after that. You're welcome to talk to Candace and set up an appointment with me to talk if you'd like. While I'm not privy to what a broken bond entails—this is completely new territory for me—I'm sure I can help you with coping with the emotions you're feeling. If you're open to that."

"We'll see," Lukas mumbled as he stood. He didn't want to blow the woman off, but he wouldn't be back. He'd never set foot in the psychology department again if he could help it.

24

Relocation

Blaire rubbed her arm, her slender fingers passing over the pale skin as if she could erase the bruising as Vincent packed away another two full vials of the blood he had just taken from her. When had having her blood taken become such a normal thing in her life that it no longer scared her? She had to wonder if soon Vincent's feeding on her would become a thing of normalcy. She shuddered at the thought.

Vincent had a schedule he didn't deviate from for blood retrieval that helped her keep some semblance of time, even if she didn't know her starting point. It wasn't as if she could even use her menstrual cycle to track time, because she completely missed the one she should have had around her birthday and barely spotted in the weeks that followed, likely because of the lack of nutrition. But she expected to make an offering every other day, and when she started keeping track, it didn't take long before she forced herself to stop.

After another week passed where no one had come for her, she stopped counting. It only served to sink her further into depression, and she couldn't afford to completely give up. In the back of her mind, she knew she would get out of this situation. While unable to fully explain the feeling, she didn't hesitate to cling to that sliver of hope burning inside like a dying flame.

"Eat your dinner. You must keep up your strength, my jewel. I don't want another episode of you passing out. You know you're susceptible to bouts of anemia."

Vincent motioned toward the kitchenette where he'd laid out a plate of barbecued chicken with sides of macaroni and cheese and fried okra. A small garden salad filled a bowl next to the plate. Blaire never understood how he expected her to eat so much.

Sighing, Blaire stood, and after a small wave of dizziness passed, she crossed to the table and lowered herself into the dining chair. She would not argue with him. He'd given her clothes back after a week of "punishment" for taking his goodwill for granted. While she didn't allow him to see her humiliation, being forced to parade around naked for his hungry eyes was degrading.

She poured herself a glass of apple juice from the carafe in the middle of the table. Vincent had made a habit of supplying her with various teas and juices. He noted she never drank soda before she came to stay with him. He said this as if she volunteered to be a prisoner; he was delusional. He rationalized that her stomach must be sensitive to carbonation.

Of course, he was completely wrong. The habit of drinking sweet and fruity teas or juice started with her stepbrother. Despite the high sugar content of both, Caleb had insisted that carbonated sodas not only held more sugar, but also more calories, and said the carbonation would bloat her. He was obsessed with keeping Blaire from gaining weight. Now she couldn't drink sodas at all without getting a terrible stomach-ache; her body wasn't used to it. So she stuck with teas and juices. Not that it was a hardship; she loved teas.

Blaire smirked, wondering how her stepbrother would react to the ten or so pounds she'd lost since being with Vincent. While she didn't look frail and bony, the loss on her tall and already slim frame was noticeable. The old Caleb would likely be pleased, and the idea turned her stomach. She needed to not think about him. The situation at hand was far more important.

She flinched when Vincent's fingers slid beneath the hair at her nape. She didn't like how he had become so at home with touching her, as if it were his right. Picking at her barbecued chicken to distract herself, she sighed as he braided her long hair.

Vincent cleared his throat after several minutes of silence. "When the school year finishes, we'll be able to go to my family's villa in Brazil. That way you won't have to deal with the Order any longer. The days of this"—he placed his hand on the bruising at the crook of her elbow—"will be a distant memory."

Blaire tensed, heavy panic settling in her stomach. They were going to leave the country? The idea shook her insides. If Vincent took her away from Blackthorn, there would be no way she'd ever escape. That small flame of hope inside her grew dimmer.

"H-how long is that from now?" The effort to mask her panic was arduous. Her heart fluttered like a caged bird.

Vincent dropped her braid and placed a hand on her shoulder. She fought not to flinch away. She took a long drink of her juice to distract herself. *Pick your battles*, she reminded herself. There was safety in compliance when dealing with someone who wasn't quite right in their mind.

"Thanksgiving is in a couple of weeks. So, another six and a half months and we can finally be free to be together without interference."

Blaire swallowed, clearing her throat. *Okay. Still mid-November. There's still time.* Weeks had passed since her birthday, but she hadn't known how many. This game he played with her had been going on for nearly two months now. Numbness crept over her again.

They actually forgot about her.

Part of her had clung to the hope that despair influenced her thoughts, but no. If she was still on Blackthorn Academy grounds, they hadn't looked very hard. They'd have found her by now. Right? If she weren't on school grounds… She had no idea how she would get back, and if by some chance they were looking for her, they'd have no way of knowing where she was.

Blaire tore tiny pieces from her chicken as her mind swirled with bleak thoughts.

The thought that no one cared about her, or about what happened to her, was sobering. No one at the academy had any real reason to be attached to her, in truth. Lukas was bound to her entirely by circumstance. Her friendships, which she thought to be strong and reliable, were merely a byproduct of her connection with Lukas. Riley put it best when they met—because she and Lukas would fully bond soon, the friendships would be inevitable. Riley seemed so happy about that fact then, so certain of their friendship. It didn't mean they *wanted* friendship with her as an individual. Perhaps they were just as sick of her as Lukas evidently was. Maybe they hadn't forgiven her for her calling Lukas a monster—and by extension, the rest of them—back when they first met and she was scared and lashing out.

Maybe they only saw her as a pathetic human the way Clarissa did.

Maybe they were too kind to put those feelings into words for Lukas's sake.

Now that they knew Lukas didn't want her anymore, they could walk away and stop acknowledging her existence.

Her stomach tightened, and she had to swallow the sob that tried to work its way out. Riley was her best friend. She didn't want to lose her.

Charlotte would worry about her. That was certain. But did Charlotte even know she was missing? Since she joined the academy, it wasn't unusual for long periods of time to pass without contact. Nothing would even seem amiss to Charlotte, outside of Blaire not contacting her to wish her a happy birthday last month on the twenty-third.

Besides, how would Charlotte even find out she was gone? She couldn't come to the academy grounds. Professor Velastra said it was much too dangerous for Charlotte to come, as a human. The statement hadn't settled in her mind until now. If it was dangerous for Charlotte to be there, why not her? They relied too heavily on the bond between Lukas and her to hold up and keep her safe. One wrong move and she could be someone's meal, if they felt inclined to try their hand. It had happened once before. Now Vincent was doing the same, slowly, over a long period.

"I'm very disappointed." Vincent cut into Blaire's thoughts, and she looked up at him as he sat at the table. "You've barely eaten anything once again."

Blaire looked down at the chicken she had picked apart and only eaten a few bites from. The untouched macaroni and okra sat cold. She hadn't even considered touching the salad. Her attempts to eat had become only what was necessary to make her stomach stop growling, and she relied on the high-sugar juices and tea for most of her calories.

"While I have not seen you naked in quite a while, I can see you've lost weight. It worries me, my beautiful jewel. Your shine has dimmed substantially."

"I'm not hungry," Blaire mumbled, lowering her head.

"I doubt that." Vincent rolled the ring on his index finger with his thumb absentmindedly. "I seem to recall you having quite a healthy appetite. It was surprising. Your body composition didn't match the voracious appetite on display."

Blaire looked at him, disconcerted. She shifted her gaze away and ripped pieces from the napkin in front of her. "How do you know anything about my appetite?" She wasn't about to address how he'd paid attention to her body. *Pick your battles.*

He gave a light shrug. "I watched you for quite a long time, of course." He took a drink of his wine and studied Blaire's face.

Every time he mentioned watching her, she felt violated. Vincent often brought up incidents that happened in the time before she came to be trapped by him. Mundane events like hanging out in the courtyard around the fountain with Riley, details of the conversations they all shared in the cafeteria during meal services. How he got close enough to know half the stuff he did unsettled her. Never mind that he'd stolen the files about her history from Professor Velastra.

Vincent was even versed in the conflicted way her relationship with Lukas developed over that time. It was as if he had kept her under a microscope. Stalked her. Blaire thought Caleb had been obsessed, but Vincent blew his infatuation with her right out of the water.

Vincent took her fork and scooped a bite of macaroni and cheese, then brought it to her lips. She opened her mouth to allow him to feed her. The act made humiliation burn inside her, but she didn't know what he would do if she denied him. She swallowed the food, but it landed like lead in her stomach.

"I know you love this food, my jewel. Why won't you eat?"

Blaire closed her eyes. "I just want to go home." Her voice broke with her admission.

Setting the fork down, Vincent sighed and stood, moving again to stand uncomfortably close behind her. Her shoulders instinctively drew up, and she rubbed her arms.

"You are home. With me. This is your home now, and soon we'll have our own place far away from the world where no one can disrupt our love."

A shudder racked Blaire's body before she could stop it, as Vincent pulled wayward strands of hair from her neck that had fallen from her braid. He leaned down to tenderly kiss the side of her neck.

"Don't do that," she said sharply. She wanted no affection from him. No intimate gestures that would keep him in his fantasy world. Just because she had to be there didn't mean she would roll over and allow him to believe she wanted this. No matter what he forced her into, Vincent would always know Blaire didn't accept him.

Vincent's lips pulled into a grin against her skin, and her heart beat a dissonant rhythm. "You are just too tempting to resist, my beautiful jewel." Another kiss. "Much too tempting."

Blaire choked on the breath in her throat as Vincent sank his fangs into her neck below her pulse point.

When Lukas bit her, she didn't feel pain. Only a sharp sting for a brief moment before pleasure took over. Nothing about the experience was negative. With Vincent, the entire process hurt.

In the beginning, she had a hard time keeping quiet and not expressing the pain Vincent inflicted, but she learned to clamp down on that reaction and push it to the back of her mind.

Another bite of pain lanced through her as he burrowed deeper into her flesh. Tears streamed down her face, her mouth parted in a silent cry, as he drank greedily from her.

The small flame of hope extinguished.

25

NUMB

Lukas was at the end of his rope.

The situation he found himself in with Clarissa made him uncomfortable, and he didn't know how to act. He wasn't good with awkward—certainly not good when faced with someone who so blatantly pushed themselves on him. It wasn't as if someone had never propositioned him before. Women tried to get his attention plenty of times when he visited the nightclub Haven. He'd never been interested in them. Never danced with any of them when they tried to entice him while looking up at him through their lashes, pursing pouty, over-plump lips. None of that did it for him. For the longest time, he wondered if something was wrong with him. He had no interest in relationships, and casual sex felt like a waste of time.

Then Blaire came along and rocked the entire foundation he stood on. He went from zero to a thousand in no time. Lukas's desire for Blaire before they bonded bordered on frightening when faced with situations that made him feel out of control.

Lukas shifted in his chair, trying to ignore the girl who had no intention of leaving him alone. Moving her chair closer to his across the cafeteria floor, Clarissa wouldn't even give him space to breathe.

He got the distinct impression that she thought if she wore him down, he would give in to her and it would be a done deal. That wasn't how he worked. Unfortunately, things went one of two ways when faced with saying the wrong thing or when caught in a situation that tested his comfort levels. One, he turned stoic and withdrawn—which usually made others back off until the situation resolved itself. Or two, he lashed out in anger because he felt backed into a corner.

He hated feeling trapped.

"Would you want to get away this weekend? Maybe go to the cinema before Thanksgiving?" Clarissa leaned into him, running her fingers over his chest, and putting her head on his shoulder. He hated the way she spoke. Blaire would have said movies. Any normal person would have said movies. He didn't bother responding to her question. Anytime she asked him to go anywhere, he denied her, and she then made a big deal out of it. Avoidance had become the best option.

The table had fallen silent, save for the scraping of forks against plates as they ate their dinner. No one knew what to say. Most of their meals went this way nowadays—his friends walking on eggshells around him. Lukas knew his behavior worried them, but he couldn't do anything to change it. Aiden had suggested he see a counselor in the psychology department, but honestly, it just made him think of Blaire more. The one time he visited was hard enough on him. Blaire wanted to be a grief counselor. Exactly what he needed, but he couldn't bring himself to be reminded of her, even in that capacity. He wasn't even processing Blaire's loss the right way.

Stages of grief? All over the place.

He couldn't even get that right.

He sat back and stared down at his tray of food, not able to stomach anything. His self-deprecating thoughts raged in havoc.

Mera cleared her throat and looked at Riley. "How do you think you'll do on winter finals next month?"

Clarissa got up and moved to sit in Lukas's lap. Aiden's mouth fell open. Lukas didn't hold her, but he didn't push her away, either. He had mentally checked out from everything, and all that remained was a numbness he couldn't shake. It warred with his heart that still felt like it was connected to a string that led far away from where his physical body remained, somewhere far from his reach.

"I think I'll be fine." Riley glared at Clarissa, who was running her perfectly manicured nails over Lukas's leather jacket. "Vincent tutored me last week, and he'll give me another session a couple of days before the finals."

Aiden growled under his breath. Riley's forehead wrinkled as she looked at her brother.

"What's wrong?" Seth asked.

Shaking his head, Aiden sat back in his chair and stabbed a straw into his blood packet. "Nothing."

The sweet scent of jasmine filled Lukas's nose as Clarissa nuzzled into the side of his neck. It was so artificial to him. While it smelled like Blaire, it didn't. Blaire's jasmine perfume mixed with her natural scent to create something uniquely her. This cloying imitation made his stomach sour.

Lukas needed to move on—get over her. He was convinced Blaire hated him at this point. She left him. But he couldn't do that. He adored her. He loved her so much. How could she have left him like this? It was his own fault. He drove her to it. So desperate to hold on to her that he pushed her away.

When he closed his eyes, Clarissa must have taken it as

confirmation that he enjoyed what she had been doing to him, accepting it as an invitation to push the boundaries further. Her breath tickled his neck before she pressed her lips against his skin. He jerked, his eyes snapping open, and he shoved her from his lap, reality coming back to him like a slap to the face.

Clarissa caught herself on the table before standing upright. She looked at him, and a smug smirk formed on her face as she straightened her uniform skirt. "I need to go meet with Daddy," she said as if being shoved away didn't faze her.

"Leaving so soon?" Riley feigned disappointment.

"Unfortunately, yes. Daddy is getting things prepared because I'm going to Europe at the end of the week, so I've got to make plans." She flipped her hair over her shoulder and gathered her belongings.

"Europe?" Mera asked.

"To our sister academy. It's really important stuff. Can't talk about it, sorry," Clarissa said with a shrug. She didn't seem the least bit sorry that she couldn't share whatever she deemed so important, as if she were better than them.

"Such a shame," Riley quipped, and Seth cut his eyes at her.

Clarissa gave her a sickeningly sweet smile as she put additional lip gloss on. "Oh, don't worry, I'll be back real soon to take care of Lukas." She put the gloss away and caressed her hand down his arm before leaving the group sitting there in stunned silence.

Reality came back to Lukas, and he glanced around the cafeteria before his eyes fell on his friends, who were staring at him from around the table.

"How can you let her just crawl all over you?" Aiden sat back and narrowed his eyes on Lukas, crossing his arms across his chest. "Blaire would be devastated if she could see this."

"Blaire left me. She doesn't give a shit."

Riley's mouth fell open. "I don't believe that for one second. Blaire does care about you."

"The mark is gone." He rubbed a hand down his face. "The last time she tried to leave, I discovered what she was doing, and we talked it out… this time, she didn't even bother to pack or talk to me, ensuring she wouldn't be discovered. She made sure I couldn't stop her."

Riley shook her head. "You could never make Blaire do anything she didn't want to."

It was true. Even at her most withdrawn moments when they first met, Blaire always put him in his place if he crossed a line she set. Maybe the first time she wanted him to discover that she planned to leave so he would stop her, but there was no mistaking that this time she left no way to find her. She really was done.

Seth cleared his throat. "I thought you loved her."

Lukas slammed his fist down on the table, startling everyone as he glared at Seth. "I will *always* love her!"

"That's the most emotion I've seen from you in weeks." Aiden gave him a look that made his insides twist. He hated seeing pity in his best friend's eyes. "You've been completely numb, and I was beginning to think you stopped caring about anything. Especially with how that girl acts with you." He looked in the direction Clarissa had exited the cafeteria. "You don't even stop her anymore. It's not like you, man."

Aiden was right. Lukas had been so lost in his inner turmoil that he failed to recognize the lust-driven glint in Clarissa's eyes, but it was hard to miss it now. At this point, he didn't even care. Would he accept her advances? No. But he didn't have the strength to put the girl in her place anymore like he once had. Pushing her off him when she pushed the boundary and kissed him today felt like he stepped out of whatever haze he'd been under.

"It's all my fucking fault. I did this to us."

"What are you talking about?" Seth asked.

"I pushed her. I pushed her to be one of us. I thought it would protect her. Keep creeps like Vincent off her back. Keep those who were prejudiced to her species like Clarissa out of her hair. I fucked up. What am I supposed to do now?" His shoulders slumped, and he looked at his best friends as if they had all the answers.

Kai shifted in his seat and sat forward, elbows on his knees, his hands clasped in front of him as he met Lukas with assessing eyes. "You can start by not letting someone who isn't your Korrena touch you like it's her right."

"I don't have a Korrena anymore," Lukas mumbled and motioned to his bare neck.

Riley burst into tears. "I'm not giving up on Blaire! I can't believe you would either! She'll come back, I know it!" She pushed her chair back so hard it fell over, and then ran from the cafeteria, drawing the attention of several students around them.

Seth looked toward Riley and stood from his seat. He cast a glare in Lukas's direction and abandoned his tray to chase after Riley.

"You need to get your shit together, man." Aiden's no-nonsense tone broke through Lukas's surprise at Riley's outburst. "Something is going on. I get that you're blind to most everything in your grief, but you need to get your head on straight."

Lukas stood abruptly and narrowed his eyes at Aiden, gripping the edge of the table so hard his knuckles turned white. "You just don't get it."

Without another word of explanation, he turned away from them and made his way out of the cafeteria. He couldn't deal with their judgmental stares. He could barely deal with himself and his own thoughts. How was he supposed to explain to them what this felt like?

None of them had experienced it before. Only Kai and Mera were paired, but they never had to encounter rejection or losing each other. Riley, Aiden, and Seth hadn't yet found their pairs, so they couldn't possibly understand the blackness that threatened to overtake him daily.

Making his way across the courtyard, he wasn't paying attention to where he was going and slammed into another body. "Shit." Lukas bent down to pick up a bag of takeout food that had dropped along with several papers that had fallen all over the smooth cobblestone. Pausing with his hand around a container from Blaire's favorite Chinese place in the plaza, he swallowed the lump in his throat.

"In a hurry?" Vincent's deep timbre made him flinch, catching him off-guard, and he looked up. Lukas really hated him, and knowing he was the last person outside of the Order to see Blaire made his blood boil. Did he know Blaire intended to leave? Did he help her? When Lukas didn't respond, Vincent smirked. "Well?"

Lukas finished bundling the papers and shoved them at Vincent as he stood to his full height, handing over the bag of takeout food. "It's none of your business," he grated through clenched teeth.

Vincent chuckled, apparently amused at getting a rise out of him. "No word from your lovely jewel?"

Lukas was seconds away from launching himself at Vincent. Anger, despair, disbelief… all had been building for weeks, but he'd kept it inside, welcoming the numbness like a blanket of protection when it would grant him a reprieve. Now, everything was reaching a boiling point, and Vincent seemed like the perfect person to unleash the repressed rage all over.

In an effort to calm down, he ground his teeth and shifted his gaze to the administration building, looking up at the large clock face, counting the second hand's movements as it ticked.

"None. What about you?" His voice was clipped, and it took concentrated effort to speak normally.

"Of course not. What reason would she have to reach out to me if she's no longer a student?" He frowned at Lukas and gave a quick shake of his head. "You really are convinced there's something between us, aren't you?"

Lukas swung.

"Shit, man, don't!" Aiden hooked his arms beneath Lukas's armpits, pulling him back before his fist could connect with Vincent's face. He jerked in Aiden's hold, trying to break free.

Seth stepped in front of him, glaring at Vincent, who had the audacity to laugh. "Leave him alone, Vince."

"Oh, come now. I'm not the one throwing fists like a prepubescent schoolboy."

Seth growled low and clenched his fists. "Seriously, man. Back off."

Vincent sucked his teeth. "I have something to attend to, anyway. I don't have time for this."

Before they could say anything else, Vincent turned on his heel and made his way toward the administration building. When he reached the large door, he turned to look back at them, meeting Lukas's eyes as he held up the bag of Chinese takeout. A grin that made Lukas's skin crawl crossed his features.

26

DISCOVERY

Aiden rubbed tired eyes and fought the urge to put his head down on the desk and sleep. Riley, Seth, and Lukas sat nearby, along with Kai and Mera, working or not, like him. Seth and Kai's cousin Vincent was their TA for this free study period, thankfully the last class of the day. Aiden's theory was the teachers threw study periods into their schedules to keep students in the main building—and supervised—while they handled staff meetings. Treating them like high schoolers up to no good. The one positive thing about the free study period was it integrated several levels of the university program so he and the other average students could share a class with more advanced students.

He'd much rather be back in his dorm playing video games.

He stared at the clock, ready to get out of class. They didn't have to do any work if they didn't want to. As soon as the bell rang, the day would be over, and he could go to his room and crash. Seth had kept him up last night playing *God of War: Ragnarök*. The only reason he didn't sleep while his friend played the single-player game was because Seth kept muttering about Riley wanting a tattoo.

The two always bickered, but Seth seemed increasingly agitated around Riley lately. Aiden figured he should say something, but they always sorted out their mess. That's the way it had worked since they were children.

"Will you take me?" Riley's voice cut through his thoughts and intense focus on the clock that had barely moved forward a couple of minutes.

"What?"

"I asked if you would take me to get my first tattoo. Haven't you been paying attention?"

Aiden frowned and shook his head, giving his sister his best look of remorse, but she glared at him. This must be what Seth was going on about last night.

"I've seriously been sitting here talking about it for the last ten minutes. I'm about to turn eighteen, and I want to get it done." She sighed dramatically and gave him the same look she always did when trying to get her way. "I've been waiting all year."

"Fine, fine. I don't see any reason I couldn't take you. What do you plan to get?"

The look on her face immediately morphed into excitement as she sat up straighter and clapped her hands with a huge smile on her face. "So, I actually thought about getting a really feminine tattoo on my shoulder. Like, peonies of different sizes with dainty chains hanging from them and maybe a butterfly—no, a dragonfly." She snapped her fingers and pointed. "Yeah, a dragonfly. I want it shaded black, but with a few pink accents, like on the dragonfly and maybe gems on the chains?"

"Pink. Of course you want pink," Aiden said with a smirk.

"You don't need to mark your body."

Riley whipped around to glare at Seth. He stared back at her with narrowed eyes. By the disgruntled sound of his voice and his expression, he wasn't happy.

"What the hell?" She poked a finger toward Seth. "You don't have any room to talk. You went and got a full sleeve over the summer." She gestured to his left arm.

"Your point?

"You're a hypocritical twat." With a scowl, she turned back to her desk and flipped pages in her text.

Seth ran his fingers over the beautiful rendition of Medusa's crying face with serpents around her head at the top of his arm. "I've already booked myself in to get the other one done this coming summer as well." He shrugged. "I'd already have it if my preferred artist didn't have a wait list a mile long."

"Why not go elsewhere?" Mera asked.

"Nah. I like this artist. She did an incredible job on my first one, and I want to keep the same style. Besides, she gets it. Her work captures the emotion of a piece."

Aiden had asked Seth why he chose the design in question, and Seth had told him the common interpretation felt right to him. Not what social media had turned into a mainstream symbol to represent sexual assault, but a symbol to protect and ward off the negative. He said it was also a reference to saving yourself through art. Aiden didn't fully understand what Seth felt he needed saving from, but he had been spiraling out of control since his birthday.

Seth had always seemed on edge since around the time he turned sixteen, but after turning nineteen back in August before Blaire disappeared, he started getting into fights with others more often, like when they were younger. He'd also started complaining a lot more about Riley. While it wasn't uncommon that he complained about her, it seemed she was always rubbing him the wrong way lately. Seth acted laid back and calm one minute, and then incredibly stand-offish the next.

Riley spun around again, not done chewing on this bone. "Why the hell are you getting so much done, anyway?"

"It's a good distraction." Seth shrugged again.

She blinked. "From what?"

Seth fixed her with a look that made Aiden question if this would be one of those times where Seth went off. He didn't exactly look angry, but his steel gaze definitely conveyed a heat Aiden couldn't place. A shiver ran down his spine as he tried to interpret the difference.

"Don't worry about it. Just don't go marking up your body."

Riley huffed and crossed her arms over her chest. She always tried her best to look intimidating and angry when Seth antagonized her, but she came across like a spoiled child being denied a cookie.

It made Aiden want to laugh, but he refrained, cutting his eyes at his friend. "What's with you? There's nothing wrong with Riley getting a tattoo."

Seth crossed his arms and avoided eye contact, drawing air through his teeth.

Aiden didn't want to stir things up further, but he didn't like how Seth thought he could tell Riley what to do like that. Why was Riley getting a tattoo such a big deal? Seth never cared what she did before. He'd had always been bossy with her, but never with such enmity.

Riley kept at it. "I mean, why in your tiny mind is it okay for you to have one but not me? Is this some sort of sexist nonsense about 'it's not ladylike'? Make it make sense."

Seth tensed, the muscles in his forearms tightening. "You only need one mark on your body," he said through gritted teeth, his jaw muscle ticking.

Before Riley could protest or ask what he meant, Seth got up with a calm ease that contrasted the tension in his posture. He gathered his books and strode out of class without a word to anyone. Vincent—the TA for their study period—didn't care all that much about his cousin's departure; he barely spared a glance as Seth left. The class ended in ten minutes anyway, and the free study didn't actually need anyone to be there, but it still was a requirement. Aiden doubted Vincent would call Seth out on it after the confrontation in the courtyard.

"What's his problem?" Riley asked in bewilderment as she looked back and forth between Aiden and the door. "What mark is he talking about?"

Mera tilted her head back, brows drawn, watching the door. "He means the Korrena mark."

Riley faced Mera with her lips parted in surprise.

Aiden wasn't sure how he felt about that revelation.

Kai lifted a black brow and looked at his mate. "I thought Seth was against the whole pairing thing."

Mera shrugged. "It's merely a guess. The only mark Riley could have that she wouldn't put there herself or didn't result from an injury—which I strongly doubt was his intention with his words—would be the mark she shares with her Korrena, wherever it will be on her body."

Riley frowned. "He's just so damn moody and weird. I don't get him."

Aiden laughed. "If you're serious, we can talk to the artist who did my raven. As long as you don't go getting a Chinese character you don't know the meaning of." He frowned as he considered Mera's words. "But have you seriously thought about the Korrena mark? I mean, you're talking about something fairly large, right? What if by some chance your Korrena mark appears in the same spot, but then it's marred by a permanent tattoo?"

"Ugh. Seth has a whole sleeve and is getting another. *He* doesn't care, so why should I? I doubt I'll have a mark on my shoulder."

"Explain that logic," Kai said. "Your logic always seems to confuse me."

Riley laughed. "I like to keep you on your toes."

Kai rolled his eyes.

"But seriously... lots of other unpaired Vasirian have large tattoos. You have one on your shoulder blade too." She pouted.

It was true. The raven on Aiden's shoulder blade was pretty large, with its spread wings that trailed loose feathers that moved over his spine to his other shoulder blade. He only hoped his Korrena mark didn't show up there—if he even found his pair at all. Shaking his head, he pushed the thought away before it soured his mood.

Aiden turned to Lukas, who had remained silent and in his own world the entire class. While it would normally worry Aiden, introverted silence had become Lukas's norm lately. Not that he didn't worry about his friend, but he knew what was eating away at him, and it was best to keep a distance. No news had come in about Blaire. Professor Velastra had no additional information, and Charlotte hadn't spoken to him since they met not long ago. There was nothing any of them could do to make it better for Lukas. All they could do was give him the space he needed to process the loss and be there if he reached out.

"Hey, man... you wanna come with?"

Lukas shrugged non-committally.

Riley met Aiden's gaze, concern in her smoky blue eyes. He shook his head at her. The shrug was as good of a response as any at this stage—more than they got from Lukas a week ago. Aiden didn't want to push him harder than necessary.

With the class nearly over, Vincent walked up the aisle with a stack of papers in his arms. He handed each student a small stack of stapled papers. "These study guides are to prepare you for the winter finals next month. Please review them, and should you need any supplementary assistance, I have a couple of additional spaces available in my tutoring group."

Lukas jerked in his seat, snapping out of his daze. He gripped the edge of the desk, staring at the papers. The last time anyone saw Blaire was before she met Vincent for one of those tutoring sessions.

Vincent had claimed not to know anything, but something about his behavior was off. With Professor Velastra backing up Clarissa's claims, they had no choice but to believe them true. Riley still insisted something wasn't right, but Lukas had lost his will to fight once the Korrena mark faded, and Aiden didn't push.

Vincent held out a stack of papers to Aiden. As he took them, his eyes locked on Vincent's arm. His dress shirt sleeves were rolled up his forearms, revealing the silver bracelets he always wore, but one particular bracelet stood out, making Aiden's stomach drop. He knew that leather bracelet anywhere. He had given it to Lukas for his birthday two years ago. It was custom made, with a hatched design embossed into a thicker piece of leather held between lengths of braided leather. Lukas had let Blaire wear the bracelet after they bonded. She never removed it, from what he remembered.

How the fuck did Vincent get that bracelet?

There was no way Blaire gave it to him. Was he wearing it when they asked him about Blaire's disappearance?

Aiden dropped his gaze before Vincent could notice the attention on him, shooting Lukas a look in an effort to get him to notice him, but failing.

Did Vincent know where Blaire was after all?

He gritted his teeth as his head spun with the possibilities of how Vincent could have gotten his hands on that bracelet.

Lukas seemed too far gone to notice anything. Aiden wanted to help him, especially after hearing how Clarissa had tried to take advantage of him in his sleep. The audacity she had to think that her privilege extended to Lukas's body made Aiden sick. Yes, she wanted Lukas, but her way of showing it was loathsome.

He clenched his fists on his desk, his gaze intent on the bracelet as Vincent turned and sauntered back down the aisle.

He knew how to help his friend now.

He at last had something to focus on that might give him answers to where Blaire might be.

27

EVIDENCE

Blaire shifted on the bed, sitting back against the pillow she'd wedged between her back and the wall as she turned the page of the novel Vincent had given her. He presented it as a reward for being a "good girl" and not fighting him anymore. What was she supposed to do? Fight and have him overpower her, or worse yet, drug her? Between his ability to take away control of her body with his Vasirian voodoo and the threat of drugging her… what was even the point? She didn't see a way out of his trap, aside from getting lost in fantasy.

She escaped into the pages of as many novels as she could get her hands on. To a place where she could avoid reality. A place where things were happy. A place where she wasn't being used as a blood doll. A place where instead of the hero abandoning the heroine, he fought for their love.

Her stomach rumbled, and a ripple of pain followed low in her belly. Sighing, she looked over as Vincent approached with a small bowl in his hand.

"You need to eat," he said softly, holding out the bowl to her as he took a seat on the edge of the bed. "Of all the hills you could choose to die on... I don't understand why you insist on a hunger strike."

Blaire shook her head and took a piece of melon from the bowl. "I'm not hunger striking... I eat." She made a point of putting the cantaloupe in her mouth and taking an exaggerated bite. "See?"

Vincent chuckled. "Touché. But you know what I mean. You're going to waste away if you continue like this."

"I just don't want anything to eat... It's not an act of defiance." It wasn't. Blaire had lost the desire for food. She ate enough to get through, but overall, nothing appealed to her as it once had. Couple that with her stomach shrinking after not eating for so long, outside of basic necessity, that she didn't see the point.

"I still don't approve, all the same."

Vincent placed the bowl on the bedside table and brushed invisible dust from his black slacks. Even in the most relaxed settings, he dressed immaculately in pressed slacks, button-down shirts with vests, and jeweled accessories. Blaire's gaze fell to his wrist, and she swallowed around a lump lodged in her throat as she stared at Lukas's leather bracelet. She didn't dare question why he wore it, but she knew he wouldn't give it back to her. It was the only remaining proof that what Lukas and she previously shared was real. That Lukas loved her once. He'd given her something to wear that was important to him.

"I have good news for you."

Blaire looked away from the bracelet and met his eyes. Something about them had changed over the time she'd been in this room. After he began feeding on her, on occasion a disconnect showed. Like something had snapped, and the Vincent from before—while still delusional—was gone, leaving in his place someone even more deranged. She doubted whatever he perceived as "good news" was going to be good for her. She knew better than to hope for that.

"I'll be able to spend more time with you very soon." He patted her leg, and she subtly slid her foot away until he removed his hand. Yep. Not good news for her. "After winter finals next week, I'll have open availability until spring, when I have to begin tutoring sessions again to prepare for spring finals."

December.

Winter finals happened the first week of December before the second semester started in January.

She'd been here just shy of two months.

She could not allow herself to process what so many weeks passing meant: her friends had abandoned her—*Lukas* had abandoned her. She looked back down at the book in her hands to read again.

Vincent continued to talk, but she ignored the words coming out of his mouth, her eyes lingering on the page. A page that Blaire had now read over for the third time and was about to pass over a fourth, but the words became blurry as her eyes filled with unshed tears. She expelled a breath and closed her eyes, tears now free to slide down her cheeks as if to run away from reality themselves. She wished she could join them. Fall and evaporate.

A warm hand touched her cheek and she flinched, looking up to see Vincent looking at her in concern.

"What's wrong? Where'd you go?"

She had stopped listening to him, so she had no idea the last thing he said.

Pulling in a shaky breath, she held up the book with unsteady hands. "It's… just the book."

"What happened?"

He caressed her cheek, wiping away a tear. His words sounded sincere, and his tone implied concern, but deep inside, she knew better than to believe either. Falling for his manipulation was exactly what he wanted. For her to fall for him and develop some version of Stockholm Syndrome. Blaire shook her head and pulled from his hand.

"It's nothing really… just… the main character of the story professed his undying devotion to Arabella, his mate, saying he would rather die than lose her, all while staring down execution by the royal court of the fae in her place." Blaire shut her eyes again and rested her head against the wall.

"Is this about Lukas?"

The familiar sinister edge was back in his tone, and when she met his eyes, she could see that warped shadow beneath the surface flare to life. Sick of how he disparaged her feelings for Lukas, knowing that it was the next thing to come when Vincent got this way, she looked away.

"I know it is hard for you, jewel, but you need to let go. He doesn't want you anymore."

She flinched at his callous words and clenched the blanket in her hands at her sides to keep from physically responding in a way that would draw attention.

"You're just torturing yourself to continue harping on him when *I* am right here for you." He leaned forward to put his face in her line of sight. "If Lukas had really wanted the bond as much as he claimed, it wouldn't have broken so easily, remember?"

Blaire already knew this, but the words sank into her stomach and settled like a cinder block at the bottom of a river. Her chest tightened, and she felt phantom pain on the side of her neck from the blood ritual Vincent performed that had stolen their bond away.

Oblivious to, or not caring about, the inner turmoil that warred inside her, Vincent continued. "He's moved on."

"What do you mean?" she asked hesitantly, not sure she heard him correctly.

"Lukas has found himself a compatible partner."

Noting her blank stare, Vincent explained. "Some of us who have not found our Korrena take a partner as a compatible pair. Similar to forming a relationship like humans do when they become boyfriend and girlfriend or husband and wife. Something more like the latter, really. You commit to a compatible pair just as you would your spouse or Korrena, though you lack that soul-deep connection."

"I know what compatible pairs are. It's just..." Blaire twisted the ends of her hair around her fingers. *How could he do that?* She wasn't even sure she believed Vincent. That kernel of doubt helped her take it a lot better than she'd expect to take something like that.

"Lukas didn't want the bond anymore, Blaire. He wanted someone who would age slowly with him, not someone he would outlive by centuries."

"You're lying."

Vincent stood abruptly, and she followed him with her eyes as he walked over to the dining table with purpose, grabbed his phone and returned to sit in front of her. "I can prove it."

Blaire's stomach twisted and her heart raced. The last time he wanted to "prove" something to her about how Lukas didn't want their bond, she experienced the worst pain she ever had in her life. Not physically, but a pain so deep-rooted that it may as well have been physical. She never wanted to feel that again.

When Vincent found what he was looking for, he passed the phone to her. Looking down at the device in her hand made her stomach drop. A bitter taste filled her mouth. She stared at the picture, frozen in place. Lukas sat in the cafeteria, surrounded by their friends. Clarissa leaned against him, her head on his shoulder, and her hand resting on his chest.

"Swipe right." Vincent's words sounded muffled to her ears, but she did as he said, and her hand shook as she gripped the phone. Clarissa was sitting in Lukas's lap in the next picture.

Vincent inhaled slowly, and as he breathed out, he whispered, "Once more."

Blaire didn't know if she could take anymore, but her fingers moved of their own accord. She swiped right and brought up a picture that had her trying to suck in a breath, but there seemed to be no air in the room for her to draw from.

Clarissa was kissing Lukas's neck, and he had his head back with his eyes closed in enjoyment. His groans echoed in her head.

Blaire dropped the phone as if it burned her hand, and Vincent moved to set it on the bedside table. He shifted back to cup her face as she struggled to take in air; the breaths coming from her mouth were only small gasps as she stared ahead with wide, unblinking eyes.

"Blaire… look at me."

Her wild eyes darted to him, and a tear slipped down her cheek from eyes that burned.

"Breathe. I need you to breathe. Slowly… *That's* it. *Good* girl."

Blaire's gasping breaths slowed, but she still couldn't get enough air into her lungs. She grew dizzy like she was going to pass out, and her fingers tingled. Bile rose, and she had to swallow it back down before she choked on it.

"I'm sorry I had to show you that. I didn't want to show you that… But you needed to know the truth so you could move on."

Before Blaire could say anything—if she could speak at all—Vincent leaned in and closed his eyes, kissing her lips gently. She didn't return the kiss, didn't close her eyes. The tears that had blurred her vision in her panic attack now tracked freely down her face and dripped from her chin.

"I told you not to cry for him." Vincent lowered Blaire back onto the bed and crawled over her.

She stared up at him with wide eyes. "What the hell are you doing?" Her mind was in a riot; her body exhausted. The need to vomit shifted to fear that prickled up her spine like spider legs. Now this? Why couldn't she escape from this torment?

"I love you, Blaire. You don't have to hurt again," he said with a hushed tone as he ran a hand up her thigh, edging her nightgown higher.

She threw her hands up and shoved him hard, putting all the strength she had into the move before he got the fabric more than an inch or two above her knee. "Stop!"

Vincent gripped her wrists in his large hands, and she winced in pain as he pinned them above her head with one hand and leaned down. Blaire shuddered in disgust at his hot breath against the shell of her ear as he whispered, "Soon you'll give in to me, my jewel. But I won't force you."

Blaire had only relaxed a fraction at the reassurance before his sharp fangs pierced the skin of her throat. Yelling out in the room's silence, Blaire tried to push him off her. She squirmed beneath him as he pressed her down with his body weight, drinking from her with reckless abandon. As she grew dizzy, he pulled free and sat up, licking the blood from his lips.

"You… you said you wouldn't… force me." Her words were a cracked murmur, her vision hazy and black around the edges as she stared at his blurry face twisted by madness.

"Mmm, and I won't. I would never force you to bed me." He stood from the bed. "That said, I can't resist the sweet temptation of your lifeblood. I must say, your fear is almost sweeter than the taste of your compliance."

Blaire's eyes widened to saucers as she took in his words. Vincent had truly gone insane.

A malevolent smile crossed his lips as he lifted the cuff and chain from the floor, shackled her ankle and locked the cuff. He grabbed his phone from the bedside table and put it in his vest pocket before moving to the door, and once unlocking the many locks, gave her one last pitying look before stepping out. As she heard each lock engage, she let go of the last bit of hope she had of being free and finding Lukas.

Even if she escaped, Lukas didn't want her. Her family was dead. Her friends had abandoned her. Her stepfamily hated her—the only one in the family who didn't hate her was a monster, and even if he didn't remember that fact, she would never forget it.

Nothing remained for her outside the walls of this small room.

28

Suspicion

Aiden tossed the controller down on his bed. "Take over. I'm not feeling it." He collapsed onto the bed and rubbed both hands over his face as he exhaled a heavy breath. He couldn't focus enough to keep his character alive long enough to make any progress, and Seth was getting frustrated.

"What's going on with you?"

That certainly was the question of the month. Aiden's thoughts constantly gravitated toward what could have happened to Blaire. Not just because he missed her, but watching his best friend have a complete mental collapse killed him. There was no way to miss the significant impact Blaire's disappearance had on those she left behind.

Aiden had poked around like everyone else had, but nothing substantial turned up. Professor Velastra hadn't come up with anything either. He checked. Riley continuously checked. The radio silence from Blaire got under his skin. He thought they were friends. It wasn't as if he was going to attempt to hook up with her or anything. Sure, he developed feelings for her last semester, but he got himself straight after her rejection of him. Seeing how happy she was with Lukas made it easier for him to let those feelings go. Even if she couldn't bother to reach out to him, why not Riley? They were best friends, and Riley was suffering.

"Earth to Aiden," Seth said in exasperation when Aiden hadn't responded.

"Ah… Yeah? What? Sorry." He rubbed a hand over his face again. "I just have stuff on my mind."

Seth opened his mouth to speak, but Aiden's phone pinged. Pulling it from his pocket, he looked at the screen. Charlotte. He hadn't spoken to her since they met three weeks ago. He didn't have any information to give her, so what was the point? Maybe she had something for him. He quickly sat up and opened the text conversation.

Charlotte:

Have you heard anything yet from Blaire?

Aiden:

No… I don't know what the hell is going on.

Charlotte:

It's almost Thanksgiving! How can anyone not know where she is? >:(

Aiden:

I don't know that either.

Charlotte:

I'm really worried. :(

Aiden:

Yeah, me too.

Aiden sighed and looked up at his ceiling. How could someone disappear without a trace like this? Sure, he'd heard horror stories about humans who vanished into thin air only to turn up years later, or worse… dead. He pushed that thought from his mind before it had a chance to turn into something that would fester.

"Shit." Seth threw the controller down when his character died and looked back at Aiden, who still had his phone in his hand. "Who is it?"

Aiden sat up and shrugged. "Charlotte."

"The redhead from the diner? Blaire's friend?"

"Yeah."

"Has she seen Blaire?"

Aiden shook his head and opened up the text thread again as another message popped up.

Charlotte:

Let me know as soon as you know something.

Aiden:

I will.

He tossed his phone on the bed and dug his fingers into his tired eyes as he rubbed them.

"They've known each other for years. Riley said they were friends since they were kids… it doesn't make sense that Blaire would stop contacting her, too."

Aiden released a weary sigh. "I know, man… I know. I was just thinking the same about Riley. Even though they hadn't known each other for as long, Riley and Blaire were best friends."

"Blaire didn't seem like the type of person to just up and abandon everyone without a word."

"Blaire isn't the type of person to just abandon anyone, period. Why do you think we've been trying to find her to get her side of things? Lukas is blaming himself for it all, and if what he and Riley says took place, I understand his guilt. He shouldn't have pushed her.

But was that really enough to drive her away?"

"Didn't it almost make her leave before?"

Aiden closed his eyes again and sighed. "That's the thing that has me concerned. That when we do get to talk to her, we're not going to be able to convince her to come back if she did up and leave because of their fight." He pinched the bridge of his nose. "Riley stops by Professor Velastra's office every single day for updates, but there's nothing. No trace of Blaire."

"Well, if she didn't just walk off and leave everyone, where is she?" Seth dragged a hand through the long strands of hair on top of his head before smoothing his hand over the shaved back. "How did she disappear without even the smallest hint left behind?"

Aiden shifted on the bed. There may have been a hint she left behind after all. The bracelet he'd seen on Vincent's arm a couple of days ago crossed his mind and he slid to the edge of the bed. "Actually… I think something is going on."

"What?"

Leaning forward and resting his elbows on his knees, Aiden met Seth's eyes and took a deep breath. "A couple days ago, in one of our study periods, Vincent was passing out study guides for the winter finals. Right after you bailed, actually."

"Okaaay?" Seth dragged the word out like he didn't get where Aiden was going with his train of thought.

"Let me finish." Aiden rolled his eyes at Seth's impatience. He cracked his knuckles and shook his head. "See, Vincent had been tutoring Blaire, right?"

"Yeah… but what's that have to do with study guides and the other day?"

"Okay, hold up… So, a couple days ago, I saw Lukas's bracelet on his arm."

"Dude! You could have started with that."

Aiden sighed. His thoughts were so scattered lately, and he wasn't saying things in a coherent order. It was as if he needed to get out every thought in his head all at once, and his brain to mouth filter failed him. "Yeah, sorry. So anyway, I knew it was Lukas's bracelet because I gave it to him for his birthday, and it has this unique pattern embossed into the leather. I specifically requested the designer to combine two different designs picked out of a catalog to make it unique to Lukas. He gave it to Blaire, and she never took it off."

"Shit."

"Yeah. And Vincent had it on his wrist. He didn't notice that I saw it, but why the hell was he wearing it?"

"Maybe he found it?"

"I find that highly suspect. I mean, the last place Lukas knew Blaire went was to a study session with Vincent after school… the day she went missing. No one else has seen her since then."

"But Clarissa said—"

"I don't trust that girl as far as I could throw her. If that."

"So, do you think Vincent had something to do with Blaire's disappearance?"

Aiden nodded. "I do. And as far as Clarissa goes? I've seen her going into Vincent's study labs since I started watching him the past couple days."

Seth's brows drew together in confusion. "Maybe she needed tutoring. Lots of students go see him or one of the other TAs."

"Yeah, but none of those students had advanced a grade—in university—because they are supposedly too smart for where they were. She wouldn't need tutoring."

"So, you think she's in on it?"

"I don't know, but I sure as hell intend to investigate Vincent more."

Vincent already had an unhealthy focus on Blaire. Aiden and Lukas had plenty of conversations about it. Even seeing the way Vincent interacted with Blaire made him feel uncomfortable. He didn't call other students beautiful, and referring to her as a jewel? The creeper factor was definitely pinging at the high end of the scale.

Clarissa was obsessed with Lukas. Was her obsession so deep she would have done something to Blaire just to have Lukas all to herself?

"I'm in."

Aiden nodded at Seth. If he was going to figure out what happened to Blaire, he'd need all the help he could get. "For now, keep it to yourself."

"Are you sure we shouldn't tell Lukas?"

Shaking his head, Aiden glanced at his phone on the bed as a text from Lukas popped up, as if summoned by Seth's words. "I don't want to create any unnecessary drama and upset Riley or Lukas more than they already are." Aiden sighed. He wasn't sure how much his friend could take. He already questioned if Lukas was stable enough not to do something drastic, if not to himself, then to others.

Seth's jaw twitched as he tightened it. "I can see that… Sure."

"I'm not going to keep them in the dark forever. But if there's no reason to say anything, I just don't want to get anyone's hopes up, or have Lukas fly off the handle at Vincent. He told me yesterday he nearly attacked him in the courtyard again outside the administration building."

Seth's head pulled back and his face scrunched. "Again? Why?"

"Vincent didn't really do anything, but Lukas felt like he was provoking him again. He's never liked your cousin."

"Not many do… he thinks he's better than everyone."

"Yeah, but his disdain for Vincent increased tenfold when Blaire came along."

"Why?"

"Lukas seems to think Vincent wants her. And honestly? I do too. He's just way too familiar with her."

"Shit… really? I hadn't noticed."

"Do you pay attention to anything, though?"

"Oh, fuck you. I pay attention."

Aiden chuckled. Seth used to be more involved in their conversations and the things they did, but he'd pulled away from the group since he turned nineteen. Not only fighting again, but he was sleeping around with unpaired Vasirian women. Aiden had been locked out of their room enough times to know the rumors spreading around were true. He didn't know what was driving Seth to act so reckless. It wasn't his business. It worried him to not know what sent Seth down the path he was on, but with everything going on with Blaire, and trying to keep Lukas together, Aiden was already stretched thin. So unless Seth reached out to him, he would have to assume his friend could handle himself.

Picking up his phone, he checked the message Lukas sent.

Lukas:

I'm going to kill her.

Aiden:

What? Who?

Lukas:

Clarissa.

Aiden:

What now?

Lukas:

She keeps getting into my fucking bed.

Aiden:

What? Like a couple weeks ago?

Lukas:

No. I keep coming back after dinner to find her in my bed wearing some slutty outfit, like she thinks it'll entice me. She won't get it through her thick skull that I'm not interested.

Aiden:

Did you ever ask about switching rooms?

Lukas:

Yes! Weeks ago. The same day she came to the room. And again, recently. They gave me some runaround answers, but it basically came down to they couldn't change anything. Maybe next year. Like, what the fuck?

Lukas:

Even asked Professor Velastra, and she hasn't been able to do shit.

Lukas:

I wish Seth hadn't moved into your room this semester.

Aiden:

She could have roomed with Riley. It's not like you are Korrena pairs.

Aiden winced. Bringing up a Korrena pairing might not have been the best move. He watched the three little dots pop up, showing that Lukas was typing, and then disappear, only to pop up again before his message came through.

Lukas:

Riley hates her.

Yeah, he messed up bringing it up. He knew Lukas had typed more than that and didn't follow through.

Aiden:

I'm sorry, man. I shouldn't have said that.

Lukas:

No, I get it. But Riley would seriously claw her eyes out.

Aiden:

LOL Without a doubt.

Aiden laughed, and Seth raised an eyebrow at him. "Lukas." He held his phone up. "He wants Clarissa out of his room, and when I suggested Riley's room, he said Riley would claw Clarissa's eyes out."

"It's true. I've been trying to keep her off the girl for weeks."

They definitely needed to not bring down the ire of the Order, and harming Angelo Moretti's only daughter would be a fast track to just that.

"It's good to at least see you working with Riley and not against her, like usual."

"What the hell is that supposed to mean?"

"Seriously? You complain about her all the time. At least playing guard to keep Riley off the girl has given you something else to focus on."

"Whatever. Nothing's different."

"Whatever you say, man."

The sound of his cell phone ringing broke through the forest's quiet and startled Lukas. It was already dark in the thick cover of the trees, but the setting rays of the sun peeped through the edge in the distance. He had sought refuge in the calm of nature behind the school to get away from Clarissa. He was so close to the edge, ready to hurt something. Deep down, should that something actually be a someone… namely Clarissa Moretti, he'd be screwed.

Digging the phone from his jeans pocket, he looked at the missed call notification. His mother. Could he handle talking to her? Telling her that Blaire left him? But what if something was wrong? It wasn't the holidays yet. Getting a call this time of year was peculiar.

With a heavy sigh, he hit the notification to return her call.

One ring.

Two rings.

Thr—

"*Poika?*"

"Hi, Mom. Sorry I missed your call."

"No, no worries. How are you? How is your pair?"

Lukas cringed, slumping back against a nearby tree. "About that..." He took a deep inhale through his nose. "What brought this call on? Everything okay?" he asked, chickening out and deflecting.

"Things are well. Your father is at dinner with a few associates to discuss business, so I stayed behind at the hotel. I wanted to call and check on you."

"That's different."

"What do you mean?"

How did he say this without sounding like an asshole? "Well, I'm just used to getting calls at the holidays. I wondered if something was wrong. I didn't expect to hear from you for another month. You normally don't call for Thanksgiving."

"Oh no! I'm so sorry if I worried you. Now that you have a pair, I only wished to see that things were well. I know it can be difficult at the beginning."

Lukas failed to mask the dry laugh that slipped free.

"Is something wrong?"

He closed his eyes, breathing in the scent of the surrounding pine woodland. Orange and red leaves danced across the forest floor from the few trees lining the back of the academy that weren't pine.

"*Poika?*"

"Sorry, what?"

"What is happening?"

Lukas slid down the tree to sit on the mossy ground and held his face in his hand. "She's gone," he said, barely above a whisper.

"What?"

"Blaire… she's gone."

"Gone? What do you mean?"

"The bonds broken. She left me."

The sharp intake of breath on the other end of the line made his chest tighten. Would his mother be disappointed in him that he wasn't strong enough to hold on to his Korrena?

"*Poika*… the bond cannot break. You need to explain to me what you speak of."

"My Korrena mark is gone. Professor Velastra believes the bond is broken too, but she's never heard of it either."

"Gone?"

"Yeah, I watched it disappear," he mumbled, his voice cracking.

"That's… no, there's only one way to break the bo—no, absolutely not."

"What?" He sat up, fully alert. Did his mother know something that even the professor didn't? "What are you talking about, Mom?"

"It's taboo. The only reason I know of it is because your great grandmother told me how her sister performed the ritual for an acquaintance for a marriage of convenience. Both sides of the pair agreed to break their bond, though. I… can't imagine how that felt. How they could come to the decision to throw away such a…" She huffed loudly, clearing her throat. "It's a practice that took place often long ago, but is considered taboo now. While not forbidden or punishable by our laws, it is a nasty practice that rips apart fated bonds."

Ritual? They hadn't done any ritual other than the claiming when they sealed their bond. He didn't understand. When he didn't speak, his mother's voice came over the line again.

"Lukas…" Her serious tone sent a shiver of trepidation down his spine.

"Is there… is there any other way for the bond to break?"

"Not that I'm aware of."

"What is this ritual?"

"A blood ritual that requires a specific incantation to be recited over runes drawn on the body in the blood of the Vasirian performing the ritual mixed with blood from one of the pair being un-bonded. The runes must cover most of the body and score out the Korrena mark. That's all I know. What happens during the ritual… I couldn't bring myself to hear. The whole thing sounds dreadful."

Had Blaire gone to someone and had the ritual performed? That sounded far-fetched. But if there was no other way to break their bond, then what was going on?

"You said she left?"

"Yes. The Order pardoned her, allowing her to leave the academy. She…" He swallowed thickly, a tear escaping and trailing down his cheek. "She said she couldn't be with a Vasirian."

"What? She told you that?" His mother's voice was high, and the shock was obvious.

"No… I didn't know she was leaving. She didn't tell me anything. She just… didn't come back from her tutoring session one day."

"Oh my. And did you try to talk to her?"

"No one knows where she is."

"What? Are you sure she chose to leave?"

"Huh?" A heavy dread settled in his stomach separate from the eery quiet of the forest now that the sun had disappeared and only the blackness of night remained.

"Korrena pairs… bonded pairs in love… they don't walk away

from each other."

"But this is different. She's human. I didn't want her to grow old and die, and I was pushing her—"

"No, Lukas. Listen to me."

He pulled in a breath. He hadn't heard his mother speak so sternly before.

Even her Finnish accent seemed fainter, as if she were speaking in her business voice. "Had she done this before the claiming, I'd have believed it. But she accepted the bond in full. Small doubts like that would not keep her from you."

"Then what the fuck happened, Mom?"

"Language."

"Sorry… shit. Sorry!"

She chuckled. "Lukas, I need you to listen to me… something is not right about this situation. Can you tell me more?"

"Like what?"

"What happened before? After? Who knows she left?"

"Before, things were fine. We were making birthday plans… She was taking tutoring so that she had more time with me. We had a fight."

"A fight?"

"Yes." He squeezed his eyes shut and swallowed the guilt he felt. He had to own his mistake. "I pushed her to become one of us. I wanted to protect her, but I didn't go about it the right way."

"I still don't think that's a strong enough reason for her to throw away the bond."

Lukas took a shuddered breath at his mother's conviction.

He rubbed his hand on a jean-clad thigh as he tried to tamp down the agitation that rose in him. "After she disappeared, they packed her belongings into storage, and I got a new roommate."

"Storage?"

"Yeah, she left everything behind." His statement was met with silence. "Mom?"

"I'm sorry. You said you got a new roommate?"

"Yes, Clarissa Moretti."

"Moretti? Angelo's daughter?"

Lukas's upper lip curled in disgust at the name. "The one and only."

"Why is she rooming with you? She is not your pair."

"They transferred her to a higher grade and supposedly I was the only one she could room with. I've tried to get it changed, but no one will change it. And worse yet…" He wasn't sure he should tell her this part. He sighed. "She wants to be my compatible pair. She's trying to replace Blaire!" His voice rose, and he gripped the hair at the back of his neck, squeezing his eyes shut. "Mom, I'm so lost."

"*Poika…*"

Lukas threw his head back against the tree and cried. He hadn't been able to cry in a long time since the numbness had crept in, but it was cycling back, and despair threatened to cripple him. After his sobs finally calmed down, he said hoarsely, "Mom?"

"Yes? I'm here."

He breathed a sigh of relief that she hadn't hung up on his breakdown. Wiping his face with his hand, he stared at the dark canopy over his head, barely able to see stars through the pine branches.

"Lukas… Who all knows of Blaire leaving?"

"Uh… Aiden, Riley, Seth, Mera, Kai… Professor Velastra, Blaire's counselor, the Order who pardoned her, and I'm sure other students and teachers know, obviously. My new roommate."

"What about friends outside your circle? Human friends she may have contacted?"

"Rue and Liam, a Korrena pair who are in the academy. Rue is in Blaire's major. She hasn't heard from her either. But outside the academy? She only really had one friend, and she had no clue when I asked if she'd seen her. I didn't tell her Blaire left."

"Hmm. Have her teachers said anything? Her tutor?"

"Oh, yeah, I forgot about that asshole Vincent."

"What do you mean?"

"Kai and Seth's cousin, Vincent, is… was… Blaire's tutor. He was one of the last to see her."

"Has he said anything?"

"Nothing more than his usual antagonizing. I swear I'm so close to rearranging his face it's not funny."

"Oh my. What's going on there?"

"Blaire didn't believe me, but I swear he wanted her."

"What do you mean?"

"He's always calling her beautiful. Finding excuses to touch her. I just… it sounds stupid, but I just *know*. It's like something on an instinctual level, you know? I've confronted him three times already."

His mother hummed on the other end of the line. "A strong bond can trigger an awareness of threats. It's not just a matter of jealousy."

This was more than jealousy. He didn't feel this bone deep rage toward Aiden when he knew for a fact his best friend had feelings for Blaire and that she returned them. It would stand to reason a situation like that would bring this feeling about, but no. He rationalized it after he addressed it. This was so different.

"Lukas… I think Jyrki and I should make a trip to Blackthorn."

"No."

It meant a lot that his mother would even suggest it, but what would they do? If Blaire left of her own accord, he didn't want to force her to come back to him. But if something bad happened…

"We can help find her."

"No, Mom. I… need to do some thinking."

"*Poika*, keep vigilant. Do not give up on that girl. Do not let go. And keep your eyes open for anything. You told me that the Order had been out for her blood. There has been too much unrest surrounding your pairing not to be suspicious of the circumstances surrounding this situation. I know you are grieving and may not be fully focused, but I need you to try to push that aside. You may be missing some important details."

Lukas licked his lips and rubbed the thigh of his jeans with his free hand. "I will … I'll… call you when I know more, or if anything changes."

"And *poika?*"

"Yeah?"

"I love you."

Lukas took a shuddering breath. It had been so long since he heard that phrase, that even hearing it from his mother broke his heart. "I love you too," he whispered before ending the call. He rested his head against the rough bark of the tree and closed his eyes.

Was there more to this than just Blaire not being able to handle being with a Vasirian? Was this more than just her reacting to the fight they had? If he thought back to before his grief took over his life, he hadn't believed the flimsy story Clarissa fed him.

Even if Professor Velastra backed the claim, had his initial instincts been correct? Was Blaire in trouble?

His stomach soured, and he turned quickly, expelling the early dinner he'd eaten. She could be in trouble. Forced into a sick ritual… He needed answers. But he didn't know where to start. Should he tell Aiden and the others? No. If something was going on, he didn't need to arouse suspicion. He had to face this alone. He needed to watch for any signs of what happened to Blaire. His mother was right; he had been so lost in his grief and the numbness that he wasn't paying attention to what was happening around him.

Many things made little sense when he thought about them. Clarissa's transfer to their class. Blaire's belongings left behind. How Clarissa ended up in his room, and the school refusing to make any concessions to the arrangement. Clarissa's father ran the show; the Order had a hand in the room situation he was stuck in and why he couldn't get out of it.

Yeah, something was amiss. He needed to figure out what—and soon. He needed to suppress the urge to wallow in his guilt.

He would not give up Blaire.

Not if she didn't walk away willingly.

29

Investigation

Today was the day. Aiden stood next to his desk watching Vincent with his arms crossed over his chest, his jaw working as he ground his teeth. Something was going on with Vincent relating to Blaire. Call it instinct, or maybe even paranoia, but something was definitely off, and he was going to get to the bottom of it. A hard push on his side had him dragging his hardened gaze away from Vincent.

"Wanna go to the movies tonight?"

Aiden shook his head at his sister. "Can't."

Frowning, Riley scrunched her brows. "Why not? It's not like you have a date or anything."

"Do you always have to be up your brother's ass?"

Riley glared at Seth and rounded on him, shoving a finger at his chest. "I'll have you know you're the one lodged up his backside, not me. It's just…" Her voice softened. "I usually go with Blaire, Lukas, and…" Her words trailed off as she lowered her hand from Seth's chest, sadness filling her eyes.

Seth looked away and muttered an apology, and Aiden put his hand on Riley's shoulder. When she turned to him, he forced a smile, looking down at his little sister's face. "I'm sorry, okay? I just have some things I need to take care of. Maybe we can go tomorrow, or next weekend? That way, Seth can come too."

Riley spluttered, the sad expression shifting as color crawled up her neck and over the sides of her face. "He doesn't need to come!"

"I don't want to go anyway," Seth said, rolling his eyes. "I bet you never shut your mouth through the whole movie."

Rubbing the back of his neck, Aiden looked away. Seth nailed it, but he wasn't about to confirm it and get Riley started. Riley knew he agreed just by the incredulous look on her face.

"Really?" Riley put her hands on her hips. "You too?"

Seth smirked. "It could be entertaining. Whatever. Yeah, I'll go." He shrugged and picked up his bag. "Let me know, man. I'll meet you outside." He brushed past Riley and was out of the classroom before she could fire a comeback as she stared after him, gaping like a fish.

Aiden gathered his things as Vincent packed his belongings, most of the classroom now empty. Even Professor Yarborough had left.

"Listen, I need to get going. Just text me movie times for tomorrow and we'll work something out, okay?" He couldn't stand to see his baby sister suffering. It was one reason he was doing exactly what he was about to do. For her and for Lukas. She was using the movies to distract herself because she hadn't left the academy grounds since Blaire disappeared other than to purchase necessities, and one time to visit Charlotte to try to find Blaire.

Riley hadn't gone clothes shopping or to get food, outside of what they served in the cafeteria or canteen. Her entire routine had changed. It was the same for him and Lukas as well. Neither had set foot out into the Valley for entertainment or other treats. It was a struggle sometimes just to get together in the same room, and it felt like a black cloud hung over them whenever they did.

Aiden watched Vincent go out the door before rushing down the aisle toward the exit. He needed to make sure he kept his distance, but he couldn't afford to lose his quarry. He followed Vincent through the corridors and down a flight of stairs into the main hallway, cast in a deep red glow from the sun shining through the black and crimson stained glass that lined the front of Blackthorn Academy's main building. The entire hallway looked bathed in blood.

Seth was waiting outside the entrance of the main building when Aiden passed through the massive wooden doors.

"He went that direction." Seth motioned left where Vincent was making his way across the courtyard at a quick pace.

"Let's go."

They rushed down the large stairs, along the front of the building, and past the massive fountain in the center of the courtyard. Early blooming camellias infused the air with their light lemony, jasmine, and anise scents. Dry leaves from the live oaks blew about the courtyard as they hurried along; their sweet, dark brown acorns littered the ground, signaling that December was closing in on them.

Two months.

Blaire had been missing for almost two months.

When they noticed Vincent's pace slow as he rounded a set of smaller buildings after passing through a narrow pathway, they stopped and lingered in the shaded path, peering around the corner of one of the buildings.

"Where's he going?" Seth asked.

"It looks like he's going to the administration building. This isn't the first time I've seen him go there."

"What's odd about that?"

"Aside from the fact that students aren't allowed inside there? Most of the teaching staff meet in the building where Professor Velastra's office is. Outside the Order's council floor, I have no idea what's in the admin building."

"Well, I know they host members of the Blackthorn Clan and other council members from all over the world when they come on diplomatic stuff."

"How do you know that?" Aiden raised a brow, looking back at Seth as Vincent took the steps up to the front of the administration building.

"Research I had to do for one of my writing classes."

"Huh. Okay."

Aiden pulled his phone from his pocket and snapped a photo of Vincent entering the building. He wasn't sure if it would matter, but it was proof worth having. This was the second time he'd seen Vincent enter the building. The last time he had a bag of takeout with him. Vincent wasn't a member of administration, wasn't on the council, and certainly wasn't a teacher, no matter how much he paraded his aide status around as if he were one. Students weren't allowed in the building, so why was he going in there? At most, Aiden had only been to the doors when he handed over those students who attacked Blaire to Blackthorn security last year.

"Come on. Let's go see Professor Velastra."

The view through Professor Velastra's office window included the administration building. Aiden hoped to see Vincent leaving so he could point it out to the professor firsthand, but he probably wouldn't be so lucky. It was for the best; they could keep what they were doing on the down-low for the time being.

"So, to what do I owe this impromptu visit? Riley left about fifteen minutes ago. If you're here for the same thing, I'm sorry to inform you I have no new information."

The professor ran a hand over the front of her black pencil skirt, smoothing it, before taking a seat in the large leather chair behind her desk. Folding her hands, she rested her elbows on her desk as she studied Aiden and Seth. While she maintained her professional front, delivering the news that she had no progress to report clearly bothered her.

Her eyes softening around the edges as she looked at them said it all.

Aiden folded his arms over his chest, stepping between the two leather chairs in front of her desk as Seth took a seat, pulling loose his uniform tie to hang low around his neck.

"I want to know where Vincent's room is."

A slender brow quirked, and the professor's lips flattened as she cast her searching gaze over to Seth. "Vincent Brandt?"

"My cousin, yeah," Seth confirmed.

Surely there were other Vincents in the academy. But the only one they would be interested in would be Seth's cousin, so it didn't surprise him Professor Velastra assumed correctly. He suspected she wasn't going to offer up the information though, with the way her gaze moved between them, the lines between her brow becoming more severe with each pass. Finally, she sat back in her seat and deflated with a sigh.

"Do I want, or even need, to know why?"

Aiden kept his features stoic as he held his gaze locked on hers. "Can you turn a blind eye just this once? We'll let you know after."

They stared at one another in awkward silence. Aiden would wait her out if he had to. It wasn't a coincidence that the hairs on the back of his neck rose when Vincent was around. Something was off about him, and seeing him with Blaire's bracelet… he had to know. He would do whatever it took.

Pursing her lips, the professor nodded. "While I'm reluctant to agree to this, considering the trouble one of you has consistently found himself in recently." She cast a look at Seth, and he rolled his eyes. "I believe you are level-headed enough not to go against our most basic rules, Aiden."

She folded her hands on her lap, the pearl accent buttons on her wrist catching the amber light of the room. "But I expect to know what all this is about as soon as possible because I'm sure it's more than a social visit that has you dropping in on your cousin's room."

Seth shrugged.

"I may not always be around, but it's not hard to miss how different you are from your cousin, and I have seen none of you spend time with him. Furthermore, you could ask him directly for his room number. I won't ask what this is about yet, but if there is anything worth mentioning, I expect to be informed."

Seth stood, and Aiden gave the professor a nod of farewell after she gave him the room information, then followed Seth to the door.

"Oh, and Aiden?"

Aiden turned and looked at the professor, who now stood behind the desk with a grave expression.

"Do not break the handbook's guidelines. Right now, the Order may be looking for any reason to come down on all of you to clean up what happened last school year." She narrowed her eyes. "Do not give them any reason. Do not draw unnecessary attention to yourself."

Aiden nodded without a word and left the room, taking the professor's warning to heart.

Knocking on a door in the hallway on the third floor of the dorm building farthest down a line of several identical buildings where all the student housing was located, they waited in the hallway.

"What's your plan?" Seth asked as he glanced down the hallway.

Vincent wouldn't be there. He was still at the administration building, and Aiden wasn't sure when he'd be back. He didn't know entirely what he was going to do, but if Vincent had a roommate, then he or she could at least let them know more about Vincent's habits in recent weeks. How often Vincent went into the Order's building, if nothing else.

"We need to know how often—"

The door opened and a lanky guy wearing an army green pullover with dark wash jeans opened the door. He rubbed at his bleary eyes, and his short, sandy blond hair stood out in all directions like he'd just awakened from a nap.

"Yeah?" he asked, his voice hoarse.

"Hey man… We're sorry to bother you, but we wanted to ask you something about your roommate. Got a sec?" Aiden slid his hands into the pockets of his uniform's slacks.

The guy ran a hand over his face and met Aiden's eyes. In a thick London accent, he said, "I don't even know if I have a roommate, though." He chuckled, sounding unsure.

"What?" Aiden's brows pulled together in confusion.

"Yeah, mate… Vincent hasn't been here this year. I thought he changed rooms after everything went down last year." He shrugged. "Thought I had the room to meself."

Seth crossed his arms. "Last year?"

"Yeah, we didn't get along all that great. He said I was too messy.

I think he was too much of a tightwad, though. Well obsessed over his appearance. He was overbearing, always causing a kerfuffle, is it?" He leaned against the doorjamb and crossed his arms over his chest. "Figured he wanted a different roommate and buggered off."

"What the hell is a 'kerfuffle'?" Seth's eyebrows rose to his hairline.

Laughing, the guy shrugged and said, "It's a Brit thing. Or more like my dad's thing." He laughed to himself and looked up as if he were searching for the right words. "A fuss? That's what you Americans call it, is it?"

Seth shook his head slowly, and Aiden turned his attention back to the guy in the doorway. He needed to see if he could get any additional information that might help them because, so far, they'd come to a dead end. "So, you haven't seen him since the last school year?"

The guy shook his head. "No, he was here the first couple months then made himself scarce around the end of September."

Aiden and Seth both looked at each other at the same time.

Seth cursed under his breath. He must have been thinking the same thing Aiden was. Two months into the semester was when Blaire went missing. The last week of September.

"Everything okay?"

Aiden turned his attention back to the guy, who looked between them with concern on his face. He couldn't tell him what was going on. Not when they didn't even know themselves, or even if they could fully trust the guy.

"Yeah, we've just been looking for him. Looks like a dead end." He shrugged like it was no big deal. "Listen, mind contacting me if he moves back in?"

The guy pulled his cell from his back pocket. "Yeah, mate. What's your number? I'll ring you if I hear anything." He passed Aiden the phone and Aiden put in his number before handing it back to him.

"Thanks, man. I appreciate it." He looked down the hall before a thought crossed his mind. "Oh, and can you not tell him we were here if you do see him?"

The guy made a strange face at that and then shook his head. "Yeah, sure, mate. Well, I'm knackered. Didn't sleep studying for my final last night."

"Yeah, no worries, man. Sorry to have woken you up."

"S'alright."

Aiden and Seth stepped back as the door shut. Once they got to the end of the hall, Seth looked at Aiden. "What in the hell does knackered mean?"

Aiden laughed. "Tired."

"How do you know all this?"

"My roommate at the high school branch was from Chelsea, an area in west London. He didn't talk a lot like that, but his mom visited often, and in those four years, I learned tons from her."

Seth shook his head. "Despite growing up in Blackthorn, I will never wrap my brain around some of the weird shit some of these people say."

Considering Blackthorn Academy took in students from all over the world, it was a melting pot for many nationalities. There were three other Blackthorn locations in the world. The one in Europe was even more exclusive than the American branch, mostly catering to the various councils' children and their extended families, and the Blackthorn Clan themselves when they were younger. It was less than a quarter of the size of this location. He was honestly surprised Clarissa hadn't gone there, since it was closer to Italy. The two others in Africa and Asia were a similar size to this location. There simply wasn't enough space and staff to go around without drawing unnecessary human attention for all children of Vasirian to go to one area for education.

Heading down the stairs and out into the courtyard, Seth stopped and turned to face Aiden. "Should we go tell Professor Velastra?"

"No. Not yet."

"But if Vincent has been all weird since Blaire disappeared—"

"But has he? He's always been weird. Is this just normal for him, considering he didn't get along with his roommate, and it was just a coincidence that it aligned with when Blaire disappeared? We don't know for sure."

"You can't be thinking it's not related."

"Honestly? I think it's related, but we can't prove it. We don't need to bring unnecessary attention to ourselves with the Order watching our every move. We need to get more information before we say anything, because once we bring attention to this, Professor Velastra will have no choice but to act. What that action will be, I don't know. I wouldn't be surprised if it doesn't involve a formal request for investigation with the council."

"And then hello spotlight." Seth's brows pinched.

"Exactly. For now, just watch Vincent. If you notice anything out of the ordinary, tell me immediately. We're going to figure this out. Not just for Lukas and Riley's sake, but for ours. Blaire's."

"Yeah, but what if she really wanted to leave?"

Aiden looked up at the sky as clouds rolled in and shadowed the courtyard, a strong breeze blowing and stirring the palmetto trees.

"Then we let her go. But I can't just accept this lying down. I can't accept the words of that brat who's obsessed with Lukas. Even if her father told Professor Velastra the same thing. I wouldn't put it past them to be in cahoots. Doesn't it strike you as funny that they're the only two providing the story? I mean, did the rest of the Order follow through? Even then, I wouldn't put some shady shit past them with how they nearly killed Blaire at the end of the last school year."

Seth's eyes narrowed. "Yeah… Whatever it takes, man. I'm in."

Maybe he was chasing a ghost and Blaire really did just get a pardon and leave, but he couldn't rest properly until he had solid answers. It wasn't as if he could ring up the Order and ask about Blaire. They weren't allowed to question the Order, even if they weren't already under a microscope.

"Let's go kill something," Aiden said figuratively. He had been a fighter when he was back in the high school branch, but he didn't do that anymore. Wound too tight, he needed to take his aggression out on pixels before he did something stupid like hunt down Vincent and demand answers with his fists the way he'd been trying to keep Lukas from doing.

30

Madness

The hedge maze was heavy in shadows, with the moon hiding behind the thick cloud cover. A rare November storm was inevitable. Vincent wanted to hurry and get this over with so he could return to Blaire. Even in the enclosed room with no windows, it was still possible she could hear the storm if it was bad enough.

Vincent moved deeper into the maze and stopped in the center, where a circle of benches surrounded a small marble fountain. Before he could take a seat, rustling came from behind him.

"You're early. That's good. I don't enjoy being kept waiting."

Angelo Moretti's thick Italian accent lilted in the night, and Vincent turned to face the robed man as he approached. Angelo looked little older than Vincent did at twenty-two, with no fine lines or wrinkles, but he knew the man easily had another seventy years on him. While not the oldest member of the Order's council, the former king of the Blackthorn Clan still deemed Angelo worthy of leading the group that kept the Vasirian of the Americas in line.

"You have what I need?"

Vincent held up the small black box in his hands.

"Come. Show me." He waved a hand with jeweled rings on each finger to beckon Vincent toward him. Even Vincent thought the look was gaudy, despite the fact that he loved to accessorize himself. Angelo and his daughter were similar, going over the top with whatever they assumed was desirable and made them look beautiful to those around them.

Vincent stepped forward and opened the lid on the box, revealing several vials of dark red liquid.

"Excellent."

Looking down at Blaire's blood in the box, Vincent clenched his jaw as his head ached. Ever since he began feeding directly from Blaire and not drinking the blood packets provided by the school, he'd been feeling off. Sometimes it was physical, and he would get headaches. If he went long enough without feeding, he'd get the shakes like an addict going through withdrawals. Other times, just the sight of her blood was enough to send his heart racing, his body alight, and it was as if he was losing his mind. But he couldn't stop. No. He wanted—no, *needed* her blood. He snapped his gaze up to meet Angelo's as he held his hand out impatiently. He missed what the man said.

"Pardon?"

"I *said*, give me the box. But I must ask, are you feeding on the human?"

Vincent's brows lowered.

"I ask not to punish you for breaking our laws. We are breaking plenty with what we are doing now, but..." He waved a hand toward Vincent's face. "Your eyes, how they glow as you stare longingly at the girl's blood. You're feeding from her, aren't you?"

Vincent squeezed his eyes shut to ward off the reaction. His jaw worked as he ground his teeth and he nodded, finally meeting Angelo's eyes.

"Mm… you must be careful. We do not know the effects that her blood can bring to our kind."

"We drink human blood out of the packets daily."

"Yes, but this girl's blood is special. She is a Korrena, Vincent. She is not like our regular donors. I have to wonder…" He tilted his head as a few wayward black strands fell across his forehead. "Have you felt any different since you started consuming the girl's blood?"

"No," he lied.

"You will report anything abnormal to me immediately. Is that understood?" Angelo's eyes flashed a vibrant amber that softly illuminated the naturally tanned skin of his cheeks.

"Yes."

"Excellent. Now, hand me the box," he said more firmly.

Vincent's hands tightened on the wood. As he passed over the box, he asked, "What are you doing with her blood if the rest if the council thinks Blaire has left the academy?"

A chuckle was the only answer he received as Angelo pried the box from his fingers that held the wood so tightly they had turned white.

"It is no concern of yours. Just continue to supply me as you have and you'll be able to keep your human pet."

Vincent growled low in his throat, and when Angelo raised an eyebrow at him, he swallowed down the sound. "She's not a pet; she's my pair."

Angelo closed the box and laughed loudly, mocking him. "Now, you know that simply isn't possible. Only that boy can be her true pair. Do not delude yourself while you play house."

Vincent tightened his fists, the bite of the metal of his ring pressing on his skin a distraction from his frustrations. He couldn't afford to have Angelo angry with him. He'd put an end to his help in keeping Blaire hidden away. A few more months to go and Vincent could take her away from here. He had to remember that.

"She… She can be my compatible pair," he said slowly, taking measured breaths to calm himself.

"That may be so, but I find it hard to believe you'll be able to sway the girl. She seems to be a stubborn one from what I have heard."

Vincent struggled to remain calm and collected with Angelo antagonizing him. Blaire's blood was doing something to him on an emotional level. He couldn't stop himself from feeding on her; that should be warning enough. He had become addicted to her blood, and she wasn't even his Korrena. He steered the conversation away from Blaire, determined to remain detached. "How is Clarissa fairing with Lukas?"

Angelo waved a hand dismissively. "Clarissa says it seems as if the boy is losing his will, so she believes it will be easier now to sway him to her side."

"Why is she so fixated on him?" She'd asked him to come to the nightclub the night Blaire and Lukas fought. She said Blaire would need him. He hadn't fully understood until he saw the distress on Blaire's face as she ran from the hallway into his arms.

"Why are *you* so fixated on Blaire Wilcox?"

Vincent's nostrils flared as he took a deep inhale. "I knew from the moment I met her she was perfect for me. I had to have her."

Raising his eyebrows, Angelo gave Vincent a pointed look. "It is the same. I will not deny my only little girl what her heart desires." He pulled up his hood as the rain started to fall. "Now, if you'll excuse me."

Tucking the box into the depths of his robe, Angelo disappeared into the shadows of the hedge maze as the bottom fell out of the sky. Vincent allowed the rain to pour heavily over his face, soaking him in mere seconds. He hadn't expected rain. It hardly ever rained in the last months of the year.

He couldn't risk Blaire's well-being. He couldn't tell the head of the Order he felt like he was losing his mind half the time—much less the other effects. They would demand her body for experimentation, and he couldn't let her go. They would demand he stop feeding from her, and he couldn't stop that. He needed to endure until he could take Blaire away from the academy. It was harder to do with each passing day. He kept messing up. A few days ago, he left the door unlocked. It would have been over if Blaire hadn't been chained to the bed and had checked the door, or decided to once more get an independent streak and try to escape as she did not that long ago. The thought sent a shiver of unease over his body.

He was thankful she had lost her fight now that she'd seen the photos he took of Clarissa and Lukas before Lukas pushed the girl off of him. The timing couldn't have been more perfect. If he wanted to keep Blaire by his side, he had to make fewer mistakes. Breaking her would come, he was sure of it. She needed more time to accept his love—to love him back. It would come.

31

Fragmented

Staring blankly at the familiar cream envelope in his hand, Lukas didn't know whether to scream or cry. Luckily, he had returned to his room before Clarissa. Had she found the envelope with his name written in stylish black calligraphy, he didn't want to think of the fallout. The smell of wet pine hung heavy in the air from the freak storm last night, and the wind rustled through the trees around him as he sat against a tree deep in the forest behind the school. He didn't want to be caught. Blaire had received a similar letter at the end of last term, but whoever sent this one addressed it to him.

He shifted uncomfortably, before flipping the envelope in his hand. Taking a deep breath, he edged his finger beneath the paper and popped the burgundy wax seal with a feather emblem, pulling a cream parchment paper from the envelope that had the same stylish calligraphy.

Your heart may be fragmented, but not all hope is lost.
Part of you is missing, that much is true,
but do not forsake the fire inside your soul.
It calls to her.
It knows her.
Do not allow yourself to be caught up in the lie.
Do not disappear.
Do not allow the self-imposed purgatory to eat away at your mind.
You teeter on the edge of a cursed eternity, but this is not your epilogue, not your destiny.
The girl waits for you.
A broken heart that is merely an echo,
a fractured melody that has been denied its harmony.
Step through the fog that consumes you and see the vultures circling.
They seek to destroy, to take,
to suffocate you in your own despair.
But she waits.
Fragmented, but waiting.

Lukas's hands trembled as he stared at the delicate paper in his hands and thunder cracked overhead, lightning splitting the sky and illuminating the canopy overhead. The weather reflected the turbulence in his heart. If he didn't know better, he'd think mother nature was responding to his sorrow with how stormy the dry season had been.

Did this mean that Blaire really hadn't abandoned him? Was this the piece of evidence he needed to confirm everything he felt after speaking with his mother?

He rested his head against the tree after folding the letter, placing it back in the envelope, and tucking it inside his leather jacket to protect it from the droplets of rain that made their way through the foliage overhead as the rain fell. He stretched his leg out, leaving the other knee bent with his arm resting on it, his hand hanging limply. His body ached, and his eyes burned. It felt as if he were running on fumes emotionally, and he didn't know how much longer he could push forward before either his mind or his body gave out on him. But he couldn't allow that. No matter what it took, he had to hang on.

"I knew I'd find you out here."

Lukas opened his eyes to find Riley standing in front of him, wearing clothes that were abnormally subdued compared to what she usually wore. She had paired black skinny jeans that were ripped on the thighs with combat boots that had a small platform to give her additional height. A black oversize hoodie with a design that looked like skeleton hands cupping her small breasts hung down to mid-thigh, and she had the hood pulled over her head to shield herself from the rain. Gone were the buckles and chains. Her face was even void of the heavy eye makeup she always wore. She looked tired with the dark circles under her eyes.

If he didn't know any better, he would think Blaire had been Riley's Korrena with the way she mourned the loss. But he wasn't a fool. Nothing anyone else was experiencing could compare to the soul-sucking despair that ate away at his very being. His girl was gone, and he had to get her back, no matter what.

Riley crouched in front of him, her knees up to her chest as she wrapped her arms around her shins, her butt resting against the back of her calves. "Why are you out in the rain?"

"I needed to get away." It wasn't a lie. But it wasn't the whole truth, either. He had to open the letter in private.

"From the c*agacazzo*?"

Lukas blinked. "What the fuck is that?"

"Pain in the ass."

"Fuck you. I don't know what that means. I'm not a—"

"No, you dipshit. *Cagacazzo* essentially means 'pain in the ass' in Italian. The bitch is Italian, so why not give her an appropriate title?"

Lukas ran his hand down his face before huffing out laughter that felt foreign to him. It had been so long since he felt anything amusing. Leave it to Riley to be the one to bring that back to him, if only for a moment. "Yeah, I come out here to get away from her, since they won't change my room."

"Aiden told me about that… That's why I figured I'd find you here."

"Yeah… So what do you need?"

"Can't I just want to hang out with my buddy?"

He rolled his eyes and gave her a knowing look with his brow raised, calling her bluff.

"Alright, fine! I was worried about you. I mean…" Riley tugged on the sleeves of her hoodie until they ate her hands and only her small fingertips stuck out. "I've been worried about you, but you've been so unapproachable." She looked up, her smoky blue eyes colliding with his and he felt his chest tighten. He'd been so lost that he hadn't stopped to think of the impact his behavior was having on those around him.

"So you wanted to check on me, then?"

Riley shrugged. "Something like that. I also wanted to get away from Seth."

"Why would you want to do that?" He hadn't been following the drama around those two in a while, but he knew things had gotten tense between them in the last few months, and Seth lashed out at everything that even looked at him wrong.

"Just…" She shook her head. "No, never mind."

Lukas nudged her knee with his hand. "No, come on… I need the distraction."

With a resigned sigh, Riley waved a hand in frustration. "He's just become so controlling! He's always tried to run things before, like an overbearing big brother, but he's gotten ridiculous."

"How so?"

"Well, the other day he scared the shit out of Reinaldo from our math class when he was just trying to ask if I wanted to study with him since Blaire wasn't around to be my partner. Like, he straight up broke the dude's desk. Cracked it right down the middle with his grip alone when he stepped between our desks to block Reinaldo's view of me." She sighed. "Told him I had a study partner, and then Seth proceeded to drag me out of the chair and out of the classroom."

That seemed like a substantial leap from last he paid any attention to the dynamic between them, and it was hard to imagine Seth being that violent. Sure, when they were younger they got into fights all the time. Aiden, Seth, and he always got into trouble for starting shit with others.

Lukas needed an outlet for the pain he felt being left alone at an academy with no genuine family to speak of, and Aiden was just along for the ride. Seth was so desperate to be like his substitute big brother that he went along with whatever Aiden and Lukas got into. But when Lukas finally mellowed out, realizing that acting out at everything wasn't bringing him any peace, the other two followed suit. That was, until recently. He didn't know what was going on with Seth, but he couldn't focus on it while Blaire was still missing.

"So, between that behavior, and him acting like a guard dog to keep me from eviscerating that *cagacazzo*, I'm about to lose my mind."

"Did you Google that word just so you could use it as an insult for her?"

"Fuck a duck, Lukas. I'm trying to vent here." Riley glared at him from beneath her hood. Without the dark makeup, it was less effective. Not that it was effective at intimidating him to start with from such a small girl, anyway. "Do not distract me."

He chuckled and shrugged one shoulder as silence descended between them; only the sound of the rain hitting the trees filled the space.

"Have you heard anything from her?" Riley asked. "From Charlotte?"

"Nothing."

"Aiden said that Charlotte said she would tell him if she heard from her. Do you think she was telling the truth?"

Lukas shrugged. "Yeah. She seemed pretty upset to find out Blaire left Blackthorn from what Aiden said."

"I miss her."

Something cracked inside Lukas's chest, and he squeezed his eyes shut to push away the tears that burned behind his eyelids. "Yeah,"—he swallowed thickly—"me too."

"She belongs here," Riley whispered with a sniff.

Surprising her, and even himself, he reached forward and tugged Riley into his arms. She fell to her knees between his legs as he wrapped a strong arm tightly around her, resting his other hand on the back of her hooded head, holding her close. She buried her face against his chest and sobbed.

He let her break in that secret place in the forest where no one could see their shared pain, and he made a silent vow, not only to her, but to himself, that he would not allow himself to stop until he knew the truth of what happened to his pair.

32

Message

Turning over in bed for what felt like the tenth time in as many minutes, Blaire stared into the darkness of the room. The red numbers on the digital clock glowed dimly from the small table beside the sofa. Vincent had gotten her a clock when she complained it was disorienting to not at least have a sense of the time of day, and he relented, giving her something that she was sure he interpreted as a domestic shift with them. Where she was accepting her "home" with him.

The clock let her know it wouldn't be long before Vincent returned from his remedial sessions. She was glad to at least be able to track his movements better this way. With winter finals coming to an end, he would spend evenings this week reviewing final exam results with those he'd tutored to prepare them for reexamination if they needed it.

Blaire slid up on the bed and sighed when her leg met resistance; the chain attached to her ankle rattled against the side of the bed.

She didn't see the point of being shackled like this every time Vincent left the room. Not when she had no hope of getting through the six different locks he had on the door without the keys he wore around his neck. Blaire shifted to where she could be comfortable with her pillow against the wall at her back. Reaching to turn on the bedside lamp, her hand froze on the switch as a rectangular blast of light from the table's surface illuminated the room.

Vincent's cell phone. Could she be so lucky?

She darted a glance at the door and listened for any sounds. When she heard nothing, she reached out with shaking hands to pick up the phone. To her relief, there was no lock on the phone. No face recognition or thumbprint necessary. No pass code required. Most people kept their phones locked up tighter than Fort Knox. Of course, nothing Vincent did made much sense to her.

Her entire body vibrated with nervous energy as she stared at the screen.

This was her chance.

She didn't know anyone's phone number offhand, but student emails were the first initial and last name, followed by the generic email server for the academy. Opening the mail app, Blaire hoped like hell that Riley checked her student email. For good measure, she CC'd Aiden. She wished she remembered Professor Velastra's contact information; the professor would definitely check email. She didn't want to chance getting her address wrong, in case the email bounced; Vincent would see that. She didn't reach out to Lukas, though. He made his choice.

Blaire focused to rid herself of the intrusive thoughts about Lukas. She hoped those she once called her friends wouldn't abandon her altogether if she reached out, because she needed to get out of here, and this email was her final Hail Mary before she found herself with a one-way ticket to Brazil.

Blaire's fingers trembled as she hurriedly tapped away at the screen, using Vincent's email account because there was no way she could log out of his account, into hers, back out, and into his again and still cover her tracks. She barely had any experience using a smart phone. She didn't trust how fast she could pull it off.

What should she say? Keep it short: Vincent took her. She thought she was still at the school. Anything about what he was doing to her was irrelevant toward rescue. She didn't have enough information to say where in the school she was, and she wasn't one hundred percent sure she was actually on the academy grounds. She went with her first impulse.

It's Blaire. Vincent is keeping me somewhere I don't know, but I think I'm still on school

The locks on the door rattled as each lock disengaged. Blaire's hands tightened around the phone to control her nervous tremors. She added "grounds" to her sentence and hit send. That had to be enough.

Staring at the outbox, waiting for it to show as delivered, she held her breath as the final lock snicked. "Email sent" flashed on the screen. Blaire breathed deep, deleted the message from the sent mail folder, and closed the app. She pressed the button that showed all open apps. The door opened as she swiped up to clear the mail app entirely to ensure Vincent wouldn't realize she had the app open in the first place. Riley had closed out a ton of apps she had open on her screen one day and explained something about active memory or data usage. Blaire was so thankful she'd been watching her in that moment and asked what she was doing.

"Wake up, my jewel. I brought you dinner—"

Vincent paused in the doorway with a bag in his hand as his eyes narrowed on her hands still clutching the phone. He stepped inside and slammed the door shut before rushing to the bedside, setting the bag of takeout on the floor, and snatching the phone out of Blaire's hand.

"What did you do?" he bellowed.

Blaire flinched, wrapping her arms around her midsection and shrinking against the wall. "I-I-I… I just wanted to browse the internet. I finished my book." She licked her lips. "I was bored."

She swallowed the ball of anxiety and tried to give Vincent a remorseful look, but she couldn't mask the fear as she took in the Vasirian sitting next to her on the bed. His chest heaved as he pulled in deep breaths. The veins in his forearms stood out as he remained tense, gripping the phone in his hands. But what had her shrinking back in fear the most was his eyes. Glowing brighter than she'd ever seen before, his eyes showed he wasn't in the right mindset to reason with. His lip pulled back a fraction, revealing his fangs, as he stayed focused on her face. She felt like a mouse cornered by a cat. Absolutely terrorized and waiting for the inevitable pounce.

"I'm sorry," she whispered. She pushed through the fear to touch his arm, her hand trembling as she did. She had to appease him. She needed to survive this just a little longer. If her email reached either Aiden or Riley, she had to believe they would find her.

Vincent relaxed at her touch, and his fangs receded, but a dim glow remained in his icy orbs. Eventually tearing his eyes away from her face, he swiped through his phone. He checked his call log, text messages, and emails. Satisfied with finding nothing untoward, he put the phone in his vest pocket and turned to face her fully.

"It's too dangerous," he finally said in a low voice, taking a measured breath as if trying to control himself. "They'll take you away from me."

"Why would they do that?"

She didn't ask who these people were. She didn't want to provoke him into a state of unstable anger again. The school wouldn't come for her if the Order knew what he was doing. He'd have their full support. Lukas wouldn't come either, all things considered. His words made little sense outside of her friends, and she didn't entirely know if they even cared anymore, anyway.

"Quit asking questions." He walked to the door, pulling his keys out and locking the bolts down the doorjamb.

While she didn't want to provoke him, Blaire needed to keep him talking. He was calming with each passing minute. She treaded carefully. "But I just… I want to understand, so I don't mess up again," she murmured faintly, toying with the edge of her nightgown. "Didn't you leave the phone for me to give me something to do? To make me happy because you love me?"

She felt like such a tool. Her skin crawled with revulsion at appealing to his delusions.

Vincent's features relaxed as he looked at her from where he stood at the door after he engaged the locks. "I apologize, my jewel." He moved back to the bed and sat down next to her. "It was a simple mistake. On both our parts. I should not have left my phone. You didn't know any better." Standing, he bent down to pick up the bag of takeout. "Now, shall we eat?"

Blaire relaxed her shoulders now that he was no longer an immediate threat. Like usual, her appetite was nonexistent, but she wouldn't cross him tonight. She would make herself choke down the food to keep the fragile peace. "What did you get?"

Vincent's lips pulled into a warm smile as he carried the bag to the table and set it down before returning to sit on the bed, lifting Blaire's leg into his lap. "A shrimp and noodle stir-fry for you, and spicy ginger beef for me from Happy Panda." He unlocked the cuff on her ankle before letting the chain fall to the floor.

"And crab rangoon?" She offered eager eyes and hoped she wasn't overselling it.

When Vincent winked at her and walked toward the table, she knew he bought into her compliant act. She needed him to stay relaxed, and if the gentle way he handled her leg was any indication of his mood, she'd made it past the worst of it—for now.

"I can't get Chinese food and not get your favorite, now can I? That just wouldn't do." He turned to look at her after he set their containers on the table. "I take it your appetite has returned?"

Blaire chewed the inside of her cheek anxiously and nodded. "The past couple of days I've been more hungry."

Vincent hummed and set another container of white rice on the table next to his beef meal. "I'm glad to hear it. I'm happy to know you're coming around." He moved to the refrigerator and pulled out a carafe of sweet tea. "Come." He gestured to the table. He set down the carafe and retrieved two glasses from the cabinet. "Let's eat."

Blaire ate until she felt sick. It was the most she'd had in one sitting in two months.

33

PANIC

It was only the first class of the day, and Riley was already ready to ditch. It felt like statistics class would never end. Professor Osmond was too animated for this time of morning.

He waved his hands around in frustration as he droned on and on about some equation she didn't understand, but it seemed none of the rest of the class understood it either, considering they were currently being lectured on how over half of them failed to identify the correct formula on the winter finals.

Groaning, Riley sat back in her seat and pulled her cell phone from her messenger bag on the floor beside her desk. She needed to check whether Vincent got back to her about remedial tutoring yet or not. She hated the idea of meeting with him, but he was the only tutor for statistics available. Without his previous tutoring prior to the exam she'd have done a lot worse—she at least passed the class—but the professor was convinced she could do better, so he'd asked her to retake the final. She didn't know if her score on the test itself was failing or not. He didn't tell her—likely to give her a push to do a retake. Remedial tutoring was supposed to allow her to address the weak points from the exam to try to bring the grade higher.

Riley tapped anxiously with her pen on her desk. When the guy sitting next to her glanced over with an annoyed expression, she shifted, dropping the pen. "Sorry," she mumbled. The guy looked away without responding.

Her mind was scattered. There was no way she could flunk out of this class. She would not take it again, but the course was required for her degree. It was extremely difficult to concentrate on most things. It had been two months since Blaire disappeared, and while it became easier to handle everyday life, it still felt like she was grieving the death of a loved one.

The pain of loss never fully faded, but she learned to live with it. Learned to fake a smile when inside she was tearing the walls apart, trashing the room, and screaming at the world how unfair it was to take someone she loved away. But none of it brought Blaire back. She may never come back. So she was forced to pick herself up from the debris and move on. *Fake it 'til you make it*, Riley told herself.

Opening her student email, she scrolled through all the unread messages. She rarely opened the thing unless she needed something specific, opting to use her personal email for what she deemed most important. Vincent hadn't emailed like he said he would today, judging by the most recent unread messages; she'd have to talk to him after class. Bypassing several emails that informed her of the upcoming new semester's class schedule for January, she paused as she reached the newest unread message. Riley blinked several times as she stared at the screen. *Blaire?* There wasn't a subject, but she could see a preview of the email's first line, and Blaire's name clearly written.

Clicking on the message, Riley's eyes moved across the screen, and she nearly choked on her own saliva. She bolted up from her chair, drawing the attention of the entire class as she stood staring wide-eyed at the screen of her phone in her shaking hand.

"Are you alright, Miss Easton?" Professor Osmond asked with a sigh, frustration that she interrupted his class apparent in his tone.

"I-I'm fine. Cramps," she stammered, her eyes darting to where Vincent glanced up from the side desk where he was reviewing papers for the professor. "Just cramps. Can I go to the medical wing?"

The professor waved his hand lazily and went back to his lecture as the students turned their attention back to the front of the room. Riley snatched her bag from the floor and looked two desks over to meet Aiden's eyes. He arched a thick black brow at her to ask if she was alright. She could only stare at him with wide, panicked eyes. Turning away, she all but ran from the classroom, wincing as the door slammed shut behind her.

The buckles of her boots jangled, and her footfalls were heavy as she raced down the hallway, down two flights of stairs, and through the heavy front doors of the main academy building into the morning sunlight. She didn't stop running until she was deep in the hedge maze, out of sight of any staff or other students. It took a moment to catch her breath and stop the side-stitch that seized her, but she had to focus. She still had the cell phone gripped in her hands, so she fired off a 911 text to Aiden to meet her.

She walked in a circle before deciding to reach out to someone else too. It might be too risky to call Lukas. If he acted without thinking... Riley opened her contacts and pressed the screen, lifting the phone to her ear with a shaky hand.

"Riley?" Seth's deep voice filled her ear, and she had to ignore how her body responded to the sound. Now was not the time to get all melty over her older brother's friend's stupid, sexy voice.

"I need you," she said, her voice breathy as she tried to contain her panic.

Silence.

"Seth?"

He cleared his throat, and she could hear movement on the other end. "You what now?" His voice was huskier, and it sent a shiver skittering across her skin.

"I need you to meet me. Where are you?"

"Shit, woman." He sighed heavily. "I'm in the courtyard heading to the canteen. What do you want?"

Ignoring the frustration and impatience in his voice, she said, "Come to the hedge maze. I'm in the middle garden, near the fountain."

"Why should I?"

"Please, Seth!" She stomped her foot, her buckles rattling. "It's important. It's an emergency!"

"Are you okay?" There was obvious concern in his voice, and it sounded as if he'd stopped moving. She could hear the fountain in the background.

"Yeah, I think." She spun around and gripped the hair on top of her head, trying to get her bearings. She cleared her throat and exhaled slowly. "Yeah. Just… hurry."

The call disconnected before she could say anything more, and she hoped he wouldn't bail on her. He could be a real ass to her when he wanted to, but he had always been there when she needed him growing up.

Riley paced in circles as she waited, hugging her waist, still gripping her phone like a lifeline. She kept the email app open in case another email from Blaire came through. She didn't want to miss it. What was she going to do? All these weeks she thought Blaire just ditched them. It didn't seem real. She didn't believe it for the longest time, but with Lukas revealing how hard he actually had pushed Blaire to become a Vasirian, and then losing his mark… it seemed plausible Blaire chose to walk away from them all, and that hurt. She wasn't even Blaire's Korrena, and she felt gutted by the loss. Blaire was her best friend, and the fact that Blaire had just picked up and left without so much as a goodbye had broken her heart.

"Riley!"

Riley spun around as Seth came out of the maze to the central court, stopping to look at her. He wasn't in uniform, having no classes for the day. Instead, he wore a pair of light-wash jeans and a plain black t-shirt with the sleeves rolled up to show off his tattoos. His eyes were wild, as if he were ready for a fight. Ready for bloodshed. When his stormy steel gaze connected with hers, he crossed the distance between them quickly and grabbed both of her arms in a tight grip. He was out of breath, so she assumed he must have run here.

"Are you okay?" Taking in her tear-filled eyes, his eyes widened. "What happened?"

She shook her head quickly, trying to control her trembling, breathing slowly through her nose in an effort to push down the emotion.

"Please tell me what happened," he whispered, and he tilted his head, studying her, as if uncertain of what to do.

Before she could get her words out, Aiden appeared around the corner of the hedges, rushing into the central court of the maze where Seth and Riley stood next to the marble fountain surrounded by flowers and stone benches.

"I got your message. Why did you run out of class like that?"

Aiden approached them as Seth released Riley's arms and stepped back, dragging his fingers through the long strands on top of his head.

Riley unlocked the screen that had gone dark and passed her phone to Aiden, unable to form the words. His eyes narrowed and his jaw tightened as he stared at the screen for what felt like forever before he passed the phone to Seth.

"It's Blaire. Vincent is keeping me somewhere I don't know, but I think I'm still on school grounds," he read aloud.

"I fucking knew it," Aiden said sharply. His face twisted with anger as he clenched and unclenched his fists at his sides.

"Knew what? What are you talking about?" Riley said. Did Aiden already know what was happening with Blaire? That he would know and not tell her, or find Blaire, pissed her off. She glared at her brother.

"When did you get this email?" Seth asked, passing the phone back to Riley, and she looked at the timestamp.

"It came in two days ago… December seventh."

"Seriously? It took you two days to see it?" Aiden crossed his arms, glaring at his sister.

"Hey, you're CC'd on this email too!" Riley thrust the phone in Aiden's face, pointing at the screen. "She emailed both of us! And you said you knew it. Why didn't you do anything?"

Aiden cursed under his breath as he turned away, gripping the back of his neck. "I didn't know *this*. I don't check my school email."

Riley growled. How could he be frustrated with her, when he was just like her? *Idiot.*

"Why didn't she just call one of you?" Seth asked.

"She probably doesn't know our numbers… Lukas never got around to giving her the phone he purchased for her birthday. Hell, I don't even know your number off the top of my head. School email is easy to remember. Also, we don't know if she sent this from a computer or a phone." Aiden dragged his hands down his face as he turned around and looked back toward the school buildings. "She could be anywhere."

If Blaire was still on school grounds, then why hadn't they seen her, and what did she mean by Vincent keeping her? Riley didn't know what to make of any of it. Vincent was a creepy guy, but none of that made sense. She looked at the email again and sucked in a shallow breath, dropping to sit on one of the stone benches.

"What?" Seth asked, moving to her side to sit.

"Look." She held up the phone so he could see the screen. "I didn't even think to check the sender's email address. I panicked when I saw Blaire's name in the preview line and didn't pay attention to anything else. I just assumed Blaire used her own account, but no… Look. VBrandt is the username of the email."

"Vincent Brandt," Aiden ground out through clenched teeth, turning back to face them.

"What's going on, Aiden?" Riley looked up at her brother, her brows drawing together and lifting as she looked at him in concern. "You said you knew something."

"I've had my suspicions that Vincent was connected to the reason Blaire disappeared for a while now."

"What? Why?"

"Well, for starters… you remember that custom bracelet I had made for Lukas for his birthday?"

"Yeah." She didn't see where he was going with this.

"Well, Vincent was wearing it one day in class."

"Huh?" Riley's brows bunched, and she looked over at Seth in confusion. "I thought Blaire wore—Shit." She looked back at her brother with her mouth parted.

"Yeah. Lukas let her wear it after they bonded… but Vincent had it on his wrist." Aiden crossed his arms again. "I don't think he knows it was Lukas's bracelet. I doubt he'd be stupid enough to wear it so openly in front of Lukas if he did know. He's creepy, not dumb."

Aiden was having a hard time standing still, talking and not taking action. She knew her brother. He was normally the calm and collected one who thought rationally before he acted. Now he vibrated with repressed rage.

"And then there's the whole roommate situation," Seth said.

Riley turned to face him. "What do you mean?"

"Vincent hasn't been in his assigned room since around the time Blaire went missing. His roommate said he disappeared a couple of weeks before the end of September, which would have been just before Blaire went missing. What he was doing up until her disappearance, we don't know."

Riley rounded on her brother and glared. "Why didn't anyone tell me?!"

"We had to know for sure. We can't just go throwing around accusations and stirring up chaos," Aiden said.

"You still could have told me." Her voice broke with the insight they didn't trust her with the information.

Aiden squatted in front of her and rested his hands on her knees. "I knew Blaire devastated you by leaving. I didn't want to upset you further. It's not that I couldn't trust you not to do anything. Lukas was the one we didn't want acting on the information."

"He doesn't know?" She swiped a tear from her cheek.

"No… and he shouldn't know for now."

"Why?"

"Clarissa is leaving at the end of the week, and if she hears about this situation, she might interfere."

"What? Why?"

Aiden glanced at Seth and then back to Riley. "I suspect something is going on with her as well. What, I can't say. Not that I don't want to… I just don't know. But I've seen her around Vincent enough to think they're in each other's pockets with whatever is going on."

Riley felt like throwing something. Her hands bunched her uniform skirt in her lap as she tried to calm down. That stupid girl had been a nuisance from the beginning, and knowing that she might have had a hand in whatever happened to Blaire made Riley's blood boil.

Interrupting her thoughts, Seth spoke up. "I don't know how Blaire got that message out to you two, but it doesn't feel complete. I dunno if she was caught or what, but something bad could have happened, and now it's been days."

Aiden stood. "We need to tell Professor Velastra."

34

Meeting

Professor Velastra crossed the room to the other side of her desk after everyone filed into her office. Vanilla incense caused Aiden's nose to itch. Every time he came into the professor's office, the smell was different. At least in Kai and Mera's room, where incense was always burning, it was a consistent scent.

Riley had called Mera and told her to bring Kai and meet them in the professor's office, but kept the information vague because they didn't know who might be listening. Aiden didn't know how deep this was, whatever the situation, or who all was involved, but he knew better than to take chances.

"Now that everyone is here, can you please tell me why we are all gathered like this?" Professor Velastra asked, lowering herself into her large leather chair and crossing her legs.

Riley slumped down into the chair in front of the professor's desk, and Mera took the other seat, Kai standing behind her with his hands on her shoulders. Aiden hadn't seen much of them in the past several weeks. Their group felt like it was falling apart with what happened between Blaire and Lukas.

Halting that line of thinking, he stepped forward. "Riley and I received an email that appears to be from Blaire."

The professor tilted her head, clearly waiting on the follow-up.

"An email sent from Vincent Brandt's school email address."

Kai arched a brow. "Blaire used my cousin's email?"

"It would seem so. But that's not the weird part. Riley." Aiden gestured to his sister. "Read the message."

Seth leaned on the back of Riley's chair, crossing his arms as she opened the email and read the message aloud.

"Vincent is keeping her? How does she not know where she is?" Kai's lips pressed into a thin line and his brows pulled low.

"This is all we know," Aiden said. "She sent that to both Riley and me a few days ago. From the way it's composed, she might have had more to say. There's no period at the end."

The professor hummed. "I now understand why you asked for his room assignment if there was suspicion, but I don't see the connection, given the email is from days ago." She motioned toward the phone in Riley's hand.

"Well, it first started with a bracelet he wore."

"A bracelet?" Mera asked.

"A bracelet I gave Lukas for his birthday that he let Blaire wear."

Mera pursed her lips. "You're sure it's not one of similar design?"

"I had the leather embossed with a custom design."

"Ah."

"Anyway, Vincent had it on in class one day. I already had a weird feeling about him, but that had me really suspicious. After that, Seth and I caught him going into the administration building."

Professor Velastra sat up in her chair. "He has no business in there. Are you sure?"

"It's true," Seth said. "And it's not the first time. Lukas has seen him go in there, and we've seen him go a few more times since we started watching him. Don't know what he's doing, because he'll disappear for hours, and sometimes we never see him come out, but he's going in there, alright."

The professor stood, her expression giving nothing away as to her thoughts on what they were saying as she crossed to the window, looking out toward the administration building. "Is that all?"

"No," Aiden said. "Once we saw him go there, we came to you about his room assignment because we wanted to ask his roommate for any information we could get."

"And?" She turned from the window to face him.

"He hasn't seen Vincent since just before Blaire disappeared." He shook his head. "He hasn't been staying in his room at all."

Kai crossed his arms and arched a brow. "Where is he sleeping, then? Even without the email from Blaire, this all seems suspect." He glanced over at Riley. "But having Blaire reach out in such a manner…"

"That's all we know, man." Aiden rubbed the back of his neck and let out a heavy sigh. A weight lifted from his shoulders through sharing this with everyone now. Sure, Lukas didn't know what was going on yet, but it gave him great relief to know he wasn't being paranoid or seeing things that weren't actually there to support the theory that Blaire hadn't abandoned all of them.

"And don't forget Clarissa," Riley said.

"What does Miss Moretti have to do with this situation?" the professor asked.

"Well, we don't know if she has anything to do with Blaire's disappearance, but we've seen her visiting Vincent a lot," Aiden said. "We all know she doesn't need tutoring."

Riley rolled her eyes.

"I wouldn't be so quick to write off her potential involvement," Kai said with a sour expression. "The girl has practically been trying to replace Blaire from day one." His nose wrinkled as his face scrunched in a sneer of disgust.

Kai took the Korrena bond seriously, and the way Clarissa walked all over it and treated Lukas like a shiny new toy had rubbed Kai the wrong way from the start. Regardless of his personal feelings, he was absolutely right. Lukas even told Aiden himself that Clarissa proposed replacing Blaire.

"She did suggest being Lukas's compatible pair."

"She did what?" The professor narrowed her gaze on Aiden and crossed her arms as she stood in front of the window. The morning sunlight coming in behind her made her more of an imposing figure than she actually was, even with her sky-high stilettos.

"The girl has been trying to get in Lukas's pants since Blaire disappeared," Seth said.

"Probably even before that," Riley muttered under her breath. "She latched onto him from the first day she showed up in class. No tact. No sense of awareness. She was told on day one that Lukas and Blaire were a Korrena pair, but that didn't stop her."

Aiden sighed. "She suggested not too subtly that she could give him what Lukas lost with Blaire, and she has since spent weeks trying to wear him down. He complains about it all the time and tells me what's happening between them." Frowning, he shook his head. "Well… not between them… but what she's tried to initiate between them." He scratched at his jaw. "He tried to change rooms, but he can't seem to get anyone to move him."

The professor frowned. "Yes, I tried to push for a transfer, but they denied the request. They weren't too polite about the denial either. It is likely Angelo Moretti didn't want to deny his daughter the roommate she wanted, if what you say is true about her extreme attachment to Lukas."

"That's putting it nicely," Kai said with a roll of his eyes.

Picking invisible lint from her silk blouse, the professor sat. "Right. Well, I will begin an immediate investigation to determine where Vincent is staying and where he has been residing this semester. Hopefully, I can uncover some information, but for now, I advise you all to continue as if you know nothing."

"What?" Riley sat forward and smacked the edge of the professor's desk. "We can't just abandon Blai—" Riley paused as Seth's hand came down on her shoulder. He squeezed gently, and she sat back with a sigh, whispering, "I'm not abandoning Blaire."

"No one is abandoning Blaire." The professor's expression softened as she looked at Riley. "I simply want you all to continue in class in the same routine as usual. Do not engage with Vincent in any way outside of the ordinary. This is imperative to not disrupt a proper investigation, one I will conduct in private." She glanced out the window toward the administration building. "If he suspects something, there's no telling what actions he may take if, in fact, he did do something untoward with Blaire. If he makes a move before we can find Blaire and get her away from him, we might not be able to save her."

"You won't be informing the Order?" Mera asked.

"No." Professor Velastra looked back at Mera with a shake of her head. "Considering how they felt about Blaire—the supposed opposition they had to Angelo pardoning Blaire—I feel it would create bigger waves than we're prepared to deal with."

Mera's brows pinched. "But what about Clarissa?"

"I'll also look into that, but it's not of foremost priority with her spending the next two weeks in Europe. That said, I think it best

Lukas remains in the dark for the time being."

"Why?" Seth asked.

"Until we know something for sure, he should continue as he has. Should he find out that Blaire did not voluntarily leave him…" She sighed, her face turning grave. "He will be out for blood. Until we know where Blaire is, it is important that Vincent remains alive."

"You think Lukas would kill him?" Seth wrinkled his forehead and stood from where he leaned against the back of Riley's chair.

Kai glanced at his little brother with a pitying look. "You don't understand how powerful emotions can be within a Korrena bond… After experiencing such a devastating loss—one where the bond was actually broken…" His voice was thick with emotion. Mera touched Kai's hand as a look of pain crossed his features, as if imagining it hurt him. When he composed himself, he spoke clearly again. "I would destroy anyone who had a hand in it, if it were me. And this is Lukas we're talking about. He's a lot less composed than I." He shook his head. "Lukas wouldn't hesitate. You saw what he did to that trash Blaire calls a stepbrother. Blaire was right there with him, and he nearly killed Caleb Wilcox in that alley the night he tried to take her away from Lukas." He curled his upper lip. "That had nothing to do with their bond. Further, it was before they had sealed the bond, intensifying his reaction tenfold."

"Shit." Seth tucked his hands in his jeans pockets.

Professor Velastra said, "As I said, you all need to proceed as if nothing is different. That includes any interactions you have to have with him as a teacher's aide."

"I'm waiting on his email to give me remedial sessions about my grade on math finals."

The professor looked at Riley and frowned. "I need you to attend if he contacts you about it. You can't make him suspicious. Keep your wits about you."

"I doubt he'll do anything to you, considering his tunnel vision on Blaire," Aiden said to reassure Riley, taking in her pensive expression. He hoped that was the case. The idea of being alone with Vincent made her nervous, but she'd been to his pre-exam tutoring sessions in the two weeks leading up to winter exams and nothing had happened. If she suddenly freaked out now and avoided him, he'd become suspicious.

"Hopefully, I find out something before you have to meet with him, but should it come, you need to go."

Riley nodded quietly.

"Now, leave this with me. I will contact you all as soon as possible. We can't allow this to linger. Knowing that email was from days ago"—the professor pressed her lips into a thin line—"means time is of the essence."

They moved into the hallway, Professor Velastra stepping out behind them.

"What do you plan to do?" Riley asked.

"A direct approach is best, considering how much time we've lost. We need to act quickly. I will find Vincent and shadow him as discreetly as I can."

"We've already done that a couple times," Aiden said.

"Yes, but I can freely move about without bringing attention to myself. He wouldn't find any suspicion in my presence moving throughout the school during the day or evening. You all are bound by schedules he would be privy to. If you aren't where you should be, it will raise red flags. Especially if you keep turning up where he is."

Riley frowned.

"Now, go. If you see me about, move along. I will reach out to you the moment I know anything."

35

Kidnapped

Sighing, Lukas rubbed his tired eyes as he made his way across the moonlit cobblestones toward the staff building, headed to Professor Velastra's office. He didn't know what he'd done now to be summoned right after dinner.

Despite his crippling depression, his friends refused to let his grades suffer further. They cornered him last week in an intervention, and both Mera and Kai held him hostage in their room, force-feeding him information he already knew to help him salvage his grades and pass the winter exams. It would have been easy to bail, but the concern on their faces made him realize something had to give. He couldn't live this way forever.

Well, he could… but not at the expense of everyone else, so he could at least keep his grades at passing. He did. He barely passed his winter finals, but he passed them, so he didn't know why he was being summoned to the professor's office.

Near the marble fountain in the courtyard, the cool spray caught on the camellia-scented breeze and misted his face. A chill settled as night descended on the courtyard. A cold front more in line with December had come in on the tail of the freak storms that passed through the area over the past couple of weeks. He pulled his leather jacket closed around his torso.

He'd rather be inside asleep than out in the chilly air.

Things that normally didn't matter annoyed him more and more these days. He thought having a couple of weeks' break from that nightmare who called herself his roommate would give his mind a much-needed vacation, but all it did was remove the convenient target he'd had for his festering agitation. Clarissa's unwanted advances, her constant need for attention, and her push to engage him in conversation at all times of the day and night allowed him to channel his irritation. She didn't seem to care that he snapped at her; it almost seemed like she delighted in his aggression. While it wasn't healthy, it was better than turning it inward like he had before and becoming numb to everything around him.

A large crow landed at the edge of the fountain, surprising him. They didn't come out at night from what he knew.

It hopped around before pausing and facing him. The silky black corvid tilted its head as if to ask a silent question, but that seemed ridiculous. He was too in his head. They stared each other down for the longest time before a smaller crow landed next to the first and buried its beak in its friend's neck, preening its feathers.

Mates.

Kai had gone on and on about how crows, like many birds, mated for life. Something about it being a romantic parallel to the Korrena bond. At the time, Lukas thought his obsession with dark gothic stuff fueled his ramblings, but seeing the two corvids bonding in front of him soured his stomach.

"Yeah… lucky you," Lukas said bitterly as he turned away from the fountain and increased his pace, his leather boots tearing through the yellow leaves that scattered over the cobblestones beneath his feet. He needed to focus, not get distracted by a pair of stupid birds that reminded him of everything he'd lost.

There wouldn't be much time to get his head straight though, because Clarissa would be back eventually, and he wasn't sure he was ready to deal with it. Her absence made him realize he hadn't been moving forward but simply redirecting—avoiding the pain that had him waking in the night and stealing his breath as he sat in the darkness of an empty room with sweat rolling down his body. He thought he'd gotten used to the nightmares, but they still wrapped their blackened hands around his throat and threatened to drag him into a never-ending abyss of agony.

His unspoken, and unfulfilled, vow to Riley and himself from weeks ago sat heavy in his stomach.

Pushing open the door to the staff building, he stepped into the dim lighting, shaking off the chill from outside as the warmth of the interior settled on him. Candles cast the foyer in a soft glow. He walked down the central hallway, sconces with candles guiding his way. Voices came from the end of the hall, but he couldn't make out anything they said. Did the professor have a meeting in progress?

Hesitating at her closed door, he distinguished Aiden's voice through the wood. It was hard to make out what he was saying to the professor because the book-filled room dampened sound so thoroughly, but he sounded agitated. Lukas rapped on the door with the side of his fist and everything went silent before the door was pulled open, revealing Kai's stoic face.

Kai stepped back, allowing Lukas to enter, and when he did, his stomach knotted. The room was filled with his friends, all with varying degrees of discomfort on their faces, except Kai and the professor. Their faces gave away nothing.

"What's going on?"

Seth shifted where he perched on the back of Riley's chair, and Riley glanced up at Lukas with concern as Kai crossed the room to stand with Mera against the bookshelves on the far left wall. When no one answered, Lukas's gaze moved to his best friend standing with his arms crossed in the center of the room. "Aiden?"

"Sit down, Lukas," the professor said calmly, gesturing to the empty seat next to Riley.

Lukas dropped into the leather chair and looked at the professor expectantly. When Aiden's hand came down on his shoulder, he tensed, on high alert. Something wasn't right. No one was speaking to him, and Aiden was holding onto his shoulder as if to anchor him in place. Had something happened to Blaire? No. He couldn't entertain that thought.

Professor Velastra stood slowly from her desk chair and moved to the large window that allowed bright sunlight to blanket the room in its glow. She clasped her hands in front of her before speaking calmly, as if she were reporting the weather.

"I've found Blaire."

Lukas jerked in his seat, the words creating a visceral response that he felt down to his toes. Every muscle in his body seized at once. Aiden's grip on his shoulder tightened as if to hold him in place so he couldn't leap up and demand information.

"I have investigated every lead I could find after seeing her message—"

"What message? What are you talking about?"

Lukas glanced around the room, then stopped his gaze on Riley as she held out her cell phone to him. Her hands were shaking, and her smoky blue eyes sparkled under the chandelier's light with unshed tears. Snatching the phone from her hand, Lukas stared at the screen, where a single line stole the breath from his body.

When he tried to get up again, Aiden leaned on his shoulder.

"What is this? What does this mean?" He looked at Riley, but she looked away, so his eyes moved to Kai and Seth. "What is this about your cousin?" He looked at the professor. "Was this really from Blaire?"

Lukas moved his gaze around the room as he asked questions that no one answered, and his anger grew with each second of silence. His head was full of static through a minute or two that felt like hours. "Someone tell me what the fuck is going on!" he snapped, his voice a sharp contrast to the calm atmosphere of the room. A calm that infuriated him. How could they all be so relaxed?

"Settle down," Aiden said in his steady voice. "This isn't helping. Focus." The pressure of his fingers gave Lukas something to focus on.

"The email sure as hell explains the bracelet," Seth said to Riley, drawing Lukas's attention.

A crease formed between his brows as he studied Seth. Apparently, he missed something. "What do you mean?"

"I saw Vincent a couple of weeks ago wearing the leather bracelet I got you," Aiden said quietly.

Lukas clenched his jaw, and he was lucky he didn't crack a tooth. "Why didn't you tell me?"

"I had to be sure."

The custom-made bracelet was unique. There was no mistaking who it belonged to. Lukas shifted, and the muscles of his jaw knotted as he resisted the urge to call Aiden out on the omission.

As if reading his thoughts, Aiden sighed. "I knew it was your bracelet, but I had to be sure my suspicions were correct, and Blaire hadn't just lost it during their tutoring sessions or somewhere on campus. I didn't want you to freak out and kill Vincent either way, because we needed to know where Blaire is."

Professor Velastra turned away from the window and looked at Lukas, taking a slow, measured breath before speaking words that shifted his entire world on its axis.

"Blaire is still on campus. She never left Blackthorn Academy." She glanced over her shoulder for a moment before returning her attention to everyone in the room. "Vincent has her in a room in the depths of the administration building on a sub-level with restricted access. The rooms on that floor are often used for diplomats when they visit because of the security of being underground."

"'Has her'?" Lukas jerked against Aiden's grip, forcing him to put a hand on Lukas's other shoulder. "What the hell does that mean?"

The professor sighed. "While I haven't seen Blaire directly, I started shadowing Vincent this morning shortly after learning of the email. I saw him take food into the building at lunchtime."

"I've seen him carrying food there too," Aiden said. "Lukas and Seth were with me one of those days."

"While that is strange in itself, considering he shouldn't be in that building to start with, I kept watching him. An hour ago, at the start of dinner service, he obtained two meals from the cafeteria and disappeared into the building again." She folded her arms across her midsection and tapped a finger against her slim forearm. "The most damning evidence of all is that I witnessed him carry out a box with vials of blood from the administration building."

"Blood?" Riley asked, forehead wrinkling. "How do you know, if it was in a box?"

"At sunset, before Vincent collected the dinners from the cafeteria, I witnessed him meeting with Angelo Moretti in the hedge maze. I could not get close enough to know what they talked about. However, when Angelo opened the box, I saw the vials."

She waved a hand and lowered herself into her chair again. "I assume it is Blaire's blood, and Vincent is giving it to the Order in exchange for their silence and a secure location. It makes the most logical sense, based on circumstances surrounding their desire to study Blaire's blood, the email message, and Vincent's behavior. Though I have to question whether the remaining council members are aware of this or if it is just a deal between the head of the Order and Vincent alone, but it matters not."

Lukas vibrated in the chair in his fury, gripping the armrests so tightly he thought he'd splinter the wood or break his nails clean off his fingers. If not for Aiden's hands anchoring him in the seat with a firm grip on his shoulders, he'd already be halfway to finding Vincent and ripping his throat out. "We need to get her now!"

"No." The professor's words hit like a slap in the face.

"No?" Lukas's eyebrows crashed together as he looked at her incredulously. "*No?* Why the fuck not?"

Riley repeated the question, her soft voice in acute contrast to Lukas's rage, "Why not?"

"It is likely going to be dangerous to infiltrate the space if Vincent is present," Kai said from his position against the bookshelves. He stood as if unaffected, his posture tight, but his arms folded over his chest and the hard lines of his face belied this.

Kai had softened since Blaire came along, too. Joked more. The beautiful human who was Lukas's pair had influenced the entire group. While they all had been friends before, Blaire's presence, and the struggle they went through—that their friends guided them through—brought them all together on another level entirely. In her absence, everyone was falling apart again.

Professor Velastra's window had a clear view of the administration building. The building where Blaire was being held against her will. Where Lukas had also seen Vincent taking food. *The takeout containers to her favorite Chinese restaurant…* Had he known then what he did now, he would have destroyed Vincent that day. He cursed under his breath.

Mera frowned. "It will be especially dangerous if Vincent has any council backing."

Professor Velastra nodded, her thin pink lips flattening as she folded her hands together on her desk. "We need to extricate her this week, because once he is finished with his remedial tutoring sessions, Vincent is making preparations to leave the country for Brazil. He had intentions of going at the end of the next semester at the end of June, but something changed the dynamic, and he moved everything up to the end of December, just after Christmas." She shuffled papers on her desk absentmindedly before sighing. "It's not a stretch to assume he'll take Blaire with him."

Lukas exploded out of his seat, pulling from Aiden's grasp as he thundered, "Like hell he will! I'll kill him!" He pushed past Aiden toward the door. He'd make sure that scum found a place in the afterlife today, even if it killed him in the process.

Kai and Seth stepped in front of the door.

"Move the fuck out of my way," he snarled, a growl reverberating low in his throat.

Aiden's large hand came down on his shoulder again, and Lukas snapped his gaze back to meet Aiden's hard eyes filled with concern.

"Do not make me fight my best friend," Lukas said through gritted teeth.

Aiden sighed. "You need to calm down to ensure Blaire survives this, man. I want to burn everything down too. Do you think the rest of us don't feel the same way? We all care about Blaire." He squeezed Lukas's shoulder. "She's made it two months, man. We'll save her. I promise."

Lukas deflated, but Kai and Seth remained on guard in front of the door as Aiden led Lukas back to his seat.

"How do you know he's planning to leave the country?" Mera asked, watching Lukas warily. He was glad someone was asking the right questions, because he wasn't capable.

"I spoke with one professor he is an aide for about his progress as a TA. I wanted to get a feel for his behavior and habits last semester by reaching out to each of the professors he assisted. One was forthcoming with the information. They were highly disappointed he would not be available the rest of the year nor the next semester. It would seem his move is to be permanent, and he plans to suspend his degree until a later date."

Seth cursed under his breath.

"That said, tomorrow night Vincent has a study group scheduled for three hours. That is when we will strike." The professor sat back in her chair. "Lukas, do not go to class tomorrow."

"Why not?"

"It's better this way. We can't afford to have you compromise the situation, and I don't think you'll be able to keep yourself composed should you encounter Vincent. At least tomorrow night, he'll be occupied. Then, and only then, can you join us."

"I'll rip his throat out," Lukas said with an eerie calm. He wasn't even about to deny the bloodlust that hummed in his veins. He didn't care who knew it.

Professor Velastra pitched her head in his direction, giving him a pointed look. "That is precisely why you should stay locked in your dorm room until absolutely necessary."

"I'll bring you meals," Riley offered.

Aiden looked at the professor. "I'll skip too, so I can stay with Lukas in his room to keep him occupied."

"Excellent. Let us all meet in my office tomorrow night at seven. We'll formulate our plan and make our move then. Until then,"—she looked at Seth and Riley, and then over to Mera and Kai—"those of you still going to classes proceed as if nothing was out of the ordinary. Aiden, keep an eye on Lukas, and no matter what you have to do to prevent it, make sure he does not leave the dorm under any circumstances until our meeting tomorrow night."

Lukas wanted to protest being kept under watch like he needed a babysitter, delivered meals like a prisoner, but it was for the best. If he left the security of his room, he would hunt Vincent down. The only other time he had ever felt this angry was when he nearly killed Blaire's stepbrother. But this oppressive poison wormed its way through his veins, and all he wanted to do was unleash it in the most primal way possible.

He had always known something was wrong with Vincent, but that he would go so far as to kidnap Blaire?

Lukas wanted blood.

36

Found

Tears ran across Blaire's temples and into her hairline as she lay on the bed, trying to calm down. She needed to get her emotions under control now that the room stopped spinning. She had become so used to Vincent feeding from her that whenever it happened, she simply detached from reality until it was over. She became a master at dissociation in her time with Caleb, so she found it easy to go back into her safe space far away when she needed to. But this time had been different.

When Vincent drank from her thirty minutes ago, he took more than usual, as if he couldn't stop. Fresh bite marks littered her neck, arms, and shoulders. She wished Vincent could close the wounds so she wouldn't be stuck with the reminders, but only Lukas was capable of closing his own bites on her skin. Vincent left her covered in marks that bruised and didn't heal well. Vincent said if she couldn't carry his Korrena mark, he would brand her in his own way.

In the last week, he'd become even more unstable than usual and even informed her he'd moved up the date they would leave for Brazil by half a year. He'd been getting paranoid that he was going to lose her, and he wanted to ensure she wouldn't go anywhere. She didn't know why he developed those thoughts, but they meant nothing good for her.

She turned on her side and wrapped her arms around her middle as she drew her knees up in front of her. It had been days since she sent that desperate email to Riley and Aiden, and no one had come for her. She had to accept her fate, because time was up. She couldn't stop the tears even if she tried.

Blaire pretended to be asleep as the handle on the door rattled. Vincent must have forgotten something. She didn't want to explain her tears and risk angering him.

Several voices filtered through the other side of the door, whisper-arguing. Easing herself into a sitting position slowly to avoid another rush of dizziness, she squinted at the door. Vincent had never brought someone back with him before. Her heart pounded frantically.

Was it the Order?

Was he taking her away now, and not going to his study group after all?

Blaire gripped her nightgown at her chest, pulling in shallow breaths. The terror sweeping over her didn't help the haze over her mind that lingered after being fed on. The room tilted as the locks disengaged, one by one. Once the final lock clicked out of place, the door burst open, slamming into the wall, knocking over a small side table, and sending a black vase with silver filigree crashing to the floor. Dark red roses and water spilled everywhere. Blaire startled, and then she couldn't breathe.

Aiden stood there, just inside the doorway, staring at her.

Her mouth failed to form words, and she wondered if she'd passed out from her anemia and was dreaming about the man standing before her. Lukas pushed Aiden out of the way and barged into the room, followed by Riley, Seth, Mera, Kai, and Professor Velastra. She had to be dreaming. After two months with only one person, the room now felt cramped.

Blaire's eyes gradually moved from Aiden to meet Lukas's green eyes glowing like the aurora borealis as he took in her appearance in the sleeveless silk nightgown Vincent forced her to wear. Hair mussed from struggling against Vincent earlier. Eyes red from crying for the last half hour. Bruises of yellow, green, and blue in various stages of healing down her arms from blood offerings for the Order. She looked a mess.

Her friends crowded between the furnishings to come closer to her, blotting out her view of the awful burgundy and black windowless studio she'd been trapped in for so long. She heard their breath. Smelled their clothes. It wasn't a dream. They weren't disappearing like many of her nightmares teased her with. Best of all, Lukas wasn't trying to kill her.

"You got my message," she whispered, her voice cracking as she moved her gaze to stare at Riley and Aiden at the foot of her bed. When Riley nodded, tears rolling down her cheeks, Blaire pitched forward, holding herself around her midsection, and sobbed. Her relief this was real was too much to take. Her shoulders shook with the force of her cries.

When Riley stepped toward her, her knees buckled, and she cried harder. Seth had to wrap his arms around Riley to hold her up.

Lukas rushed forward instead, reaching for Blaire. Panic flooded her system along with mental images of him entwined with Clarissa. As his hands touched her bare arms, she screamed, "Don't touch me!" She threw her fists out and hit Lukas on his chest, arms, and any part of him to stop his touching her. She didn't want him anywhere near her after what he'd done. He abandoned her and didn't want her anymore, and her heart couldn't handle being in his presence. His hands on her skin felt like burning brands, brands claiming her, and it was torture for her broken heart.

"Blaire! It's me!" Lukas pleaded, shaking her. "You're okay!"

"Stop! Don't touch me!" Blaire wailed as she jerked away from him, thrashing, and kicking her free leg.

When Kai pulled Lukas away from her, Lukas rounded on him and growled, "Back the fuck off."

"This may not have been a good idea," Professor Velastra said, looking at Lukas with furled brows. "I hadn't imagined bringing a pair together would result in this."

Still holding onto Lukas in a tight grip, Kai shook his head. "Something is obviously wrong,"—he glanced at the open doorway—"and we don't have time to address it. It's clear she doesn't want you near right now."

"Why the fuck not?" Lukas roared as he narrowed his eyes back on Blaire.

She pressed against the wall, ducking her head and squeezing her eyes shut. She couldn't face him. Not from fear that he'd hurt her physically, but fear of what he would do to her heart and how it betrayed her by racing at his touch. It still called to him. Still longed for him. Her body still reacted to his presence, and it was agony. She couldn't allow herself to reach for him, to want him again. He made his choice, and that choice wasn't her.

Blaire tried to pull in air, but it was a struggle as her eyes burned from the constant onslaught of tears. She pulled her knees up to her chest, the chain on her ankle tugging back.

While Lukas argued with Kai, Aiden approached the bed

cautiously, and Blaire stared at him with wide eyes. Tears tracked her face as she clung to the wall, as far from the edge of the bed as she could get, like a frightened animal.

"Will you come with me?" he said, his voice lowered to soothe and coax her.

Blaire's gaze darted over to Lukas then back to Aiden.

"I won't let him touch you. I promise." Aiden lowered himself to her level and held out his arms and waited. "Let's get you home, okay?"

Blaire glanced at Riley, who nodded encouragement, gripping Mera's hand as she remained slumped against Seth, who held her firmly against him. Mera remained silent, but her damp lashes revealed that what was happening in that room—what *had* happened—affected her too.

With a shaky breath, Blaire crawled across the bed into Aiden's arms, where he scooped her up princess-style. She wrapped her arms around his neck and sobbed into his chest as she clung to his body. The scent of his aftershave filled her nose, and her body relaxed. The comfort Aiden's touch brought—a touch she wanted—when she spent so long without being able to control who touched her, was monumental. Her body relaxed into his, and he pulled her tighter against him in a soothing gesture as he rose to his feet, whispering comforting words against the top of her head.

"Why the hell is she okay with you and not me?" Lukas snapped, his voice edged with pain. Blaire could feel his emotions, but barely. The broken bond teased and taunted her with what she'd never have again with him, and the loss shattered her.

Kai sighed. "Aiden is her friend. There's nothing to worry about."

Lukas growled. "I know that. But I'm her damn Korrena! She's *mine*!" Lukas put both hands on the back of his neck and squeezed.

His entire body moved with the heavy breaths he took. He was on the edge.

Blaire buried her face against Aiden and whimpered. Lukas's words made no sense. The bond had been broken. It was his choice. She hadn't wanted to lose him. The mark wouldn't have gone away if he hadn't wanted it to. He couldn't change his mind now just because they found her. It didn't work that way.

"The bonds broke—" Riley started, and Lukas cut her off with a glare. Seth stepped in front of her, staring Lukas down.

Before the tension in the room could get any higher, Professor Velastra clapped her hands, drawing attention to herself in the doorway. "We need to leave as quickly as possible." She glanced down the hallway. "We can discuss bonds, and Blaire's psychological condition when we get her somewhere safe."

The professor gave Lukas a pitying look. "Blaire has been through something traumatic. We don't know what happened, but something in relation to you has put her in this state. We will look into it once she's safe. Remain calm until then."

Aiden moved from the bedside, but froze when Blaire yelped and gripped him tight around the neck as the chain extending from the cuff around her ankle rattled and pulled taut, the blanket that had been covering it falling away. She clung tightly to Aiden, her nails scoring the back of his neck in fear of being ripped away from the security his hold provided by the chain that bound her for so long.

"He had you chained up like an animal?" Kai bit out indignantly.

Lukas cursed and paced the room, and another wave of fury swept through Blaire, projected from him. She sucked in a breath.

Moving back to the bed, Aiden knelt and set Blaire on the edge, prying her hands off his neck.

"Please don't leave me," she begged.

He shook his head and smiled reassurance at her. "Never."

He lifted her leg in his hand as the professor approached. When the professor tried to remove the cuff, she huffed a frustrated breath.

"It has two locking mechanisms. One lock is simple. The other? Not so much."

Seth moved to the bed. "I got it." As the professor moved out of the way, he pulled a small tool out of his jeans pocket and fiddled with the cuff.

"Where the hell did you learn to do all this?" Kai asked in awe. "First the locks on the doors, now this?"

Seth put the tool in his mouth and shrugged as he undid the cuff from Blaire's ankle, and it fell to the floor with a loud thump and rattle of chain revealing severe bruising and cuts from the metal biting into Blaire's skin. He put the tool back in his pocket as he stood. "Learned as a kid."

Kai's slender black brow rose as he studied his little brother.

Aiden promptly picked Blaire back up into his arms, and she wrapped her arms around his neck again. She'd stopped crying, but she still held onto him for comfort, afraid he would disappear, and she'd wake up from this dream to find herself halfway to Brazil. Her arms tightened, and he squeezed her lightly in return, reassuring her as he stepped out of the room that had been her prison for two months.

The nightmare was finally over.

Lifting her head to look at those following behind, she made eye contact with Lukas, and her stomach flipped at the pain in his eyes and the tightness that gripped her chest. She didn't know if what she felt was her own emotions or his, but the more time they were around each other, the stronger the feelings became. The proximity to Lukas refreshed the bond's empathic link, and the intensity scared her.

When Lukas's eyes started glowing, Blaire tucked her face into

Aiden's chest again, digging her nails into the back of his neck. He hissed and whispered, "Shh. It's over now."

The Korrena bond was supposed to be broken. How was this happening?

Blaire lifted her head as they stepped out into the crisp night air. A gentle breeze blew yellow leaves all around the courtyard, and she shivered from the biting chill against her exposed arms and legs. Aiden pulled her closer. Her eyes scanned her surroundings intently. The sound of the fountain in the distance soothed her, and the sweet smell of lemony camellias on the breeze was a refreshing change from the staleness of being in a closed off room for so long—even if Vincent kept bringing flowers into the space. After being trapped for so long, the sights and smells outside overwhelmed her. Sadly, she had little time to appreciate it.

"We have to hurry. It's not safe to linger in front of the administrative building like this," Professor Velastra said.

Aiden shifted Blaire in his arms as the group took off at a fast pace toward the staff building across the way.

37

Truth

The world was spinning. The nightmare was presumably over, yet it was ongoing. The reality of it twisted Blaire's stomach in knots as she held onto the only certainty: Aiden wanted her once, but had become a protector and comforting friend, and he was right here with her.

"Sit her down over here," Kai's voice called from farther in the room.

Blaire lifted her head and glanced around. They were in Professor Velastra's office. The wholesome smell of old books and vanilla stood in acute contrast to the rose perfume trying to mask the staleness in the room Vincent had forced her to call home for two months.

As Aiden moved farther into the room, she caught sight of the worried faces of those who had quickly become her friends in the time she spent at Blackthorn. Shame made her bury her face against Aiden's chest once more when she was left to face the fact that she had doubted they cared about her. Could they blame her, considering how long it took to be found?

Still, the reality of her captivity didn't soften how terrible it felt to have not trusted them.

When Aiden lowered Blaire into one of the familiar leather chairs in front of Professor Velastra's desk, her gaze collided with Lukas's. The pain swirling in those green depths she hadn't seen in so long, laced with a rage she could feel thrumming through her veins from the empathic connection reigniting between them, made her grip Aiden's neck again hard enough to make him hiss in pain and curse under his breath. He hesitated before standing upright and pulling her into his embrace again, looking at Kai with a grimace.

"What's wrong with her?" Riley asked from the corner of the room, moving toward Blaire warily. Seth closed in behind her, watching Blaire hold on to Aiden like a frightened child.

Professor Velastra crossed her arms and frowned. "I don't know what happened in that room, but just looking at Blaire's physical state, it's not surprising she's traumatized."

"Yeah, but why is she clinging to Aiden like he's the only person in this room who wouldn't hurt her?" Seth said, before looking at the others, who all held equally hesitant expressions lined with a mixture of pity and pain.

Blaire couldn't handle it. She didn't believe any of them would hurt her, but whenever things got tough since she joined Blackthorn Academy, Aiden has been there to protect her. "I'm sorry," she mumbled against Aiden's t-shirt.

Aiden finally sat in the chair with Blaire in his lap and pulled her closer, cradling her in his arms as the professor passed a throw blanket she kept behind her desk to him to cover Blaire, who still wore only an emerald green nightgown. "You have nothing to apologize for. We're just worried about you. You know none of us would hurt you, don't you?" His dark green eyes searched hers for the truth, and she slowly nodded. "Then we understand. At least that much." He shifted his attention to Lukas and mouthed, "I'm sorry."

Blaire burrowed into his hold, looking around the room in silence.

She flinched when a small, warm hand touched her shoulder.

She met Riley's tear-filled eyes where she knelt on the floor in front of the chair. Blaire turned in Aiden's lap and leaned forward into Riley's embrace. As Riley's sobs echoed in the room, she trembled against Blaire. Her best friend seemed almost as broken as she was.

After several minutes, Riley's cries quieted, and she pulled back to look at Blaire. "I've missed you." She stood and Seth immediately pulled her into his arms, moving to sit in the chair next to where Aiden still held Blaire in his lap, pulling Riley down into his own lap.

Professor Velastra locked the office door, gave Lukas a long look as he gripped the side of one of her bookshelves with white knuckles, and then crossed to stand behind her desk. "We have a couple of hours before Vincent discovers Blaire is missing."

"He won't get the chance," Lukas growled, turning toward the door.

"What are you doing?" Mera said.

"I'm going to end this now," he said in an eerily calm voice.

"Lukas, no." Mera stepped in front of him to block the door, and when Lukas growled at her, Kai crossed the room and shoved him back. "Enough."

"It isn't necessary, anyhow." The professor's voice cut over the tension in the room, and Lukas swung his narrowed gaze at her. "Security is already in position to apprehend him after he makes the discovery."

Mera raised a perfectly sculpted eyebrow. "Why not take him now?"

"From my understanding, when I briefed security on the situation this morning in preparation for tonight's events, they want to gather additional evidence on him once he realizes she's gone. What actions he'll take. Blaire's physical state alone is enough to warrant investigation, but I won't begin to try to understand their methods."

The professor sat in the large leather chair and sighed. "For now, Blaire should stay here until we meet with the Order regarding this situation. Once statements are made, and evidence is collected, the protocol should have Vincent forced into a trial before the Order's council. As for what will happen, I am unsure. I've never experienced a council trial related to a crime of this magnitude."

Blaire watched her friend sitting in Seth's lap as he stroked the back of her head soothingly, noticing how tired she looked. She always had the brightest expression, and even when angry or sad, her eyes sparkled and her skin glowed. But what greeted Blaire tonight made her heart sink. Riley was missing her trademark punk rock princess makeup, revealing paler than normal skin, like she hadn't been outside in a long time, and she had raccoon eyes with heavy lines beneath them. When Riley offered that cheesy, toothy smile that made Blaire so happy to see, despite her eyes glistening as tears returned, Blaire's chest tightened.

"Lukas," the professor said. Lukas stepped away from Mera and Kai at the doorway. "There is a bedroom down the hall that locks from the inside that you and Blaire can use until we sort out this situation. The dorms aren't safe, and there's still the other matter to work out regarding occupancy."

Blaire whimpered and shook her head rapidly as her hand fisted Aiden's t-shirt at his stomach. The professor raised a brow at her, but she couldn't explain what she was feeling.

Frowning, the professor asked, "Do you want Aiden to stay with you instead?"

Again, a nod was her only response. Outside of apologizing, she hadn't had the strength to say much else. She reached her hand out to Riley again.

"I'll come too. Would you like that?"

Blaire cleared her throat as Riley's small hand clasped her fingers. "Please." The word was a hoarse croak.

The sensations from the renewed empathic connection with Lukas overwhelmed her. She didn't want to share the truth of how devastated she was that Lukas had chosen another. Did they even know? Surely, they did. They were in the photos too at the cafeteria table. They didn't stop it from happening, either. Could she trust any of them? She pulled away from Aiden as her breathing picked up, and she blinked moisture from her eyes.

"Why the fuck do you want him to stay with you and not me?" Lukas demanded

Blaire flinched when another spike of anger flooded her senses. As much as rage radiated from Lukas, an undeniable sorrow beneath it confused her.

When they first were bonding, she had the time to get used to the slow buildup of sensing his emotions and eventually could control how it affected her when they fully bonded. But with this sudden surge of everything coming back at once—which shouldn't be happening if their bond was broken—she was having a hard time functioning. Breathing.

Aiden's large hand stroked her hair, and he whispered, "It's okay."

She furrowed her brow, not sure how he could tell she was distraught until she noticed her nails were cutting into his forearm, and her breathing was so shallow that she felt dizzy.

Aiden stroked her hair in soothing motions and asked softly,

"Why are you afraid of Lukas?"

Blaire had to say something. She needed to snap out of this. She'd been able to push through and be strong for weeks with that monster. Allowing this connection and this anxiety to do her in was insanity. Swallowing hard, she mumbled, "I'm not afraid of him."

"Then what's wrong?" Riley coaxed gently, rubbing soothing circles with her thumb on Blaire's palm.

"Lukas… he…" Blaire glanced at Lukas, who had his hands fisted at his sides, his brows narrowed, his expression almost pleading. The emotions radiating off of him were almost as confusing as his expression. Pain, anger, confusion… love. It was all in the look he gave her. But it wasn't real. Or maybe now that they found her, he felt regret for going to another? Maybe that emotion was buried under the rest. She took another steadying breath and looked at Aiden.

"He doesn't want me."

"What the hell are you talking about?" Lukas snapped, and Kai grabbed his arm, giving him an imploring look.

Aiden continued petting Blaire's messy hair as he shook his head slowly. "Of course Lukas wants you. Why would you think otherwise?"

Blaire's eyes welled with wet heat, and she shook her head rapidly before looking at Lukas again, taking in the pain in his expression that overrode the anger at her words, and her stomach soured as tears tracked her cheeks. Tears she didn't even think she could cry, considering how much she had cried this night. "He wanted the bond broken," she whispered, but apparently not quietly enough for Lukas not to hear—his expression shattered. She flipped her gaze back to Aiden before this sick biological need that tried to force them together could fool her. Lukas was as much a slave to it as she was. He'd proven what he wanted.

Her gripped tightened on Riley's hand, and Aiden raised a brow at her with a look of confusion.

Mera stepped forward. “What are you talking about?”

“Vincent said the bond couldn’t be broken if both parties in a pair wanted it to remain… He… Well, he proved Lukas didn’t want me anymore by breaking the bond.”

“Lukas!” Kai called out as Lukas sank to his knees on the floor, shock and agony twisting his features.

“No,” the professor said firmly, stealing Blaire’s attention. “That is not how it works at all.” She pinched the bridge of her nose. “I looked into it after Lukas came to me when his mark disappeared. I hadn’t the information to help him then, but I’ve since discovered that to sever thc bond between pairs, a Vasirian must perform a blood ritual using forbidden runes. This severing will rid a Korrena of their mark.”

Riley looked at the professor. “But is what she said true? Is a lack of”—she glanced at Lukas and winced—“love on one side required for the ritual to work?”

The professor shook her head. “This has nothing to do with their feelings.” Turning her gaze to Blaire, she said with the utmost conviction in her voice that left no room for argument, “Any pair’s bond can be severed this way, Blaire.” Her expression softened as she tilted her head. “This ritual isn’t spoken of because it’s cruel. Vasirian in the olden days would perform it for marriages of convenience when families wanted their children to marry into other influential families. They would force the pair breaking.”

Mera gasped and covered her mouth, mumbling something about barbarism, but Blaire’s world was tilting on its axis. She didn’t understand. She stammered, “But… the… the photos…”

Riley sat forward in her seat, her hand tightening on Blaire’s. “What photos?”

The anger of betrayal rose inside her, confusion fueling it. She wanted to lash out. This was too much, and this new information the professor provided was throwing everything she believed for weeks into turmoil.

"I saw the photos of Lukas and Clarissa together in the cafeteria. She was all over him, and he just… He looked like he enjoyed it." She glared daggers at Lukas. "Laid back, eyes closed, while she sat in *your* lap like a bitch in heat. You kissed her!"

She snapped her gaze back at Riley, letting go of her hand. "Don't tell me you didn't know about the two of them," she bit out through gritted teeth. "I saw you all in the background."

The room fell silent as everyone shared uncertain glances with one another. She wondered briefly if she was being irrational. The emotions she felt, both from herself and Lukas, warred with her senses, coupled with the fact she was tired, hungry, and sore all over.

Professor Velastra raised an inquisitive brow and parted her lips to speak, but before she could, a strangled sob cut the silence as Lukas clutched his hair and bowed forward. He squeezed the back of his head as he cried in a way Blaire had never heard before, the sound slightly muffled by how close he held his face to his lap as he remained in a child's pose on the floor. His sobs rattled through his body as he caved into himself.

It was hard not to rush to his side to soothe him. Every muscle in her body tensed, her nerves firing in protest against her resistance to the lingering remnants of the bond. It had to be lingering remnants. With the mark gone, what else could it be?

"What?" Aiden shifted beneath Blaire and looked her right in the eye, his eyebrows drawn together. "Lukas has been so caught in his grief that he shut everything out. Clarissa has been forcing herself on him, but he never once reciprocated her advances. He's been trying to get away from her." He rubbed at the back of his neck the way he always did when uncomfortable, or trying to sort his thoughts, as he glanced over at his best friend. "I remember the day you're talking about, and Lukas didn't do anything. It was all Clarissa."

"He let her do it. How else would the photo exist?" Blaire muttered bitterly, before biting down on her lower lip hard enough to taste blood to keep from saying anything more.

Aiden brought his hand up to Blaire's chin to gently turn her face toward his. "He pushed her off him when *she* kissed *him*. He certainly didn't kiss her. Photos don't always tell the entire story."

"Blaire," the professor said sternly. "Vincent has manipulated you. I think it is safe to assume he took the photos if he is the one who showed them to you. He wanted you to believe Lukas abandoned you." She looked at Lukas on the floor. "But he didn't. He's been searching for you even though he thought you didn't want him anymore."

Lukas lifted his head and looked at Blaire with bloodshot eyes. "I stopped her so many times," he choked out. "She tried to come onto me so many times. Tried to sleep with me." He dropped his hands and held his fists in his lap. "She wanted to share blood with me! But I didn't do any of it. I love only *you*, Blaire. I would *never* do anything to betray you, even if you abandoned me. Even if you no longer wanted me. I still tried to find you." He took a measured breath, trying to calm down the gasping breaths he took as he laid his heart out. "You're it for me."

Blaire pushed the throw blanket from her legs to the floor and slowly stood on shaky legs from Aiden's lap. He held his hands near her body, a silent gesture of support to steady her should she fall in her weakened state. She looked at him as he stared up at her face. She could never repay the kindness he'd given her since they met, but she would always try. Placing a trembling hand on his forearm, she pushed it down so she could move forward.

She staggered over to stand in front of Lukas, who had returned to staring at the floor. The pain and defeat rolling off him choked her. Mera stepped aside, and as Blaire's bare feet came into his view, Lukas lifted his head to stare at her.

This broken man hadn't abandoned her. He hadn't given up on her.

Lukas sucked in a startled breath as Blaire collapsed into his arms on the floor, an agonized wail leaving her as she released all the pain and longing she felt for him in their separation. He held her tightly in his arms. Familiar arms that soothed her, yet held on so strongly he might break her. His shuddering cries against her hair broke her heart into pieces; his words of love muffled at her shoulder and incoherent.

She inhaled deeply and sighed. Apples. Spice. Citrus. Leather. Uniquely Lukas. Not a trace of the sour tang that accompanied his scent in the dream.

This. This was real.

After allowing Lukas and Blaire a moment to reconnect and calm down, Professor Velastra said, "Everyone needs to rest to prepare for tomorrow, because it could very well be dangerous. Especially you, Blaire. I will not ask you to relive what you went through yet, but you will need to share the information soon to solidify the punishment for Vincent Brandt. Lukas, take her to the room down the hall and help bathe and clean her wounds."

Lukas leaned back and looked at Blaire's face, that she was sure looked awful, a question in his eyes. When she didn't respond, he asked, "Will you go with me? Do you need…" He trailed off, his eyes flitting between Aiden and Riley briefly.

Blaire shook her head. "I need you," she whispered.

The professor pulled a first aid kit out from one of the bottom drawers of her desk and handed it to Aiden as Lukas stood, pulling

Blaire up with him as Riley pushed out of Seth's lap and rushed over to them. Lukas bent down and grabbed Blaire beneath the knees, swooping her up into his arms to carry her, and she wrapped her arms around his neck, breathing in the spicy apple scent that was a balm to her broken soul.

"Come on, let's take care of her," Aiden said as he strode forward.

Lukas stepped into the hall with Riley on his heels after Kai opened the door for them, and Aiden followed with the first aid kit in his hands.

38

Safe

Nudging the door open with his foot after turning the knob, Lukas walked across the hardwood floor to a queen bed pushed against the far wall in the corner. He placed Blaire gently down on the edge of the bed to rest on the black duvet and ran a hand over his mouth, trying to keep his composure.

He finally had her back.

Riley plopped down on the bed next to Blaire and curled her arms around Blaire's waist, snuggling into her side like a koala latching onto its mother. Lukas couldn't stop the smile that spread across his face when Blaire rested her head on top of Riley's.

Aiden stepped up beside him, holding the first-aid kit, staring at Blaire. Lukas rolled his neck. He didn't feel right. All of his muscles wound tight as he took in his best friend. He knew Aiden wasn't a threat. Knew that with as much certainty as he knew the sun rose in the morning, but try telling his body that. Instinctively, he wanted to snarl like a beast and force distance between them. His body hadn't caught up with his mind that it had Blaire back again, and he still felt bitter that she found solace in Aiden's arms.

"I'm sorry," Aiden said quietly as he stared at Blaire with an uncomfortable expression.

Blaire shook her head, and Lukas raised a questioning brow at both the apology and the guilty look on his best friend's face, the strain in his voice. Aiden had nothing to apologize for as far as he knew.

"I knew something wasn't right about Vincent, but I couldn't do anything, and you paid for it."

"Stop," Blaire said with a shake of her head. "You found me. I'm safe thanks to you, all of you."

Riley huffed, and Blaire looked down at her.

"Aaactuaallyyy...." Riley sat up straight. The mischievous spark was back in her eyes. "It was thanks to *me*." At Blaire's questioning look, she said, "Yep. I'm the one who saw your email. *Not* Aiden."

"Two days later," Aiden muttered.

"At least I saw it!"

Blaire snorted a laugh. The mood instantly lifted by Riley's playful side returning.

Lukas bristled when Aiden stepped forward and placed his hand on Blaire's head like he did before in the professor's office; something meant to comfort, but it grated on Lukas's nerves.

Aiden chuckled. "If anything, this has taught me I need to actually check my school email."

When Aiden's hand lingered on Blaire's head, Lukas growled, unable to handle it any longer. The urge to possess and show his claim on his pair won out over rationality.

Aiden's brows knotted briefly, but as Lukas stepped protectively toward Blaire, recognition crossed his features. Aiden was smart;

Lukas didn't have to say anything. For which he was grateful, because he didn't know if he could explain his need without losing the feeble grip he had on his self-control.

Aiden set down the kit on the bed and took several steps away.

Riley glanced between the two guys and blinked. "Um… I think we should get you bathed, Blaire." She stood. "Lukas, help me carry her to the bathroom."

"I'll be back first thing in the morning," Aiden said as he moved to the door. "Call me right away if you need me."

"Thank you," Blaire said.

Aiden opened the door and turned back. "Take care of her," he said to Lukas, his face etched with an emotion Lukas couldn't place. Lukas gave a sharp nod. He hoped his friend understood. If not, he'd have to explain later. In this moment, he needed to focus on only one thing, and she sat battered and bruised only a foot or two away.

"Lukas?" Riley said impatiently when the door shut, and his gaze moved from the door to her. "Bath? Help me?"

"Huh?"

"I figure a bath will help Blaire relax after everything."

Lukas looked down at Blaire, who nodded. She didn't stink, but she didn't smell like herself. He'd been picking up a scent he didn't recognize, and it set him on edge. A bath would wash away everything physically connected to that room they had found her in. He nodded.

He lifted her into his arms and moved her into the ensuite bathroom.

Once in the bathroom, he pulled off his leather jacket and then his t-shirt, laying it on the counter. "For when she's finished. I don't want her back in that."

"How caveman of you," Riley said with a snicker.

"Whatever."

He wasn't about to justify that with an argument. Riley needed the light mood as much as Blaire did, just as he needed to sever all ties to Vincent.

Only when he stepped out of the bathroom, and was alone again, did Lukas realize how agitated he'd been. As he scanned the room, taking in his surroundings, his shoulders lowered from where he had his back up earlier with Aiden.

An ornate Tiffany lamp stood on the small bedside table. A large Persian area rug filled the center of the room between the bed and a simple mahogany dresser with a large vanity mirror. He slowly pushed out a heavy breath and inhaled deeply through his nose, allowing the simple act of cataloging his surroundings to bring him off the ledge. The scents of the room finally reached him. Wood, cinnamon, and the jasmine scent that belonged to Blaire.

He dropped down to sit on the edge of the bed, resting his elbows over his knees. He hung his head forward, his long hair falling in front of him as he listened to Blaire and Riley giggling on the other side of the door. The sound was a balm to his soul.

Forever passed as he waited for them to finish. He had to stop himself from going into the bathroom several times. He wanted so badly to be close to Blaire after being without her for two months that his skin itched like a fiend.

When the bathroom door opened and Riley led Blaire out on wobbly legs, he jumped to his feet. Blaire paused at his sudden movements, staring at him, wearing nothing but his black t-shirt that fell to her mid-thigh. His tongue darted out to wet his lips as his mouth went dry. Her eyes tracked the movement.

"She's all clean!" Riley smiled proudly. Despite looking like she needed a six-hour nap, she was back to her spunky self.

Lukas stepped forward and lifted Blaire in his arms again. She gasped and threw her arms around his neck as he led her back to the bed to sit on the edge. He didn't want her to overdo it, even if it meant he had to carry her everywhere until she was steady on her feet again.

Riley yawned and stretched. "You want me to stay?"

"I'm okay," Blaire said, shaking her head. "Get some sleep. You'll be back tomorrow, right?"

"Absolutely."

Riley wrapped her in a warm hug that Blaire sank into, putting her arms around Riley's small body. "Have Lukas call if you need anything. I'll be back in my dorm." Riley went to the door. "See you in the morning." She blew a kiss and then shut the door.

Lukas let out a heavy breath, relaxing once hurricane Riley cleared the room.

He brought his full attention back to the broken girl sitting on the unfamiliar bed with hesitation in her eyes; waves of sadness and love poured from her unfiltered as she stared at him.

How was he able to feel her so strongly if Vincent broke their bond?

He sat on the bed next to her and reached up to gently run his knuckle across her cheek. "I missed you," he whispered, then leaned forward to press a soft kiss to her lips. At the taste of salt from her tears, he pulled back; she wasn't done crying. Her beautiful green eyes glistened in the dim light of the room.

"I thought I'd never see you again." She pushed the heels of her palms into her eyes.

She was trying to be strong after breaking earlier. He wasn't completely sure how he felt about that. Did she feel she couldn't let her guard down now that they were alone? Did she no longer trust him? She lowered her hands to her lap, fisted so tightly that her knuckles were white. He shook away the intrusive thought that would cause more conflict than anything.

"I missed you so much," Blaire whispered, looking at her hands.

Shoving aside his insecurity, Lukas reached for the first-aid kit on the bed. "You have no idea how much I've missed you." Standing, he helped Blaire to stand on unsteady legs, her too-thin hands gripping his bare shoulders for balance. His brows narrowed as he surveyed her arms. He hadn't noticed before—so caught in his grief and focused on the wounds—but she was thinner than before this all happened. Sliding his t-shirt up and over her head, he stepped back as she released him.

He wasn't prepared for the change in her. A strangled noise left his lips before he could tamp down his reaction. Blaire's chin quivered, but she didn't cry again, her arms folding over her breasts to hug herself. His stomach twisted, and a blend of anger and worry moved bile up his throat. Resisting the urge to storm from the room to turn Vincent into paste beneath his boot, he made himself face what happened to his Korrena.

He stepped forward and gently ran shaking fingertips over her right hip.

"Blaire…" he whispered, voice breaking on the emotion clogging his throat. He had her back, but for some reason, it felt like she was so far away.

She was thinner, though not sickly. The developed muscles she had when she first joined the academy had become softer and less defined, more like a non-athlete's. But that subtle change was not what bothered him; her posture, her body language showed an inhibition she never had with him before. When she looked away from his probing gaze, closing her eyes, his heart ached. Seeing her behave in such a broken manner decimated him to his core.

After several beats of silence, she gasped, startled by the growl he couldn't contain that had worked its way out of him. Her wide eyes followed his line of sight to where he inspected her arms, shoulders, and neck. He hated that this happened. Hated that her skin told such a harrowing tale. That he hadn't protected her from this.

The colorful bruising in various stages of healing that bloomed on her skin made his heart pound in his ears. Some were such a dark purple they appeared black, others a faint yellow. He wondered how many got through the complete healing phase; how many others had she endured and for what reason? His entire body vibrated with rage at what it could mean. Considering how slow she was to heal, it could be months before these physical reminders faded. His penetrating gaze finally settled on the thing he tried not to focus on the most.

The bites.

Markings that not only made it clear Vincent fed from her body, but some were so vicious that he'd left the rest of his teeth marks behind. The monster had torn into her flesh with more than just his fangs. Unnecessary. Brutal. Her arms, neck, shoulders, stomach, thighs…

He swallowed the dark thing that kept clawing at his insides. Blaire needed him.

With his gaze locked on a particularly nasty wound on her thigh, he asked the question that had been burning the back of his skull. "Did he rape you?"

Blaire snapped her gaze back to Lukas as he lifted his eyes to meet her shocked stare, simmering with the knowledge that if she confirmed his worst fears, nothing would stop him from ripping through the door to hunt down Vincent tonight.

"No," she said with confidence. "He said he wouldn't force me."

Lukas snorted derisively. "Only forced you in other ways," he muttered.

Blaire's eyes sparked. He winced; that wasn't the most delicate way to say that. He struggled to think calmly when all he had on his mind was murder. Vincent needed to pay.

"Yes... But I'm okay now."

"What did he do to you?"

Blaire looked away. "Bit me. Drank from me," she murmured.

That much was obvious. He didn't want to push her, but if Vincent didn't rape her, how had she come to such a state?

"Why are you so... injured?"

"I tried to escape once. He was rough in how he picked me up when he caught me. And just other ways he'd move me around. Hold me down. Take my blood for the Order."

"Why'd he hold you down?" He tensed in preparation for the worst.

"I fought him when it became too much. He'd use his size to overpower me. He'd also hold me down to—" She shook her head.

"What?"

"Nothing."

"Blaire, don't." His voice cracked. "Don't do that to me. I need to know."

She bit her lower lip. "Kiss me. He kissed me."

Thumbing away a tear that slipped free and rolled down Blaire's cheek, he whispered, "I'm sorry." He wanted so desperately to rip Vincent's head off after hearing her confession, but he couldn't. He couldn't abandon Blaire when she needed him most.

He touched the puckered skin of a bite on her shoulder that wasn't as severe, and she flinched. "I'm just... Shit." He ran a hand over his face and dropped his arm limply at his side with a rough exhale. "I'm angry. At him, at myself for not finding you sooner, just... so much that I'm struggling with. I'm sorry. Please don't think it's you I'm angry with."

Vincent should have known he couldn't heal her. Only those in a pair bond could heal bite wounds, and for some twisted reason Lukas didn't understand, he only had the ability to heal the marks he inflicted on Blaire himself. As much as he would loathe moving his tongue over where another man put his mouth on Blaire, he would do it if it would remove those marks. But he didn't know if healing was possible anymore with their bond broken through that sick ritual.

Lukas suspected Vincent intentionally made the marks more savagely than necessary to lay some morbid claim. The worse the mark, the longer it'd last. The more likely to scar, especially without medical attention. He hadn't needed to rip her open as deeply as he had. That was the most twisted part of all of this.

He'd wanted to brand Blaire.

Lukas knew it instinctively. The sick bastard couldn't have a Korrena mark, so he created something all his own. He inhaled deeply through his nose and closed his eyes, praying the marks wouldn't scar. He didn't know how he could face permanent reminders that another man tried to take Blaire away from him. She belonged to him. Just as much as he belonged to her.

When she looked up at him with flushed cheeks, he knew she felt that way too. When her tongue wet her dry lips, he couldn't hold back. Her need was so strong he could taste it.

He gripped the back of her head, his fist twisting into her wet hair as she pawed at his body, her fingers seeking something to hold onto as if afraid he'd disappear. The emotion mirrored his own so strongly he didn't question for a second that she shared his thoughts.

Letting go was not an option.

She whimpered against his lips as his fingers tightened in her hair, before the soft sound faded into a gasping moan as he pressed his hips against her to soothe the ache, his fingers loosening in her hair to avoid hurting her. She still felt so soft against him. He needed every point of contact he could get. He'd been denied the sunshine and warmth her presence brought to his life for far too long.

When his hand moved down her arm and she flinched and hissed in pain, he froze. Pulling away, breathing heavily, he ran a hand over his face. "Shit. I'm sorry. I shouldn't have... Now isn't the time for this."

Blaire sniffed and hugged herself tightly. "I'm sorry. I should have listened to you."

Lukas's mouth parted as he stared at her in confusion. "Listened to me? Blaire, you have nothing to be sorry for." He wrapped his hands gently around her upper arms and looked deep into her watery eyes. "This isn't your fault."

"You knew he wasn't right. I didn't listen. If only I'd listened."

Her words shook him. Did she really think he blamed her?

He pulled her down to sit on the bed, kneeling in front of her. "You couldn't have known his intentions. No one could. Even I didn't think he was capable of... *this*," he said, grinding his teeth on the last word. Blaire hung her head as Lukas rummaged through the first-aid kit, muttering curses under his breath.

"What is it?"

"We really need a nurse to look at you. But it's not safe ye—"

A knock on the door cut him off. He unfurled to his full height and grabbed the throw blanket draped over the foot of the bed, passing it to Blaire to cover her naked body. There was no telling who was on the other side, and he was itching with the need for blood. For a fight. After ensuring Blaire was appropriately covered, he opened the door, and then deflated with a heavy exhale. Just Mera. Riley's head popped out behind her.

"Riley said you might need me." Mera stepped into the room, not waiting for an invitation. "Professor Velastra said that until Vincent is apprehended, it would be wise not to inform the staff of your whereabouts."

Lukas shook his head. He'd completely forgotten Mera was studying for a career in the health field. This entire situation had scrambled his head, and he couldn't keep track of anything.

"I thought you were going to bed?" Lukas asked Riley, who skipped over to Blaire, sitting down beside her again.

"Thought about it. Decided against it." She shrugged.

Mera asked Blaire, "Will you let me take care of you for now?"

Lukas tilted his head as he looked between the girls. It was the first time he'd seen Mera so unsure. She always presented a confident front, so seeing her wringing her hands and hesitating surprised him. Though with Blaire so afraid earlier, it made sense Mera would hesitate to touch her without consent.

Blaire nodded, lowered the blanket from her shoulders, and set it aside so Mera could see what she was working with. Lukas's jaw clenched at the sight. He'd have to work hard to school his responses to the bite marks and bruising to avoid upsetting Blaire through their empathic connection.

Mera moved to sit next to Blaire, shifting the first-aid kit farther onto the bed, placing a few items she'd brought into the room with her alongside it. Her analytical eyes moved over the markings, betraying no emotion as she remained professional in the face of her friend's injuries.

Her eyes lingered on the bite on her inner thigh before she moved her gaze up to meet Blaire's. "For now, I just want to disinfect the wounds, apply ointments to assist with healing, and bandage any wounds that are open enough to be susceptible to infection by being exposed. Riley said she already bathed you, so now would be the best time to do that. While they are clean; before bacteria can settle in."

"Do you think they'll scar?" Worry creased Blaire's brow as she bit her lower lip.

Mera looked up from where she was prepping the gauze on the bed. "A few wounds are concerning." She glanced at Blaire's thigh again. "But I will do what I can to give them a fighting chance at healing properly. After this is over with, you'll need to go to the medical wing for an exam. As long as we continue a thorough aftercare regime, I think you at least stand a good chance of avoiding scarring on most, if not all, wounds."

Blaire leaned back on the bed, posting her arms behind her, her hands splayed flat on the bed so Mera had full access without making Blaire stand. She hissed at the sting of the disinfectant on the marks that were fresh, glistening with fresh blood that seeped out.

When Mera moved to her thigh, Blaire whimpered in pain.

Mera sighed. "I wish I could make it hurt less, but I have to be thorough in cleaning to avoid infection."

Blaire shook her head. "Trust me, this is a cakewalk compared to the last several weeks." Her nervous laugh cut off abruptly at the sound of Lukas growling from where he stood leaning against the door, arms crossed over his chest.

"Knock it off," Riley chastised.

Once Mera finished bandaging the last wound that required it, she stood from the bed, packing everything away as Blaire sat up. "I'll leave some cut gauze, medical tape, and ointment for you. The next time you bathe, apply fresh ointment and re-cover any wounds that haven't scabbed over. Try to keep the scabbing moist, as that will reduce the likelihood of scarring." Her brows lowered as she seemed to think of her next piece of advice. "Oh, and don't pick anything.

It'll itch as it heals, but if you pick at scabs, you won't allow for proper healing. New skin needs to form in peace."

Blaire pulled the throw blanket back over her shoulders, wrapping it around herself with a small smile. "Well, thank you Doctor Gibson." She laughed softly, and Lukas relaxed at the sound.

"Doctor Gibson was my grandmother. I don't plan on becoming a doctor."

Blaire snorted a laugh. "It was a joke."

"Oh, I know. I apologize. I'm just…" She looked back down at Blaire and tilted her head, considering her words. "It's been difficult with you gone. I think we're all a bit on edge."

Riley frowned and snuggled into Blaire's side.

That was as much of a confession of care for Blaire as any he'd heard from Mera. He'd hardly seen Kai or Mera during all this, so he didn't know that Blaire's absence had affected them, but it was easy to see now. Mera was always difficult to read, but there were small things she did and said since finding Blaire that gave away her concern. Hearing her now, he was sure he'd seen tears in her eyes earlier.

Blaire swallowed and nodded. "I'll take care of everything. Thank you, Mera."

With a sharp nod, Mera walked across the room to the dresser and lined up the items Blaire would need to tend to her wounds. She looked over at Lukas. "Make sure she does what is needed."

Lukas grunted and stepped away from the door as Mera approached.

"Okay, *now* I'm going to sleep." Riley stood and chased after Mera.

Once they exited the room, Blaire sighed. "I feel so bad that everyone suffered over this."

"Why? It's not your fault. The reason everyone is like this is because they care about you." Lukas crossed the room to stand in front of Blaire.

Reaching out, he pulled the blanket from her shoulders and tossed it to the foot of the bed. "We should get some rest." He turned and bent down, pulling off his boots and socks. When he turned back around, Blaire was staring at his naked torso, her face unreadable. He shifted, scratching his stomach absentmindedly as nervous uncertainty filled his gut. Would she want to be close to him? Should he have had Riley sleep with her instead?

Clasping her hands between her knees, Blaire looked down at the floor, whispering so softly he barely heard the words. "The pictures really weren't true?"

Lukas sucked in a sharp breath as pain rushed over his body that he knew wasn't his.

"Blaire, no." He knelt in front of her again. He reached to take her hand.

"No other woman could compare to you. Trust me. Clarissa tried. She wanted to replace you." He stood, guiding Blaire back onto the bed on her back, allowing her to rest her head on the pillows. "She even wore your perfume, but it's not the same." He shook his head as he crawled over Blaire, dragging his nose over her stomach, breathing in her intoxicating jasmine scent that was natural. It wasn't only her perfume that carried the jasmine fragrance. "No one could ever compare to the real thing."

"Lukas...."

Swallowing the desire that coiled in his stomach, Lukas lifted from Blaire's body. It took all his self-control to move away from her, but he managed. He pulled off his jeans, followed by his boxers, revealing how her proximity affected him.

"Under the covers," he rasped.

Blaire swallowed thickly, scooting up to pull the covers from beneath her and slipped under. He pulled the cover back enough to climb into the warmth with her, and she immediately latched onto him, hooking a leg over his thigh, laying her arm across his chest to put a hand on the side of his neck. The fact that she craved his closeness soothed him. Reassured him he hadn't lost her. But a tension thrummed between them that he couldn't place.

When she kissed his shoulder, he squeezed the arm across his chest to stop her.

"I want you so badly, but you're too weak." At her whimpering protest, he turned his head to face her. Her eyelids were half closed, and she almost looked drunk with exhaustion.

She was doing exactly what Professor Sinclair had said Blaire did in response to trauma: she was compartmentalizing what happened and redirecting toward sex. He wouldn't let her close in on herself that way. She was exhausted, but he could feel fear beneath the surface.

"You need rest. Tomorrow we'll straighten all of this out. I'm not going to leave you. This is not me rejecting you. You don't have to worry about that." He guided the hand that had been on his neck to his aching cock, groaning when she squeezed it in her grasp.

"Trust me, I want you," he said, clenching his jaw and grinding his teeth against the pleasure her strokes brought him. It took a herculean effort to remove her hand, but her needs were more important than the burning desire he felt.

Blaire snuggled into his body, resting her hand on his chest, releasing a contented sigh.

"I love you, Blaire. I'll never stop loving you."

He tried not to worry when she didn't respond, already asleep on his chest.

39

Aftermath

A groan left Blaire as a bead of sweat rolled across her forehead. It was boiling. She needed to wake up, otherwise she'd be caught off guard and defenseless when Vincent came to collect the latest offering for the Order. It wasn't like she did much to defend herself against him anymore, though, so what did it matter?

She sighed when her stomach rumbled. The spasm of hunger rippling through her belly left an ache she couldn't ignore. Slowly she moved to lift herself, but froze when she couldn't move. Heaviness pressed over her body, across her legs, and over her torso. Did he strap her down? Fear slithered down her spine. What had he planned for her now?

Didn't she… Hadn't they found her?

Blinking away the last dregs of sleep, she pulled the covers back to see a toned arm draped over her, a heavy leg tangled with hers. Releasing a shaky breath, she looked over her shoulder to see Lukas's sleeping face. She breathed again as her heart resumed its normal rhythm.

They found her. She was safe. Lukas was here.

Despite the heavy bags beneath his eyes that showed a lack of sleep, he looked peaceful and relaxed. In truth, it was the most relaxed sleep she'd had herself since Vincent had taken her. Being this close to Lukas soothed something inside that had kept true rest at bay. Perhaps it was the same for him.

A heavy knock sounded on the door, and Lukas startled awake, tightening his hold on Blaire to the point of pain. When she whimpered, he loosened his hold, staring at the door warily. She shrank in place, wary as well. When another hard beat sounded against the wood, he disentangled himself from her body. With quiet focus, he extracted himself from the bed, throwing on a pair of boxers.

"I won't let anything happen to you." His tone was lethal.

"Open the door, Lukas! It's me!"

Aiden.

Blaire deflated and pulled the covers over her head, cocooning herself in the bedding now that the space heater wasn't pressed against her. Lukas's apple scent was strong under the covers, and she wanted to stay buried in it for the rest of the day.

The room fell quiet enough that she drifted back into sleep. Lukas would handle whatever was needed at the door, and she could rest in the meantime, secure that he'd protect her. Besides, Aiden wouldn't hurt her. He looked out for her like a brother.

She didn't think of Aiden as a brother, per se. Their contact had been too intimate in the past for her to feel comfortable with that label, but he was the closest thing she'd ever had to a protective older brother. What she had so desperately wanted from Caleb before he became a monster.

Nevertheless, their contact was deliberately innocent.

After she rejected him as a romantic partner, Blaire never allowed gestures that could cross the boundaries into anything more. Even when she sat in his lap last night, hand twisted in his shirt, nestled in his embrace, she sought only the safe haven he provided as a friend. So, part of her accepted him as a brother. She hoped one day his Korrena would reveal herself to him so he wouldn't be alone anymore. He deserved to know what that all-consuming love felt like.

Hearing Lukas pad back into the room, she sat up groggily, rubbing her sleep-crusted eyes.

Someone cleared his throat near the door. She snapped her attention toward Aiden and Seth standing behind Lukas. She gasped and pulled the cover over her bare breasts as Seth laughed and Aiden rubbed the back of his neck, trying to look anywhere but at her directly. A red flush tinted his cheekbones.

"What's so funny?" Riley shoved past Seth and made him stumble, barging into the room like she owned the place. He growled at her, but she poked him in the ribs, unperturbed by his annoyance with her. She held a couple of bags in her hands. "Thought you both would like fresh clothes," she said with a cheerful smile as she approached, setting the bags on the foot of the bed.

Despite the bright smile she offered, she couldn't hide the shuffle of her feet, or the dullness in her complexion—all signs that she didn't sleep well last night, if at all.

Aiden held out a blood packet, bottle of water, and a wrapped biscuit to Lukas. "Figured you'd need something for breakfast." Lukas grunted his thanks as he looked between Blaire and Aiden. He still seemed on edge, but not as bad as last night. She felt his jealousy and conflict through their lingering empathic connection, but she didn't fault him for it.

"I'm gonna get changed." Lukas walked over and kissed Blaire on top of her head. Taking the proffered bag from Riley, he disappeared into the ensuite.

Flopping down on the foot of the bed, Riley rubbed her eyes and rolled her shoulders before turning toward Blaire. "How are you feeling today?"

"Drained. Numb. Is that normal?"

"I've never been kidnapped before, but maybe it's because you know you're safe? Like, your body is letting go?"

Blaire frowned. "Maybe. It just feels like I couldn't cry anymore if I wanted to."

"I think I've cried enough for both of us since you disappeared." Riley offered a lopsided grin. "Think we could use a break, yeah?"

Blaire smirked. If only she could turn it all off, but her emotions simmered under the surface. The temporary balm of numbness would wear off too quickly. She sighed, trying to brush back the rat's nest of matted hair that looked like she'd stuck a finger into an electrical outlet. She shouldn't have fallen asleep with her hair wet, but she had been too exhausted to care.

Seth held out a juice and wrapped biscuit. "Here. You look like you could use something yourself."

Her stomach rumbled loudly in response to the smell of warm egg and sausage that seeped through the wrapping paper. Her cheeks flushed, and Seth chuckled.

She groaned at the first bite. It'd been so long since food felt satisfying to eat. But she finally felt relaxed enough to focus on the flavor. The cheesy egg was fluffy like pillows and melted on her tongue, and the sausage was perfectly spiced. The biscuit even held the right amount of butter. Before she knew it, she'd devoured the entire thing, coughing as she swallowed the last bite. Seth opened her juice, and she drank greedily to clear her throat. "Thank you," she rasped.

"You must be starving." Aiden chuckled.

"Well, she has lost weight." Lukas stepped out of the bathroom, pulling down the hem of a v-neck black t-shirt that hugged his shoulders and chest. "Is that enough to eat?"

"Gee, thanks, I'm glad you approve of my new diet," Blaire deadpanned. "Yes, I've had enough to eat."

A knot formed between Aiden's brows. "What do you mean by that? She looks fine to me."

Lukas's hard gaze shifted back to where Blaire sat on the bed, finishing the last of her juice. Riley took the trash from her to the wastebasket on the other side of the room.

"It's not much, but she's slimmer," Riley said to her brother, frowning at Lukas. "I'm not trying to be insensitive, but maybe you're overthinking it?"

"No, I'm not. She used to be heavier."

Blaire's brows rose. "Heavier? You make me sound like I used to be chunky."

Lukas groaned and rubbed his face. "That is not what I meant, and you know it."

"Lukas, relax." She shifted to allow Riley back on the bed beside her. "I'm the same size I was when I played soccer. I had more muscle then, but I have been this slim. Once I'm able to move around freely, I'll put the muscle back on and gain a little weight from eating regularly again, and I'll be good as new."

She tried to appease his worry, but she wasn't sure it was working. He seemed so fixated on how much she wasn't whole that it made her uncomfortable. Would she ever be good enough for him?

If I were a Vasirian, this wouldn't have happened.

She bit the inside of her cheek at the thought. Lukas was likely already thinking it.

"Did that monster not feed you?" Aiden finally snapped, his face a portrait of unleashed fury. He had fallen silent while they joked about her weight, but he seemed to be taking it more seriously than she was.

Sighing, Blaire met his gaze. "He did. Constantly after the beginning. More than I could ever eat." She met Aiden's stare. "I just had no desire to eat." She tried to shrug it off like it wasn't a big deal.

"What happened to you?" Riley asked, moving up beside Blaire on the bed.

Aiden growled. "She doesn't have to answer that." Turning to Blaire, he stressed more firmly, "You don't have to answer that."

"I didn't mean to upset her by asking," Riley said with a frown.

"She's fine, just worried about me. Y'all don't know what happened, and if it were her—or any of you—I'd want to know, too." Blaire shifted beneath the covers. "Even if it's no big deal to lose ten pounds," she said pointedly at Aiden, who looked pissed.

Riley shook her head. "You don't have to tell me."

"I want to. I don't mind you knowing."

Lukas sat on the foot of the bed, his firm hand squeezing her knee over the covers. "What did you mean by 'after the beginning'?"

She looked at Lukas, avoiding the heat still lingering in Aiden's gaze. He was angry, of course, but she wasn't used to seeing him so on edge. That it was because of her made guilt flare to life inside her. A gentle squeeze pulled her away before she allowed that feeling to grow into something more.

"For the first two weeks, Vincent kept me in a drug-induced daze. I barely stayed conscious." She clenched the covers closer to her as Seth cursed again, and Aiden paced. "I have no idea how he took care of me, but after that long feeling sick and woosy, I didn't have the desire to eat anymore. Human stomachs shrink when we don't eat for long periods. Considering you guys need real food too, I'd suppose it's the same for you."

"He drugged you?" Lukas narrowed his eyes.

"Until I complied."

"Complied?" Seth asked.

"Stopped fighting him. Took a bath like he told me to. Wore the gowns he brought for me until I lost the privilege of wearing clothes…" She trailed off, realizing how bad that sounded.

"Privilege? Did he—"

Lukas's growl cut Aiden's words off. "He didn't rape her."

"I tried to escape. He caught me. Told me I lost the privilege of wearing clothes as punishment. He finally allowed me to dress again after a week of compliance. Eventually, I gave up."

"But why?" Seth crossed his arms over his chest, his steel-gray eyes focused on her. "Why would you give up?"

Riley's small hand squeezed hers.

Blaire glanced in Lukas's direction before looking at Seth again. "I thought Lukas didn't want me. Between the ritual and the photos, I couldn't deny the evidence." She released a shaky breath. "Add to that, thinking everyone abandoned me… That I was just going to live my life as some sort of blood doll to a psychopath… I didn't want to live anymore."

Lukas moved up to the head of the bed, and Riley crawled over Blaire to her other side. He pulled Blaire into his arms, kissing the top of her head. "Never, ever, believe that I don't want you. You're the most important thing in my world."

Aiden's jaw worked, and he speared his fingers through his inky hair, making it stand in all directions. "Don't you ever leave us." His eyes met hers. "You can't," he said, his voice breaking with emotion. Seth nodded, his eyes holding the same conviction before he disappeared into the bathroom. He didn't want her to go, either.

She had to look away from the intensity swirling in the depths of Aiden's eyes. How she'd become so important to their lives in such a short time never failed to surprise her, but it warmed her heart to know she hadn't been abandoned when enduring the worst moments of her life.

Lukas stood and walked over to the dresser, picking up his forgotten blood packet and biscuit, making quick work of them.

While Aiden and Lukas were talking on the other side of the room, Blaire leaned over the side of the bed and grabbed Lukas's t-shirt from the floor. Sitting up, she lowered the blanket, allowing it to pool at her waist before pulling the t-shirt over her body.

Seth cursed, and she looked up at him staring at her just outside the bathroom door.

"What's wrong?" Aiden turned to look at him.

Blaire bit her lip, and Riley put a hand on her arm. Riley had already seen all the marks her body held. Aiden and Seth had only seen her arms, really. When they arrived this morning, they must not have seen much before she covered herself. She shifted uncomfortably under the scrutiny of Seth's angry gaze.

"What is it?" Lukas stepped in front of Seth. "Why are you staring at her like that?"

"Lukas, it's alright. He just saw..." She sighed.

"Saw what?"

Blaire looked up at Aiden's concerned eyes. "Turn around." At his confused expression she sighed. "If you want to know what he's talking about, you'll turn around. You too." She looked at Seth. He didn't need to see her breasts a third time.

Once they'd turned their back to her, she pulled Lukas's shirt back over her head and positioned it to hide her nakedness, only allowing her upper chest, shoulders, ribs, and stomach to show.

"Alright."

Both turned around, but Seth immediately turned away again, walking into the bathroom with a curse. Aiden's eyes locked on her body. She could feel his stare burning on her skin as he took in her wounds. She didn't have to look into his dark green eyes to sense the war playing out beneath the surface.

Blaire knew she looked terrible. Even after Mera did her best to patch her up, hiding the worst of the wounds beneath pristine white bandaging, no amount of cleanup would hide the aftermath of what Vincent had done to her.

Growing embarrassed at the lack of response in the room, she pulled the covers back over herself with a sigh and Riley immediately latched onto her. She sank into Riley's embrace, resting her head against her friend's chest.

"We need to go see the professor," Aiden said through gritted teeth. "It's obvious there's a lot more to the story, and I'm sure Kai and Mera would want to know too. Professor Velastra wanted a proper report for the Order for Vincent's trial. Better to just tell it once so you don't have to keep reliving it."

"Trial?" Blaire's brows rose.

"Blackthorn Security apprehended Vincent last night. They've had him detained in the dungeons of the admin building ever since."

Blaire's mouth gaped as she tried to process what Aiden had just explained. "We have dungeons? Like, honest to goodness dungeons, with chains and bars?"

"Yep. Like out of a medieval castle," Riley said with a strange brightness to her voice. Who got excited about prison? Maybe it was the castle part. Blaire yawned. She was too tired to try to figure out Riley's quirks this early.

"It's mostly there for Vasirian awaiting trial with the Order before either being shipped off to Cresbel Asylum, or transported to Europe to face the Blackthorn Clan's judgment. Depends on their crimes, really." Aiden shrugged like he hadn't just dropped a bomb.

Blaire shook her head. "So let me get this straight." She sat up and Riley frowned, eyes drawn to Blaire's bruised and bitten shoulders before she could pull the cover back up. "You mean to tell me the council has a makeshift prison *on school grounds* that could put us all in danger?"

"To be fair, I don't think they really care," Seth said, coming back out of the bathroom. "You saw how they treated you. You're a student."

"Well, yeah, but y'all are their own kind… I'm human. I guess I sort of thought they'd be different with the rest of the student body." As soon as the words left her mouth, she realized it didn't make a lot of sense. The Order's minions didn't have any qualms fighting Lukas when they'd come for her blood.

"I don't think they care about stuff like that. Besides,"—Riley stretched her arms over her head—"we're Vasirian, so we're not as fragile as humans. It's not the same as a human university."

"Don't I know it," Blaire muttered.

Lukas sat on the edge of the bed and leaned over to tuck Blaire's hair behind her ear. "It's nothing to worry about. They keep the lower levels heavily secured."

"Wasn't I on the lower levels?"

"Yes, and no. You were on the first level, just underground," Aiden said. "The admin building has a secured basement floor for diplomats and other Vasirian of importance when they visit, but there's another section that is actually farther underground beneath the admin building. You can't access it from the diplomat floor. I don't know what all is down there, but it's well known there is a dungeon."

"With students not allowed in the building, not everyone knows what is even in there. We only know this much with the help of Professor Velastra," Seth added.

"How do you know all that then if students aren't allowed in there?"

Aiden shrugged. "Professor Velastra had a floor plan. Saw it before we went to rescue you."

Riley opened the bag at her side and pulled out a cornflower blue sundress with short sleeves. "Um... so... your clothes aren't in the dorm anymore. So, I went out this morning and got you this dress. Figured it'd be more comfortable than restrictive clothing."

"What? Why aren't my clothes in the dorm?"

Lukas and Aiden shared a look she didn't understand.

"What's wrong?"

Lukas put a hand over his mouth and closed his eyes, leaning forward with his elbow on his knee.

"Lukas?"

"It's Clarissa," Aiden said.

Blaire's hackles rose immediately.

Lukas dropped his hand and looked at Blaire. "They moved her into our room and put your things in storage when they told me you left the academy voluntarily."

"What?"

"I tried to get another room. Tried to stay with Aiden and Seth. They wouldn't accept any solution I proposed, and they wouldn't let me stay with anyone until they could transfer me. They said they couldn't transfer me." He closed his eyes. "Eventually, they said they weren't going to and told me to stop coming by the housing department. I think the Order had a hand in it too."

Blaire didn't know what to think. What happened while Clarissa was in her space?

Alone. With Lukas.

As if sensing her inner turmoil, Lukas touched her face. "I didn't do anything with her. She tried. I told you she tried. But nothing happened. I promise you this."

Blaire's shoulders fell; she didn't realize her body had coiled tight with tension until Lukas's words calmed her.

"So what happened to my stuff? Where am I going to stay?"

"Right now, Clarissa is at the sister location in Europe for some reason. She's supposed to be back end of this week—or next—I can't remember, but I'm not sure when. Until that time, while we try to sort this shit out, you'll sleep in my bed." Lukas leaned in and gently kissed her lips. "I'm not leaving you alone, and I refuse to not share a room with you."

Blaire nodded. Nervousness and uncertainty still lay heavy in her stomach.

Riley rummaged in the bag again and pulled out a long-sleeved black cardigan. "I got this to cover…" She gestured to where Blaire's bruised and bitten arms were hidden beneath the covers.

It warmed Blaire's heart to know her friend went through the extra effort to make her feel comfortable. She knew Blaire would want to hide how bad her arms looked. She smiled at Riley, feeling the hole that gaped in her chest for so long fill even more.

Seth bringing her food. Aiden being protective. Mera making sure she was patched up. Lukas being… everything. She sniffled as the emotions tightened her chest. She couldn't ask for better friends in her life. It took so long to find them, and she found them in a species not even her own.

"Hey, you okay?" Riley's brows pinched, and Lukas thumbed away a rogue tear that slipped down Blaire's cheek.

"Yeah, I'm fine. Just so grateful to have you. All of you."

Seth shifted against the dresser in apparent discomfort, his eyes darting to the door.

"We should get going," Aiden said, rubbing the back of his neck.

Lukas stood. "I'll be just down the hall. All you have to do is scream, and I'll come running."

Riley frowned. "I've got her. I'll flay anyone who tries to get in here." The gleam of malice in her smoky blue eyes gave Blaire the distinct impression that Riley wouldn't hesitate to inflict violence on any soul with less than righteous intentions.

40

PREPARATIONS

Rain pattered against the window of Professor Velastra's office, blurring the view of the administration building beyond the dogwood trees and floral bushes. Winter was the dry season, so it surprised Blaire to see rain in December. Somehow the sky knew the mood and responded accordingly.

No one had said anything since Riley led Blaire into the office and into the leather seat across from the professor's desk, taking the other herself. Everyone seemed hesitant to broach the subject, as if they were waiting on Blaire to spontaneously describe the nightmare of the last two months. She wished they would stop walking on eggshells and ask their questions. She was willing to share with them what she went through—had already detailed some things that happened to her with Vincent—but it wouldn't be easy to talk about all of the moments she shared with him in that room at the basement level of the administration building.

A rumble of thunder penetrated the quiet room, and Lukas

stepped up behind Blaire, placing his hand on her shoulder, pulling her from her reflection. She didn't respond to inclement weather the way she used to, but Lukas still gravitated toward her in a way that made her feel safe.

"I've called a meeting with the council." Professor Velastra sat on the large leather chair behind her desk with her legs crossed. She wore pressed charcoal slacks and a black chiffon blouse, and despite wearing her usual sky-high stilettos that peeked out behind the edge of the desk, the severity on her face said she was ready to go to battle. Blaire shook her head, trying to imagine the professor wielding blades and fighting dressed like she was made for corporate America. "I haven't informed them what the meeting is about, only that I have information on a few students who need administrative correction."

"What about Vincent?" Seth asked from his perch on the back of Riley's chair.

"They are in the dark about him. Security and I wanted to ensure he was detained and we could make a proper report before informing the Order. Confining a student in the dungeons isn't typical protocol. There was a concern the Order would release him then ask questions later."

Meeting the professor's stern gaze, Blaire's eyes widened marginally. "They would release him?" She shuffled in her seat and rubbed her hands together, scratching at her palm to distract herself from the fear that coiled around her lungs, threatening to steal the breath from her like a boa constrictor.

Lukas squeezed her shoulder then urged her to stand. He lowered himself into the chair and pulled her into his lap, wrapping his powerful arms around her middle to anchor her.

"Possibly, but for now, they are not aware of anything happening on campus beyond the status quo." Professor Velastra pinched the bridge of her nose. "Now, I know this might be difficult for you, Blaire, but I need you to tell me what happened to you. The more details you are comfortable providing, the better chance we have of formulating a strong case against Vincent Brandt."

"Isn't the fact that he kidnapped her enough?" Kai asked from where he leaned against the bookshelf with his arms folded over his chest.

"And he stole their bond away." Mera's black painted lips turned down at the corners and she furrowed her brows, discomfort all over her face. "Does she have to say more than that?"

Lukas gripped Blaire's thigh possessively at the mention of their stolen bond.

"Realistically, it should be enough. But as I previously stated, the more information we have, the higher the likelihood of his conviction. And,"—the professor pressed her lips together and looked at Blaire—"the worse his punishment is based on the severity and number of his crimes. I'm sure he's guilty of much more than just kidnapping and breaking your bond, yes?" When Blaire looked down at her hands in her lap, the professor hummed. She placed a small tape recorder on the desk. "I would like to record everything, so you're not forced to retell it in front of the Order members. You've been through enough."

"He deserves to die. Slowly." Aiden's voice rumbled from behind Lukas.

"Kidnapping is not an offense punishable by execution," the professor said with a calm detachment. "There would need to be more to sway the Order to act."

Blaire closed her eyes and sighed. She didn't intend to keep what happened to herself. It wasn't like she planned to let the entire school know, but the people in this room… they mattered. They cared. They wanted to know what she went through, even if they didn't say it. She could see it in the way they looked at the markings on her body before she hid them.

Knowing Vincent could walk away with a minor punishment for what he put her through made her stomach sour. He deserved to suffer like she had. Did she want him to die? She didn't have an answer. She'd always thought of herself as a compassionate, forgiving person. She would rather someone get the help they need and live a better life afterward, like Caleb.

Vincent needed help. His mind was twisted.

When she met him, and at the beginning of her stay with him, he hadn't seemed so delusional, but as he fed on her, he lost more of himself. The man needed extensive therapy and medication. But death? What purpose would that serve? Would that bring her satisfaction?

Kai, Aiden, and Lukas were debating about Vincent's death and the trauma telling the story would bring her. She was already traumatized—by more than just what happened with Vincent Brandt in an overly decorated room while chained to a bed. Retelling the events wouldn't change that. Whether or not it would bring his death, she needed to tell the story.

But she'd only tell it once. No sense reliving it repeatedly. Professor Velastra could give the report to Professor Sinclair, and Blaire would discuss it with her from there, because there was no way she wouldn't need therapy for this. She wasn't deluded enough to think she wouldn't need it.

Opening her eyes and looking around at everyone in the room, she shook her head, cutting off the argument. "Stop. It's fine," she said with a confidence she didn't realize she could call on.

The boys quieted down, and she began her tale. She relayed in excruciating detail everything that happened from the time she showed up for her tutoring session and was drugged, to the bond being broken and Vincent manipulating her, to his feeding and bloodletting for the Order, up until the message she sent and her rescue. When she finished, she was utterly exhausted.

She'd cried, raised her voice, fought off another panic attack, and now she felt comfortably numb despite the rage that burned in her veins emanating from Lukas. He'd been eerily silent the entire time she told her story, but he radiated pain and fury. Lukas wanted blood, and not hers. She glanced around at the others, trying to get a feel for what they were thinking, as no one was volunteering to be the first to respond—not even the professor.

Riley sat crying in the seat across from her, and Seth's jaw worked as he ground his teeth, sitting on the back of Riley's chair. His gaze captured Blaire's with its intensity, and reflected a restrained storm that promised vengeance on his cousin. Had Seth always been that way? She didn't remember him having such a volatile aura, but like a rubber band pulled taut, so close to snapping, he only needed a reason.

Mera was staring out the window, but the amber light from the chandelier reflected off shiny dampness on her cheeks. Kai held her in his arms, his analytical stare searching Blaire's face. She couldn't tell what he was thinking. Only the subtle clench of his jaw gave away that he might be uncomfortable.

"Fuck!"

Blaire flinched at a crash behind her, and she spun as Aiden's fist connected with the back wall, books scattered at his feet where they fell from shelves on either side of him. His shoulders heaved as he hung his head, his breaths coming rapid and heavy.

"I think..." The professor cleared her throat. "I think we have all we need." She clicked the button to stop the recording. Her russet eyes focused on Blaire, a faint glow illuminating the irises. She stood and gathered the recorder and some papers in her arms. "I'll make sure each member of the council hears this report so you do not have to explain that again."

"He's a dead man," Aiden said as he walked back to the group and looked down at Lukas, still holding Blaire in his arms. "Either you get him, or I will."

Lukas growled. "He's mine."

"No." Professor Velastra slammed her hands down on the desk. "Neither of you is going to put himself in a position to be shipped off to Cresbel Asylum, or, worse yet, executed for murder." She straightened, smoothing her blouse, and cleared her throat, gathering the items she'd put down. "Now, I understand you want your pound of flesh. I can't say I wouldn't want to take a go at him myself."

When met with several shocked expressions, the professor shook her head with a chuckle. "I'm not immune to emotion. What Blaire went through affected me, too. Even if Vincent is my student, what he did… Well, it's unforgivable. But all that said, you boys need to be smart, not foolish. I've told you before, Lukas, if you're gone, you can't protect Blaire. That goes for you too, Aiden."

The professor put the tape recorder and papers in her desk drawer and cast her stern gaze around the room. Whatever emotion had broken through her no-nonsense, take-charge demeanor had fled, and in its place, a calm seriousness had Blaire's attention.

"It will probably take a day or so for the members to listen to the deposition and formulate whatever plan of action they wish to take. As I said, it will likely result in a trial, and there are procedures that must be followed prior."

"So, we can't just go and deal with this now? How much longer is she going to have to suffer?" Aiden crossed his arms as he loomed over Blaire in Lukas's lap.

Professor Velastra placed her hands on the desk and sighed.

"Unfortunately, no. We have to follow the proper procedures to make as little waves with the council as possible. Again, it should not be more than a day or so. Until then, Blaire has the opportunity to settle in with Lukas."

Kai shook his head. "How's that gonna work? Clarissa is still in his room."

Blaire tensed in Lukas's lap, and he tightened his arms banded around her waist.

"Angelo's daughter is still in Europe. One of the things I intend to deal with after this meeting concludes is calling for an executive order from the council to have the room assignments changed now that Lukas's Korrena has returned. Protocol is to keep all pairs together."

Blaire sighed. "But we're not a pair."

Lukas dropped his head on Blaire's shoulder. While she hated to say the words aloud, they were true. Their bond was broken. Didn't that mean they weren't a pair anymore?

"Doesn't matter," he mumbled against the hair that lay over her shoulder. "You're still mine. We're a pair in every way that matters."

Seth's brows furled. "Can't you just fuck, and everything be—" His words died on a grunt and exhale of heavy air. "What the hell, Riley?"

Riley's lips pulled tight, and she scowled at Seth as he rubbed his ribs. "Don't be so crude. Claiming is more than that, anyway. Aside from *making love,*"—she cast another withering glare at Seth, and he just rolled his eyes—"they also share blood. It's the forming of a strong emotional connection, not just…"

"Getting off?"

Another elbow to the ribs.

"Fucking hell, woman!" Seth got off the back of Riley's chair and stalked across the room out of her strike radius.

Professor Velastra sat back and folded her arms over her stomach. "Despite his colorful, simplistic description, I don't see why you cannot perform the same claiming ritual to reinstate the bond."

Lukas lifted his head to look down at Blaire.

The intense longing in his gaze raised her hackles, and she leaned away. "Just the claiming? Not..."

"What?" Lukas's forehead scrunched as his brows drew together.

"I'm not becoming a Vasirian."

Lukas groaned and dropped his forehead to her shoulder again.

She had started to come around to the idea, but she didn't want to submit to the decision under duress. In the wake of such a horrible experience, while her bond was broken, it could be viewed no other way.

"Blaire..."

Riley shook her head quickly and spoke over Lukas, "We've told you a million times before, you don't have to do that."

"It would make things a lot easier," Lukas mumbled.

Blaire stood from his lap as her fingers twitched with the urge to throttle him. Riley hopped up immediately, likely seeing the anger in her eyes, allowing Blaire to sit. Riley perched on the arm of the chair.

"We've been through this, Lukas."

"I know, but... Look what happened!" He threw a hand out in her direction. "You look like you went ten rounds with a cannibalistic boxer!"

"Lukas!" Riley kicked his chair. "This is exactly the stuff that had you freaking out when Blaire was gone. How are you still harping on this after how much it upset you before that you pushed her?"

"I'm not—"

"Yes, you are. You're pushing her again."

Lukas was never going to stop. He wasn't going to give up on the idea that she wasn't acceptable until she became like him. If she hadn't seen his behavior with other humans like Charlotte, she'd have thought Lukas just as prejudiced against humans as Clarissa.

His eyes sought Blaire's, but she turned away from his fierce stare.

"Whatever. If you don't want to do it, I can't make you."

She had to wonder if he would try if he thought he could get away with it.

41

Lies

The halls were quiet as Lukas led Blaire down the hallway toward their dorm room later that night. Lukas's continued insistence she become a Vasirian irritated her. Rationally, he only desired to protect her, and she didn't have a good argument anymore that she was fine as a human. The last two months were a testament to how fragile she was in their world.

His hand tightened on hers and she sighed, allowing the tension to bleed out of her. She needed to focus on the simple fact they were reunited. They could work out the rest of it with time. They'd been through too much just to throw it away. Even if the subject matter was monumental. Changing your species was unheard of. It could mean the difference between life and death.

A shudder passed through her as fear trickled in. She didn't want to die. But to become Vasirian required losing blood to the point of death, amounting to the same risk.

Seth and Aiden walked ahead of them in silence. Riley had stayed with Professor Velastra, trying to sort out the room situation and locate Blaire's belongings.

Clarissa was going to be furious when she returned from Europe. Blaire smirked.

Mera and Kai also stayed with the professor to assist with additional paperwork, and Mera provided an in-depth medical evaluation so the nurses would know what they were working with later on when Blaire came to see them after this finally went to trial. She wondered if rumor would spread among the students once it reached that point.

She could not hide all the bruises and bites. The ones on her neck would still stand out even if she wore her long-sleeved blouse and fully opaque tights with her uniform skirt. A turtleneck would be too obvious as well as too warm in this climate, even in winter. She could tie a light scarf around her neck and tuck that beneath her blouse, but again, that would draw attention and prompt questions.

The one nurse who did come by while Blaire slept before they met in the office had let Lukas know it shouldn't take her too long to return to "normal," at least where weight and muscle mass were concerned. A regular diet and exercise should have her body balancing itself out. Blaire had tried to tell him that the weight loss was normal. She didn't know how it worked for Vasirian—maybe they didn't have random fluctuations in weight the way humans did—but dropping ten pounds in a couple of months wasn't out of the ordinary or even extreme.

She suspected that events being completely out of his control was the real issue.

Blood sharing wasn't recommended, so how were they supposed to re-bond? Sure, she was malnourished from not eating much, but she wasn't weak and sickly looking. The nurse had reasoned that because of Blaire's marked bouts of anemia in the past, waiting to allow Lukas to drink was a cautionary route they should consider.

Lukas looked over at her when she sighed heavily. "What?"

"Nothing really. Just thinking about something the nurse said to you."

Lukas's brow furrowed.

"Also thinking about the claiming ritual."

"What about it?"

"The blood sharing."

Lukas stopped in the middle of the hall. His sudden halt made Blaire stumble back and look at him.

"What the—" Her eyes widened at the flash of hunger in his eyes; a hunger that not only spoke of the need for blood, but also of lust. His pupils dilated, and when his tongue trailed along his lower lip, she tracked the movement with avid interest.

With everything going on, Blaire hadn't had the opportunity to focus on what this all meant for the two of them. Their broken bond. The weird empathic connection that still thrummed through her veins. The overwhelming need for the man in front of her. Not in the sexual sense—though her body ached for his in ways she didn't understand. Rather, her heart needed him. She knew that instinctively.

When his emotions were tame, he brought a calming peace to her that no one else had ever been able to. She didn't need a mark, or some magical bond, to tell her Lukas was the one for her. She'd take him even if fate stole their bond. They could just be together and connect like normal humans did, right?

Blaire crossed one arm over herself to anxiously rub the other that hung at her side in a self-soothing gesture. Would Lukas want that? Would it be enough for him? The Korrena bond was a precious thing to the Vasirian, and she couldn't deny how good it felt when they fully bonded, like a piece of her missing her entire life had finally clicked into place. Since the ritual, only a hollowness remained where she'd once felt full. She may have always felt that way before she met Lukas but wasn't aware of it. Now it became a craving.

He wouldn't want to give that up, and with his unhealthy focus on her humanity being a problem, she doubted he would accept the human way of being connected as enough.

Lukas raised an eyebrow at her, likely sensing the shift in her mood.

"What's going on?" Aiden asked, turning to look at them. Seth stood a few feet ahead. Neither of them had noticed Lukas and Blaire had stopped until that point.

Blaire shook her head. "I'm just tired." It was a weak excuse; she'd slept like a rock last night in Lukas's arms and had a quick catnap in the makeshift safe room before they decided to go to the dorms after having dinner. "The past couple of days… It's been a lot to take in." At least, that was a more honest answer. Mentally, she was exhausted.

They approached Lukas and Blaire's dorm room, and Blaire turned to face the guys. "I think I'm just going to lie down." She offered a strained smile when she saw the concern on Aiden's face.

She didn't want to bring up her insecurity about her connection with Lukas. He would jump on his soapbox again about the only viable solution being to become a Vasirian. End of argument. Lukas needed to accept her no. She wouldn't leave him, but this issue could become a huge ravine keeping them apart.

"I'll be there in a sec." Lukas stepped up to her and wrapped his arms around her lower back. "I need to talk to them about something first." He tilted his head and leaned in, pressing a chaste kiss on her lips that ended far too quickly for her liking. She needed the security of his touch.

He smirked at her heavy sigh when he pulled away.

Blaire couldn't wait to be somewhere familiar again. To feel

Lukas's bed sheets and pillow. Hopefully soon she would have her own returned. Despite the luxurious items Vincent had provided her, she was eager to use her familiar cheap drugstore bath products again. She wondered if they also stored those away.

She pushed open the door, stepping inside the room she hadn't seen in two months.

A woman gasped and Blaire froze, looking up. Clarissa stood next to the beds in a pair of white booty shorts and a tank top so tight and thin the entire outline of her nipples showed through the fabric. *Classy as always.*

"What the hell are you doing here?" Clarissa spat, posting her hands on her hips with her nose wrinkled in disdain. "This isn't your room. Shouldn't you be... I don't know, flipping burgers or something?"

Blaire stood with her mouth agape, not sure how to respond. What was she doing here? Wasn't she supposed to be in Europe?

"Hellooo?" Clarissa waved a manicured hand, the charms of her bracelet tinkling as they shook about. "I get you humans are slow, but..."

Blaire glanced around, tuning out the annoying yammering of the girl in front of her, finally taking in the state of her room. Lukas's side of the room was exactly how she remembered it, but her side of the room was completely different. Despite knowing that Clarissa had moved in, it was still a shock seeing the changes.

A fuzzy throw blanket that looked like real fur lay over the foot of the bed with several ornate accent pillows hiding the pillow the school provided. On the desk at the foot of the bed sat a laptop and a cup filled with several pens with fuzzy pom-poms on the top. She hadn't seen anyone use those since middle school. A couple of stuffed bears sat behind the laptop.

Blaire's gaze shifted past a glowering Clarissa to the nightstand, and her throat tightened, her vision tunneling. The photo of her mother with her in the sunflower field was gone, replaced with a glass dish filled with jewelry. Of course, it was gone. It was probably hauled away with everything else. But that bowl sitting where her most precious picture should have been made her vision cloud with crimson.

What if they threw it away?

Had they thrown her mom away with her other stuff?

"Where is it?" Blaire barked, pushing past Clarissa so hard she stumbled into the bed and protested the action, but Blaire couldn't hear anything she said. Picking up the bowl, she rounded on Clarissa. "Where. Is. It?" Blaire kept her voice low, her control slipping. She'd been through way too much to have to deal with this loss on top of it.

"That's mine!" Clarissa reached forward, but Blaire stepped back. "Give it back!"

"Tell me where my picture is!"

"I don't know what you're talking about," Clarissa said in exasperation, putting her hands on her hips. "But that bowl is a one-of-a-kind Annette Marie Bordeaux that was custom made for my sixteenth birthday. Trash like you could not even begin to comprehend its value, so just put it down and get out of my room before you do something like drop it with your stubby fingers. Whatever you're looking for is probably still rotting in storage if your family didn't come get it."

In her blind anger, she had forgotten her stuff had been moved to storage. Her mind hooked on something else Clarissa said. Her brows rose at the audacity of the girl's claim.

"*Your* room?"

Clarissa huffed a laugh and shook her head. "Wow, you really are slow." She waved a hand toward her bed. "This is mine and Lukas's room. You don't belong here."

"You're sorely mistaken. This is my room."

"Oh, there's no mistake, human," Clarissa sneered at Blaire, looking at her as if she were gum on the bottom of her shoe. "Lukas doesn't want you. He's upgraded. This is *our* room."

Blaire gripped the bowl in her hand and bit the inside of her cheek, but Clarissa continued, oblivious to the dark thing uncoiling in Blaire's gut.

"You're not even supposed to be here. You're not needed here. No one wants you around anyway, and Lukas and I are doing just fine without you."

"Excuse you, what?" Blaire shook with the urge to rip out the perfectly styled hair of the girl in front of her. "Y'all are not anything."

"What?" Clarissa snorted a laugh. "Gods, what hick accent is that? Are you even speaking English?"

Blaire's cheeks burned in both fury and embarrassment that she'd lost the filter on her conditioned speech in her upset. Inhaling through her nose and exhaling slowly, she said as calmly as she could, "Lukas is mine. He's never been yours."

"You truly are slow. Didn't you hear me?" Clarissa crossed her arms. "Lukas doesn't want you. You're nothing to him."

"You're wrong. I saw the photos, but I know they're a lie."

"Then why would I know what Lukas sounds like in bed?"

Blaire went slack-jawed.

"We've been together. Slept together." Clarissa closed her eyes, and a look of bliss crossed her features. "I've heard his groans, you know, like—" She imitated a sound Blaire knew intimately.

Blaire's heart hammered against her ribs and her blood whooshed in her ears. Her hands shook, and the jewelry fell from the bowl to the floor as her arm dropped to her side. She already felt unstable from everything that had happened to her over the last eight weeks. Discovering half of what she had believed about Lukas and her friends was false—that they didn't abandon her like she believed; that they hadn't accepted Clarissa in her place—only to face this.

"—Oh, and the way he gripped my hips—"

"Shut up! Shut up! SHUT. UP!" She hurled the glass bowl at Clarissa, who ducked, barely managing to not get hit. The glass shattered against the door.

Clarissa opened her eyes wide, shrieking, "You bitch! Do you know what you just—"

Lukas threw the door open, and Clarissa jumped, her words dying in her throat. Blaire collapsed to her knees, gut aching like someone knocked the wind out of her. She wasn't aware she had started crying until the droplets hit the arms she'd wrapped around herself.

"Baby!" Clarissa called out in an overly sweet tone as she rushed to Lukas and threw her arms around his neck, clinging to him and rubbing her barely dressed body against him like a cat in heat.

"What the hell is going on?" Lukas gripped Clarissa's shoulders and pushed her back to arm's length.

Aiden stepped into the room, his shoes crunching over the broken glass. "Blaire?" He looked from Blaire to the broken glass and back again.

"I was just informing this infuriatingly slow human about our relationship." Clarissa looked down her nose at Blaire with obvious faux pity. "She doesn't seem to get it. Maybe you can tell her, baby?"

"What the fuck are you on about?" Seth's brows pulled together, moving fully into the room. The scowl on his face made it clear he either didn't like what Clarissa said or plain didn't like her. Blaire couldn't tell and didn't have the mental capacity at the moment to care.

Clarissa huffed and rubbed her temples, stepping away from Lukas. "Is everyone around here slow?" At Seth's growl, she waved a hand as if placating a small child. "Lukas and I are a compatible pair."

"What? No you're not." Aiden snapped, whipping his head around to look at Clarissa, his eyes narrowing. "Aren't you supposed to be in Europe?"

Clarissa shrugged. "Came home early." She continued casually, as if Aiden's burning stare meant nothing to her, "And yes, we are. We've been sleeping together."

Blaire sucked in a sharp breath at the wave of red-hot rage that swept over her. She couldn't be sure if it was Lukas's or her own; all she wanted to do in that moment was rip the wannabe princess into pieces.

Seth shook his head at Blaire. "It's a lie. Don't listen to her."

The fact that she was shaking and had wet cheeks did little to show she didn't believe Clarissa, but something in her gut told her it wasn't true. It was hard to hear. She questioned if Lukas sought comfort in Clarissa, and that imitation of the sounds he made when aroused was too accurate, but she trusted what she felt through their shaky connection. She could feel his intense hatred for the girl burning as hot as her own.

Slowly standing to her feet, Blaire clenched her fists at her side. "You—"

"I've told you before," Lukas said before Blaire could unleash on Clarissa. His tone was sharp enough to cut glass, and the low pitch pressed the seriousness of his words. "I don't want you. I've never wanted you. We are not pairs, in any form." He walked past her, bumping her shoulder hard with his, knocking her off balance. "This is my pair. Mark or no mark." He wrapped his arm around Blaire's shoulder and glared at Clarissa, his upper lip curling. "I belong to her, not you. Now get the hell out."

"No." Clarissa pursed her lips, tilting her head and staring at Lukas, challenging him. "This is my room."

"Fine." He stepped forward, wrapping Blaire's hand in his and pulling her along with him.

Clarissa's eyes widened. "Fine?"

"You heard me." He stopped next to her, and the look on his face as he stared her down with such contempt made a shiver pass through Blaire. "We'll find another room."

Blaire wasn't sure where they would go. Lukas had been denied switching rooms, would the Order so willingly let them get a different room together now that she was back? Professor Velastra made it sound as if their Korrena status offered some form of protection from being separated.

"No, wait." Clarissa reached out to Lukas's arm, but his sharp glare as he snapped his gaze to hers made her hesitate and back away from him. "Y-you can't do that. This is your room. With me. Our room," she spluttered.

"Enjoy *your* room," Blaire gave her a saccharine smile as they moved to the door. She felt good. Better than she had in a long time. With Lukas making it crystal clear to Clarissa right in front of her, the unnamed beast inside her settled, pushing away the darkness. "Oh, you might wanna clean up the glass before someone gets hurt."

Blaire had to resist the urge to burst into laughter at the affronted expression on Clarissa's face as she stared after them, gaping like a fish. Seth and Aiden shot her their own dirty looks before they all left Clarissa to enjoy the room she felt entitled to.

Blaire knew her fuss had nothing to do with the room, and she was positive the others did, too. It was all about Lukas. Control and possession. But Lukas wasn't one to be controlled, and he didn't belong to Clarissa—no matter how many underhanded moves she made to shift things in her favor.

When Seth closed the door on Clarissa as they stepped into the hall, Blaire's shoulders fell. Lukas braced for another storm from her.

"I knew she'd moved in. I just wasn't prepared for how it would feel to see it." She wrapped her arms around herself. "And then she started saying things about how she and Lukas..."

"You didn't really believe that shit she said, did you?" Seth asked.

Blaire glanced down the hall, avoiding Lukas's eyes. "I know she was full of it, but... not at first."

Lukas raised a brow. "How could you think anything she said was true?"

"I..." Blaire looked at the ceiling, as if trying to figure out how to say whatever was rolling around in her mind.

Her insecurity cramped in Lukas's stomach, and he swallowed hard.

"I might have questioned, for just a bit, that maybe... maybe you went to her for comfort." When her confession was met with silence, she added, "Physically."

Lukas dropped his head forward and exhaled heavily. "That is so beyond what I did while you were gone that it's comical." He wasn't laughing.

Blaire's cheeks turned pink. "I know. It was just a knee-jerk, reactive thought in a moment of weakness."

"You've been through a lot. No one can blame you for a thought like that," Aiden said, and Lukas nodded, reaching out to take Blaire's hand again.

Half of the time she was gone he had spent caught between ever-shifting states. If he wasn't furious, he was so distraught it crippled him. Then there was the numbness. The black thing that swallowed him up, threatening to consume everything Blaire didn't take when she disappeared.

"Lukas spent most of his time hiding from her. Either in my room or in the woods," Aiden said.

"I only really slept in the room because administration forced it. Avoided the place like the plague, otherwise."

Seth leaned against the wall and crossed his arms. "I started to suspect he was drinking or something with how he'd act so volatile then suddenly bliss out."

"Drinking? Really?" Lukas pinned Seth with a look, both brows raised toward his hairline.

"Yeah, man. Some people get stupid and try to drink away their grief when shit like this happens. That or drugs." He mimed smoking a joint.

"You're an idiot." Aiden shoved Seth's shoulder. "Wait. If you thought Lukas was turning into a drunkard, why didn't you say something?"

All eyes landed on Seth until he scratched his cheek as he glanced to the side. "I was going to, but then I got into it with this guy from my advanced English course, and..." He trailed off, clenching his jaw.

"Dude, it's fine." Aiden put a hand on his shoulder. "But we really need to do something about *your* problem."

"Huh?"

"I've wanted to talk to you for a while, but with everything going on..." Aiden gestured toward the dorm they exited.

"Just leave it," Seth snapped.

"Um. What's going on?" Blaire looked between Aiden and Seth

with a knot between her brows. Despite how much sleep she'd had, she still looked too tired.

"When's the last time you ate?" Lukas asked her, changing the subject. They couldn't deal with Seth's mess while they had their own situation to deal with. "I didn't see you eat much of the dinner Mera brought for you after your nap." The last thing he remembered her eating was a few orange slices and half a chicken burger.

"I had lunch."

"Not much of one." Lukas sighed.

"I don't..."

Her stomach growled, and Lukas shook his head, sensing the lie before it ever left her lips. "Don't say you're not hungry. You might not be used to eating, but I know you."

Blaire could eat circles around him. If he didn't watch her, she'd steal half his meal after she finished hers on a good day. Being with Vincent might have dampened her appetite, but she needed to eat, and once she did, her love for all things culinary would revive.

"First, we need to figure out what you two are going to do about a room. Then worry about food," Aiden said.

"They can't expect me to stay in that room with her now that Blaire is back. I can't continue living in a room where she tried to tear us apart." The skin around his eyes tightened. He hated to see the flicker of pain in Blaire's eyes as much as he hated the sudden punch to the gut that followed through their empathic connection.

Aiden nodded. "I figured as much." He glanced at the dorm room again and shook his head. "I guess it's back to the safe room in the staff building for now?"

They lay together in the dark, Blaire resting her head against

Lukas's shoulder. She ran her fingertips absentmindedly in circles on his bare chest as he ran his fingers through her hair.

"You do know everything she said was a lie, right?"

"Hm?" Blaire tilted her gaze up to meet his, his face illuminated softly by the moonlight from the window.

"Clarissa." He pushed her head back to his shoulder. "All that shit about us being together. Sleeping together. None of it was true."

"I know."

While she'd entertained the thought briefly, she could not accuse Lukas of being a liar. The strange connection between them made it difficult to hide a lie. She didn't feel every emotion he had—that would have driven her mad long ago—but she felt the strong ones. Surges of emotion in response to something. As far as she could tell, when someone lied, they had a strong internal reaction, no matter how good their poker face was.

He was not lying.

"I thought she was you," Lukas said so quietly that she wasn't sure she heard him correctly. "There was this one morning I woke up, but I was still caught between that haze of sleep and wakefulness. I felt you. Well, I *thought* it was you. Feminine hands, long hair… that damn jasmine perfume."

Blaire lifted her head and watched Lukas staring into the blackness of the room. His jaw ticked, and he wouldn't meet her eyes.

"She was touching me, and I thought it was you." His voice cracked on the last words. "I… shit." He rubbed a hand down his face. "I got hard."

Blaire blinked. Was he confessing to seeking comfort in Clarissa? The guilt and shame in the air suffocated her, and she had to squeeze the covers over her waist to focus.

"Nothing happened," Lukas said after a brief silence. "I mean, after she responded to me—"

"What did you do?" Blaire whispered. She hated how shaky and meek her voice sounded.

"Nothing!" Lukas met her gaze and put a hand on her cheek. "I pulled her hair, or something, and when she"—he made a face like he'd eaten something rotten—"moaned, I knew it wasn't you. That woke me up completely. I told her to get off me." He sighed heavily. "Nothing happened. She tried and failed. I would never betray what we have like that."

The tightness in her chest loosened, and Lukas thumbed away a rogue tear that trailed down her cheek. "I'm sorry," she whispered.

Lukas frowned and tilted his head, studying her. "For what?"

"For even questioning..." She looked across the room.

"Hey, no." Lukas took her chin between his forefinger and thumb, turning her face back to him gently. "With everything that piece of shit did, said, and showed you, no one can fault you, even if you believed it."

"I didn't, not fully. I still... I kept going back and forth. I wanted to believe in you, but then the photos..."

Lukas silenced her with a gentle kiss. "I get it. I'm not mad at you. Blaire, I love you."

Not enough to accept me as I am.

Blaire sniffled and pushed the intrusive thought down. Pulling from his grasp, she sat up on the bed and untwisted the t-shirt Lukas had given her to sleep in. He raised himself up to lean against the head of the bed.

She shook her head to dispel the mental imagery of Clarissa perched in his lap. They sat in silence in the dark. Lukas watched her with arms crossed and legs outstretched under the covers. He had his ankles crossed, by the way the covers were laying. He looked comfortable. Relaxed. She tried to lighten the moment.

"This isn't our same room, but I like this one okay," she said, tugging the covers straight. "That place he kept me in was more spacious than our dorm rooms, with the kitchenette and lounge area, like a studio apartment—"

Lukas snorted a laugh. "If the apartment was owned by someone wanting to be featured in *Ostentatious Vampire Weekly Magazine.* Not that there is such a thing—vampires aren't even real—but that room would absolutely get a feature."

She smiled. "The bathroom alone warranted an interior design award for Gothic allure. Is there a Vasirian equivalent to *Archetectural Digest*, or one of those magazines that put celebrity lives on display for the masses to consume and judge?"

"I don't know. Not my thing."

"Well, what happened in that space was nothing to write an article about. At least, not in a magazine about beauty and wealth. A true crime publication, maybe—or a horror magazine. Do they make those?"

Flashes of the worst night of her life picked at the back of her mind, desperate to worm its way forward. All the blood, the burning sensations, the fighting, and tears as Lukas slipped away from her.

"What was that?"

Blaire's chest heaved, and she held the covers in a stranglehold.

Lukas's brows furrowed, and he leaned forward from the headboard. "Hey, come here," he coaxed gently.

Blaire allowed him to pull her into his arms, and he settled back against the head of the bed, speaking softly to calm her. "So, tell me what that flash of emotion was about. I can still feel you, you know. I'm sure you know that… because you feel me too, don't you?"

"Yes," Blaire said quietly. He squeezed her shoulders, drawing her in closer to his body. "I can't stop remembering…"

"Remembering what?"

"The ritual."

She was thankful he didn't ask her to elaborate on the process or what she experienced during the ritual. When she'd given her statement, she gave the basics about the ritual, but not what she felt and experienced. She didn't want to go through it again. At least, not now. Maybe later when it wasn't so panic inducing. He deserved to know. She wasn't obligated to share with him or anyone else, but it was such a meaningful thing to their bond that she didn't feel right *not* telling him everything.

She sighed, looking up into Lukas's eyes that were shadowed in the dark. The moonlight accented his strong facial structure but left his deep brow in shadow.

"Is it permanently gone?"

"Huh?" His head tilted slightly, his long hair falling over his shoulder and blocking some of the moonlight. "Is what permanently gone?"

"The… bond. If we can still feel each other, is it permanently broken?"

"No."

When Blaire tried to lift herself to get a better look at him, he tightened his hold.

"When you went into the dorm yesterday, remember how I said I needed to talk to the guys?"

"Yeah…" she dragged out the last of the word.

"Well, while you napped before dinner, I asked them to talk to Professor Velastra to see if she found out anything more. When I talked to them in the hall, they told me our bond still exists."

"It does?"

"The professor talked to my mom when she couldn't find any text supporting our bond being broken. Mom has heard of this happening before, so I told Professor Velastra. The professor's speculation was correct, if what Mom said was true. We just have to go through the claiming ritual again to solidify and stabilize it. Right now, it's unstable and not coming to us in stages like it did when we met." Lukas rubbed her back soothingly. "If what's happening to me is anything like what's happening to you, I'm sure you're being driven crazy by what I'm feeling."

Blaire swallowed hard. "And our mark?"

"It'll come back with the ritual," he murmured softly, clearing his throat of the emotion he couldn't hide from his tone or from their empathic link.

42

Desperate Need

The next morning, Lukas rolled his shoulders and reached out to take Blaire's hand as Aiden led them up the stairs of their old dorm. Last night was the best sleep Lukas had gotten in two months. Sure, he'd had Blaire at his side the night before, but everything was up in the air. She was injured and emotions were high.

Last night, things felt calmer. They were freshly washed and were both on the same page regarding their relationship and the condition of their bond. That was probably what helped the most; knowing that the bond wasn't lost despite Vincent's best efforts.

He'd have still taken Blaire, regardless.

Lukas didn't need the Korrena bond to tell him Blaire was his. He'd take her however she'd allow him to have her. But he couldn't deny part of him—the Vasirian at its primal core—would have been devastated to discover the bond was gone forever. It was the part of him that wanted what his parents had. The part of him he tried to ignore when he thought he wouldn't find a Korrena because of his age.

The part of him that insisted that he convince her to become like him so he could protect her properly. So that she'd always be with him.

Blaire squeezed his hand, glancing over at him while she sipped on a bottle of white peach tea Aiden had gotten her from the canteen that morning. He'd gotten them breakfast while she was in the shower and Lukas met with Professor Velastra briefly in her office. Aiden brought it to the room, saying he figured they wouldn't want to face other students yet. He insisted they needed to hurry and eat because he had a surprise.

"What did Professor Velastra say?" Blaire had asked as they ate.

"She said they've heard the deposition and have Vincent in custody, refusing to release him until there's a trial. They want to do a sweep of the room you were in for evidence. I was going to tell you after we found out whatever Aiden is up to, but it's set for two days from now."

Lukas groaned. He didn't do surprises. At this point, he'd be happy with a fully mapped out plan for the next several years to give structure to the chaos that had become their lives.

"What do you think it is?" Blaire made her way to the door in the stairwell to the floor under Aiden's. He stood holding the door open.

"Don't know." Lukas narrowed his gaze at Aiden. "But it better be good."

Aiden laughed and slapped Lukas on the shoulder. "Lighten up, man. You'll love it."

Lukas sucked his teeth.

Blaire nudged him. "Be nice," she scolded.

He wasn't mad. He was mostly struggling with the urge not to rip Blaire's dress off. She'd put on another short sundress that Riley brought her. This one was teal green and fell to mid-thigh. The sweetheart neckline dipped to show her cleavage and made his mouth water. She still wore the little black cardigan to hide the marks and bandages on her arms. A pair of black tights provided warmth from the December chill, and hid the damage to her thighs, and the bruises the chain left around her ankle. He was glad the exposed area of her sternum was unmarred.

Lukas had done his best to hold his needs at bay while she recovered from the initial shock of what happened, but he was reaching his limit. The beast inside him was riding him hard to claim her again. He doubted it would settle until that happened, still sensing a threat to what was his birthright. Unease settled in on him as he tried to avoid the other need warring inside him. He couldn't force Blaire to not be human.

He shuddered.

"Here we are," Aiden said, pulling Lukas's attention. "I think it's the one directly above mine, actually, judging by where it's at in the hall."

"Huh?"

"Dude, are you okay?" Seth asked, passing with a box in his arms.

Lukas looked around. He couldn't see inside the room, but he recognized some of the items in the top of open boxes being carried into the room by Seth, Mera, Riley, and Kai.

"What's going on? What's all this about?" Lukas asked Aiden as Blaire let go of his hand and walked into the room.

"Your new room," Aiden said matter-of-factly. "When I went to get your breakfast this morning, I ran into Professor Velastra in front of the staff building before she went in to meet with you, and I told her what happened with Clarissa. I don't know how she managed it, considering they wouldn't cooperate to get you away from Clarissa before, but they've set up a new room." He shrugged.

"Probably because Blaire is back. They can't keep a Korrena pair apart without backlash," Mera said as she stepped up to the door. She looked at Lukas. "They retrieved Blaire's belongings from storage on the bottom floor of the staff building. Professor Velastra said she already had personnel bring your belongings so neither of you has to see Clarissa."

"I don't think so. The Order isn't aware Blaire is still on campus, according to Professor Velastra. Angelo had said she withdrew, remember? While they've heard the deposition, I think they're still under the impression Blaire voluntarily left and Vincent took advantage of it." Lukas turned to Aiden. "Either way, they've heard the deposition. It's out there now. Trial is in two days."

"Wait..." Aiden's eyes narrowed. "They think Blaire withdrew, and *then* Vincent took her?"

"Professor Velastra said that was what Angelo told her when she received feedback on the report."

"That's the stupidest thing I've ever heard. So how did you finally get to switch rooms? And what about Clarissa? Wouldn't she tell her dad?"

Lukas cracked his neck. "Man, I don't know. I know it had something to do with someone Professor Velastra was owed a favor by who just started working in housing, but the details weren't explained. Not my business. As far as Clarissa goes, I don't know if she's talked to her dad or not. I hope not. I mean, with his position in the Order, and her living on campus, I wonder how often they see each other to start with."

Seth leaned on the door frame, interrupting their conversation. "These are the last of Blaire's boxes." He thumbed over his shoulder, motioning to the room. "We already set everything up. Come check it out."

Lukas followed Seth inside, Aiden trailing him.

The room looked exactly like their old dorm, with its desk placements and a few items they had set up before. But instead of two single beds, beneath a window in the center of the room sat a queen bed framed by black curtains pulled back on each side with burgundy cords. The bed had the same black and burgundy ornately styled linens from their old room. A plush, black area rug covered a majority of the hardwood floor beneath it. A nightstand sat against the wall on each side of the bed with a small lamp like the ones they had before sitting on top of both.

Blaire sat on the edge of the bed, holding a picture frame in her hands, chatting with Riley. The look of relief on Blaire's face as she stared down at the photo of her with her mother lifted his mood. He couldn't stop staring at her. His fingers twitched as she crossed her legs, her dress shifting up to reveal more of her thigh. He cursed the black material obstructing the view of her creamy skin.

"How are you holding up?" Kai stepped up beside Lukas. Of course, Kai would pick up on his struggle. It was the same struggle as the first time around. The incessant need and longing. But it was so much worse than before. Kai wouldn't understand this part. Lukas hoped he would never have to. Losing the bond, and then feeling the need to fill that hollow space while feelings of lust and possessiveness rooted through his veins like a poison. He didn't wish that on anyone.

Before Lukas could answer Kai, his eyes met Blaire's as she looked up at him from the bed. Riley continued to ramble, oblivious to Blaire's sudden distraction.

Lukas's nostrils flared as she shifted on the bed. A red flush moved up her neck and over her cheeks, giving her away before her feelings of desire even hit him. He could hear her heart hammering from here.

It was the first time since before she disappeared he'd heard it. When the flush spread over her pale breasts above the neckline of her dress, he had to turn away before he did something stupid like claim her with everyone watching.

"That well, I see," Kai said with a low chuckle.

"Shut up." Lukas tried to sound put off, but the rasp in his tone did nothing to help his case.

Riley groaned and stood from the bed. "I'm exhausted. I need a milkshake."

"There's that new ice cream shop that opened in town," Seth started, and Riley looked at him, her brows knitted together. "I can take you to get one if you want."

Riley's mouth parted, and she stared at him until Seth's relaxed expression shifted to something guarded as his lips pinched tight.

"Who are you, and what have you done with Seth?"

Seth scowled and walked away. "Forget it."

"No! Wait!" Riley launched herself at Seth's back and wrapped her legs around his waist, latching her arms around his neck to hold on to his six-foot frame. His hands flew up to grab her thighs from beneath to keep her from falling.

"What the fuck?" He glared over his shoulder at Riley as she clung to his back expecting a piggy-back ride. Despite the glare, Lukas recognized the heat in Seth's eyes. He saw his own struggles reflected there.

Riley wiggled, and Seth lowered her to the floor. "I wanna go," she whined.

"Fine. Let's go, otherwise, I'm going by myself." Seth exited the room.

"Wait up! I was only kidding, you know!" Riley's voice echoed from down the hall into the open doorway as she ran after Seth.

Kai laughed, and Aiden shook his head.

"We're glad you're back, Blaire," Kai said, taking Mera's hand to lead her from the room.

Aiden looked between the two of them as Blaire stood, setting the photo of her mother and her on the nightstand. She smiled at the photo now in its rightful place.

"If you need anything, I'll be one floor down," he said, rubbing his neck and moving to the door.

Lukas wouldn't be surprised if even Aiden could sense the tension in the room, bonded to them or not. Neither was doing a good job of hiding it, and it was being fueled by each other. The need was stifling.

As soon as the door snicked shut, Lukas crossed the room and turned the lock, turning to watch Blaire where she stood next to the bed shifting from foot to foot.

A low growl worked its way up Lukas's throat, and Blaire gasped at the sound as he took several purposeful strides toward her, wrapping an arm around her lower back and hauling her up against his body. He placed his other hand on the back of her head and slammed his lips on hers.

Lukas groaned into the kiss as he twisted his hand in her hair. Her sharp intake of breath against his lips gave him the access he needed to plunge his tongue into her mouth. She gave as good as she got, and when he broke from her lips, her pupils were blown wide with desire.

He trailed kisses over her jaw and down her neck. "I need you," he rasped against her throat, nipping at the skin above her pulse point. "Now."

It was all the warning he could manage to give Blaire before he dropped to his knees, trailed his hands up the outside of her thighs, then pulled down her panties and tights down to the floor in one quick motion. She gripped his shoulders. He didn't hesitate. As soon as she stepped free of her undergarments, he lifted her leg and threw it over his shoulder.

A strangled cry cut off Blaire's gasp of surprise as Lukas sucked her clit into his mouth. She tasted like sweet fruit, and she smelled like jasmine and orchids. Lukas groaned as he dragged the flat of his tongue over her wet folds; her leg trembled on his shoulder.

She clutched the back of his head, fingers tangling in his hair as she bent over him, moaning and writhing against his face when he slipped two fingers inside her. He continued his assault on the sensitive nub with his mouth as he worked his fingers in and out of her warmth.

"Lukas," she panted. He loved hearing his name on her lips, but his mouth was too preoccupied to tell her that. His responding growl vibrating against her center, making her buck against his face, would have to be enough.

When he curled his fingers just right, hitting that sweet spot he'd found before, she shattered, curling into him, and crying out as her orgasm moved through her.

He didn't slide his fingers out until she stopped pulsing around him. Slowly placing her trembling leg down from his shoulder, he stood and sucked his fingers into his mouth, letting nothing go to waste.

Blaire was a sight to behold: breathless and flushed, her pupils so blown he couldn't see the green in her eyes anymore. She looked thoroughly sated, but he was far from finished.

Lukas stood and slipped the cardigan from her shoulders, pushing it down until it fell to the floor. He ignored the marks there to not ruin the mood. This was about the two of them; he wouldn't let another taint it. Her dress followed, fluttering to the floor in a pool around her feet.

With no fanfare, he made quick work of his clothes. He didn't have time to tease. He wanted her too badly. He saw the same hunger mirrored in her eyes.

Blaire climbed onto the bed, crawling to the middle, giving Lukas a toe-curling view of her ass in the air. She was stunning. Glistening and swollen and so ready for him.

He pulled open the nightstand drawer, praying that someone thought ahead when they set up their room. Arranged in the drawer were not only a bottle of lube and condoms, but also the ornate knife Aiden gave Blaire long ago for protection they ended up using the first time they sealed their bond.

What a fitting way to restore things.

Lukas smiled to himself as he pulled out a packaged condom and the knife, tossing them on the bed beside Blaire. He didn't need the lube. She practically wept for him. A shudder rolled through him at the knowledge. It was for him. He made her respond this way. The satisfaction he got from that would never get old.

Lukas crawled over her body and paused at the look on Blaire's face as she gazed up at him. Her face was relaxed, a smile making the weariness she'd been carrying recede. Her heavy-lidded stare did nothing to hide the loving way she looked over his face as she reached up to cup his cheek.

"I love you," she said softly.

He lowered his head, burying his face into her hair and breathing her in. How did he get so lucky to find someone so perfect for him?

Lifting himself, and sitting back on his heels, he said, "I don't want to hurt you. It's been awhile."

He wanted to be careful with her. She'd only ever been with him, and it'd been a long time. He really didn't know if that would affect how it would feel. It wasn't like he could ask her what it was like to go two months without sex after only four months of activity since losing her virginity. Not a conversation he wanted to have.

"You'll tell me if it hurts, right?"

"Of course, but I don't think—"

"Just do it. Tell me if anything hurts. If you're uncomfortable, if my bite…" His jaw clenched. "If it's too much."

It wasn't just the long dry spell without sex that worried him. She was fragile. With how Vincent had hurt her, Lukas was afraid to bite her. But he couldn't shut down the beast that crept into the back of his mind. He needed this.

Humans are so breakable. If only she would accept…

He shook his head quickly.

He didn't want to hurt her physically with his body. And then there was her mind. Would his bite trigger something in her after what Vincent did? His jaw clenched so hard he thought he'd chip a tooth, and he had to tamp down the bubbling anger that tried to rise to the surface.

Blaire ran her hand over his cheek, across his jaw, and cupped the back of his neck, pulling him down until his forehead met hers. "I'm fine, Lukas. Your nerves are making me nervous. I'm not afraid of you."

Lukas closed his eyes as he exhaled shakily against her lips and nodded.

He repositioned himself between her parted thighs, her lower legs draped over his thighs. He stroked his erection slowly, a bead of moisture glistening the tip. She licked her lips, then bit the lower one in a way that always drove him crazy.

"I'm not going to want to stop, so…" He grabbed the knife and cut into the soft fleshy area where his neck met his shoulder muscles, clenching his jaw at the sharp bite of pain. Blood spilled down his chest, over his ribs, and continued trailing into the defined V at his pelvis. He cut a little deeper than last time to ensure the wound wouldn't heal too quickly and would last until they were ready.

If she had fangs, I wouldn't need to do this…

Lukas growled, squeezing his eyes shut as he forced back the dark, intrusive thoughts.

Tossing the knife to the side, he grabbed the foil packet and tore it open with his teeth, then rolled the condom down his length.

"You ready to be mine again?" His voice was low, strained.

"I was always yours," she said, staring into his eyes as he slowly pushed into her.

Blaire's head lay back on the pillow as she moaned, long and low, her back arching as his hips pressed flush to her center.

He had to hold himself still for a moment, his arms posted on the bed on either side of her head. Her walls fluttered around him, squeezing him as if she were on the edge of another orgasm, and it was taking everything he had not to blow from that alone. It had been way too long. He hadn't even masturbated the entire time she was gone. He hadn't wanted to. Now, it felt like he could come just from sitting still inside the warmth of her body.

"Please move," she whined, and squirmed her hips, making Lukas's eyes roll back.

He cursed under his breath. "I don't think I can hold back."

"Then don't."

"Tell me if it hurts," he rasped.

Dark thoughts, that he didn't want to entertain the meaning of, took a backseat as lust took the wheel.

He lifted himself up and took hold of Blaire's thighs in his hands as he pulled almost all the way out before pushing in quickly, fully seating himself inside her.

When the only response to his deep and forceful thrust was a gasping moan, he took it as all the encouragement he needed to let go. His hard thrusts made her breasts bounce as she clawed at the covers and over his chest, painting her fingertips with his blood.

He curled over her, and his hair hung over his face, sticking to his skin as sweat run down his forehead. Leaning in, he trailed his tongue up between her breasts over the soft flesh before sucking her nipple into his mouth, his other hand pinching the opposite bud. She rewarded him by rocking her hips up to meet his, grinding herself against him.

They were smearing his blood all over her skin as they rubbed against one another, but he didn't care. He'd mark her in every way possible. Blaire's nails dragged over his back, the sting letting him know she broke the skin.

Mark me. Make me yours.

His thrusts grew frantic, and the bed rocked violently, the headboard banging against the wall as each slap of their skin connecting echoed in the room. He was sure their new neighbors hated them already. They'd have to move the bed farther from the wall or ditch the headboard all together.

As he felt his end racing down his spine, making his balls draw tight, he licked a path up to the column of her throat. His fangs descended. She shuddered and goose bumps rose along her pale skin as he grazed the sharp teeth over her delicate, bruised flesh.

He growled at the reminder of what had happened to her. She was so fragile.

Blaire's slow tilt of her head was the only invitation he needed. Lukas pushed past the nagging in his mind to plunge his fangs into the soft spot on her neck, and she cried out. Her pleasure and a brief flash of pain pushed against him through their bond. The combination of that, and the sweet taste of her blood flooding his mouth, made his head swim. She tasted divine.

He was grateful she knew what to do, latching onto the cut he made and sucking on the skin like a starved animal.

The sensation of her drinking his blood was too much. He couldn't hold back. His rhythm became jerky, faltering, as her thighs clamped tighter around him; her insides gripped his cock like a vise.

Blaire released his skin from her mouth and screamed against his shoulder, her nails digging into his skin. She clung to him desperately as her orgasm crashed into her.

Lukas thrust a last time, driving deep inside, and spilling into the condom, groaning against where he was still latched onto her neck.

Her pulse was strong, and her sweet lifeblood coated his tongue. Reason became lost in the desire to consume.

Protect her. It's the only way to protect her.

Blaire fell silent, and her arms slipped from his back to the bed as he drank deeply from her neck. He was sure she said something, but it was so faint it didn't breech the swirling thoughts in his mind.

When her pulse slowed, alarm bells went off in his head. The fear that slammed into him was enough to make him force himself off her, scrambling to the other side of the bed on his ass.

She didn't move.

Her eyes were closed.

"Blaire?" he croaked.

The taste of her blood still sat heavy on his tongue.

He crawled toward her, looming over her body that looked paler than usual. "Blaire?" he tried again. "Say something."

When she groaned softly and her eyelids fluttered open, his heart nearly stopped beating.

"Oh, thank the gods."

"W-what… happened?"

"I went too far." Lukas clenched his fists, and then climbed from the bed, making quick work of disposing of the condom. It was taking everything in him not to put a hole in the wall of their new room. He'd almost killed her. His bloodlust, and that gnawing need to turn her so she would be safe, nearly cost him everything. Ironic. In his desire to protect her, he nearly killed her.

He stalked back to the bed and stared down at Blaire as she shifted farther up on the pillows, looking thoroughly wrecked.

"What do you mean?" She sounded so tired, and her eyes were half closed. "How'd you go too far?"

"Drinking. I took too much. How do you feel?"

"Why do you sound so angry? I'm a little dizzy, but I'm fine, Lukas. Why are you ruining this moment?"

"I'm not—"

"You are. This is supposed to be a sacred thing, is it not? You're so focused on not hurting me that you are hurting me. Just not physically."

Lukas sat on the bed and pushed his hair away from his sweaty skin. He was so angry with himself. How could he tell her he lost control in his need to have her be just like him?

Blaire gasped and stared wide-eyed at him.

"What's wrong? Are you hurt?"

"Where is it?" Her voice broke on the words as her eyes sparkled under the overhead light.

"What?"

"It's not there. Why is it not there?" She clawed her hair away from her neck. "Do you see it?" She sounded borderline hysterical.

Lukas cursed and stood, pacing the floor.

Her soft voice reached him, broken and scared. "It's not there, is it?"

"No," he growled.

"Why not?"

"I don't know!" He lowered his tone when she flinched. "I don't fucking know."

When he felt her shut down and pull the covers over her body, he roared and threw a punch at the wall. How was he messing up after just getting her back?

He reached down and grabbed a pair of boxers, jerked them up his hips, snatched his cell phone from the nightstand, and went into the bathroom, slamming the door.

43

Fractured

Blaire flinched when the door slammed shut. Lukas had lost it. She hadn't seen him this angry in a long time. She didn't know how to respond. With their mark failing to return, she didn't know what to think.

She roughly swiped away a tear that trailed down her cheek.

Then there was the fact that Lukas hadn't been able to stop drinking her blood.

He could have killed her.

When they first came together, her biggest fear regarding the claiming ritual centered on the concern that he wouldn't be able to stop, and she'd die. He'd promised he could stop. And he did. Every time she allowed him to consume her blood from that point on, he stopped with no struggle whatsoever.

Why had he been unable to stop this time?

The bathroom door opened, and Lukas stepped into the room with his head down. He trudged across the room, retrieved the knife and condom wrapper from the bed, and then cleaned up their space without saying a word. She bit her lip anxiously when he didn't even bother to look at her.

Was he mad at her? Did he blame her for the mark not returning?

He walked around to the other side of the bed, pulled the covers back, and then climbed beneath them. He pulled her into his arms, burying his face in her hair. The only sign he might feel more than anger was the way his shoulders shook. For some reason, she couldn't feel his emotions the way she had before they had sex.

What was happening to them?

"Lukas?" she asked hesitantly, and his shoulders tensed.

She gently pried herself from his hold to get a better look at him, ignoring the woozy sensation that moved over her. His cheeks were wet, and his eyes looked haunted.

"What's going on?"

"I couldn't stop. I wanted..."

Why couldn't she feel him? The emotions on his face and in his eyes spoke of anguish, but nothing from inside him reached her. She felt absolutely nothing but her own emotional turmoil; the echoed emotions that mirrored hers were missing. The empathic link that burned so strongly after her rescue had flickered out without warning.

"Wanted?" she whispered, pushing down the panic rising in her chest at the realization she'd lost that empathic tie with him again.

"I wanted to turn you... I don't even know fully how to do that." His voice lowered, but she heard his next words clearly. "I could have killed you." The words sank heavily into her belly, filling the hollow left from their disconnection with fear.

He looked away from her, but not before anger flared in his eyes.

"Y-you what?" She pulled farther away from him, and he didn't fight her. "You tried to... Lukas, I don't understand. Why would you do that? *How* could you do that to me?"

"I wasn't thinking straight!" He leaned forward and held his head in his hands. "It's this *thing*… what I am… pushing me to protect you in the only way I know how."

"You talk like a Vasirian is two separate beings."

A dark look clouded his features, making him appear defeated and worn out.

"It sometimes feels that way since you came along."

Blaire shook her head. "What? Why?"

"I know the right thing is to give you space. Let you decide on your own time—if you decide to do it at all. But then there's the other side of me that wants to own you completely." She wanted to untangle his hand that pulled his hair strands so hard the tautness at the roots along his hairline made his scalp white. "I know you're not an object, but that primal part of me won't stop digging its claws into me."

The anguish in his voice allowed her to empathize, but the anger overriding it didn't allow her to ignore the crossing of this boundary.

"You violated my trust."

"What?" he choked out. "No—"

"Yes, you did." She climbed out of bed on shaky legs, a wave of dizziness crashing over her. She had to hold the side of the bed for support. Yeah, he took way too much blood. "You were going to force me—"

"No! I stopped! I would never!"

He started to move toward her, but stopped when she retreated a step.

"I got carried away… I'm sorry." His voice cracked. "Please… I would never hurt you."

"But you did."

A knock sounded on the door, and Blaire quickly pulled on her dress, forgoing any undergarments. She opened their door as Lukas stared at her, frozen in shock.

Aiden stood there with his phone in his hand.

Her nostrils flared. "What are you doing here again?"

His brows rose at the irritation in her voice. He held up his cell phone. "Lukas texted me."

Blaire spun so fast she lost her balance.

Aiden reached out to steady her. "Whoa. Hey, are you alright?"

She shrugged him off and made her way over to a desk chair to sit away from Lukas, hating how unstable her movements were. "Peachy." She glared at Lukas.

"I texted him in the bathroom. I needed someone to talk me down."

"What's going on?"

Aiden's gaze moved around the room, taking in the situation. Blaire's tights, panties, and cardigan lay on the floor at her feet. Lukas sat in bed in nothing but his boxers, covered in dried blood; his clothes remained scattered over the floor. She was sure the same blood that coated Lukas's skin stained the dress she rushed to put on.

Between the bruises and bites that littered her body, the bloody clothes, Lukas's skin, the rumpled bed, and the discarded clothes, it probably looked like snuff porn.

She couldn't even laugh at the ridiculousness of the thought.

"Oh, not much. Just Lukas trying to kill me."

Aiden's eyes widened, and he stared at Blaire in stunned silence.

"I didn't try to kill you!" Lukas's pale green eyes flared with rage. The anger that had faded with his pleas returned to his voice.

"Fine. You almost *accidentally* killed me." She rolled her eyes. "You know… while you were drinking my blood, convinced I should be a Vasirian. Do you hear how unbelievable that sounds?"

"Wait..." Aiden's gaze darted between the two of them. "You tried to turn her?"

"No, not on purpose. I was thinking about how I wish she was one of us. We were in the middle of..." His gaze flicked over to Blaire and back again to Aiden. "When I bit her, I couldn't stop myself. It scared the fuck out of me, man."

Blaire tilted her head. "Scared you?" That was the first he'd mentioned fear, and it had the strange effect of lowering her hackles.

"Of course, it scared me! Blaire, your heart slowed. You stopped moving." He scored a hand through his long, tangled strands of hair, damp from sweat. "That fear brought me back from the brink. I can't lose you. Even if our mark never returns, I still don't want to lose you. I *need* you."

Aiden perched on the foot of the bed. "Never returns? Didn't you—"

Lukas growled. "It didn't work. We had sex. She drank my blood. I obviously drank hers... It didn't return."

Blaire sat forward and put her elbows on her knees, scrubbing her face with her hands several times in rapid succession, groaning loudly into her palms. She didn't know how to respond to that. Lukas loved her, but he really would not be satisfied as long as she remained human. If he truly had no control over the darker side of being a Vasirian, could she trust he wouldn't go through with it the next time they were together? Or outright kill her?

Could *he* say for certain he trusted himself not to do it? He seemed as surprised by it as she was.

"So, what does this mean?" Aiden asked hesitantly when no one said anything for a long while.

"I don't know," Lukas mumbled. "Blaire, please don't leave me." The desperation in his voice poured acid on her open wounds.

She lifted her head from her hands, sitting upright. Wetting her lips nervously, she looked back at Lukas and sighed at his expression. Begging like he had long ago when she threatened to leave him gripped her heart, and she had to look away from him to keep from breaking. "I'm not leaving, but this isn't going to work."

"What do you mean?"

"I can't be with you if you're going to keep crossing that line. If instinct won't let you do anything else." She closed her eyes and took a breath, revealing a truth she had avoided telling him before Vincent kidnapped her. "I considered it before Vincent took me. Strongly. I didn't tell you because I knew you wouldn't stop backing me into a corner about it if I did."

Aiden's eyes widened in surprise at her confession.

She let out a dry laugh, void of humor.

"It doesn't matter though, because you've done it already. Backed me into a corner. And after all this… the kidnapping, what you've done here tonight… I don't know anymore. But I won't leave you. Not while you're still trying to figure this out. If you didn't have as little understanding of everything that is happening with this whole Korrena thing as I do, then it would be a different story, but I'm not so callous and stupid as to not recognize you're just as lost as me. I'd be a horrible person to abandon you over that."

"Blaire—"

She held a hand up. "But, Lukas?" A tear rolled down her cheek. "I don't trust you. You hurt me. You promised to protect me, but you were the one I needed protection from in the end."

Lukas sucked in a breath, and his eyes glazed with liquid emotion. He probably hurt as much as she did, but she couldn't feel it.

Why couldn't she feel it?

"We should probably talk to Professor Velastra about this. About the mark, not what you did."

She didn't want everyone to know what Lukas did. She believed he was as clueless as she was. If he got lost in his emotions, swept up in the moment, in instinct, then maybe he had lost control and it wasn't a malicious thing. But it still didn't mean it was right—or anything less than terrifying.

The more pressing issue to her was why the mark didn't return, given the oneness she'd felt with Lukas in that moment of shared orgasm. That's where she needed to shift her focus; solving the mystery of their severed bond.

"You still want my mark?" His hopeful tone twisted her stomach, and her heart raced at the relief in his eyes.

At least she still responded to him physically. If it meant more good sex like they'd just experienced, she was down for that.

"I do," she drawled. "If we split up over every single negative thing that happens between us, we'd have a pretty shitty relationship. Though, admittedly, nearly killing your partner is a bit more than just a spat, but you get what I mean."

Aiden barely suppressed a snort of laughter at her lighthearted tone. She was trying to shift the mood in both her thoughts and environment.

Lukas ran a shaking hand over his face. "Yeah." He swallowed. "Let's go talk to her."

"I'm surprised to hear the mark didn't return with your joining." Professor Velastra frowned, sitting back in her large leather chair.

Blaire had described their lovemaking in basic terms but left out the part about Lukas nearly killing her in his blind bloodlust. She couldn't bring herself to reveal something she could tell caused him distress. She might not be able to feel it, but she'd been in his presence long enough with the empathic connection between them that she'd picked up on the physical cues that came with the emotions she felt from him.

Several worn tomes sat open on the professor's desk. Scrolls, old parchments, and newer papers were scattered around them. Blaire had never seen her desk so messy.

"After speaking with your mother, Lukas, and finishing preparations with security for the trial, I have been thoroughly researching this phenomenon of your bond's severance in case we ever run into this situation with other bonded students. I assumed once you both performed the claiming ritual, all would be well."

Russet eyes cast them a pitying look. If Blaire hadn't been watching the professor closely, she would have missed it.

"Before we found Blaire, I hadn't been able to find any information in our main library, but I've since been able to access the archives in the administration building."

Blaire's face screwed up in confusion. "Why couldn't you check before?"

"I must confess my methods weren't exactly pure. It matters not my excuses, but they were deemed valid enough to allow me access to the archives that are typically only accessible to the Order themselves, diplomats, and the Blackthorn Clan. The books and scrolls kept there are some of our oldest, and they date back hundreds of years. Several tomes have been restored and added to our library, but there are still many kept hidden away." She motioned to her desk. "These three, for example."

"So, did you find anything?" Lukas asked.

The professor's frown deepened as she studied him. Blaire didn't need to hear her response to his question to know she didn't find anything useful. Her shoulders slumped, and she lowered her gaze to the floor.

"Unfortunately, nothing we don't already know. Nothing about the situation you're facing."

Lukas collapsed heavily against the back of the chair from where he'd been sitting on the edge. He smoothed a hand over his face, his other hand gripping his thigh.

"I know this is difficult for you, but I think our modern knowledge of the Korrena bond can help in this case."

"How?" Blaire crossed her ankles to keep her leg from shaking. Seeing Lukas so upset bothered her more than she wanted to admit after what he'd done to her. He hadn't meant to do it, but she struggled with accepting that as the full truth.

"The Korrena bond is a connection we're born with. If we are destined to have a pair in our lifetime, we leave the womb with the spark of that attachment deep inside our souls. Once we find our pair, that link begins to burn deep inside until we're drawn together. Naturally, an emotional attachment develops, fostered by trust, protection, and all the other intense emotions that accompany the bond. With this blend available, when the pair chooses to perform the claiming ritual—claiming each other in both body and blood—the bond fully seals, turning the spark into a burning flame."

"What of it?" Lukas's voice was gruff, and he sounded impatient, but there was an underlying hint of despair.

"The point I am trying to make is that more than just physical desire and biological need fuels the Korrena bond. The bond requires an emotional attachment."

"We have that." Lukas leaned his head on his hand, propping his elbow on the arm of the chair.

"Do you?" The professor glanced between the two of them.

They sat far apart in opposite leather chairs, the choice unconscious. Previously they'd been unable to stop touching each other, after Blaire discovered the truth the night of her rescue.

"It's more than just longing and missing what you had. It's more than just loving someone. It's clear to anyone to see that you are emotionally attached to one another, but you both are missing an important aspect, essential for the Korrena bond to flourish."

"And that is?" Lukas said bitterly.

"Trust."

"I trust her," he retorted quickly, sitting up and slapping a hand on the arm of the chair.

"But I don't trust you."

Blaire's words were a whisper, and if Lukas's head hadn't whipped around so sharply, his pained green eyes boring into hers, she wouldn't have been sure he heard it.

"And therein lies the problem. As long as Blaire doesn't trust you, your bond will remain fractured. It's there, but not whole. This is likely what is preventing your mark from returning."

"Is that why I can't feel her anymore?"

Blaire raised her eyebrows. He couldn't feel her either?

"What do you mean?" Professor Velastra asked.

"When I…" He glanced at Blaire nervously, and she nodded acquiescence. "Fuck it. I almost killed her."

"Excuse me?"

"We were in the moment, and I bit her… but I didn't stop feeding. All I could think about the entire time was how fragile she was. How I needed to protect her. How if she were like me, she'd be safe. It went round and round in my head until she went limp. I panicked."

"Oh, well, that's certainly a problem."

"I didn't mean it!" Lukas's fists clenched on the arm of the chair and Blaire reached out to squeeze his hand, unable to take his pain any longer. He deflated at her touch.

"Your connection was already unstable. You had lost her for an extended period—which is why we mandate that pairs room together, as absence weighs heavily on the psyche. While the end result is surprising, it isn't surprising to know that there was a breaking point from the pressure."

When Blaire first came to Blackthorn Academy, the idea of girls and guys being assigned to share a dorm room freaked her out. The culture she was raised in didn't allow that sort of thing. In fact, if students wanted to sleep together, they usually had to sneak to different dorm buildings entirely. In Vasirian culture, not only was it accepted, but they encouraged it. They still had the decency not to put unpaired Vasirian in dorm rooms together, which made the practice feel less like "Let's let our kids have sex all day" and more simply what their truth was: Korrena pairs needed to be together.

When she came out of her drug-haze, they had been separated for two weeks, and she felt sick with the longing to be near Lukas. Two months nearly killed her, and half of that, their connection was severed. She couldn't imagine a full school year apart.

Sure, they'd see each other every day, and at first, she questioned why that wouldn't be enough, but after bonding, and spending her nights in his arms, sleeping didn't feel right without him.

"I can't feel him either," Blaire admitted with a sigh.

"When did you stop feeling his emotions?"

"Same time, I think. It's become easy to read his body language, so I didn't notice it at first, especially with being dizzy, disoriented and panicked about not seeing the mark, but I realized it when he came back from the bathroom. When he told me…"

"His intentions?"

"Yes."

"I suspect that was the breaking point. In revealing that he did the one thing you were so afraid of before your union, he shattered that trust you both had worked so hard to build."

Lukas sat forward and put his elbows on his knees, holding his face. He'd stopped talking a while back, but he was taking everything in. His rigid posture. His constant shifting. He was ready to explode.

Blaire looked away from him and swallowed down the sadness bubbling up in her throat. Lukas broke her trust when he refused to protect her. Acting on selfish instinct. He claimed it was an act of protection to make her less fragile. But she couldn't fully see it that way.

If he truly didn't feel like he had a hold on what was inside him, and treated it as if it were another being, then he hadn't protected her from the beast that he was aware lived inside him.

The beast didn't want to protect her.

44

Blood Magic

Angelo paced the lab, watching the insufferable men and women at work. His lip curled at the sight of their white lab coats, their disheveled hair from hours of constant work, and he was sure a few of them needed a shower. It was beneath their kind to be so uncouth.

"There's enough blood in the stockpile you discovered to make a proper concentrated effort on discovering what makes the human's blood so special," a woman said from where she sat in front of several boxes of vials filled with dark crimson liquid. He didn't acknowledge her as he passed the boxes and continue through the room, followed by Tobias, his right-hand man.

Of course, there was enough. He'd saved every vial Vincent provided him during the two months that he held the human girl in the basement of the administration building, doing only the gods knew what to her. Angelo didn't care. As long as he got the blood.

Vincent had once questioned how Angelo explained to the council where Blaire's blood came from if she was supposedly gone from the academy, but he didn't elaborate. He didn't have to explain himself to a student.

Eventually Blaire would end up dead at Vincent's hands, and then all the saved blood would be fine to use. A mad student who'd gone so far as to kidnap a human was bound to want her blood. He hadn't suspected Vincent would actually go mad. Something wasn't right about this human's blood. He'd tasted human blood before—had it every single day with his meals—and it never affected him in that way.

"I find it so very strange how you found so many vials," Tobias said, brushing white blond hair from the alabaster skin of his forehead with long, slender fingers.

Tobias Nilsson came to the Order from Sweden twenty years ago, and had stood with Angelo ever since. He was more loyal than the other men, but more vocal than Angelo cared for. He was clever, and his ever-assessing gaze often gave Angelo pause. He didn't know if Tobias would still stand with him if what he did to assist his daughter came to light.

Tobias was a mere forty-seven, young in comparison to the other members, four of whom were well over one hundred years old. However, outside of a council setting, he acted much younger, as if he belonged more with the university students of Blackthorn Academy. Age could never be a true measure of maturity with their kind.

"Mm. I'm sure Mr. Brandt was stockpiling the human's blood for feeding." He looked over his shoulder at Tobias. "I found the stash in the back room he apparently slept in away from the girl, after security had done a sweep."

"Why didn't security find the vials?"

"Perhaps because the room looked like nothing more than a disused storage room, save for a single bed." The excuse was weak.

Blackthorn Security was highly trained and thorough. They'd have checked the storage room. He hadn't banked on so many questions, but Tobias was one of the smarter members in the Order's council.

Tobias hummed and didn't press further.

With his youth, it wasn't surprising he was sharp and clever. He had the advantage of modern resources at his disposal, while most of the other members balked at societal progress. Several of them had wanted to hear the human's testimony in person, rather than through a small recording device. This request had more to do with intimidation than an abhorrence of technology.

Angelo changed the subject. "His obsession for her existed before he fed on her, by the reports from the other students. Knowing the effects the human's blood had on Mr. Brandt, how it drove him mad, I am positive there is something more to her blood."

Vincent had lost it. While currently held in the dungeons underground, they'd received reports he was manic. Throwing himself into the walls in a desperate bid to escape. Screaming for the human girl. Shifting from pleading, to anger, to sobbing in a corner like a child. Security had noted in their report that his physical responses were like that of a junkie. Sweating, pale with heavy bags beneath his eyes, shaking. His appetite was gone, and he would often ramble incoherently.

The symptoms set in the night he was taken into custody and grew worse in the following days. Only in the last twelve hours had the physical symptoms dissipated. Though he was now eating, and his color was returning, he still suffered manic episodes that made him too unstable to be left unattended—even if he was behind bars.

Tobias frowned. "While it is taboo to feed on a human directly—since it is a crime to bring them harm—it is not unheard of, and this is not the typical reaction, no. So, I am inclined to agree with you."

They stepped from the lab into a long hallway that led to the stairs to the public area of the administration building.

"Are we truly going to allow the human to return to classes?"

"I don't see the harm. Should we run out of blood, she'll be there to provide a limitless supply."

Tobias nodded. "We can't exactly ask for her voluntary donation after everything, no matter that she is now willingly sharing with her pair."

"Master Moretti! Master Nilsson!" A man in a white lab coat, wearing thick-rimmed black glasses, came running from the room they exited, barreling down the hall as if afraid for his life. His face was pale, and he looked panicked as he held up a paper in shaky hands. "We've discovered the anomaly!"

Councilman Kirill sat stiffly in his seat at the top of the platform. "What is all this about, Angelo? The trial is tomorrow. We have no reason to be here."

Angelo approached with Tobias trailing him. The council had gathered at Angelo's command. He glanced at the men on each side of him as he took his seat. "I know we have been holding meetings frequently of late, but for once it is for something we are all eager to hear about."

"Quit with the vague prattling and get on with it," Maxwell said, raising a dark blond brow at him. "I'm thirsty and have a date with a rather curvaceous professor this evening."

Angelo sneered. Eighty-three years old and still thinking with his cock like a young one. Ever since Maxwell lost his Korrena pair in an accident he still had never elaborated on, he drowned his sorrows in gorging on the blood and warm holes of willing women.

Only three of the seven members of the council of the Americas were younger than one hundred—Tobias, Maxwell, and Angelo himself, at ninety-five.

The large doors that led from the outside stairs to the main council chamber opened. Five researchers wearing white lab coats in varying degrees of disarray walked hesitantly into the room.

Several members of the council sat up in their seats, obviously surprised by the sudden appearance of the researchers.

At Angelo's nod, the man in the middle cleared his throat and stepped forward to the podium, placing several papers on its surface. His hair stood up in several directions. The light brown strands looked almost black from oils in some places around his forehead where he'd clearly been sweating. He pushed his wire-rimmed glasses up his nose and pushed a hand through his hair, mussing it up further.

"W-we believe we have discovered the secret behind Blaire Wilcox's blood."

He waited until the whispered murmurs from the men around Angelo ceased. "Her blood reacted when near certain runes."

"Runes?" Tobias questioned.

"Yes. Y-you see, Vincent Brandt had to use runes written in his blood to perform the bond breaking ritual—"

"Yes, yes. We know how the ritual is performed. On with it," Maxwell snapped.

"Ah, y-yes. Apologies, Master Ballentine." The researcher pushed his glasses up his nose as they slid down again from the sweat that coated his skin. "W-we used Vasirian blood to draw runes to test her blood's response. Our hypothesis was that perhaps there could be a connection there." He glanced at a woman at the end of the line of researchers who had the good sense to remain quiet. "My c-colleague had the idea. It was a long shot, but something happened."

Angelo steepled his fingers, resting his elbows on his lap. "Go on," he said in a low, measured tone.

"The human's blood reacted in the strangest way. Some runes would cause it to boil, while others would turn it black. Some created a spark, and one even caused the blood to ignite." The more he spoke, the more excited he became, his nerves replaced with the excitement of scientific discovery.

"We were concerned it would mean something dangerous for the human herself. Our first tests exposed her blood alone to the runes. We then tested how her blood responded in proximity to Vasirian blood without a rune, and nothing happened at all. We then tested another hypothesis. If her blood came in contact with a Vasirian's blood, would it harm her? Would different Vasirian blood samples have different reactions?

"We initially used one Vasirian sample and had myriad reactions. The same results occurred no matter the Vasirian sample we used. When we poured one of the human blood samples into a vial containing the blood of a Vasirian donor, nothing happened to the blood mixture within the vial. But…" He shifted his gaze to look at the other researchers. Several were wringing their hands, and the agitated energy amongst them made the hairs on Angelo's arms stand. Something was very wrong.

"A stack of files we had on a nearby table burst into flames."

Excited murmuring broke out through the council.

"Silence!" Angelo glowered at the head researcher. "Is that all?"

"N-no, Master Moretti." He looked back at the others, and then flipped a page on the podium. "We tried it again, and again… Each trial produced the same response, or other responses."

"Like?" Angelo's voice was like ice, cutting through the thick tension in the room.

"Glass beakers shattered. Objects were thrown from the table as if picked up by wind."

"What does this mean?" Nathaniel interrupted from the end of the platform. He rarely spoke, like several of the council, but his bass level voice echoed in the room, demanding attention.

The researcher jumped at the deep sound. "W-well, it means Blaire Wilcox's blood contains base magical properties."

"Come again?" Tobias shifted from his casual position in the chair to sit up straight.

"She has esoteric blood. Magical blood," the researcher said in a calm, low voice that was in sharp contrast to the nervous and excitable energy he had filled the room with before.

"Magic? How is this a thing?" Tobias questioned, his brows drawn.

Angelo stood and focused his sharp gaze on the researchers. "Do not speak of this finding to anyone. If I find out this information goes beyond this room, I will place your heads on spikes outside this building as a testament to what happens when you defy the Order."

Several recoiled as they should, which pleased him greatly. He drank in the fear on their faces as if it were the finest wine.

"Destroy the evidence of what you've found," he added.

"Until we know what this means for our kind, we cannot allow this information to fall into the wrong hands." Maxwell shifted in his seat with a scowl on his face. "With the human's blood driving students to madness, it is unwise to keep it around. We should destroy the samples and only extract what we need from the source in only the amounts we need, if we need it further."

Several nods and voices of agreement came from the rest of the council.

"Destroy the blood samples as well," Angelo said darkly. "You're dismissed." The researchers fled the room, and he lowered himself into his seat with a weary sigh.

"We need to speak to the Oracle immediately."

45

Lost Power

The scent of lingering pansies and hellebores drifted into the room through the open window over the bed. Even on the top floor, the rich fragrance that floated on the chilly December breeze reached her nose.

Blaire stretched out her legs on the bed, admiring her freshly painted toenails—a dark glittery purple. In the right lighting, or if she turned her feet just so, the color appeared inky as the night sky. She wasn't a girly-girl by any stretch, but it had been so long since she enjoyed the simple things like this that she derived even more pleasure from it.

It was the perfect distraction from the sadness at what happened between her and Lukas. They still hadn't talked about it, and with the trial tomorrow, she wasn't sure she was ready to add the stress of another fight on top of it.

A door closing out in the hall followed by a light scraping noise grabbed her attention as a cream envelope slid through the gap under the door.

She jumped from the bed and rushed to the door, throwing it open. Silence greeted her. Not a soul stood in the hall. No retreating forms, no sounds of doors closing in the corridor. The stairwell door a few feet away was closed. Her brow furrowed in confusion as she turned to stare at the familiar envelope on the floor with the feathered wax symbol sealing it.

The Oracle's signature.

It'd been a while since she dreamed of the secret place where the Oracle revealed herself in the guise of her mother. She still didn't know what to make of it, and she had to wonder if it had been a fever dream in her weakened state. A world and a presence she created to disassociate from the trauma of what she had to endure in that room. Or perhaps residue of the drugs had played with her mind after Vincent stopped forcing them on her.

Shaking her head, she picked up the envelope from the floor as Lukas opened the ensuite door, stepping out with a towel tied low on his hips.

"What's that?"

Blaire closed the door and locked it, watching his back muscles shift and flex as he walked across the floor to the clothes he left folded on his desk. Beads of water trailed down his back from his long, damp hair, disappearing into the towel.

"Blaire?"

Her eyes snapped up to meet his and her face heated. A smirk graced his full lips as he gave her an appreciative look. He was well aware of the effect he had on her, and he took advantage when he could. Even when they fought, they couldn't hide from the physical attraction they had for one another. He turned away with a shake of his head and a grin, then dropped the towel.

Blaire's mouth went dry.

Lukas sported lean, tight muscles; he wasn't bulky and broad in the way someone who spent lots of time lifting weights would appear. His rounded backside was no different. With just the right shape that dipped in on each side, she imagined how it would look flexed while he—

"Seriously, Blaire." He chuckled, and the sound made her heart flutter. "What's up?"

He pulled on his boxers and turned around to lean on the desk. He still had the playful grin on his face, but his eyes focused on the envelope. She hadn't seen him smile since the day before yesterday, when everything fell apart. It bothered her.

Blaire cleared her throat. "Yeah, um, sorry." She sat on the edge of the bed.

"Don't ever be sorry for wanting me." Lukas crawled onto the bed beside her, guiding her up to the pillows to lie on her back. "Just because we're going through something hard doesn't mean I want you any less. That I love you any less."

He kissed her softly, lingering over her lips. "Besides, I love it when you want me." When she groaned, embarrassed, he smiled against her lips and sat up.

"What's it say?"

Blaire sat up and popped the seal, pulling out the same delicate parchment from the last message she received. Delicate black calligraphy littered the page.

The stars have revealed new truths.
A danger to both your kind and mine.
The balance and restoration are at risk,
saved only by a friend's sacrifice.

An untapped, lost power is the conduit
for a bond deeper than that of lovers
to overcome even death itself.
But the heart must be open.

Blaire frowned at the message. "Death? Sacrifice? This one is more confusing than the last."

Lukas sat back against the headboard, crossing his arms over his bare chest, and closing his eyes in contemplation. The breeze passing through the open window fluttered his long hair around his shoulders.

Blaire folded the page, but paused when she saw the same delicate writing on the back.

Your doubts are unfounded.
I will meet you in the clearing.
You know real from delusion.

She gasped, and Lukas's eyes popped opened. "What's wrong?" He snatched the parchment from her hand and read the message on the back. "What's this about? It's not the same as the riddles."

Blaire bit her lower lip and twisted the hem of her t-shirt around her fingers. "Um…"

"Blaire, what's going on?"

She huffed a heavy sigh. The Oracle couldn't seriously expect her to hide this from Lukas. He wouldn't tell anyone. "So… while I was in confinement, I had these dreams, but they weren't dreams. I mean, I was sleeping, but it was real."

A knot formed between his lowered brows.

"I know it sounds crazy, but it's true. I dreamed of this place unlike anything I'd ever seen before. There were forests that looked strange."

"Strange?"

"Like they were influenced by different elements. Anyway, there was a deer."

"A deer?" he deadpanned.

"Yes," she huffed, glaring at Lukas. "Let me finish."

Lukas raked his hand through his hair. "I'm just trying to understand."

"Just listen first." She drew her legs up to sit with them crossed beneath her, facing him on the bed. "The deer didn't look like deer around here, or anywhere else in the world. It had a huuuuge rack." She held her arms out as wide as she could. "And there was all this beautiful blooming foliage dripping from the rack's points. Oh, and its eyes! Absolutely beautiful. Gold, and they seemed so intelligent, like it was aware of me in a way a normal animal wouldn't see a human."

Lukas nodded, remaining quiet as requested.

"So, then I heard this singing, and I followed it away from the view of the other forests. There was this clearing. I saw my mom."

"Your mom?"

Blaire couldn't fault him for questioning. Her mom was dead. This couldn't be anything but a dream, but it was true.

"It was, but not. It was the Oracle. She presented herself in a form I'd be more inclined to listen to her in, she said, and one that would bring me the most comfort in my time of… you know."

Lukas looked down at the bed and clenched his jaw. Only a grunt of acknowledgment encouraged her to continue.

"So, she told me these messages were from her. She's lost her memories. Well, actually, Rosendo Blackthorn sealed them away."

"Rosendo?"

"Apparently your king's great grandfather."

"But why?"

"I don't know. She doesn't remember anything."

"So, what else did she say?"

Blaire exhaled heavily and explained the entire experience, from the Celestial Conclave, to the insistence that the world she woke up in was important to Blaire's purpose. She even told him about the dragon she'd seen. By the time she finished, his mouth hung open. An odd look for a man as serious as Lukas.

"So, the gods don't exist? Just some council called the Celestial Conclave? Isn't that like gods?"

"I don't know. The way she described them makes them sound like they are the shapers of fate and why we're here, so I guess it is like gods. But the way she spoke of them, they didn't sound like a council of real people."

Lukas raked his fingers through his hair and flopped back on the bed. "This isn't going to get easier. From this message alone, even knowing nothing about your dreams, it means this is far from over." He turned his head on the pillow to look at her. The haunted look in his eyes pleaded with her.

"Lukas… I can't do it. Not after…"

He gave a stiff nod and didn't press the issue. "We need to tell Professor Velastra."

"We can't. I wasn't supposed to tell anyone about it, but I just… I couldn't keep it from you."

Lukas folded the parchment and put it back into the envelope before climbing off the bed and retrieving the letter Blaire received at the start of summer and another she'd never seen before from his nightstand.

"Why are there two?"

"I received one while Vincent had you." He tossed her the envelope. "It was for me. You can read it."

Blaire took the envelope in her hands and pulled out the

parchment, reading over the message of pain and a plea to not let go. She swallowed thickly and tucked the delicate paper back in its envelope. "I'm glad you didn't give up," she whispered.

Despite everything that had happened afterward, she was still grateful he didn't stop searching for her. That none of them had stopped.

Lukas cleared his throat. "Yeah, me too." He ran a hand over his forehead and sighed. "We at least need to let the professor know about these messages. The Oracle didn't say to keep those secret, did she?"

"No."

"Then we should tell her. Maybe she can help us figure out what the hell it means."

Blaire gathered the envelopes and looked up at him. "We shouldn't tell anyone else, though. I don't want others getting hurt."

Lukas nodded tightly.

"Okay," she said, letting out a measured breath. "Let's go."

Lukas grabbed his jeans and tugged them onto his hips. "Can't today. Professor Velastra is off campus until the trial tomorrow. But when this is all over, we tell her."

The Oracle stepped across the marble floor through the red hue reflected on its surface from the large stained-glass window. The tension in the Order's meeting chamber was stifling. The seven men on the thrones they used to lord over the students of Blackthorn Academy, and a large portion of Vasirian kind, shifted restlessly. She didn't have to ask what had them in such a state. The shift vibrated in her old bones, and her dreams whispered truths.

Vasirian of all ages held faith in many gods watching over them, gods who created them and were physical beings on another plane.

They believed no one being had the ability to create everything, and they were correct about that, but their details were skewed.

The Celestial Conclave comprised several voices without a face. They shaped this world into what it was and who lived within it. Not several gods or one god. The Celestial Conclave were not corporeal beings, to the best of her knowledge. They didn't exist on a physical plane like the planets, or even an imagined plane such as heaven and hell.

If she were splitting hairs, then yes, the Celestial Conclave shared aspects with the gods humans and Vasirian believed in. Regardless of what type of all-seeing being each species' various religions believed in, the principles of how fate and free will worked were the same. In the end, the Celestial Conclave were the real thing.

Standing before the Vasirian Council, she pushed her hood back and looked at Angelo's pinched and tired expression. "You summoned me?"

"We have made a discovery," he said.

The Oracle nodded, clasping her hands in front of her. "I'm aware of what you've learned."

Angelo sat up in his seat with a snarl. "You knew her blood was magical and said nothing?" He had the nerve to look at her as if he could command respect from her.

"No. I was gifted a dream last moon. They informed you of the findings shortly after my discovery."

Angelo sneered. "Convenient. So, tell me, what else have you seen?"

Angelo was a child compared to her. She was not so blind as to underestimate the position he held, but while she respected his position's authority, she would not bow to him. "The Celestial Concla—"

"Enough with this Celestial Conclave nonsense. We were created by the gods, not governed by mysterious beings in the stars," he snapped.

To question a being older than all Vasirian who could see beyond the veil was a fool's arrogance. The Oracle shook her head. "Very well. I have been shown new pieces of our history. It differs greatly from what we have come to believe, and it sheds light on our current situation. I had not mentioned it, as it did not benefit the current Vasirian, and gaps in my memory prevent me from seeing the entire story."

The council exchanged confused glances as she continued.

"In the days of old, long before the birth of all living Vasirian, humans and Vasirian co-existed differently than they do today. There were special humans with magical blood known as witches and warlocks. They knew of our kind. Our kind found their Korrena pairs with them. Blood was shared between these pairs as we now share between each other."

"Where are these witches and warlocks now? If magic is real, why are there not more of these special humans?" Maxwell asked.

"I assumed the bloodlines had died, but it seems that is not the case."

Angelo stiffened in his seat.

"What this means for the present world, I cannot say, as a dark cloud obstructs my vision, but I am certain the human girl, Blaire Wilcox, is a descendant of one of the witches of old. I believe old magic flows through her veins. How much, I also cannot say."

"This is insanity. We must destroy her before she causes irreparable damage," Nathaniel said, his cold eyes cutting to the Oracle. "Does anyone know where she is now?"

Angelo gave a slight shake of his head. "After her rescue, I assumed she crawled back into whatever hole she went to after her withdrawal."

Maxwell's nostrils flared as he exhaled heavily. "We need to find her and handle this, immediately."

"I advise you to tread lightly, to not awaken a dormant power lost in our bloodline long ago. I cannot predict all potential outcomes."

Angelo's lip curled, and he narrowed eyes on the Oracle, gripping the arms of his chair. "Where does your allegiance lie? The human is a threat to our kind and should be dealt with as such."

The Oracle didn't flinch, didn't breathe differently, didn't give any outward indication that Angelo's words affected her. His intimidation tactics were juvenile at best. She chose what information to hold close and what seeds to plant. His communication style would not sway her. "I am for the betterment of our kind, and if that happens to involve humans and the restoration of old magic, then so shall it be."

As she turned from the platform and walked to the doors to leave, pulling her hood over her head, the men spoke amongst themselves.

"We must harness this magic, if we cannot destroy her. Remove it and use it before she discovers it for herself and brings harm to us all."

The Oracle pinched her lips together.

46

Judgment

Vincent's trial had finally come, and Blaire wished she was not required to attend. With everything that had happened with Lukas and their bond being so damaged, she wanted to be anywhere but toe-to-toe with the mysterious Order. Professor Velastra hadn't said the others' testimony was needed at the trial, but she was thankful all of her friends had come with her. She didn't have the strength to handle this alone. Even Lukas's brooding presence gave her comfort, despite the tension between them. The group of friends climbed the long, winding stairs to the top floor of the administration building into a dark hall lit only by candlelight.

Professor Velastra waited for them in front of a large set of double doors with the ornate insignia for the school carved into the dark stained wood. Sculpted branches with sharp thorns stood in high relief, a pair of crows flying out of the thorns' reach. Flickering candles made the birds look like they were moving. If she weren't grappling against a riot of wasps in her stomach, Blaire might have been able to appreciate the artistic beauty of it all. Instead, she was trying not to throw up.

"It's going to be okay," Lukas said, stepping up to her back and pressing against her. She relaxed, allowing his warmth to seep through the fabric of her clothes. Breathing in his apple spice scent, she looked over her shoulder as he looked down at her. "They won't hurt you with all of us there."

"I'm fine. I'm not worried about the Order." Which was true. It was Vincent she didn't want to see again.

"Remember what I said." Professor Velastra stepped forward to take hold of the bronze handles of the doors. "Let me do the talking."

"What if they ask her to explain what happened?" Riley asked. A sconce on the wall containing a lit red candle—to signify a meeting in session—cast a dim light across her face.

"Of course, you should comply with their inquiries, but it isn't necessary to volunteer more than the bare minimum." Her eyes moved from Riley to the door. "They have all heard the recording."

Professor Velastra had told Blaire that while not all of the council members were pleased with not hearing from her directly, they had accepted her recorded testimony as evidence.

"Let's go." The professor pulled the long handles of the heavy doors, and they creaked loudly, echoing into the room they stepped into.

The spacious room with a vaulted ceiling of carved wood timbers dripped with dazzling opulence like something out of medieval times, a stereotypical vampire castle. Tall candelabras with black and red candles cast an ominous glow over the gold-veined marble floor. Large drapes of black and burgundy covered the walls in fabric. A floor-to-ceiling window to one side of the room overlooked the forest surrounding the school. A massive, round, stained-glass window threw crimson light onto seven high-backed chairs of black stained wood and burgundy upholstery perched on a high dais like thrones.

The seven robed men in those chairs wore faces of varying degrees of shock and anger as Blaire and her friends filtered into the room. This didn't look like they were off to a good start.

As everyone finished making their way into the room, the man on one end of the dais held his hand out, pointing at Blaire and friends. "What is the meaning of this?" His high cheekbones flushed red, and his dark blond brows narrowed in suspicion. "What reason have you to bring so many students to a simple disciplinary hearing?"

The man in the middle, with tanned skin and long black hair swept away from his face, lifted a hand, the light catching on the jewels adorning his rings. "Now, now," He chided in a thick, Italian accent. "We've heard the report. I'm sure these good students are here as witness to events prior to the terrible fate that befell our unfortunate victim." His piercing eyes narrowed on Blaire momentarily before cutting to the professor. "Yes?"

Before the professor could respond, another council member on the opposite side spoke up. "What is the reason for bringing the human girl when she is no longer a student? She has no place here. The recording was enough. You insisted we accept it as evidence. There is no reason for the girl to be here."

Professor Velastra stood silent, presumably to gauge if they were done with their questions and outrage, before stepping forward in the center of the room to stand behind a podium. It was the only item in the large space aside from the chairs at the top of the stairs and the candelabras that adorn the space around the room.

In the strained silence, the ticking of the clock from the front of the building echoed into the room. The seconds ticked like a taunt, counting down the time to where she would have to face Vincent again.

Tick, tick, tick, tick.

"As I'm sure you are aware, the victim in the report you've received is Blaire Wilcox, the human student. Yes, these students with me today have all witnessed the progression of events surrounding what occurred two months ago. But there is one fact you have wrong. She never withdrew from Blackthorn Academy."

Ignoring the mutters rising between the council members, she continued, "She did not withdraw only to fall into Vincent Brandt's hands as you assumed." Her eyes locked on the Italian man in the middle, whom Blaire assumed to be Angelo Moretti given the accent, his position in the center, and what he had told the professor the Order believed.

"Miss Wilcox has been held against her will as a hostage for the last two months. She underwent varying degrees of torture while also being fed on by one of our own, a student in the later university years who abused his teacher's aide privilege to get close to her, and garner her trust, only to drug her and sequester her in the diplomat wing of this building."

Angry and shocked whisper-yells rose amongst the men on the platform, and it was difficult for Blaire not to wilt under the scrutiny as several looked at her in disbelief. Instead, she focused on her friends, who stood with her. Had they not truly listened to the report? The professor wasn't saying anything they hadn't already heard. Maybe it really did matter to hear it firsthand instead of over a recording.

Aiden and Lukas had her pinned between them—shoulder to shoulder—a protective front against anything that might threaten her. Seth stood silently at her back, a calmness over his features more in line with what she was used to seeing from him in the past. Kai stood to the left of Lukas with a focused expression, his eyes soaking up everything taking place on the platform, while Mera held his hand. Riley stood on the other side of her brother, wringing her hands in front of her. She seemed to have difficulty with being in the room with the men in charge, but as her blue eyes found Blaire's, an understanding passed between them. Riley had her back, no matter what.

The man in the middle—Angelo—waved both hands to bring order to the council. "I was under the impression that Miss Wilcox was done with the academy." His heated glare made Blaire shift from foot to foot, her gaze dropping to the floor to avoid the glow flaring to life in his eyes. "I approved her dismissal myself," he added matter-of-factly, as if he hadn't just been shooting murderous looks at her.

A dark chuckle came from the man a couple seats to the left of Angelo. "I find it highly doubtful that a student managed to not only capture another student, but hold her prisoner for… What was it?" He tapped a gloved finger against his chin. "Ah yes, eight weeks?" His tone was light, as if the entire thing was absurd.

"Beneath our very feet, at that," a man with alabaster skin seated on Angelo's right said with an incredulous shake of his head.

"*Dermo,*" a man with a thick Russian accent spat.

Blaire looked around with wide eyes. The entire situation was falling apart. They didn't believe the report. But hadn't they been the ones who overlooked her captivity as long as Vincent supplied them with her blood? Surely the professor cut that out of the recording to avoid conflict and further backlash. She had to believe that. So why were they acting as if this was all news? The only one who seemed like he wasn't being honest with his reactions was Angelo.

"Angelo, I can assure you that Miss Wilcox did not voluntarily withdraw. Your daughter informed these students that Miss Wilcox met with the Order and received approval to leave without retribution if she left immediately." Professor Velastra lifted her chin. "You said yourself she requested a withdrawal."

Angelo—Clarissa's father—spluttered, "Of course she didn't meet with us. Clarissa must be confused." He waved a hand dismissively. "I received a written request outlining the human's desire to withdraw. This is what I meant when I informed you of what I knew." A sheen of sweat coated his brow, and his hands gripped the ornate arms of the throne he sat upon. He was lying.

"No, you didn't," Blaire protested before she could think better of it. She gasped and put her hands over her mouth as seven sets of eyes turned their ire her way.

Tick, tick, tick, tick.

"Do you have something to say, human?" the one with alabaster skin asked with a sneer.

She didn't like the way they were looking at her, assessing her as if they were waiting for something. Unease prickled her skin. Blaire looked at Lukas, and he nodded, giving her hand a squeeze. "I… I didn't put in a request to leave."

The council members shifted curious stares to Angelo, who looked like he wanted to launch himself off his chair and throttle Blaire. Aiden stepped in front of Blaire, easing her behind him.

"Clearly, someone must have forged the document," Angelo said with a chuckle and a shake of his head. "Likely the rogue student who apparently pulled the wool over all of our eyes."

The council members nodded their agreement, speaking amongst themselves. When it seemed like they would no longer question his words, Angelo relaxed in his seat.

He had to have been the one in contact with Vincent, unless the others were top-tier liars. Blaire prided herself on reading people's intentions. With the Wilcox family—especially her stepbrother—she learned real quick how to pick apart someone's darker motives. That was why everything with Vincent took her by surprise. She'd gotten comfortable here and felt safe enough to not consider a teacher's aide a threat.

Aren't they vetted or something? Apparently, a psychological evaluation should be included for Vasirian TAs.

"I say we bring in the accused and have him answer for his actions." Angelo sat up straighter, his leader mask back in place now that he had garnered the backing of the others again. He flashed a grin at Blaire with his fangs at the ready.

She tensed, reaching for Lukas.

The leader of the Order must be getting a sick thrill out of her discomfort. He was as prejudiced against her kind as his daughter. The apple didn't fall far from the tree with these two.

Tick, tick, tick.

Blaire's eyes tracked the movement of a robed woman as she made her way across the room, away from the large doors they'd entered through. She climbed the stairs to the platform, stopping in front of the large, round window that took up most of the wall above the thrones. Blaire had seen it from the outside and often wondered who was behind such an extensive work of art. In shades of red and black—like most things in the academy—a murder of crows flew over blackened brambles. It was even more stunning up close.

The woman looked no older than sixty, so she must be extremely old by human standards. Riley had said for a Vasirian to look that age, they'd have to be one hundred fifty or more. She had black hair pulled up into a French twist with silvery strands streaking through it. It was difficult to ascertain her eye color, but her expression was soft and open. She didn't seem as guarded or severe as the men of the council. Who was she to them?

Even her robe was different.

Her robe was a deep burgundy, accented by black feathers embroidered at the bottom around her feet, as if they were falling from her knees; a black filigree lined the wrists of the large sleeves and hood that rested on the back of her robe. Dainty silver chains draped in looping swoops from a chain around her waist. A few chains hung straight down, small rubies glittering in the light from their ends. With the feathers, jewels, and chains, her robes were certainly more ornate than those of the seven men of the Order.

They wore black robes with little embellishment save for burgundy filigree that lined the bottom hem and wrists for every member except Angelo, who had golden accents—because of course he had to be "extra" to show his leadership status. If he was anything like his daughter, it wouldn't be too far of a stretch to assume it was by his insistence that the design of the robes worked that way.

Heavy doors opened on the other side of the room and a commotion echoed into the large room. Three members of Blackthorn Security escorted a struggling Vincent into the room.

Icy blue eyes met hers, flaring brightly as they glowed. Blaire instinctively stepped back as her breathing picked up.

Lukas snarled, charging at Vincent. "You're dead!"

Before Lukas stepped more than a couple of feet forward, Kai wrapped his arms around Lukas's body. He jerked wildly as Kai restrained him, fangs at the ready, eyes glowing fiercely.

"Control your students, professor!" the council member with alabaster skin boomed.

Angelo sat forward, watching Lukas thrash, wild eyes focused on Vincent. "If you cannot control your students, we will be forced to dismiss this trial, and disciplinary action will be taken."

Professor Velastra bowed her head, then turned toward Lukas, sighing when Seth moved forward to help a struggling Kai restrain him. "This is not helping. Blaire"—Lukas snapped his wide-eyed gaze from Vincent to the professor at the mention of Blaire's name—"needs you to remain calm. If we're dismissed, there is no telling what will become of Vincent. I know you wish to protect her, but if they take you, you cannot do that."

Aiden blocked Blaire's view of Vincent and took her face in his hands. "Breathe," he said, his soft command grabbing her attention.

Looking up at Aiden through blurry eyes, she hadn't realized she was panicking. She'd been so focused on Lukas she hadn't kept herself calm, and the anxiety built to ricochet behind her ribs, her heart fluttering like a hummingbird.

"Breathe," Aiden repeated, keeping her locked in his dark forest stare.

Blaire's chest swelled and caved with each fast and heavy breath she gulped down. She tried to suck up all the oxygen in the room, finding none. She gripped the hands that held her cheeks like they were a lifeline.

"Breathe."

Closing her eyes, Blaire took a deep inhale through her nose and released it on a shaky exhale from her mouth. Slowly, her heart rate returned to normal, but she had to fight to calm down. With Lukas at war with the beast inside, she was having difficulty separating her emotions from his, and it was making her ill.

Wait a minute…

Her mind whirled with questions at how she suddenly felt Lukas's emotions. Thankful for this connection, she smiled, leaning on Aiden with her body.

A gentle touch from a small hand on her lower back, Riley's, had her releasing the last of her tension as her body slumped.

"That's it. We can get through this," Aiden whispered.

Blaire dropped her hands from Aiden's, reaching out to Riley, taking her hand, and squeezing it. Riley's expression was fraught with worry, and the slight tremor in her hand that held onto Blaire made it clear how uncomfortable she was here. But she stood alongside Blaire against seven men who had the power to shape their fate into something miserable.

With Riley's nervous tension, and Lukas borderline feral, Aiden became the only reasonable anchor to focus on. Seth and Kai had their hands full, and Mera… Blaire felt guilty to say she couldn't find the grounding she needed with her. Not that she cared any less for Mera, she just needed greater strength than calm rationality could yield. Despite her need to be near Lukas—and the thrill that she could feel his fury—he wasn't in the right head space. What she needed was the unwavering resolve of Aiden, and she had the feeling he sensed that, which kept his own rage at bay.

Until she could handle the assault of emotions crashing into her from the sudden return of the empathic connection she shared with Lukas, they would not be much good to one another in situations of stress. He likely was suffering the same issue, and it did nothing but pour fuel on the fire.

They needed the grounding the others provided or they would feed off each other's turmoil. The damage wrought might destroy them.

While she was happy it had returned, this was probably the worst time for it to happen. But he was trying to protect her against the monster that had held her captive. His protective vengeance sparked deep in her belly and warmth built there.

Angelo gave one last withering glance to Lukas, held rigid between Seth and Kai, a riot of repressed rage boiling beneath the surface that nearly suffocated Blaire with its intensity. Shaking his head, Angelo turned his sharp eyes to Vincent, snapping, "Explain yourself."

Vincent shrugged off the guards and pressed his hand over his long sleeves to smooth the wrinkles, tugging his vest down to straighten it. Gone was the fire she'd seen in him when he entered the room, replaced with the calm demeanor he'd always worn before he kidnapped her. The abrupt change in his mood used to unnerve her, but for weeks he'd shift in such volatile ways that she'd gotten used to it.

"The girl is my compatible pair." Once the murmurs passing between the council members quieted, he continued, "Lukas no longer wanted the bond fate blessed him with. I was merely helping her get through her grief."

"By kidnapping her?" the man with the Russian accent asked. By the look on his face, and that of several other members, they thought Vincent was a few screws short of a hardware store.

"I didn't see it that way." Vincent shrugged. "I felt keeping her shielded from the… stressor"—he narrowed his eyes on Lukas, who was practically vibrating with fury—"would assist in healing."

Professor Velastra calmly interjected, "Vincent Brandt fed on Miss Wilcox. That clearly isn't helping her heal. Especially with his inability to heal the wounds like her true pair would be able to." When Vincent curled his upper lip at her, she added, "Furthermore, breaking the Korrena bond with a taboo blood ritual is reckless."

"I love Blaire!" Vincent roared. "She would have loved me too if given the chance!"

Blaire's eyes widened at the declaration. He'd been saying that for weeks, but the fact that he still insisted it was truth, while staring down who knew what punishment, was shocking.

Angelo steepled his fingers, resting his elbows on the arms of his chair as he gave a faint smirk in Vincent's direction. "It is clear this rogue student, whose obsession with the human was so great it led to this elaborate scheme, has tricked us all." He narrowed his eyes and looked at his fellow council members. "I, for one, am appalled that this happened under our noses."

Murmurs of mutual consent broke out across the platform. Angelo licked his lips, smiling wide with a malevolent grin that didn't reach his eyes, making him look like a deranged lunatic. Something was seriously wrong. Blaire felt more than ever that he had something to do with why she had been hidden away for so long. But without proof, she couldn't accuse the leader of the Vasirian for this half of the world. Even if she could prove it, she doubted they'd take her word over his. Strong prejudice remained against her kind being involved in their world.

"I call for the immediate expulsion of Vincent Brandt," he quickly said while the others were caught in discussion. He was clever to make a move before anyone could dig deeper into motive or method.

A man on the end closest to the door, who'd remained quiet throughout the trial, said, "Just expulsion? Surely his crimes warrant a stint in Cresbel Asylum. Vasirian law is clear about what it means to harm a human." The others nodded, whispering, and glancing at Blaire.

"Very well. Until we can run this by King Blackthorn and get his seal, he shall remain in the dungeons."

"You can't do this!" Vincent shouted desperately, struggling against security as they led him away. "Angelo told me if I supplied you all with her blood, it was okay! I've committed no—"

"Take him away!" Angelo barked, standing, and pointing at the door.

"Wait!" Lukas stepped forward, and Kai grabbed his arm again as all eyes moved to Lukas. "I want my bracelet back," he said in a calm voice that belied the turbulent emotions Blaire could feel. Even his face held an impassive expression.

Angelo scoffed and waved dismissively. "We do not have time for such foolishness, boy." When Lukas glared and pulled against Kai's firm hold, Angelo asked, "Is such a trivial thing necessary at a time like this?"

Before Lukas could say or do anything, the professor cleared her throat. "The stolen bracelet in question was a gift that should be returned."

Angelo sucked his teeth and sneered at the professor, but she didn't flinch, keeping her hands firmly clasped in front of her, chin held high. He waved a hand to the guards, and they circled Vincent, removing his many bracelets, bringing them over for Lukas's inspection. Once Lukas picked his leather bracelet from the pile, the female guard turned away, pocketing the remaining bracelets.

Lukas pulled away from Kai and moved to Blaire as Seth watched him warily. "This is one of the ways Aiden was able to figure it out," he said, slipping the bracelet over Blaire's wrist, tightening the straps.

"I love you, Blaire!" Vincent cried out as security hauled him toward the door.

Blaire flinched.

He pulled free briefly and stepped forward a few feet before being apprehended again. He thrashed, yelling, "We were meant to be!"

Lukas pulled Blaire into his arms as she fought against the sting prickling her eyes. She would not let that monster see how he damaged her. No, she wouldn't allow there to be damage. She survived. Lukas squeezed her tightly, likely feeling her resolve as she straightened her spine. That warmth in her belly spread over her skin as Lukas held her close.

"He's gone mad after feeding on human blood like an animal. Security has kept us informed of his behaviors away from the human's blood. His mind is broken." He *tsked*, shaking his head as if he cared. "Such a shame."

Vincent once again broke free from the guard's hold, charging toward Blaire and Lukas with a manic expression laced with rage. "Don't touch her! She's mine!"

Blaire tensed as icy fingers shot down her spine before a blazing fire licked its way through her, stealing her breath. Before she could question the sensation, Lukas pushed her into Aiden's arms and lunged at Vincent so fast neither Kai nor Seth had the chance to stop him.

They crashed to the ground as guttural growls and snarls echoed throughout the room. Despite Vincent being larger than Lukas, he didn't have the upper hand. Vincent was running on his madness, and it clearly affected him. He roared as Lukas grabbed him by the hair and smashed his head into the floor. The resulting crack from where Vincent's skull impacted the marble branched out like lightning splitting the sky.

Lukas didn't give him a moment to get his wits about him. He drove his fist into Vincent's face, shattering his nose. In the brief moment Vincent was dazed, Lukas roared his fury, his fangs flashing in the light as he tucked in and tore into the side of Vincent's throat. Before he could fully latch on to rip his throat out in a move designed to kill, Vincent managed to throw Lukas off him, staggering to his feet as blood poured from his nose like a faucet. A chunk of skin flapped loosely at his neck where blood flooded down to saturate his clothing.

Vincent launched himself at Lukas, who spun out of his

grasp. Lukas grabbed hold of Vincent's arm and wrenched it back, overextending it until a sickening snap filled the space, followed by a scream of pain.

Unlike when Blaire witnessed Lukas attack her stepbrother, she wasn't afraid. While Aiden tried to get her to look away, she couldn't. She couldn't ignore the tingle in her gut at the beautiful brutality of Vasirian anger.

No, not Vasirian anger, Lukas's anger.

The raw passion and love.

The animalistic power in his movements as he met Vincent blow for blow. His deep need to protect burning in the depths of his glowing, bioluminescent eyes. His body moving with a primal grace as he brought down the threat to what mattered to him.

Realization took her breath away.

She wasn't scared of the monster that lurked beneath the surface.

Maybe she'd finally snapped and gone crazy, or perhaps she'd grown in her time with Lukas, but she wasn't the same girl who stood in that alley and hid from the reality of what slept beneath the surface of Lukas's skin.

Lukas grunted as Vincent landed a blow to his jaw with his good arm, spitting blood across the floor.

"She belongs with me," Vincent sneered, but it was obvious his words lacked the same bite as before. He was getting weaker. "You don't… deserve her. You… don't want her," he panted.

"You know nothing!" Lukas tackled Vincent, and they slid across the floor, crashing into the stairs that led up to the platform where the council members sat watching the spectacle at their feet.

They did nothing to stop it; several members watched with gleeful smiles, others with a bloodlust that longed for the fight. Angelo raised a hand to stop security from intervening, and cast a scathing glare when both Seth and Kai tried to interfere. Of course he wouldn't want to stop them from potentially killing each other. If that happened, he wouldn't have to deal with questions. But if they didn't kill each other, or if Lukas killed Vincent—which, judging by how limited and sluggish Vincent's movements had become while Lukas still ripped into him, it was a real possibility—he would be exiled.

Her pair could not be exiled—she wouldn't survive that.

The only thing that would stop the beast raging with murder in his eyes was their connection. It thrummed beneath her skin in the face of his protection and love. His rage for the man who'd held her captive for so long twisted in her stomach. She could taste his desire to kill. It was strangely heady, and a little arousing, which confused her. Maybe she was going crazy.

She shook her head, vaguely aware of Riley rubbing her back and Aiden standing close. She needed to focus. Needed to move past the looping thoughts of *beautiful-anger-want*, and the overwhelming thought of *mine*, because that was exactly what this powerful force in front of her was. Hers. Nothing about the way he ripped into Vincent said that Lukas willfully abandoned her, that he wanted to kill her.

Mine.

His.

She was always his. Mark or no mark.

Maybe she was the child of an unholy union, after all. How else was it possible to feel so alive in response to such brutality wrenched forth by a being that in mythology would be considered evil incarnate? He was beautiful.

Shaking her head again, Blaire forced herself to focus on the reality that Lukas was going to be exiled away forever if she didn't bring him back from the brink. The swirling thoughts clouding her senses crashed down, replaced by a much more familiar feeling—fear. She couldn't lose him again. She needed to do something—anything—to bring the feral animal in front of her to heel.

Without second guessing the move, Blaire broke away from Aiden and Riley and ran across the floor.

"Blaire, no!" Riley shouted as Aiden cursed.

Lukas pulled Vincent up close to his face, declaring, "Blaire is *mine.* She was never yours." He threw his head back and roared like a savage beast before moving in for the kill.

Blaire collided with him, wrapping her arms around him. "Lukas, no!" she cried, and he staggered back, pulled by her momentum and weight, dropping a nearly lifeless Vincent to the floor. Blackthorn's security team, which had somehow increased in number while Blaire was focused on the fight, moved in on Vincent.

Lukas whirled around to face her, his face twisted in rage, and he snarled at her. He was feral. Lost to the beast inside that still desired blood.

Blood.

Ignoring the shouts of her friends to get away from him while he was in this state, Blaire didn't let go. Instead, she pulled her cardigan down and tilted her head. "Drink," she snapped. If her theory was correct, if they still had any connection at all, her blood might bring him from the edge, calm him the way words couldn't.

He growled low in his throat and gripped her upper arms so hard she had to fight against the urge to recoil in pain. He eyed her neck, no doubt focusing on the pulse point that beat erratically.

"Drink," she urged again, gentler this time.

If he couldn't stop, the others would stop him before he could do something he'd regret. She had to trust that. It was the only way she knew to save him from being exiled, or worse yet, death. She had to trust him. Trust he wouldn't kill her. Lukas wanted to protect her.

He wouldn't let the beast win.

The rumbling in Lukas's chest grew louder as he lowered his head to Blaire's throat. He breathed in deeply, scenting her, before licking her exposed skin. She shivered at the movement, warmth pooling low in her belly.

"Mine," he murmured, his tone twisted with the growl that spoke of the Vasirian strength within.

Sinking his fangs into the soft spot where her neck and shoulder met, Lukas groaned as he fed on her, her blood running in rivulets down to soak into her clothes from where his mouth latched onto her. His hands moved from her arms to her hips, where he pulled her tightly against him in a bruising hold. His arousal pressed against her through his jeans. She lost all care about who was watching.

The rage and frantic discord that had clouded her mind receded like the morning tide. Her blood was soothing the beast within.

As dark spots clouded her vision, she faintly heard Aiden's voice. "Enough, Lukas. You'll kill her."

Something about that statement, or the tone, made Lukas break away. He stared down at Blaire with concern in his sea-glass eyes. "I'm… fine," she breathed, feeling a bit drunk.

He stopped.

Lukas had regained control of his most primal self.

"Look at that!" Angelo waved a hand at them. "Clearly, her blood has also driven the boy mad, if he's resorting to such barbaric behavior in front of us, knowing the consequences. He nearly killed another student!" He looked to where security was carrying a limp Vincent from the room.

"It's the Korrena bond," Professor Velastra said, raising her voice to be heard over the hushed conversations happening on the platform. "Mr. Virtanen is merely responding to having his bond broken in the most literal sense. This is something we've never witnessed before, so none of us can truly say how we would react to coming face to face with the person who would dare sever our fate's pairing."

Words of agreement reached Blaire's ears as the council spoke animatedly, and she had to hope it meant they wouldn't punish Lukas for what he'd done to Vincent.

Angelo looked seconds away from fleeing the room, spluttering, "Well, yes, that may be something to consider." He sat on his chair with a flourish of his robe. "Something you can use as a counterargument at his trial."

"Trial?" Professor Velastra asked.

Blaire looked up at the platform. The expressions on the council members changed, and her heart sank. They were catching on to what Angelo meant and nodding their agreement.

"Yes, trial." Angelo sneered. "A student cannot attack another student in a violent manner. We must follow protocol and hold a disciplinary trial to decide how we will deal with this… deplorable situation."

Blaire gripped Lukas's arm, and he pulled her close.

Her head was filled with cotton. Professor Velastra's mouth was moving, and responding arguments came from the platform. Aiden yelled something, by the looks of the anger on his face, but both Seth and Riley grabbed his arms in an attempt to calm him before he got himself in trouble. Mera had moved to Riley's side, while Kai stepped forward to stand behind Lukas and Blaire in silent support.

What was going to happen to Lukas?

He didn't kill Vincent. He beat him up, sure. Okay, beating him up was putting it lightly. When security dragged him out of the room, Vincent could barely hold his head up. Even with his healing abilities, it would still take time to become whole again, from her understanding of Vasirian healing abilities.

Lukas hadn't harmed a human. She was his Korrena. Even if the mark wasn't there currently, and the bond was in a state of discord, they still were soul bound. He didn't harm an innocent human.

"Lukas Virtanen," Angelo stated with a louder voice that broke through the cotton and made Blaire flinch. "You are to be confined to the dungeons until such a time as we can conduct a proper trial to decide your fate."

"No!" Blaire pulled on Lukas as security grabbed onto his arms.

Aiden pulled Blaire away from Lukas, whispering in her ear, "Don't fight them. If you do, they'll lock you away too."

Blaire sagged in his arms with heavy breaths, tears rolling down her face. "Please don't take him." Her words were soft, pleading.

The man with alabaster skin leaned his head against his palm on the arm of his throne and tutted. "We have rules and protocols we must follow, little human." His voice had softened, sounding sympathetic. He was the only one, though. The faces on the platform held varying emotions—disinterest, anger, smug satisfaction, except the man with alabaster skin.

When Blaire looked at him, pleading with him to stop what was transpiring, his jaw ticked, and he looked away.

She wasn't going to get any help from him. Whatever she saw in that brief moment wasn't enough to change anything. Her stomach tightened.

Lukas twisted in the guard's grip and looked back at Blaire with so much pain in his eyes that if they hadn't already recovered their empathic connection, she would have been able to see how devastated he felt. He mouthed "I love you" as they pulled him out of the room.

"Lukas!" she shouted.

Aiden tightened his hold. "Blaire, please…"

"This is why we keep occupancy to a minimum during these trials," one of the council members muttered, disgust clear in his tone at the emotional display before him.

Angelo shook his head and looked at Blaire as if he felt pity for her, but it was all fake. This man was as wicked as his daughter.

"But what about Vincent's punishment?" Riley asked, her eyes shining in the light.

It wasn't clear if Vincent would go to Cresbel Asylum or just face expulsion, but Blaire didn't care anymore. She needed to save Lukas.

The man with alabaster skin held up his hand. "It is wise that you do not press further. You are lucky that we are letting the human girl return to her studies at the academy and not terminating her contract for this… disruption." His upper lip curled.

"Disruption?" Riley shouted. "He kidnapped h—"

"Silence!" the Russian man boomed. "Leave, small one."

Aiden pulled an unsteady Blaire by the shoulder as he led her from the room, her gaze falling to the silent woman with the crow robes as they left. The woman's lips pinched into a hard line, but her eyes were soft and worried.

Maybe it was the blood loss playing with her mind, but Blaire couldn't get the woman's eyes out of her head as they made their way out of the building.

47

Bait

Lukas cracked his eyes open as he rested against the cold stone wall, blinking back exhaustion and a strange aching hunger in his stomach. The dim lighting from sconces on the walls outside his cell only gave him enough light to see into the cells directly across from him, and to his left and right. He didn't know what lay in the darkness beyond.

When security first brought him into the cell that was about the size of a small public bathroom, he'd had a bag over his head. He hadn't been able to see how he got here, what else was down here, or how to get out of the place if he managed to get free. Which he spent several hours trying to do, unsuccessfully.

He'd taken out his rage on the small cell. The small single bed that had seen better days, originally against the wall, now lay overturned, its meager threadbare linens spread in disarray. The bucket in the corner they expected him to piss in also felt the brunt of his rage. That was, until he actually needed to use it. It did nothing to sate his rage when he had to stand over a metal bucket and piss into it.

The chains binding Lukas's wrists weighed down his arms. He'd lost his strength after spending the last several hours trying to break out of the cell.

The look on Blaire's face as he disappeared through the door remained burned into his mind, cracking his heart in two. He didn't know how it happened, but after he attacked Vincent, everything flooded back in.

Her emotions.

Her love.

He felt everything.

But he didn't get the chance to celebrate. He had messed up significantly in the eyes of his kind, but he felt no compunction. Nothing, save for the regret that he didn't finish Vincent off. If Lukas was going to be exiled regardless, he wished he'd gotten the opportunity to watch the light fade from Vincent's eyes. Anything to exact vengeance against the monster that harmed his Korrena.

He lay his head back against the cold stone wall, a chill passing over his skin from the cold, stagnant air that filled the dungeon. Closing his eyes, memories of the last moments with Blaire ran through his mind.

She'd risked herself for him.

Despite what he had done to her when they tried to reseal their bond, she still threw herself into stopping him when he thought himself lost. Never in his life had he thought what lived within him could be so out of control. Never had he been driven so hard to kill. The desire he felt to destroy Blaire's stepbrother when he tried to take her away from him was only a drop of water in an immense sea compared to what he felt when Vincent declared Blaire was his.

A low growl reverberated in his chest.

Blaire was his. But she owned him too. No one was going to come between that. Not while he still breathed.

Lukas lifted his hands, the chains clanking, and the thick metal cuffs pulling on his wrists as he rubbed his face. He hadn't even bothered to sleep, choosing instead to fight against his captivity, desperate to get back to his heart.

But with fighting came exhaustion; forgoing sleep, and suffering with a strange ache in his stomach he hadn't felt before, he didn't have any fight left in him. He sat on the cold stone floor with his back to the large stones stacked tightly together with mortar and smoothed flat. Metal bars separated him from the surrounding cells. If someone was in the next cell over, he'd be able to reach out and touch them, but he was the only one down here as far as he could see.

Where was Vincent?

From the obvious signs of erosion, and the worn cobblestone beneath him that appeared smooth from years of foot traffic, it was clear the dungeon was old. He didn't know how old Blackthorn Academy really was, but they renovated often to keep with the modern times. This area of the school didn't receive the same treatment, despite being kept clean.

He half expected to see puddles of water and an infestation of rats and bugs.

"I see you don't appreciate our hospitality."

Lukas dropped his hands into his lap and drew his right knee up, leaving his left leg extended on the floor as he looked up toward the voice. If he had more strength, and wasn't bound like an animal, he'd try to reach through the bars and snap the man's head off, but as it was, he wasn't in a state to fight back. He'd tried, and that's why he now sported chains, despite being locked in a cell. The bars hadn't kept him from punching out at least one security guard from his confinement.

He couldn't help but grin at that.

"I'm glad you find it funny."

Lukas glared at Angelo. The man was as ostentatious as his daughter. Perfectly styled hair, eyebrows that looked like they received professional upkeep, gaudy rings adorning fingers that looked as if he'd never worked a day in his life. Lukas's nose wrinkled.

"Nothing to say?"

The man sucked his teeth and tossed a blood packet into the cell, which skidded to a halt at Lukas's feet. When Lukas only looked down at it, with no indication that he was going to drink, or thank Angelo for his gift, Angelo hissed.

"Despite your outrageous display of feeding on that human during Vincent's trial, it has been twelve hours, and if you continue to go without, you will succumb to *sanguis manie*."

Blood mania.

Lukas had heard of the condition but never witnessed it firsthand.

They taught them in school that once a Vasirian went an extended period without consuming blood, they would enter a state of mania where they would lose control of the beast inside them. What they would do, and how strongly they were affected, depended on the Vasirian themselves. How long it would take for the mania to set in was much the same. Typically, younger Vasirian had it the worst because the school system accustomed them to having a limitless supply of blood.

"Drink," Angelo snapped.

As much as Lukas wanted to take pleasure in defying the man who put him in a cage, he wasn't stupid. He didn't want to lose himself.

Tearing into the top of the blood packet with his fangs, Lukas tilted it up, eyes locked on Angelo's as blood filled his mouth and burned a path down his throat. He felt it immediately. A calm washing over him. He didn't even realize his body was already in a state of unrest because of how long it'd been since he drank Blaire's blood.

Angelo gave him a knowing look.

Lukas drained the packet and cursed, the relief exposed on his face. He hated that the asshole saw him in a moment weakness.

"Now with that settled—"

"Where's Vincent?" Lukas cut Angelo off in an icy voice. He didn't like that, judging by his glare, and Lukas got satisfaction out of provoking the man.

"We've taken care of that."

"Where is he?"

He exhaled heavily. "King Adrian Blackthorn sent word for his banishment to Cresbel Asylum. He is going away for quite a long time for what he did to your precious human."

"And me? What's going to happen to me?"

"Well, that all depends on our special little human."

Lukas's arm hairs stood up at the way he said that.

"What do you mean?"

"Mm..." Angelo ran his fingers over the bars as he paced in front of the cell. "I wonder if telling you would matter. After all, you won't be able to stop anything." He lifted his fingers from the bars and his upper lip peeled back as he stared at his fingertips as if they were filthy.

"Stop what?"

Panic rose into his chest, reflected in his voice, bringing a gleeful smile to Angelo's twisted face.

"Oh, you shall see. Or perhaps not. It all depends on if you're around for the events that come."

Lukas scrambled to his feet and lunged at Angelo through the bars, the chain connecting his wrists catching on the bars and keeping him from extending his hands the way he wanted to.

Angelo stepped back with a hearty laugh. "I guess the blood re-energized you after all."

Lukas stepped back, glaring at the man.

"Enough playing around. All you need to know is that you are simply bait. If you sit down here and behave like a good little boy, you will return to your life, without harm or exile, as it was before Blaire Wilcox ever came to this academy."

"Before she came? Bait?"

A door opening echoed through the low-lit space.

Angelo lowered his head and breathed out as if exhausted by Lukas's inability to understand things he hadn't even offered to tell him. Lukas wasn't a mind reader.

"The girl will come for you. And when she does, I'm sure we will be able to work out an arrangement that will appease everyone." He tapped his lips. "Well, most everyone."

"What the hell are you talking about?"

"The Wilcox girl is quite special, Lukas. Her blood holds something we have never seen before, and we cannot simply overlook it."

They figured out why Blaire differed from other humans? His entire body prickled with unease.

"What are you going to do?"

With only a smirk as answer, Angelo turned away from the cell and made his way down the hall as two members of security walked past him. They stopped in front of Lukas's cell and slid a tray with a sandwich and a bottle of water through the small slat at the bottom of the cell door.

"Eat well. You'll need your strength," Angelo said in warning as he left, followed by the security team.

What was he up to?

Lukas kicked the piss bucket, sending its contents splashing into the next cell, filling the air with the harsh scent.

He needed to get out of here. He hoped his friends were watching out for Blaire, because as much as he promised to protect her, everything around them was conspiring to keep them apart.

48

Warning

Thunder rumbled in the distance. Birds scattered from the surrounding treetops into the sky darkened by storm clouds. Blaire glanced around the clearing, but found no one. The tree stump the Oracle had sat on with the face of her mother stood empty as the grass blew wildly around its edges.

Rustling at the edge of the clearing drew Blaire's attention. The deer with the expressive golden eyes stood quietly, observing her. She had no idea how a creature with such a large rack made it from the cliff and through the forest without getting stuck.

"Do you know where she is?" She felt stupid asking a deer for directions, but what else could she do?

Slowly, the deer turned its head toward a small footpath to the south of the clearing that she'd never noticed before.

"Thanks."

The deer turned away from her and moved into the forest, the darkness swallowing it whole.

Blaire moved to the south end of the clearing as lightning split the sky overhead. Rain scented the air, and she hoped she would find shelter before the bottom fell out of the sky.

She walked the darkened path lit by dozens of fireflies for what felt like hours before she emerged on the other side of the forest at the edge of a river. A woman stood on the opposite bank with her back turned toward the water. The wind whipped Blaire's hair around her and she tucked the strands behind her ears to keep them from her face as she approached the river.

"Oracle?"

Crows cawed as her only answer. The pair from before landed on a cluster of rocks at the edge of the river.

"What's going on?"

Thunder boomed loudly overhead, and Blaire yelped. She hadn't been afraid of storms in a while, but something about being in this place with the raging elements felt different.

"They are coming for you, child." A lilting voice echoed in her mind as the rain fell in heavy sheets, consuming everything.

Blaire looked at the woman and all around her. "Who? Who's coming?"

"Your time is running out. Only your blood can save you. But it will not save your friend."

The riddle.

Blaire shouted over the hard rain that pelted her, chilling her to the bone. "What did you mean? What friend? What's going to happen?"

"You must find who you are before it's too late."

Blaire threw her hands up in frustration, clenching her teeth. "Stop speaking in riddles! Help me understand!"

She couldn't handle anymore cryptic messages. Her world was

falling apart. Lukas was locked away just after she reconnected with him, but their bond was still unstable. Unsealed. She didn't want the distance to destroy them.

"My child, I can only push you, but I cannot aid you. Not directly. I cannot upset the balance more than it already is."

Lightning struck a tree nearby, and Blaire screamed as it burst into flames.

"This world is in chaos, but only in your mind. Its fate depends on you, and right now, you stand on the precipice of life and death. The choices you make will determine who lives and who dies." The woman who'd worn her mother's mask slowly turned toward her, but with the blinding rain and darkness, Blaire could barely make out more than a blurry silhouette. "Including yourself."

Lightning flashed, illuminating the woman's face, and Blaire shrieked.

Her mother's face was the stuff of nightmares. Flesh melted from the bones of half of her face. Blood and muscle pulled away from white bone to reveal hollow cheeks and rows of teeth that should never be seen outside the body. Her eyeball was barely held in the right socket, as most of the bottom of that side of her face was gone. Is this what her mother looked like after the fiery car accident?

It was a closed casket service. They hadn't allowed her to see her mother.

Blaire stumbled back and fell over a rock on the shoreline, landing on her backside. "You're not real!"

The voice echoed in her mind again. "She's not. I would not allow you to see the truth of what happened to her if I had control right now. I cannot reach you, child. Not like before. Not right now. You are in grave danger, and you must prepare."

Blaire choked on a sob. "I don't understand!"

"Befriend the captive. It's your only way to get free." The Oracle's voice echoed in her mind as the world grew dark.

Blaire jerked upright in her bed, sweat pouring down her forehead, and she raked two hands through her hair as she drew her knees to her chest, resting her elbows on them. She shook her head quickly, trying to chase away the image of her mother melting in front of her, swiping a tear from her cheek.

Her eyes fell to the empty space beside her on the bed, and she crumpled into the space, burying her face in Lukas's cold pillow that still held his apple spice scent, her sobs swallowed by the plush material.

Something bad was coming.

She didn't know what the Oracle meant, but danger was coming. Death was an inevitability. Someone was meant to free her, but from what?

With Lukas gone, she couldn't process it.

"I have been unsuccessful in my attempts to get the Order to release Lukas." Professor Velastra stood from her desk to look out the large window behind her chair. "I strongly feel he won't be exiled to Cresbel Asylum, but I cannot say I share the same optimism when it comes to the possibility of expulsion for his behavior."

Blaire sat in the chair in front of the professor's desk, numb and drained. Emotions that weren't hers teased her from the edge of her senses. Rage was the most defined. An all-consuming inferno. If she moved close enough to the edge of campus, she could feel it lick through her veins.

She suspected the dungeons were too far away for their connection to remain constant. It made her feel even more hopeless, especially after seeing what happened at the trial didn't trigger their mark's return. She'd asked Professor Velastra if they needed to make love and both exchange blood at the same time to make it return, and while the professor confirmed that to be true, she speculated there might be something more holding their connection at bay.

The dungeons were underground beneath the administration building, but where, she didn't know. She'd thought they were a floor down from where Vincent kept her—as did others—but she picked up Lukas's emotions best standing near the tree grove at the front of the campus, at the edge of the courtyard, well away from the administration building. She suspected there was a lot more to the area beneath Blackthorn Academy than the basement levels of the administration building.

Professor Velastra was more optimistic than Blaire. With how the Order targeted her, she wouldn't be surprised if they found a way to remove Lukas from the equation, by any means necessary. If they shipped him away to Cresbel Asylum—wherever that was—there wasn't a need for her to be at Blackthorn Academy. If Lukas was exiled, the Korrena bond wouldn't matter, so they wouldn't have to respect it.

The Order didn't care about how they felt anyway, or how much the separation would hurt them. They would dispose of Blaire once they got Lukas completely out of the picture.

She honestly didn't think a simple expulsion was on the table.

The professor adjusted the bottom hem of her champagne-colored chiffon blouse and smoothed her hands over her black pencil skirt as she turned to face Blaire, Seth, Aiden, and Riley. "Mind you, I believe Lukas acted in a manner to be expected, given the situation. I think what is happening is unjust, and I would like to put a stop to it."

"He should have just killed Vincent," Seth said in a low voice.

"Then he would be rotting in Cresbel Asylum." Riley frowned.

"And that's different from rotting in a dungeon below the academy?"

"Seth! Riley! Shut the hell up. Can't you see what you're doing to Blaire?" Aiden pointedly looked at Blaire, whose eyes filled with tears.

"I'm so sorry, Blaire," Riley murmured, moving to sit next to her.

Blaire lowered her head. She'd come to talk to the professor about a lot of things, but hearing this about Lukas, she had her answers regarding him. It was a waiting game until they could set a trial.

She wondered if he was being fed properly. If the dungeons were like what she'd seen in movies and read about in books.

Dirty. Damp. Rat infested.

Her eyes burned, and her head hurt.

"Well, Vincent will get what he deserves for his crimes. Last night, members of our security team transferred Vincent to Cresbel Asylum. King Blackthorn sent word ordering Vincent's banishment to the Asylum. I am uncertain about the length of the sentence, but he should be away for a very long time. Our laws about harming humans carry severe penalties. Furthermore, I have other news."

"News?" Riley asked.

"Clarissa Moretti has been permanently transferred to the sister location in Europe. With the object of her affections indisposed, her father took the opportunity to make it happen. Apparently, he wanted her there all along. She leaves in a week."

"Thank fuck," Seth said.

Professor Velastra sighed softly and sat back down in her chair.

"I had a couple things I needed to talk to you about. Besides Lukas," Blaire ignored the painful memories poking at the back of her mind regarding Clarissa. She twisted the ends of her long hair between her fingers.

"Yes?"

"Well." Blaire looked over at Aiden, whose brows knotted in confusion. "Do you remember how that one guy made me freeze back when we first met?"

Aiden clenched his jaw. "Yeah, I remember."

Blaire looked at the professor and sighed. "Vincent apparently tried to compel me. Before he drugged me in the hedge maze, during another session, we were sitting in the tutoring room, and I felt a terrible headache. I could have sworn his eyes glowed. It was unnerving, and I didn't know what was happening, and then, just like that, it was gone.

"He told me he tried and it failed. I had hoped he wouldn't use the hypnosis to paralyze me, but he realized he could too soon, and that's how he forced me into the ritual. So, it seems I can lose control of my body, but not be forced to comply with the wishes of whoever does it. Is that normal?"

Blaire tried not to laugh at her own question. It wasn't exactly normal that someone had the ability to hypnotize someone, steal control of their bodily functions, and then compel them to do their bidding.

Professor Velastra tapped her chin. "I haven't heard of the abilities of those gifted with such a power to only be able to halfway perform." She glanced at the phone on her desk. "Might you indulge me in an experiment? I promise you will be safe, but I would like to test this for myself in a controlled environment."

Blaire pivoted to look at Aiden, Riley, and Seth to see what they thought.

"I promise you, no harm will come to her, and you three can be here the entire time, of course."

Riley looked at Blaire, and she nodded. What else could she do?

If this helped determine whether she at least could rely on not being controlled beyond body autonomy, then it would go a long way in reassuring her she had some form of control over her own life in this place.

The professor picked up her phone, pressing a single number. After several silent moments, she spoke, "Professor Galloway, could you please come to my office?" A pause. "Yes, now if you can." She hung the phone back into its cradle and sat back in her chair.

Moments later, after a knock at the door, a tall, slender man with slicked-back black hair stepped into the room. He reminded Blaire of refined butlers with his pressed slacks and vest on his straight frame. He didn't appear to have much muscle mass, and his height—which easily surpassed Lukas—added to his willowy appearance. His steps were graceful as he moved to stand alongside Professor Velastra's desk.

"How may I assist you today, Soomin?"

"Soomin?" Seth raised an eyebrow.

Professor Velastra slowly shook her head. "My name. Professor Marcus Galloway is more familiar with me, as he was my late husband's cousin. He oversees students who have chosen career paths in engineering." The professor waved her hand in their direction. "This is Blaire Wilcox, our human student who joined us last year, Seth Emerson, a second-year university student, and Riley and Aiden Easton—siblings, also in their second year."

The man inclined his head slightly in greeting.

"Yes, now that we've gotten introductions out of the way. I summoned you to ask a favor."

"A favor?"

"It would seem Blaire has a bit of an issue with compulsion." At Professor Galloway's raised brow, she continued. "This must remain in this room, and I know you are known for discretion, but while she has the ability to be hypnotized, she is immune to commands."

Professor Galloway arched a thick brow and studied Blaire. She squirmed in her seat.

"Professor Galloway is one of our strongest Vasirian in the way of compulsion. I wanted to see if he is capable of not only subduing you, but also controlling you. This will determine if it's an immunity or just a matter of Vasirian strength."

Aiden walked to Blaire's side.

"I'll be okay," Blaire whispered, looking up at him. She could see he was protecting her in Lukas's place, and she was grateful to have him by her side.

"I will not allow harm to come to her. I trust him, and can assure you of her safety."

"Dear boy, I have no desire to harm her. I shall be quick."

Aiden didn't move, but he relaxed a fraction as Professor Galloway crouched in front of Blaire.

"This may feel uncomfortable, but I promise it will be over soon."

"I've felt it before."

Professor Galloway nodded and closed his eyes briefly. When he opened them, he stared up into Blaire's eyes. His glowed a vibrant amber.

Just like before, her body locked up. Her eyes widened, but she couldn't make herself move, not even a finger twitch. Even though she expected it, and had experienced it before, it still scared her. To lose complete control of her body was maddening. Rapid, quick breaths came from her nostrils, and Aiden tensed beside her.

Riley moved to Blaire's side and lifted her hand, stroking the top of it in a soothing gesture.

Her body could move. Just not with her control.

"It'll be over soon," Riley said softly, her tone meant to reassure and calm.

"Hurry up," Aiden said in a measured tone, but Blaire could hear his agitation.

"Aiden, please," Professor Velastra admonished. "Let him concentrate."

A wave of dizziness swept over Blaire, and her heart sped up, hammering wildly against her rib cage. This was different. The intense migraine she expected, but this time, it made her nauseated. It was so much worse than before.

Professor Galloway's face twisted in confusion with an edge of anger. It wasn't working the way he wanted, and he wasn't happy about it. Her breathing got heavier, and she shot Professor Velastra a panicked look as a tear slipped free from her open eyes to roll down her cheek.

"I think that's enough," Professor Velastra announced, standing, and walking around the desk to place a hand on Professor Galloway's shoulder. He flinched, and the spell was broken. Blaire fell forward, the envelopes on her lap falling to the floor.

Aiden knelt, drawing her into his arms, and she clung to him.

"She is quite powerful against my gifts," Professor Galloway said, panting from the exertion of trying to gain control of Blaire. "I've never heard of anything like this. A human should be the easiest to compel."

"What does this mean?" Aiden asked, still holding onto a shaking Blaire as he looked up at the two professors.

"It leaves us with more questions than answers, I'm afraid. We now know she's somewhat protected, but the how is unknown." Professor Velastra looked at Professor Galloway, who still stood baffled by what he had witnessed. "I believe that's all we need. Please keep what occurred here to yourself for now."

"Of course." With one last parting glance at Blaire, he exited the room.

"I'm sorry you had to go through that. I assumed he would have stopped sooner, but the man is a stubborn one, and we needed to be thorough."

Aiden slowly stood as Blaire sat back in her chair, scooping up the envelopes that fell from her lap.

"Now, the second reason you came?" Professor Velastra moved to look out the window.

Blaire shifted in her chair and toyed with the edges of the two envelopes in her lap as she took a steadying breath. She'd left the personal message for Lukas in their room. It wasn't relevant to the situation any longer. "I think we might have a problem."

A perfectly arched brow raised.

Blaire held out her hand with the two cream envelopes to the professor. "I've been receiving messages. I received one right after Lukas and I bonded and another the day before the trial."

"Messages?"

Blaire nodded at Riley as she took her seat again.

The professor took the envelopes and lowered herself into the large leather chair behind her desk, sliding forward and placing the envelopes on the desk's surface. "Why didn't you say something sooner? Who sent these?" She opened the one on top and read aloud:

There is more to your blood than a lover's bond eternal.
A long ago buried secret,
An unknown history stained crimson,
A balance broken to hold control and power.
The stars have aligned;
Your awakening is nigh.

The Dark Kiss is the key,
But the consequences are shrouded.
A child born of a love tested and won
holds the key to salvation for a king bound.

Blaire studied the professor's face for any sign of understanding, but the woman gave nothing away. Her pink lips relaxed, her facial muscles neutral. The professor was the queen of the poker face—either that, or she didn't care as much as Blaire hoped.

"What does that mean?" Riley slid forward on the edge of her chair, trying to see the parchment in the professor's hands as if it would help her figure it out.

"Some of it seems obvious," Aiden said, and Blaire look back at him. "Lover's bond eternal—the Korrena bond."

"Lukas and I thought the same."

"And the Dark Kiss? I've heard the phrase before with vampires turning humans in movies, so wouldn't that apply to Vasirian, too?" Riley sat back and twisted her lips in thought.

"I would suspect as much," the professor said calmly, rereading the parchment in her hands. "I'm interested in this unknown history. A massive amount of Vasirian history has been lost to time. There is barely any documentation of King Rosendo Blackthorn's reign, aside from the last thirty years. He ruled for three hundred years, and yet we know nothing of his accomplishments or what came before him."

Blaire stiffened in her seat. She wanted to tell the professor what she learned in her dream, but if the Oracle was to be believed, it might put the professor in danger, or potentially upset whatever this balance thing was.

"And what of the child?" The professor's brow lowered marginally. "Key to salvation for a king bound…" She looked up at Blaire and the others. "It doesn't completely make sense. Perhaps there are further answers in the other envelope? Again, who sent this to you?"

"The Oracle."

The poker face cracked.

Professor Velastra sat up in her seat, her lips parted as she stared disbelieving at Blaire with a slackened expression. "Come again?"

"The Oracle sent me these. Lukas received one too, but it isn't a cryptic message like these. More like encouragement while I was locked away."

"What?" Riley's voice pitched high in shock.

Aiden moved to Blaire's side. "How do you know it was the Oracle?"

Blaire tensed and looked from Riley to Aiden. "I… I can't say. I'm sorry." At the professor's confused expression, she added, "Apparently sharing that detail would cause conflict that may put others in danger."

The professor hummed and sat back in her chair, picking up the next envelope, once again reading aloud:

The stars have revealed new truths.
A danger to both your kind and mine.
The balance and restoration are at risk,
saved only by a friend's sacrifice.
An untapped, lost power is the conduit
for a bond deeper than that of lovers
to overcome even death itself.
But the heart must be open.

She didn't flip the parchment over as she slipped it back into the envelope.

"This seems a little more straightforward, but just as obscure in its presentation. Why did she choose to communicate in such riddles?"

"I think she can't directly tell me anything because it could mess with whatever is meant to happen."

"Mmm. I suppose that makes sense."

Blaire relaxed at her words, thankful she was taking it all at face value without prying deeper.

"Doesn't make sense to me," Seth said, crossing his arms.

"Me either." Riley frowned.

"Ever hear of the butterfly effect?" When they looked at him, Aiden continued, "Chaos theory. Basically, if one small thing happens—like telling Blaire a piece of the future—it could change things on a large scale, and that isn't always a good thing."

"Oooh, I get it," Riley said. "Still, she could be a little less vague." She crossed her arms and sat back in her chair.

"This one sounds more like a warning than the first. The first sounded like a message of guidance." The professor sat back in her chair and crossed her legs, resting her hands over her knee, interlacing her fingers.

"That's why we wanted to come talk to you. Before Lukas was taken away, we planned to come after the trial," Blaire said. "To see what you make of it. But now..." She sniffed as emotion bubbled to the surface.

"I see a couple of patterns between the two messages. Talk of a balance, and of a lover's bond. We know the lover's bond must be between the two of you. In this message," she said, tapping the top envelope. "There is a power that a bond deeper than what you two share needs to rise above death itself. I don't know what power it means, or even what bond you have that is deeper than the Korrena bond, if such a thing exists."

Blaire couldn't imagine having a bond stronger than what she shared with Lukas, even if it was currently damaged. Of course, she couldn't imagine half of the things she experienced in her time at Blackthorn Academy. A balance, power, death, sacrifices… She had no clue what any of it meant, but between the messages and dreams, she knew one thing for certain.

This was only the beginning.

Where Lukas and their fractured bond fit into it all, she didn't know.

A firm triple-knock sounded against the wood of the door, and Blaire tensed as the professor walked around the desk to open it. A burly security guard stood on the other side.

Shorter than the other guards she'd seen, he still towered over the professor, so everyone got a good look at him. Clean shaven olive skin with dark brown hair that was cropped close to his head like a military cut, and muscles upon muscles, he exuded what Blaire came to expect from the beefed-up security of Blackthorn Academy.

"They want to speak to the girl," he said in a gruff voice.

"The Order?"

Professor Velastra glanced back at Blaire when the man grunted his response, before turning back to the man. "Thank you, Alexander."

He grunted again and turned from the door, disappearing down the hall out of sight.

The professor moved back into the room. "I will go with you. The rest of you need to go back to your dorms."

"What? No way." Riley rose out of the chair to stand beside Blaire. "I don't want to leave her alone with those maniacs." Riley gripped Blaire's hand and gave her a reassuring smile.

"She will not be alone. I will be with her. I'm sure Blackthorn's security team will also be there."

"But—"

"Don't make it harder than it has to be," Seth said, his eyes locked on Riley. "None of us like it. But the sooner she goes, the sooner she gets out of there."

Blaire didn't know what the Order could possibly have to say to her after locking Lukas away. Would they demand she leave the academy? Lock her away themselves for more experimentation? Terminate her contract and take her life? The possibilities swirled in her mind, making her dizzy.

Whatever they wanted, she had to go.

They had Lukas, and despite what happened when she and Lukas tried to reseal their bond, she knew he was still her pair. The spark of flame flickered inside. He got control of his dark side.

For her.

Everything he did for months was for her. Now she needed to do something for him. She would do whatever it took to save him.

Stay in Touch

Join Stephanie over on Facebook in Stephanie Denne's Book Sanctuary Facebook Group! It's a place to discuss current works, future works, and interact directly with Stephanie.

https://www.facebook.com/groups/743979797516659

Social Media

- TikTok: https://www.tiktok.com/@stephaniedenneauthor
- Facebook: https://www.facebook.com/stephaniedenneauthor
- Instagram: https://www.instagram.com/stephaniedenneauthor/

Newsletter

Sign up for Stephanie's Newsletter to keep up to date on the latest news around the Blackthorn world and future series, and get special sneak peeks at the writing process and chapter previews for future books.

http://eepurl.com/h_N5uP

About the Author

Stephanie Denne is an author of Paranormal Romance and Dark Fantasy for new adults and adults. The Blackthorn Saga marked her debut in the literary world.

Inspired by art and music, she felt the need to give life to characters that had been rolling around in her mind for 12 years. Never having written anything before, when she sat down and started drafting, she discovered she had a passion for the craft and the story naturally grew into something much bigger than she could fit into one book—much less a few, or even one series!

Born in the United States of America in the Southeast, Stephanie has now called Ontario, Canada her home since 2011. When not writing, she can be found reading her favorite stories, playing video games with her husband, painting with watercolor, or cuddling with her two Golden Retrievers. But not the cat—the cat has her own agenda.

Acknowledgments

As always, I want to thank my amazing husband for his support and constant patience as I ramble about characters that have made a home in my mind. Your reassurance through moments of self doubt and uncertainty have kept me going. I appreciate and love you very much.

To my editor Kelly, as usual you have been invaluable in bringing out my voice and keeping my characters from going off the rails—or pulling their hair out.

I also want to give my appreciation to my ARC readers from Mark of the Vasirian who provided invaluable feedback that helped my writing improve for Stolen Bonds. Thank you so much!

To Dom, Sean, Brian and his partner, Denys, and other members of HTLOZ that helped me with foodie questions, and helped with the voice of Europe, I appreciate you all!

And to every reader who has made it this far, as always, thank you for picking up (or downloading) my book and completing it. I hope you loved it as much as I loved creating it (even if this one was emotionally taxing at times) and that you will stick around through the saga to come. I appreciate each and every one of you. Thank you from the bottom of my heart.

Printed in Great Britain
by Amazon